W9-ARD-082

DESTROYER OF WORLDS

Larry Niven AND Edward M. Lerner

DESTROYER OF WORLDS

A TOM DOHERTY ASSOCIATES BOOK

New York

This is a work of fiction. All of the characters, organizations, and events portrayed in this novel are either products of the authors' imaginations or are used fictitiously.

DESTROYER OF WORLDS

Map by Jon Lansberg

A Tor Book
Published by Tom Doherty Associates, LLC
175 Fifth Avenue
New York, NY 10010

www.tor-forge.com

Tor® is a registered trademark of Tom Doherty Associates, LLC.

Library of Congress Cataloging-in-Publication Data

Niven, Larry.
    Destroyer of worlds / Larry Niven and Edward M. Lerner.—1st ed.
      p. cm.
    "A Tom Doherty Associates book."
    ISBN 978-0-7653-2205-0
    I. Lerner, Edward M.   II. Title.
    PS3564.I9D45 2009
    813'.54—dc22

                            2009031593

First Edition: November 2009

Printed in the United States of America

0 9 8 7 6 5 4 3 2 1

For Werner Heisenberg—maybe

CONTENTS

DESTROYER OF WORLDS
INTERSTELLAR SETTING
(worlds not to scale)

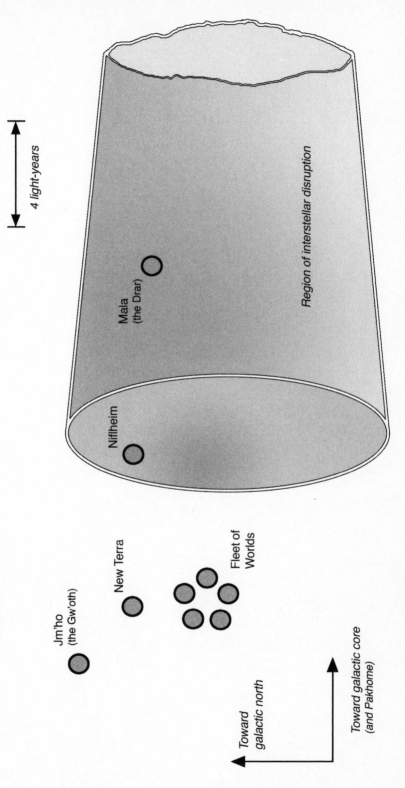

DRAMATIS PERSONAE

HUMANS (*)

Sigmund Ausfaller
  Defense Minister of New Terra (and head of the undisclosed intelligence service); Earth native
Sabrina Gomez-Vanderhoff
  Planetary governor of New Terra
Eric Huang-Mbeke
  Hero of New Terra's independence movement; engineer
Alice Jordan
  Sol system refugee
Penelope Mitchell-Draskovics
  New Terran government biologist
Kirsten Quinn-Kovacs
  Hero of New Terra's independence movement; math whiz; pilot and navigator of Don Quixote
Omar Tanaka-Singh
  Hero of New Terra's independence movement

(*) New Terra native and resident, unless otherwise noted.

CITIZENS/PUPPETEERS

Baedeker
  Engineer; disgraced former employee of General Products Corporation; self-exiled to New Terra
Minerva
  Baedeker's research assistant
Nessus
  Concordance scout

Nike
  Hindmost of the Concordance and chief of Experimentalist political party
Vesta
  Deputy Minister of Foreign Affairs; chief of Clandestine Directorate

PAK

Thssthfok
  Climatologist turned refugee turned castaway
Phssthpok
  Instigator of the Librarians' War; pilot of the rescue ship sent to find the Lost Colony

GW'OTH

Ol't'ro
  A 16-plex group mind (i.e., a Gw'otesht-16 ensemble)
Er'o
  Physicist and explorer; lead mind within Ol't'ro

PROLOGUE

1

Intelligence was overrated.

Not unimportant, merely not the *everything* that many made intelligence out to be. Intelligence leapt instantly, inexorably, from the merest observation to subtle implication to profound deduction to utter certainty. Intelligence laid bare the threats, vulnerabilities, and opportunities that lurked every-where. Intelligence understood that other minds all around raced to similar conclusions—

And that countless rivals would take immediate action thereon.

To become a protector, awakening into intelligence, was to lose all in-nocence, and with it the ability ever to let down one's guard.

But here, now, so *very* far from home, things were different.

Thssthfok stood alone atop a glacial vastness, clad only in a thin vest, worn for its pockets rather than for warmth. His hard, leathery skin was proof against the cold, at least for short periods. A portable shelter stood a few steps away, his shuttlecraft not much more distant.

The air was clean and crisp and bland in his nostrils. The oceans of this pristine world teemed with life, mostly single-celled, but the land remained barren. There were no native predators to fear here. As for protectors, the most formidable of predators, within a day-tenth's travel, there was only himself.

The children and breeders Thssthfok lived to protect were all on Pakhome, incommunicably distant. Their safety had been entrusted to kin and further guaranteed, to the extent that was possible, with hostages, prom-ised rewards, and dire threats. Without such measures, Thssthfok could never have come. That would have been unfortunate, for if this mission succeeded, *all* in clan Rilchuk might enjoy the greatest possible protection—

Release from the endless wars of Pakhome.

The only sound, but for the wind, was the whir of powerful electric motors laboring to extract deep core samples. Locked into the glacier was a story eons in the making, written in layers of ice, traces of ash, and microscopic bubbles of trapped gases.

Thssthfok was here to read it.

The concentrations of trapped gases would speak of the evolving climate. The traces of ash would reveal the frequency of volcanic eruptions. Occasional dustings of rare metals like iridium would disclose the impacts of large meteors. Patterns in the thickness of layers would speak to fluctuations in ocean volume and worldwide ice cover. That information, and the detailed observations of newly emplaced satellites, and the measured orbital parameters of this world . . . together they would reveal much about the long-term suitability of this place.

For this world offered far more temperate climes. Suitably prepared, much of the land here might be as pleasant as the great savannahs on which the Pak had evolved—*if* present conditions persisted. Planetary engineering took time and great resources. To relocate the entire clan—hundreds of protectors and many thousand children and breeders—would be a massive undertaking. Thssthfok had crossed a hundred light-years to answer a single question: How variable was the climate here?

He needed core samples, drilling as far back in time as he could get. A climate forecast rooted only in today's data was no more than a guess, and no basis for casting the fate of everything he held dear. The ice would yield its secrets, but the ice refused to be rushed. . . .

And so, remote from danger, removed from any clues to the circumstances of his breeders, Thssthfok was safe. Safe—unlike almost anywhere, anytime, on Pakhome—to disregard the outside world. Safe to ignore past and future. Safe to immerse himself, unprotectorlike, in an unending present. Safe to return to an age before thought.

Safe to dream of his time as a breeder . . .

THSSTHFOK REMEMBERED.

He remembered hunting and mating and fighting and exploring, always with zest. He remembered being curious about everything and understanding almost nothing. He remembered his pride in the ability to fashion a pitiful few tools: sharpened sticks, chipped-stone implements, straps cut from cured animal hide. He remembered staring, awestruck, into campfires. He remembered conversing with family—if the concepts expressible in a few hundred grunts and gestures could be called conversation.

The world then was ever new and exciting and usually inexplicable. Sometimes, when people died, a reason was obvious: torn by wild beasts, or fallen from a great height, or impaled on a spear. But many deaths came without warning or reason, with only the onset of bad scents to explain.

For scent was everything: how one found or avoided one's enemies; how one bonded with one's family; how one was drawn to mates and knew one's own children.

He remembered the rich, warm scent of family. Every person had a unique smell, and yet the subtleties of that aroma declared one's lineage for generations. He was not called Thssthfok then. There *were* no names, for names were not necessary. To smell relationships sufficed.

Scent was everything, and death was everywhere, and life—

Life was intense.

Lightning and starlight, seasons and tides, the ways of beasts and the wants of the mysterious beings occasionally glimpsed at a distance (and even less often, intervening) . . . all were unfathomable and wondrous.

For all their poignancy and grip, those memories were indistinct. A breeder merely dipped a toe into the great sea of sapience.

And then, one day, as happened to all breeders who reached a suitable age, he smelled . . .

Heaven.

Heaven was another vague concept for breeders. As they threw rocks and spears, so, obviously, far mightier beings hurled the lightning. Who but gods could carry sun and moon across the sky? Who but gods could arrange the stars and command the phases of the moon? Perhaps, as many thought, the gods descended from heaven and took mortal form to visit their people. It would explain the mysterious strangers and their magic implements. And since heaven was surely a better place, it would explain why the mysterious strangers came so seldom.

Heaven, it turned out, was not in the sky.

Heaven was a tree, scarcely more than a shrub, ordinary in every way, passed many times before, entirely familiar. On that day it exuded a scent of irresistible potency. Suddenly he had found himself prone at its roots, scratching with his bare hands at the rocky soil. The smell urged him forward, downward, indifferent to torn fingernails and flayed skin and the blood streaming from his hands. He must find—

He did not know what.

Fingers digging madly found a gnarled, yellow-orange length of tree root. The scent grew overpowering. When next he was aware of himself, his stomach was painfully engorged. His jaws worked mindlessly on a mouthful of something almost too fibrous to chew. He was flat on his back beside a length of exposed tree root, from which a few rough-skinned tubers still clung. Sap oozed where more tubers had surely been ripped loose. In some dim recess of his thoughts, he knew it was a tuber like these on which he helplessly gnawed.

All around was a stench that part of him wanted to flee and part of him recognized was somehow *himself*. That his very scent could change was terrifying. Yet another part of him noted, with unusual clarity, that whatever had overcome him had left him helpless. This reek, if it repelled others as much as himself, was all that kept away his enemies.

The new smell was already fading, changing to yet another odor, something strangely right for him. How could that be? What more had changed? In a panic, he explored his body.

His hair had fallen out in clumps, from head and chest and limbs. His knees and elbows and hips protruded, magically become enormous. The knuckles of his hands were sore and enlarged. His mouth felt odd, the skin pulled unaccountably taut. When, fearfully, he explored with the hand unencumbered with a half-eaten tuber, his lips and gums were becoming one. His cheeks felt like cured animal hide. He patted his chest and legs and other arm. They, too, were becoming tough. He peered fearfully at his most personal parts—and they were gone!

He howled, his anguish muffled by a mouthful of the root that had maimed him. And yet . . .

Despite pain and shock and confusion, he could not help but notice: His thoughts had never been clearer.

He continued to chew.

THE DRONING OF MACHINERY CHANGED pitch as another deep ice core neared the surface.

Thssthfok returned from the eternal present of a breeder into *this* present, awakening into a deep sense of loss. Breeders *felt*. Then, he had been one with the land, one with his family, passionate about every experience.

Intelligence was a pale substitute.

Only one emotion remained to him, all the more intense for subsuming the rest: He *must* protect those left behind. Not his children—for they were long gone, whether dead or transformed like him by tree-of-life root—but *their* children's children's children, and their children besides.

As many generations must pass again before Thssthfok would return, while by ship time, coming and going at near light speed, hardly six years would have passed. He himself would have aged even less, his biological processes slowed to near immobility in cold sleep.

Scent and memory were inextricably linked. With home fresh in Thssthfok's thoughts, the sterile, scentless air above this windswept ice oppressed him. Perhaps he would return for a while to the expedition's main base on the south-temperate continent, where the geologists and biologists labored. There he would find the scents of relatives, if only the weak emanations of other protectors. Shipboard, at least, there were synthesized scents. The best work of perfumers paled beside the heady, blended redolence of home and family, but it was *something*.

A *thunk* announced the arrival from deep below the surface of the latest ice sample. Working with tongs lest any detail be lost to the heat from his hands, Thssthfok put the slim cylinder into a clear, insulated bag. The layers had been automatically scanned, the results already displayed, but Thssthfok studied the ice for himself. When it came to winnowing pattern from noise, no machine could compete with eye and brain and eons of evolution.

Correcting effortlessly for the compression that varied with depth, Thssthfok pondered the strata in the ice. Some layers were thicker than others, the precipitation at this spot a clue to the extent of snowfall worldwide. At a glance he discerned cycles upon cycles upon cycles.

Sun and moon and neighboring planets, each in its own way, each at its own pace, tugged on this world. And so the shape of its orbit changed, and the tilt of its axis, and the slow precession of its axial tilt. With each shift, the strength of sunlight varied across the globe.

Of such minutiae are climates made.

As had the samples before it, this latest core spoke of ice ages. Orbital variation explained most and volcanic ash layers the rest. The ice gave no reason to expect another ice age for many thousands of years.

Almost certainly, Pakhome would face an ice age sooner. If Thssthfok was lucky, that next ice age would arise from Pakhome's own astronomical cycles, long after his death. (If he was unlucky—well, with only normal luck—war would be what killed him. War killed most protectors. The competition for resources was ever fierce.)

A part of Thssthfok would find an ice age—especially one hastened by a nuclear winter—fascinating, but he was a protector more than climatologist. With his family at risk, too distant to defend, the prospect filled him with dread. Even a limited nuclear exchange would make the temperate zones uninhabitable for many years. Every family from those regions would set out to conquer new living space for his breeders. The struggles for equatorial territory would be brutal.

Rilchuk, the island of Thssthfok's birth, the home of his family, straddled the equator. Their land would be prized. Breeders with the wrong scent—his family!—would be slaughtered by any conqueror.

Thssthfok thought: I *must* find a New Rilchuk, whether on this planet or another, a place to shelter my descendants for many generations.

If I am not already too late.

As he had a hundred times since reawakening from cold sleep, Thssthfok suppressed that qualm. Let doubt once blossom and he would lose the will to live. It was better not to dwell on circumstances that could not be known.

He refocused on the ice core with renewed dedication. In his bones, he knew: *This* is the world. The sooner he could prove it, the sooner he could bring his descendants from—

Within a sealed vest pocket, Thssthfok's radio shrieked. It was tuned to the command channel, and the harsh warble was unambiguous: immediate emergency recall.

Recall? Thssthfok needed deeper cores to prove this world safe. To make his breeders safe. Even to wrap the ice cores properly and recover the drilling equipment would take half a day. He took out his radio. "Commander, request another day. The cores—"

Bphtolnok, commander of the mission, was stationed on their orbiting ramscoop. That the commander was Thssthfok's grandfather's sister would merit no favors. Everyone on the mission was family.

Bphtolnok cut off Thssthfok. "Aboard in two day-tenths, or be left behind."

2

The recall of everyone from the planet brought chaos to the landing bay. Thssthfok was still securing his shuttle when he was again summoned.

He pressed through jammed corridors noisy with grumbling and the roar of ventilation fans. The full ship's complement was never meant to be awake onboard. Whatever had inspired the recall, these conditions could not persist. Life support could not sustain so many at once. Already, some must be queuing for the cold-sleep pods.

Even as Thssthfok struggled through the crowd, *New Hope* launched on full acceleration.

He entered the commander's cabin to find, besides Bphtolnok, four people. Three, like the commander, were warriors, marked honorably with scars. The last, his half brother, Floshftok, was an astrophysicist.

Abandonment of a promising colony world. An emergency departure— and the commander away from the bridge. An urgent meeting that involved strategy, astrophysics, and climatology. Any of these circumstances was extraordinary. But all? There could be only one reason: Their breeders were at risk!

Any message from Rilchuk had been a hundred years on its way. Despite his first scent in days of family, Thssthfok knew despair. Protectors without breeders had no purpose. They lost the will to live, and their appetite, and starved to death.

And yet.

Bphtolnok, at the least, knew what peril loomed—and she had acted decisively. There must yet be time. The danger must originate elsewhere than on Pakhome.

Floshftok's presence demonstrated an astrophysical dimension to the threat: something detected from afar. An unexpected neutrino flux, perhaps, from fusion reactors in a neighboring solar system. Or the hungry maw of a ramscoop approaching, or the white-hot exhaust of a fusion drive, ramscoop or otherwise, decelerating in this direction.

It was to distinguish remote threats from natural phenomena that an astrophysicist was part of the expedition.

Pak or alien, the response would be the same. If Pak, then certainly a rival for the pristine world *New Hope* had just deorbited. If alien, then at least potentially a rival. Thssthfok had no interest in another intelligent species. Curiosity was a breeder behavior, long outgrown.

Pak or alien, intruders or neighbors, those whom Floshftok had seen must be destroyed.

All this flashed through Thssthfok's mind as he crossed the small cabin and took a seat. He leaned forward, desperate to know more.

"Recap," the commander ordered.

Floshftok evoked a holo display of the stellar neighborhood, expanses of false color washing past nearby stars. Each color denoted a type of radiation.

Thssthfok studied the image, too extensive to be other than an astronomical phenomenon. Lots of neutrinos and the radiant glow from . . . what?

"Supernovae," Floshftok offered.

Plural. But how many? The wave front showed no curvature. Many supernovae then, the spherical wave fronts from each explosion averaging out. "The galactic core?" Thssthfok asked in wonderment. The closer an end-of-life star was to a supernova, the more likely—

"A chain reaction," Floshftok agreed.

And so the meeting went, with seldom more than a word or a short phrase offered. The breeders for whose safety Thssthfok feared required many words to convey the simplest concept. Protectors wrung meaning from the subtlest clue, their minds racing faster than their reasoning could be put into words.

No supernovae shone in the night sky over New Rilchuk. What Floshftok had detected was the leading edge of the wave front. The radiant glow, in frequencies across the spectrum, must blaze from stellar remnants lagging behind the neutrinos. The shock wave would be coming on at one-tenth light speed, thousands of light-years thick, sterilizing every world in its path.

No wonder *New Hope* fled.

Neither warrior nor climatologist nor astrophysicist could defeat exploding stars. He looked around the table. This time, one of the warriors beat Thssthfok to a conclusion.

Klssthfok, their most senior strategist, said, "The end of cycles."

. . .

FOR MILLIONS OF YEARS—how many, the historical record had too many gaps to ascertain—Pak had battled for their families and clans. Every possible advantage was embraced; every horrific consequence excused. In the process, Pak had visited upon themselves every imaginable disaster. Ecological failure. Gengineered plague. Nuclear winter. Bombardment from space. Toxic deserts and radioactive wastelands. The legacy spanned Pakhome, the home system's asteroids and rocky moons, even the colonizable worlds of nearby stars.

The return from each collapse was harder, the recovery time longer. Petroleum and coal were long gone from Pakhome, as were most fissile materials. Deuterium and tritium had all but vanished from the seas. Metals were more often stripped from ancient ruins than found as ore in new mines. Only knowledge—sometimes—persisted to alleviate the suffering.

And to hasten the *next* collapse.

Only there could be no recovery from a world sterilized.

"ONE FINAL COLLAPSE," Thssthfok said. *This* was why he had been summoned. Once imminent disaster was recognized, every protector on Pakhome would have a common goal: escape with his breeders.

The resources did not exist to evacuate a world.

There would be war over the few starships, and any resources that might be used to build more. There would be war over every type of supply necessary to provision a ship. And because this was, inevitably, the final war, it would be fought without restraint.

However closely *New Hope* approached light speed, the ship could not *quite* catch up to the wave front now rushing toward Pakhome to presage disaster. And yet, they must return for their breeders. They would arrive, inevitably, during the fiercest of all wars.

No Pak living had seen a nuclear winter, and the strategists needed the best possible information about the conditions in which they would fight. While most crew slept through the coming flight, Thssthfok would be analyzing the conditions into which they would arrive.

Wondering, with no answer possible, if he had breeders left to rescue.

3

Pakhome was a world in torment.

Its sky was banded in muddy black. Its continents were adrift in snow. Icebergs dotted its oceans. Day side or night side made little difference: Where the smoke was thickest, all was dark; everywhere else, the glare from the galaxy's core ruled the sky.

Rubble circled the world, the debris of this era's space stations joining the detritus of cycles passed. New craters scarred the moon, where colonies had thrived. The fourth planet had lost one of its moons, the fragments still distributing themselves into a new ring.

Up to a light-year distance, the fusion exhausts of small fleets showed that some clans had gotten away. Much of the ruin here came from their preparations: raiding for provisions for themselves and destroying what they could not steal lest rival clans pursue.

How had clan Rilchuk fared? That remained to be determined.

At maximum acceleration, Thssthfok's shuttle was three days' travel from Pakhome. *New Hope* was similarly distant, in another direction, hidden. Only scattered rock-and-ice balls registered on the shuttle's instruments; a beam weapon from any of them would arrive without warning. He could do nothing about that, so, while he waited, he redirected his main telescope back to Pakhome.

If protectors could, Thssthfok would have cried.

Only charred ruins or still-roiling columns of ash and soot marked where great cities had stood. The great dam on the river Lobok had been destroyed; most things that had not washed out to sea were now embedded in a sheet of ice. Nothing remained of the onetime great island of Rabal but a volcanic stump, lurid on the ocean floor. Thssthfok could not tell from this distance what had set off such a cataclysmic eruption, but his mind seethed with theories.

The ancient, sprawling Library complex near the center of the south-polar desert looked unmolested, at least at this resolution. In their need to escape, what all Pak sought was better weaponry, and weapons technology was knowledge no family ever deposited to the Library. The onrushing radiation would leave none to use the knowledge long accumulated there.

After millions of years and countless cycles, the great repository had become irrelevant.

THE LIBRARY . . .

For many breederless protectors, the Library was life itself. For as long as they could convince themselves they served the good of all Pak, they retained their appetites and managed to outlive their descendants.

For others, the Librarians were abominations, crimes against nature, and the Library a depressing place.

Thssthfok remembered visiting the Library before *New Hope* set out, poring over ancient records of Pakhome's climate. Every archway was inscribed with the symbol of the Library: the stylized double helix that represented life and cycles. The upward spiral spoke to the promise of better times, of past collapses mitigated with the Library's knowledge. The downward spiral represented the inevitable next collapse for which they must always prepare.

His work had gone slowly. Most information existed only as written text stamped into nearly indestructible metal pages, survivability taking precedence over ease of use. It was said that neither absence of electricity nor obsolescence of format could devalue the data—never that the archaic representations made work for Library staff, painstakingly transcribing from old languages to newer.

Thssthfok had worked quickly, eager to get away, vowing that if misfortune ever befell his bloodline, he would have the decency to fade away.

THE LIBRARY WAS ONE of the few Pak institutions to extend beyond narrow family interests. All would pass.

Some already had.

New Hope had approached the home system just in time to witness the destruction of the final space elevator. The structure was too thin to discern even at maximum magnification, but there was no mistaking the slow-motion destruction as half of the long cable crashed to the ground, or the scattering of the blockading fleet as the counterbalance end of the cable writhed free. With their mutual enemies all but stranded on the planet, the fleets of the space-based civilizations immediately turned on one another.

The island of Rilchuk, inconveniently remote from newly frozen lands, blessed with a paucity of natural resources, remained, for the moment, largely unmolested. Messages encrypted in family codes were answered with pleas for rescue. It wasn't too late.

Just all but impossible.

Three years of endless war gaming gave consistent results. *New Hope* alone could not evacuate Rilchuk. Even to approach Pakhome would be folly: A single starship could not defend itself against those who would be eager to seize it. But in addition to their ship, irreplaceable, the crew had one asset to trade. . . .

RADAR SIGNALED THE APPROACH of another shuttle and Thssthfok turned off his telescope display. The other craft was expected: Rilchuk was not the only clan bereft of options.

The ships exchanged authentication codes and rendezvoused. Thssthfok waited for his visitor to board. Despite connected air locks, the stranger wore a pressure suit. What appeared to be a medical scanner dangled from his utility belt.

The device could easily be a disguised weapon, but Thssthfok did not ask to examine it. Only unconsciousness or death could keep Thssthfok from protecting the secret he was here to trade, and a failsafe would blow the ship's fusion reactor at the first anomaly in his vital signs. Given the stakes, his visitor would expect no lesser precaution.

Warily, the stranger removed his helmet and sniffed the cabin. "Qweklothk," he introduced himself.

No clan name. Perhaps no snowball differed from another. *Rilchuk* emanated a heady bouquet, changing with the seasons, spiced with salt tang from the sea. *Rilchuk* was a place, a home, a proper clan name. Comet dweller would suffice, Thssthfok decided.

Qweklothk exuded not the faintest aura of kinship, and Thssthfok's skin crawled at the first new scent in years. He had not expected to find family here in the cometary belt, of course, but smell is a primitive sense, directly wired to the hindbrain. His mind and instincts warred. "Qwek-lothk," he repeated.

It was a label only, without meaning, the very concept jarring. *Thssthfok* was no arbitrary set of symbols but who he was: the dominant pheromones of his grandparents, represented in sound.

He, surely, was as alien to his visitor. "Thssthfok of Rilchuk."

"Show me," Qweklothk said.

The shuttle's small cargo bay held a cold-sleep pod. Thssthfok had been chosen for this meeting for what he did not know and could not reveal: the secrets of cold-sleep pods.

Qweklothk expected nothing different. Asking no questions, he slowly circled the pod. The scanner, now in his hand, hummed. He compared the readings from his instrument to the display on the pod control panel. He brushed rime from the dome to peer inside. A still figure lay within; with patience, the slow rise and fall of the chest was visible.

Qweklothk took a probe from a pouch of his pressure suit. Without asking—they would not be here unless Thssthfok was willing—Qweklothk retracted the dome to remove a tissue sample. The scanner chirped its approval.

New Hope had carried no breeders on its long voyage. The breeder in the pod had been captured in a supply raid on an outer-system colony. Its family was as good as dead, anyway.

The pod slowed metabolism, and with it pheromone release, to almost nothing. So, although this breeder was as foreign as Qweklothk, the gaping pod did not add to the stench—

Until Thssthfok woke her. Successful revival was central to the demonstration.

Thssthfok and Qweklothk smelled as alien to her. The breeder's screech trailed off into the silence of abject terror. She quivered in the pod, her eyes flicking between two unknown protectors. To the extent a breeder could think, she knew she lived at their whim.

Qweklothk poked and prodded her, gauging her reflexes. He scanned her where she lay. He lifted her from the pod and set her on her feet, running more scans as she stood shaking.

"Acceptable," Qweklothk said. That concluded their business, and he turned to leave. Almost as an afterthought, he snapped the breeder's neck.

Comet dwellers had resources to build starships and flee the oncoming radiation, but that would only prolong their extinction. Even at near light speed and measured in ship's time, the flight to safety in the outer galactic reaches would be an epic endeavor. Without cold sleep, most of all for the children and breeders, the comet dwellers could not possibly survive the trek.

Living quarters on a ramscoop were limited and austere. In less perilous times, it had been thought cold sleep would allow clan Rilchuk's migration to a new home—a world distant enough that rivals without cold sleep would not follow. How ironic, Thssthfok thought, to have found such a world only to abandon it. And that one hundred light-years once seemed a great distance.

Now cold-sleep technology might save his bloodline in another way.

Many comet dwellers would die rescuing breeders from Rilchuk, in exchange for cold-sleep technology.

THE ARMADA DESCENDED ON PILLARS of fusion fire. Airplanes and spaceships rose to intercept. Beam weapons, missiles, and railguns lashed out from every vessel. Plummeting like stones or bursting like fireworks, mortally injured craft disappeared from the sky. The evacuation fleet fought its way ever closer to the island of Rilchuk. At the appointed time, encrypted in clan codes, ships radioed the prearranged radio call signs.

From the developed end of the island, protectors unleashed their weapons to cover the landing of their rescuers. On the opposite, primitive end of the island, children and breeders cowered from the noise and chaos.

After massive losses to both sides, the enemy ships broke off their attack. The surviving evacuation ships, still broadcasting family recognition codes, vectored toward landing zones at the island's unpopulated waist. At the last moment, the oncoming ships swerved—

Incinerating with fusion flames the Rilchuk protectors on the ground. The comet dwellers could hardly rely on Rilchuk protectors to stand by passively while strangers captured their breeders.

Thssthfok would have done the same. Protectors were always—except, possibly, to themselves—expendable.

Through comm relays and by remote sensing, from the comparative safety of far-off New Hope, Thssthfok watched the comet dwellers round up, gas, and load children and breeders.

The comet dwellers now held Rilchuk breeders as hostages. Clan Rilchuk had been granted an ample supply of comet-dweller breeders as its own hostages. One clan needed cold-sleep pods and expertise. The other clan needed additional ships. Apart, they would surely die. Together, they might survive.

Thssthfok wondered how long the alliance could last.

THE RILCHUK/COMET-DWELLER FLEET RECEDED into the void. Thssthfok's final glimpse of Pakhome, before he lost it in the sternward glare, was of the southern hemisphere. At this distance, the Library complex was no longer visible. The stamped metal pages of the Library would survive the catastrophe soon to kill everyone left on the planet.

Thssthfok redirected *New Hope*'s telescope forward. Toward the galactic arm, and beyond.

Toward, if the fleet had one, its future.

IMPENDING DOOM

4

Sigmund Ausfaller always knew he would die horribly. Oddly enough, he had been optimistic. He had died horribly—twice. So far.

Modern medicine being all but miraculous, he was, all in all, pleased with how things had turned out.

That worried him.

Familial chaos surrounded Sigmund. Like a third lease on life, domestic bliss had taken him by surprise. He took a moment to bask in the commotion.

Hermes was tall for his age and skinny as a rail, with masses of dark curly hair. He had boundless energy, an impish grin, and creative excuses for the mischief in which he invariably found—and, as often, put—himself. The god of everything that involved skill and speed and dexterity had proven an apt namesake.

How old was Sigmund's son? Eight, as years were reckoned here on New Terra. And on old Terra, on Earth? Nobody on New Terra, not even Sigmund, remembered how long an Earth year might be. For that one vanished detail, at least, he had a decent approximation. He remembered that pregnancy took nine months on Earth, out of twelve. Here, where they didn't count in months, pregnancy lasted five-sixths of a year. That made New Terra's year about ninety percent of the ill-defined norm, and Hermes scarcely seven years standard.

And what, rather than gathering his things for school, was Hermes doing? Teasing his little sister, of course.

Athena was another perpetual-motion machine. She had a sweet face, a delicate frame, and an aura of fine blond hair. Barely four New Terra years old, she already showed signs of her mother's athletic grace. Athena was precocious; time would tell whether she achieved the wisdom to befit her divine namesake. As for her brother's teasing, Athena appealed, with eyes round and innocent, with theatrically quivering lower lip, for maternal intervention.

Scarily precocious.

Penelope, harried and overworked, funny and smart, struggled to set everyone on their way for the day. Penny was beautiful, with rosy cheeks and twinkling blue eyes. Waves of ash-blond hair flowed past her shoulders. She was as tall as Sigmund and much fitter. She was Sigmund's wife, best friend, and anchor.

Without hesitation, Sigmund would die or kill to protect any of them.

"What's the ETA on breakfast?" Penny asked. Tone of voice asked why he didn't just synth their meals.

Because Sigmund preferred to cook. Cooking centered him. "Two minutes." He flipped the Denver omelet, and that was the most anyone on this world knew about Denver. He started toast and poured juice. "Everyone sit." He and Penny together got a few bites into the kids before they rushed off to school.

Penny stayed long enough to fret about the latest crisis pending in her lab and to gently chide Sigmund about his jumpsuit programming. She didn't touch her fork until he set the nanofabric to a pattern and texture befitting his august stature. She patted his arm. "That wasn't so hard, was it?"

Before New Terra and Penelope, Sigmund had worn only black. No bother, no ostentation. But that was in other lives, on other worlds. He failed to see the logic of encoding social cues into programmable clothing. If anyone could project anything onto their clothes . . .

That, somehow, was why the *choice* made such a statement. Sigmund stubbornly refused to learn more. Clothing rules was one of the few mysteries he could afford to ignore.

He leaned back in his chair and, smiling, watched Penny eat. Did the pattern of the stripes on her outfit indicate that she ran the wildlife lab where she worked, or was the signal somehow a function of the faux-velveteen finish? He never quite understood her selections and did not care. That they both wore pastels—Hey, we're mated!—was all that mattered.

Sigmund tapped his wrist implant to bring up the clock mode. Good, he had a few more minutes. "So, a problem with the crabs," he began.

"They're adapted to a tidal environment. We had tides. Now they're gone." She glanced at her wrist implant. "That's the short answer. The full answer is much longer, and it's getting late. Ask me tonight. If you're home tonight, that is." They exchanged a quick kiss and she left.

Yes, Sigmund would die or kill without hesitation to protect his family. He would die or kill for his adopted home world and the people who had embraced him.

The difficult part was to wake every day wondering if this was the day. . . .

SANITY WAS OVERRATED.

The near infinite universe has a near infinite number of ways to kill you. Any rational mind acknowledges that simple logic and is appropriately wary.

Any rational mind, perhaps—but individuals do not define sanity. Groups do. Somehow, among humans, respect for the near infinity of dangers fails to qualify. Rational or sane? Those are very different standards.

Sigmund had not been born paranoid—not quite. Not until he was ten had his parents vanished in hostilities that failed to rise to the level of a numeral in the official reckoning of Man-Kzin Wars. They had died in a mere "border incident."

Everyone knew the Kzinti devoured their prey.

Sigmund had bided his time, kept his own counsel, and told the therapists what they wanted to hear. For more than a century, he lay low, set traps, marshaled his defenses, watched and waited. Until—

A precaution the sane disdained as paranoid had saved him. By then a midlevel United Nations financial analyst, his investigations had inconvenienced a criminal syndicate. Arguably, he wasn't saved soon enough—he died with a dagger through his heart—but UN police arrived in time to revive him. A trap Sigmund had set with his own wealth as bait had alerted them.

He had emerged from the autodoc with someone else's heart, and an invitation into a new life: as an agent of the UN's Bureau of Alien Affairs. For sniffing out threats to Earth's interests, the UN *liked* paranoids.

Eighteen years later Sigmund was killed for a second time. This time the police were too late to reach the body. Still, Sigmund *was* saved: spirited away by a covert agent provocateur who had stalked Sigmund—and vice versa—for years.

Sigmund and Nessus shared more than rivalry. Nessus, by the standards of his own species, the three-legged, two-headed Puppeteers, was also insane.

Sane Puppeteers were philosophical cowards. Sane Puppeteers never left home, nor allowed non-Puppeteers to know where home was. Sane Puppeteers ran from any danger—as they fled, even now, from the supernova chain reaction recently discovered onrushing from the galactic core. Because sane Puppeteers never left home, and the level of their technology was truly advanced, they brought home with them. Their evacuation fleet was a literal Fleet of Worlds.

And, as Sigmund soon learned after waking on New Terra, the Puppeteers also fled from their own sordid past.

5

Sigmund strode across the central plaza of Long Pass City. He studied his destination, the unassuming, four-story Governor's Building. He took in the bustling crowds. Trees and bushes dotted the plaza, and he looked at the stately pines and oaks and poplars, at the whimsical topiary animals, at—

Snap!

Sharp crack and unexpected movement drew Sigmund's eyes, unwillingly, to a shoulder-tall snarl of red and purple tendrils. As he stared, a second purple tendril lanced out. It was an alien hedge, snaring and devouring alien insects.

His eyes jerked away, down—

To find two clusters of shadows at his feet, one group extending to his left, the other to his right. His eyes jerked away again, skyward—

Where tiny artificial suns shone in two parallel arcs. A glow on the eastern horizon hinted at another string of the orbiting suns about to rise.

With a shiver, Sigmund forced his attention back to the plaza. His escorts glanced at Sigmund sidelong, and he realized he had skidded to a halt. He resumed his purposeful walk toward the Governor's Building.

Thirteen local years on this world, and the strangeness could still take him unawares. One of the few things Sigmund knew about Earth was that it orbited a star—that on Earth, a year *meant* something. Free-flying habitable planets like New Terra were the exception. That Nessus had left intact the memory of a life-giving sun could only mean that the knowledge *wasn't* a clue to Earth's location.

Unless, that was, Earth *was* like New Terra, and Sigmund's memory of a normal star had been planted as a false clue. . . .

It would be nice to know something for certain.

At one time he could have gone in one step directly from home or office to his meeting with the governor. How insane was *that*? Stepping-disc access to the world leader's own office! Everyone here trusted the teleportation system, no matter that the Puppeteers had designed and deployed it. No matter that, until a few years ago, the humans on this world had been unwitting slaves, the Puppeteers their absolute masters, and this world, then one among the Fleet of Worlds, was known simply as Nature Preserve Four. And it wasn't terrestrial life the Puppeteers had cared to preserve here, outside of the enclave that sustained their slaves. Pines and oaks, not purple bug-eating hedges, were the oddities here.

None too soon, Sigmund completed his march across the plaza. Outside the Governor's Building armed guards saluted. The squad leader extended a hand, palm up, for identification. "Good morning, Minister," she said.

"Good morning, Lieutenant." The lesson had taken years to set in, but *everyone* was to be checked for proper identification. Even the minister of defense. Even the world governor herself.

Sigmund took an ID disc from his pocket. He pressed his thumb against the sensor pad, and up popped a holo bearing his name and likeness against a shimmering backdrop of New Terra.

Beyond the security checkpoint people milled about the foyer. So did the occasional Puppeteer—only Puppeteer was a term from Earth and politically incorrect here. The aliens—locals—called themselves Citizens. After independence thousands of Citizens had chosen to stay. Native New Terrans saw nothing strange in that: Life anywhere off the home world marked a Citizen as low-status or an outcast, if not insane. Why not make a new life here?

Sigmund had another explanation. Many of the stay-behinds, surely, were spies.

Spy or not, one could never mistake a Puppeteer for anything else. He—females never appeared in public—stood on a tripod of two forelegs and a massive, complexly jointed hind leg. The torso reminded Sigmund of an ostrich, only the leathery hide lacked feathers. Two serpentine necks—vaguely sock-puppetlike, hence the nickname on Earth—emerged from between muscular shoulders. Each flat, triangular head had an ear, an eye, and a mouth. The mouth also served as a hand, with tongue and knobby lips substituting for fingers. The bony hump between the necks, padded with a thick mane, encased the brain.

Except for a belt or sash for pockets, Puppeteers wore no clothing. Like fabric selections among New Terrans, mane coiffures indicated status among

Puppeteers. Even the few Puppeteers in the lobby exhibited a wide range of braids and curls, ribbons and jewels.

As Sigmund's eyes swept across the lobby, at people and Puppeteers alike, he wondered: Which of you are spies?

The lieutenant finished her scrutiny and returned his holo ID. "Thank you, Minister."

An aide waiting just inside the main entrance led Sigmund to the governor's outer office. More sentries stood there; Sigmund presented his ID again before he was permitted inside to meet, alone, with the governor.

Sabrina Gomez-Vanderhoff looked more like a doting grandmother than the planetary leader. Her office was spartan and unassuming, decorated only with potted plants—all, blessedly, of terrestrial green—and holos of her family. Sigmund had known junior accountants with fancier offices.

No wonder he liked her.

"Morning, Sigmund," Sabrina said. Titles came out only on public occasions or around junior staff. Her slacks and blouse combined a riot of color and texture that doubtless—he would need Penny to truly understand—befit Sabrina's position. Her massive progeny ring glittered with four small rubies and a dozen emeralds: tokens of children and grandchildren. This was a farm world, all but unpopulated. Small families were a rarity here. That, too, was different from Earth—but a welcome change.

She gestured at a built-in synthesizer. "Help yourself."

"Black coffee," he told the synthesizer before beginning a slow circuit of her office, scanner in hand, checking for bugs. "We're clear, Sabrina."

They both knew he lied.

High on the wall behind Sigmund the grille of the air duct had a panoramic view of Sabrina's office. The screws that fastened the grille did double duty as stereoscopic optical and audio sensors. The bugs Sigmund pretended never to have found were far beyond New Terran technology—but not that of the Puppeteers.

With such an excellent source of information, Puppeteer agents might look elsewhere with less diligence. Such was Sigmund's hope.

Not that he placed much stock in hope.

They took their seats, Sabrina behind her desk, the better to squarely face the hidden cameras. She said, "So, Sigmund. What's scary today?"

What wasn't? But they rarely discussed the truly scary stuff within range of the bugs. "*Don Quixote* is overdue checking in, though not yet alarmingly late. A training accident at the Army academy. Defect rates remain too high at Munitions Plant Three."

"An accident? Not serious, I hope."

Sigmund kept his voice level. "We lost a young man." The cadet would arrive, soon enough, someplace the Puppeteers and their sympathizers might not suspect existed: the New Terran intelligence academy. Spy school.

"Remind me. Where did *Don Quixote* go this trip?"

"Routine mission, scouting ahead of New Terra," which world, in turn, flew ahead of the Fleet of Worlds. Sigmund suspected this world's erstwhile masters didn't entirely mind New Terra making its own way. By rushing ahead as fast as its planetary drive would take it, New Terra served as a lightning rod. Any hostile aliens that human scouts encountered in their path would more likely strike the world in the vanguard than those that lagged behind. "Sabrina, the delayed report may not mean anything." It wasn't even delayed. Not everything the scout ships did was intended for Puppeteer consumption, even though the Puppeteers paid well for scouting reports, and in the only currency that truly mattered: ships.

Which served only to replace—slowly—the ships destroyed in Hearth's nearly successful attempt to reclaim its errant farm world. Sigmund kept his expression stoic, not letting his resentment show. It wasn't as though Sabrina didn't share the anger.

Item by item, Sigmund updated Sabrina on New Terra's fledgling military and defense industry. Only someone born off-world could hope to grasp the concepts, let alone manage the undertaking. He was a talent pool of one.

(Who but the off-world paranoid even saw the need for a military? The only planets nearby were the Fleet of Worlds, whose inhabitants outnumbered the New Terrans almost a million to one. This world remained free at the whim of the Puppeteers. And among those Puppeteers, Nessus, at the least, expected Sigmund—somehow—to protect New Terran interests. That was why Nessus had brought Sigmund here. A very complex individual, Nessus.)

Sabrina asked for background on a long list of topics. He grumbled about a few. And finally the session was done.

Sigmund stood to leave. "Getting you those answers will take a while," he warned.

That, as they both knew, was another lie. It would serve to explain his absence for a few days—while he did his real job.

. . .

THE SQUAT AND RAMBLING STRUCTURE that was headquarters to the defense ministry existed in a state of perpetual flux. The disorder served both sides. Ongoing construction provided the perfect cover for Puppeteer sympathizers to hide sensors, and for Sigmund's most trusted inner circle to "accidentally" damage or discard the most troublesome of those bugs.

Amid organizations and reorganizations, drills and exercises, the ebb and flow of defense contracts, the ongoing construction, the cycles of plans and budgets . . . who could possibly detect the critical resources Sigmund siphoned off to where they could do some actual good?

From the governor's office Sigmund made his way across the plaza to the defense ministry, past layers of security personnel, deep into an area of ongoing remodeling where a few stepping discs had been deployed temporarily to facilitate the delivery of construction materials. Noise-absorbing partitions and stacked boxes "happened" to shield him there from anyone's view. His hand dipped into his pants pocket for his transport controller, thumbprint-*and* DNA-authenticated. He stepped onto one of the discs—

And off another disc, half a continent away.

Officially, this facility did not exist. Its funding was laundered through the Ministry of Defense. Its staff appeared, if at all, in the files of the Office of Agricultural Research. The stepping disc here had never been entered into any directory of the transportation network; only a few biometrically triggered transport controllers could override the system to access this location.

Few in the crowded, windowless room took note of Sigmund's arrival. Among those who had, he rated only desultory waves in greeting. These were the best of the best, handpicked and personally trained. It had been years since they needed much in the way of direction.

The Office of Strategic Analyses managed the real defense of New Terra.

SIGMUND SPENT A WHILE REVIEWING routine intelligence reports.

New Terra's military was mostly for show. It had to be capable enough to discourage meddling, if only to hold down interference to manageable levels; it dare not even hint at growing into a serious force. The Puppeteers would strike at the first sign New Terra might become a threat. All that deterred the Puppeteers from reclaiming their former colony, truly, was fear of disfavor with the Outsiders. Sigmund had ferreted out enough secrets to play off one species against the other—and extortion was a precarious way to live.

If New Terra was ever to achieve long-term security, he must find Earth.

With a sigh and a hand gesture he dismissed the latest report file. "Jeeves," Sigmund called.

"Yes, sir," his computer answered in a British accent. Some days, the AI understood Sigmund better than anyone or anything with whom he spoke. And with good reason: Jeeves, too, came from Earth.

Nearly half a millennium earlier, Puppeteers had established their slave colony using frozen embryos from a captured starship. To this day, no one in Human Space knew.

Until recently, no one *here* had known, either. They had been taught for generations to believe themselves the fortunate survivors of a derelict found adrift in space, and that the Puppeteers were their generous benefactors. Happy, grateful slaves they were—

Then the Puppeteers found out about the core explosion. Who better than expendable human slaves to scout ahead of the Fleet of Worlds?

More of Nessus' doing.

To give humans a starship, even under supervision, was a mistake. In time, Nessus' scouts found *Long Pass*, their supposed ancestral derelict. It wasn't afloat in the vastness of space; it was stashed inside a Puppeteer cargo ship orbiting another Nature Preserve world. The whole tissue of lies collapsed.

Much of the colonists' true history lay hidden in the ancient shipboard AI. Alas, Jeeves also had holes in its memory. Its ill-fated crew had managed, under attack, to erase all the astronomical and navigational data that might reveal the location of Earth. Not that the Puppeteers hadn't eventually found Earth anyway. . . .

"We're two of a kind, Jeeves," Sigmund said. We're brain-damaged fossils from Earth.

"Indeed, sir."

Jeeves's mellifluous voice brought England to mind, the accent reminding Sigmund of Shakespeare in Central Park. That, uselessly, Sigmund remembered, but not the shape of England, or its size, or where on Earth's surface it resided. Or, for that matter, what Central Park was at the center of.

Damn Nessus! He had violated Sigmund's mind, and Sigmund hated the

Puppeteer for that. But in bringing Sigmund here, Nessus had acted to protect the New Terrans from the darker instincts of his own kind. Here, Sigmund had started a new life. Here, he had the family on whom he doted. On New Terra, if he only could learn to embrace it, he might find actual happiness. So thank you, too, Nessus.

"The usual, sir?" Jeeves prompted. "If I may be so bold."

Sigmund had to smile. "Please."

A holo globe appeared over his desk, slowly spinning. Land, sea, and ice appeared on the surface, their boundaries ever changing. Jeeves invented topography, subject to the facts, and glimmers of facts, and wild speculations from facts—anything the two of them managed to dredge up. Occasionally, one of the random variations struck a chord, and then they had one more datum to guide a search for Earth.

The globe spun on, bringing into view twinkling motes atop an island peak. A city. It evoked the omelet Sigmund had had for breakfast. "Denver, the mile-high city," he said to himself. Whether on an island or in the heart of some continent, at least one major Earth city sat at that approximate elevation. Useless of itself, the random phrase from his subconscious had woken up Sigmund, his heart pounding, years after his arrival. Where one descriptive detail had surfaced from cultural trivia, others must lurk unsuspected.

New England clam chowder. Did England, wherever it was, have an overseas colony? It implied England had coastline.

Baked Alaska. The recipe involved ice cream and baked meringue. An implication of glaciers and volcanoes in proximity? That vague speculation evoked a second trace of memory. Who, Sigmund wondered, was Seward? Why was Alaska his folly?

Jeeves knew more than ten thousand recipes, replete with terms that might be place names or mythological references or—Finagle knew what.

Jeeves had more than cookbooks in his memory, and Sigmund was working systematically through it all. Legends and literature. Song lyrics. Not 3-V movies. A rotating globe, the outlines of Earth's oceans and continents plain to see, had been the logo of a movie company. The memory remained tauntingly just out of Sigmund's reach. In the rush to hide Earth from those who were boarding *Long Pass*, the entire film library had been erased.

That Earth had a moon was another fact Sigmund believed he knew. Month and moon went together—didn't they?—yet the months he remembered ranged from twenty-eight days up to thirty-one days. Not that he knew the length of an Earth day. Perhaps Earth had several moons, each with its own orbital period . . . but no. He remembered tides, twice a day. One moon.

Recently he had been sifting Jeeves's musical library for clues. Lyrics cited a blue moon, a silvery moon, a harvest moon, an old devil moon, even a paper moon. What was fact, what metaphor, what—

Sigmund started at a sharp rap on the door. The door swung open.

A man, short and stocky, dark-skinned with a long, black ponytail, stood in the doorway. Eric Huang-Mbeke was the first person Sigmund, fresh from the autodoc, had met on this world. Now Eric was the chief tech wizard for the Office of Strategic Analyses. He usually managed to get made just about any gadget Sigmund could need—and like most New Terrans, Eric was too innocent to know what needed making until Sigmund asked.

Eric looked—grim? No, stunned.

The alarms were silent. New Terra was not under attack. What, then?

"Is it *Don Quixote*?" Sigmund asked. Eric's wife, Kirsten, was aboard *Don Quixote*, its navigator and chief pilot.

Eric shook his head. "You have to see this, Sigmund. Jeeves, the incoming hyperwave message. Time—"

"I have it, Eric. A distress call, looping."

Like a soap bubble pricked, the spinning globe vanished from above Sigmund's desk, replaced by a 3-V playback. The text crawler was all squiggles, and Sigmund did not understand a single symbol. But that was not why he stared.

The figure in the image looked like a cross between an octopus and a starfish.

6

Cowardice was overrated.

The notion was insane, even seditious. Baedeker dared to think it anyway. He lived on New Terra in voluntary exile, far from home. Among Citizens, that choice alone branded him as insane.

He crouched over his redmelon patch, patiently weeding. The suns warmed his back. Both necks ached and the joints in all three legs, but that would pass.

Besides, few things tasted as fine as vine-ripened redmelon.

Cowardice was not a Citizen concept, of course. Citizens were prudent. Cautious. Sensible. Where humans had their leaders, Citizens sought direction from their Hindmost.

Once, the flight instinct was unassailably correct. To stray from the herd was to meet the jaws and claws of predators. Any tendency to wander had been bred from his ancestors long before the first glimmerings of sapience.

But things change.

Through fear, technology, and ruthless determination, Citizens had exterminated predators from the land surface of Hearth. They could not eliminate the lifecycle of stars. Now the Fleet of Worlds fled the sterilization of the whole galaxy—

Headslong into unknown perils.

THE DAY WAS ENDING, all but one arc of suns gone from the sky. Purple pollinators had begun to emerge from their nests, thrumming their delicate tunes. Far overhead, a lone terrestrial bird circled, effortlessly soaring. A cool breeze ruffled Baedeker's mane. He continued his weeding, trying to lose himself in the moment and the company of friends.

"I'm ready to stop," Tantalus said, his voices raspy from the dust they had raised. In truth, he had just arrived and scarcely started, hoping to hurry Baedeker along to dinner.

"And I," Sibyl agreed. "Food all around and nothing here to eat." His heads swiveled to look each other in the eyes. Sibyl was partial to irony, not least in the human-pronounceable label he had chosen for himself. Human independence had freed him from hard labor in a reeducation camp—not exactly how he had foretold regaining his freedom. "Baedeker, how about you?"

Baedeker was hungry, too, and so what? "I'll work a bit longer," he sang.

"A glutton for punishment," Tantalus answered. It was a human aphorism, and as he delivered it in English, it required only one mouth and throat. With his other head, he was already gathering his tools.

Tantalus' gibe was hardly fair, but Baedeker saw no reason to comment. Why match wits with his friends when to match wits with these weeds was the limit of his ambition?

He toiled all day, every day, not as punishment, although once he had been banished to another farm world and condemned to hard labor, and not as penance, although he had much for which to atone. He gardened as therapy.

With trills of farewell (and grace notes of disappointment) Baedeker's friends brushed heads with him before cantering off. They dropped their loads of weeds through a stepping disc, to a composting facility, perhaps, or into a food-synthesis reservoir, before they disappeared themselves, leaving Baedeker alone in the sprawling garden.

He knelt, picked up a trowel (carefully—it was a bladed instrument!), and resumed his task. When he had worked long enough, and hard enough, sometimes he lost himself in the rhythm of the task and forgot to think.

Thinking was the root of his problems. Thinking about impregnable hulls that weren't quite. About how to manufacture neutronium without exploding a star into a supernova. About the great sealed drives purchased from the Outsiders that moved whole worlds, and the all-but-complete mystery of the drives' operation, and of the stupendous energies involved, and—

No!

With grim determination, Baedeker refocused on gathering weeds to add to his pile. After a while, when not a single weed remained within his reach, he stood, joints cracking, to shuffle to a new spot. The sky was nearly dark now. He would have to stop soon.

The breeze hesitated, then returned from a new direction. He caught a whiff of something foul. The wind stiffened: a sea breeze.

His nostrils wrinkled at the stench. The coastal ecology had all but vanished, killed by the lack of tides.

As Nature Preserve Four, as a part of the Fleet, this world had been one of six worlds orbiting about their common center of mass. It had experienced ten tides a day. As New Terra, this world traveled alone. It had no tides.

Imminent nightfall and the reek of long-dead . . . whatever . . . that had drifted ashore to rot. Baedeker sighed, with undertunes plaintive in his throats. He would get no more relief from thought this day.

His examinations of an Outsider drive had not been entirely in vain. The mechanism somehow accessed the zero-point energy of the vacuum. Tapping the energy asymmetrically was inherently propulsive, enough so to move whole worlds. What if, he mused, one somehow superimposed the slightest of vibrations into the propulsive fields, applied a bit of a torque? Perhaps waves could be induced in the oceans, sloshing back and forth, to simulate tides.

And then? The force would not limit its effects to the oceans. A bit too much stress might topple buildings. And more than a bit too much? The strain could unleash seismic faults. An unintended resonance might build the surges higher and higher, until tsunamis crashed across the continents and washed away entire cities.

Baedeker trembled with the mad hubris his years of exile had yet to purge.

Perhaps, in these modern and perilous times, cowardice was overrated. When danger is everywhere, you cannot escape it. Except—

Quivering in shock and fear, Baedeker collapsed to the ground. His heads darted between his front legs, beneath his belly, into a Citizen's refuge of last resort: a tightly curled wall of his own flesh.

BAEDEKER COWERED IN HIS APARTMENT, picking disinterestedly at a bowl of grain mush and mixed grasses, still shaking from his latest panic attack. A holo played in the background, the ballet troupe surrogates for the companionship he craved but remained too shattered to handle. He would eat first, and comb the tangles and burrs from his mane, and bathe, and sleep. Then, perhaps, he would be fit to see and be seen.

From the pocket with his comm unit, a glissando sounded, cycling up and down the scale. He ignored the music until it stopped. Moments later a fanfare rang out, louder and more insistent, denoting a higher priority call. He ignored that, too. Before it could interrupt a third time, he dipped a head into the pocket and powered off the unit, averting his eye from the display. He did not want to know who had called. The matter could wait, or it was beyond his present ability to cope.

More tones, harsh and discordant, and from a new source: an emergency-override alert from his in-home stepping disc. Who? Why? Baedeker sidled away in fear.

A human stepped off, short and thickset with a round face. He was entirely unimposing—until those dark, intense eyes impaled you. Baedeker knew those eyes. He dreaded those eyes. He flinched and looked away.

It was Sigmund Ausfaller!

"Don't be alarmed," Ausfaller said.

Baedeker backed off farther, ready to bolt in any direction. Instinctively, he spread his heads warily, one high, one low.

"Do you know who I am?" Ausfaller asked.

It had been years since they last spoke, but of *course* Baedeker knew the human. Even if they had never met, he would have known. Ausfaller was the planet's lone Earthman, and the minister of defense.

The question made Baedeker wonder: How deranged do I look? He dared a sideways glance, and the mirror disclosed a slumped and disheveled figure. Despite himself, he plucked at his tangled mane. "Yes-s. Why have you come?"

Ausfaller looked for a place to sit, and settled for a mound of overstuffed pillows. If he had hoped to make himself seem less threatening, he had failed. "Baedeker, I need your help."

"You don't." Baedeker shivered. "I am a simple gardener."

Ausfaller leaned forward. "I know, and I'm sorry. You were once much more than that, a brilliant engineer. I need you to be one again."

Because who shares their best technology with their servants? Only fools, and Citizens were anything but.

Baedeker looked himself in the eyes. He remembered the cocky engineer he had been—and cringed at the memory. "I'm sorry. I can't do that."

Lips pressed thin, Ausfaller considered. "There is a serious danger. . . ."

Once again, one of Baedeker's heads had plunged itself deep into his mane. He pulled it out to fix the human with a frank, two-headed stare.

"The old Baedeker you seek? *He* is a serious danger. It is for the best—for everyone—that no one sees him again."

"And if a whole world is at risk? Perhaps many worlds? What then?"

His necks shook from the struggle not to plunge between his legs. Cowardice was overrated, he thought. All he said was, "Perhaps, Sigmund, you should tell me more."

Ausfaller shook his head. "Join a crucial, off-world mission or return to Hearth." When Baedeker said nothing, the human added, "Sanctuary is a privilege, not a right."

Many worlds at risk? That was no choice at all.

7

Hurtling through space on parallel courses a thousand miles apart, two ships prepared to swap crews. Cargoes had already been exchanged. Fuel had been transferred.

"Ready on this end," Kirsten Quinn-Kovacs called over an encrypted radio link from *Don Quixote*.

"After you, Eric." Sigmund gestured at the stepping disc inset on the relax-room floor. He was sweating. The ship-to-ship jump scared the crap out of him.

A stepping disc could absorb only so much kinetic energy. The velocity match had to be all but exact: within two hundred feet per second. That limit wasn't a problem when the velocity differences arose from planetary rotation. Then it was straightforward geometry to calculate the velocity difference between start and end discs. As necessary, the system relayed you through intervening discs.

The void held no intervening discs.

As a safeguard, send and receive discs were built to suppress transmission if they sensed a velocity mismatch approaching the threshold. The odds were all but infinitesimal that his two ships would cross the mismatch threshold during the light-speed-limited, under-a-millisecond interval between send and receive.

Maybe if Sigmund had trained as a physicist rather than an accountant he would have been reassured. He settled for the simple truth that the bigger risk was delay. To rendezvous and dock would take time they might not have.

"On my way," Eric replied. He stepped forward and disappeared. "Nothing to it," he radioed back.

Sigmund's mouth was dry. He cleared his throat. "Send them from your end, Kirsten."

One of *Don Quixote*'s crew popped over, and then a second. Both did double takes at seeing Sigmund. "Minister," one began.

Sigmund returned a too-slow, self-conscious salute. "You didn't see me. Captain Tanaka-Singh is on the bridge. He'll explain." Omar would keep these two hidden until *Don Quixote* returned from its upcoming, unannounced mission.

"Yes, sir," they chorused.

Alert clicks came over the comm link, then Eric's voice. "Sigmund, are you coming?"

"In a minute." Sigmund waited for the footsteps to fade. He muted the inter-ship link before connecting the intercom to Baedeker's cabin. "It's time."

Silence.

"Now, tanj it!" Sigmund said.

Finally: "Acknowledged, Sigmund."

However grudging, the answer was delivered in a breathy contralto. Puppeteers always spoke thus to humans. Given that a Puppeteer could imitate most musical instruments—and whole orchestras when he wished—the sexy voice had to be a conscious, manipulative choice.

A moment later hooves clattered on the metal deck of the corridor. Baedeker hesitated in the doorway, ready to run in either direction.

"Baedeker," Sigmund coaxed. The Puppeteer edged into the relax room. "Baedeker, it's your turn to cross."

With a bit less cajoling than Sigmund had expected, Baedeker sidled onto the disc and vanished. Sigmund allowed Baedeker a moment to vacate the receive disc before stepping to *Don Quixote*—

Where Eric was red in the face. Baedeker had backed away. His heads were swiveling about in panic, searching for somewhere to bolt. He found refuge behind the crates of weapons and battle armor Sigmund had transferred before the crew exchange.

"You!" Eric hissed. "How dare you—"

"He's with me," Sigmund snapped. "Eric, back off. That's an order."

Kirsten was listening over the intercom. "Who? Is everything okay?"

"Fine, Kirsten," Sigmund said. "Radio the shuttle. Tell Omar, 'Well done, and have a safe trip home.'"

Eric's hands were fists, white-knuckled, as he kept moving toward Baedeker. "Do you know who this is, Sigmund? What he tried to do?"

"Eric! Who is it?" Kirsten asked.

"It's Baedeker!" Eric shouted back. "Baedeker!"

Sigmund chose his words carefully. "He did what seemed best to protect his people and his home. As you and I do."

"He hid explosives aboard my ship!"

The late, lamented *Explorer*. "The ship you stole, Eric."

"That's not the point!"

It was precisely the point. In another life, on another world, Sigmund had hidden a bomb in another ship, and for the same reason: lest the vessel be stolen. Sigmund had done it first, and—unlike Baedeker—deterred a theft.

Not that Sigmund was proud of what he'd had to do. "Baedeker was doing his job. Eric, do yours."

Eric winced. "I always have."

Sigmund permitted Eric the last word to lessen the sting of the rebuke. "All right, Kirsten." Sigmund recited a set of coordinates. "Whenever you're ready."

Kirsten knew how Sigmund felt about spaceships and she allowed him no time to get cold feet. That, or she recognized their destination. "Dropping to hyperspace in five seconds . . . four . . . three . . ."

HYPERSPACE!

It was a place (dimension? abstraction? shared delusion?) that defied description. Whatever hyperspace was, or wasn't, when you were in it a hyperdrive shunt carried you along at a prodigious clip: roughly a light-year of Einstein space every three days.

Leave a view port uncovered in hyperspace and—if you were lucky—the walls seemed to converge in denial of the nothingness. If you were unlucky, your mind simply got lost. Whatever hyperspace was, or wasn't, the mind refused to acknowledge it. Hyperspace had driven many minds mad.

And so, ships sped through hyperspace with their view ports painted over, or hidden behind curtains, or powered down—and their crews, all the while, brooded on the oblivion that lurked just outside the hull. They dropped back to normal space, more and more frequently as a trip continued, just to know that something besides the ship still existed. And they found themselves, again and again, unable to stay away, on the bridge staring obsessively at the mass pointer. For whatever hyperspace was, or wasn't, the hyperdrive did something strange if it came too near to a large mass. Approach a star or a planet too closely while in hyper-space and—

Well, Sigmund didn't know what. No one did. Perhaps the ship ceased to exist. Perhaps it was hurled into another dimension, or a deeper level of hyperspace, or far across the universe. The math was ambiguous.

What Sigmund *did* know was that he feared hyperspace and that he wasn't alone. Nor was an aversion to hyperspace merely a human frailty. Before New Terra, Sigmund had known many spacefaring species. He remembered every one, just not how to find them. They all recoiled, in one manner or another, from hyperspace. Puppeteers exhibited one of the most extreme reactions. Most—Baedeker was among the exceptions—would not, under any circumstances, travel by hyperdrive.

The Fleet of Worlds would be a long time in its flight.

With a shudder, Sigmund pulled himself together. He pressed his cabin's intercom button. "Everyone, join me in the relax room. It's time for a mission briefing."

A VID PLAYED above the relax-room table. Sigmund's crew watched the holo. Sigmund watched them.

Kirsten stared, her eyes shining, her fingers drumming absentmindedly on the tabletop, at the final, frozen scene of the vid. She was trim and athletic, fair-skinned with delicate features and high cheekbones. Her auburn hair was cropped short.

Eric and Kirsten—husband and wife, reunited—sat together on a long side of the table. Baedeker occupied the parallel side, closest to the hatch the better to flee.

(Or perhaps Baedeker merely maximized his distance from the pointy corners. Puppeteer design shunned edges and corners. To Sigmund their furniture looked half melted, like the Y-shaped overstuffed seat on which Baedeker sat astraddle. The chair was a small part of the mission supplies that had been teleported aboard.)

Sigmund had taken the chair at the head of the table, the better to preside—and to separate Baedeker and Eric. The table end opposite Sigmund was flush with the bulkhead. When not in use, the table folded up against the wall.

"The Gw'oth," Kirsten said in wonder. "They mastered interplanetary travel."

Baedeker stared, too, but in horror. Like Kirsten, he was seeing this recording for the first time. "Another spacefaring race?" he said. "And you know of them? Explain."

Kirsten couldn't take her eyes off the image. "It was our first mission away from the Fleet. Eric and I, and Omar, and Nessus."

Baedeker bleated something two-throated and discordant. He didn't translate and he didn't need to. No love was lost between him and Nessus.

Kirsten frowned at the noise, then continued. "Unexpected radio broadcasts had just reached the Fleet. We backtracked, found these guys, tapped their communications. We learned a lot about them, without—at Nessus' insistence—ever making contact. They call themselves the Gw'oth. Individually, a Gw'o. They're from the ocean beneath the crust of an ice moon. We're heading to their solar system."

Baedeker pawed nervously at the deck. "And you left these Gw'oth a hyperwave radio beacon? Why?"

Eric and Kirsten exchanged unhappy looks. "It's complicated," Kirsten finally offered.

In other words, they didn't want to tell Baedeker. Tanj it, Sigmund thought, I need to build some trust among my crew. Distrusting Puppeteers is *my* job. "We have time," he prompted.

"We were testing the little guys," Eric offered. "We fried one of their primitive comsats with a laser to see how they'd react. The Gw'oth launched a replacement very quickly. That got Nessus wondering about the extent of their sky watching. The Fleet would've been passing by in about seventy years, moving at three-tenths light speed by then. If there was any possibility the Gw'oth could lob something stealthy into the Fleet's path . . ."

Sigmund shuddered, even though the back story wasn't new to him. You didn't have to be a Puppeteer to find kinetic-kill weapons frightening. "Go on."

Eric stalled for a few seconds with a bulb of hot coffee. "Nessus ordered us to rig a cometary-belt object with a thruster. The idea was to temporarily modify the snowball's orbit enough to seem a threat to the Gw'oth. He wanted to see if and how they reacted."

Baedeker's forepaw scraped the deck. "And did they?"

Kirsten shook her head. "We never did alter the snowball's orbit. *Explorer* was recalled to the Fleet first. Nessus was needed on Hearth. He never explained. And of course the Fleet has altered course to avoid the Gw'oth."

Mention of *Explorer* brought sad reminiscence to Kirsten's face and a flash of anger to Eric's. Baedeker intoned something deep in both throats.

There was a lot of shared history among these three, and Nessus, and the late ship *Explorer*. Sigmund tried, and failed, to interpret the Puppeteer's reaction. Maybe it was emotional, not verbal.

"Why leave the comm buoy?" Sigmund prompted.

Eric and Kirsten exchanged looks again. Kirsten said, "Soon after, Eric, Omar, and I went out again to scout ahead of the Fleet. Just we three. Either we had passed a test on the previous mission, or no one could be spared to chaperone us."

More soft, low-pitched chanting: jarring chords in some exotic key or scale that made Sigmund uneasy. Mournful? He guessed Baedeker had opposed the unsupervised mission.

Kirsten shivered and kept going. "Instead, we went hunting for *Long Pass*. Given what its discovery revealed about our people's own history, it was impossible to believe the Concordance"—Hearth's government—"wouldn't lob a comet at the Gw'oth.

"After independence, Omar and I went back. Removing the thruster from the snowball prevented that particular remote-control attack. It didn't guarantee the Gw'oth their safety. That's why we left a hyperwave radio buoy in the cometary belt: to monitor Gw'oth radio chatter. I programmed the buoy to signal New Terra if it sensed any significant changes."

Baedeker squealed like an abused bagpipe, still pawing the floor. "In just a few years the Gw'oth went from simple comsats to visiting the cometary belt? And you gave them a hyperwave radio to reverse-engineer? They could have hyperdrive in a matter of—"

"Not from us," Kirsten said firmly. "They won't find the buoy."

"And yet here they are using it," Baedeker retorted.

Kirsten shook her head. "We left behind a standard radio beacon, omnidirectional, on another moon near them, and directions for contacting us in major Gw'oth languages.

"The hyperwave buoy forwards to New Terra any radio signal from that beacon. The comm channel runs only one way—they can't follow a reply to locate the hyperwave relay. It was all strictly for the Gw'oth to reach us if they needed help."

Sigmund restarted the holo. The signal had repeated for days, but the message was short.

Amid fronds like drifting seaweed, a not-quite starfish—a Gw'o—undulated before them. Orifices puckered and relaxed rhythmically at the tips of its five tubular tentacles. Breathing? Speech? The shipboard translator rendered the runes that flowed across the bottom of the image.

"Friends, come at once. Something is rushing our way. Something very dangerous."

8

Sigmund tossed and turned to the accompaniment of faint moans from the adjoining cabin. He didn't blame Kirsten and Eric, reunited after what only Sigmund thought of as more than a month. His empathy didn't make their urgent lovemaking any easier to overhear.

Sigmund missed his entire family, terribly, but right now his thoughts were on Penny. Well, not his thoughts, exactly.

He had to laugh. You would think someone approaching two centuries old could handle a bit of celibacy. Only you would be wrong. His memories—such of them as he retained—reached that far into the past, but he had arrived on New Terra in the body of a twenty-year-old. Only Carlos Wu's nanotech-enabled, experimental autodoc could have put Sigmund back together. Soon after, Nessus had whisked away the prototype. The *lone* prototype. No one else on New Terra would be rejuvenated as Sigmund had been.

Well, Sigmund had saved Carlos's life once. Use of the autodoc made them even.

With a groan, Sigmund collapsed his sleeper field and settled slowly to the deck. He wasn't going to sleep, so he might as well get up. A bit of exercise, he decided, and maybe a snack. Then, if sleep remained elusive, something productive.

Away from the crew cabins, *Don Quixote*'s corridors were deathly quiet. The name was Sigmund's little joke. How did one explain a quixotic pursuit to people who had never read Cervantes? When asked to explain, Sigmund would say, "It's a long story."

He paced from stem to stern, engine room to bridge. The ship was basically a cylinder with rounded ends, about 110 feet in diameter. It provided ample pacing room. He whistled tunelessly as he went, patting the hull for its reassuring solidity.

Don Quixote was one of the few vessels in New Terra's tiny fleet made by the Puppeteers' General Products Corporation. The vessel was built in the #3 hull model. Before vanishing from Known Space, fleeing from the core explosion, General Products had advertised their hulls as all but indestructible.

Yes, but.

There are many obscure ways to die. Once upon a time, Sigmund had voraciously read and vidded mystery stories. The more impossible the crime, the more educational. Locked-room mysteries were the most instructive of all.

GP hulls were sort of like that.

As only a paranoid mind could, Sigmund began obsessing on the ways this hull could fail to protect him.

Hit something hard enough and passengers became stains on a still-unblemished hull.

And: Antimatter in sufficient quantities would destroy *anything* made of normal matter. But antimatter was scarce. The trick was to find enough.

And: Visible light passed right through the hull. The Puppeteers considered transparency a feature, not a flaw. You painted a GP hull where you wanted to block the light. So: A laser beam held on target long enough would vaporize the coating and overcome any antiflare shielding and pour unabated through the still-intact hull.

And: Each GP hull, it turned out, was a single artificial molecule, its interatomic bonds massively reinforced by an embedded power plant. It took an extremely lucky shot—or a nearby, stationary target—to fry the embedded power plant with a laser, but it could be done. Without the power plant, air pressure alone would burst the weakened hull.

And: There was at least one other way, one Sigmund had yet to fathom, to destroy a GP hull. Puppeteers had once destroyed a GP-hulled ship with a crew of ARMs aboard. Another time, they had destroyed, all at once, every GP hull in New Terra's tiny navy.

Baedeker had worked for General Products Corporation, and Sigmund sensed the engineer knew more than he would admit—which was nothing—about these events. An autodestruct code, Sigmund guessed, transmitted through the hull on visible light.

He did what seemed best to protect his people and his home. Sigmund found it much easier to dish out that line to Eric than to accept Baedeker's deeds himself.

Sigmund continued his aimless pacing, still seeking reassurance in the solidity of the hull. Seeking in vain. No material could protect a ship in hyperdrive from the hungry maw of a gravitational singularity.

He looped back to the bridge to peek again at the mass pointer. Not that there could have been—he had checked just minutes ago—but the instrument revealed nothing massive nearby. With a sigh, he changed course to settle in the relax room. "Jeeves," he called.

"Here, sir," the familiar voice answered. Most New Terran ships carried a copy of Jeeves. Puppeteers, predictably, suppressed AI development—why build a potential rival?—making Jeeves, centuries old though he was, more advanced than anything else available.

A snake-crowned image popped into Sigmund's mind. Medusa, his one-time AIde. Medusa was largely self-directed. *She* would have finished mining Jeeves's archives long ago, correlated everything with everything, calculated probable relations, inferred much—

While Jeeves had to be led by the virtual hand. Sigmund said, "At home I've been looking at references to Earth's moon."

"How may I help?"

Sigmund had been making his way through the music library, but in the faux-night of the ship's third shift, music seemed antisocial. He didn't feel like reading lyrics. What, then? "Literature with moon references. Most recent publication first."

Jeeves offered things that were diverting or amusing or aggravating or depressing, but nothing useful. Nothing scientific, of course, not even in the fictional sense. All such had been erased. Eventually there was *Goodnight Moon*, a charming little bedtime story which Athena would surely enjoy, and *A Moon for the Misbegotten*, which Sigmund couldn't imagine anyone enjoying. Broadening the search parameters to works with "moon" anywhere within the text gave a ridiculously long list. Sigmund had tried that before.

He synthed a bulb of hot milk, opting to read simply for relaxation. A few titles on the list of books mentioning the moon looked diverting. *A Connecticut Yankee in King Arthur's Court*, he decided. Connecticut sounded familiar, somewhere near a place he had once worked, he thought. Or maybe it was only that Mark Twain could be droll, or that King Arthur, like Jeeves, was English. Sigmund thought he might have seen a 3-V adaptation as a boy.

He straightened in his chair at the first mention of an eclipse. A solar eclipse. Something stirred in the back of his mind. . . .

"May I join you?"

Sigmund looked up. "Hi, Kirsten. Of course, I'll be glad for the company. I thought you were in for the night shift."

"Couldn't sleep." She covered a yawn. "Appearances to the contrary. What about you?"

"Same." He gestured at the text projected from his comm. "Maybe a bit of reading and some warm milk will do the trick."

She got herself tea before joining him at the table. "What do you think the Gw'oth saw?"

The four of them had gone round and round on that. The obvious answer, assuming the Gw'oth had seen *anything* and this wasn't a trap, was the Fleet. *Explorer* had found the Gw'oth precisely because their transmissions came from along the flight path of the Puppeteer worlds. That flight path had been changed, but the divergence was not yet significant.

The worrisome answer was that the Gw'oth had detected some kind of Puppeteer preemptive strike. If so, *Don Quixote* would almost certainly arrive too late to intervene.

"Gremlins," Sigmund finally answered, and then had to explain what gremlins were. *Gremlin* was as good a term as any for the final possibility: something altogether unexpected.

She yawned again. "So, what are you reading?"

Sigmund slid his comm unit toward her. "An Earth story from way before my time. Before spaceflight."

She blinked through a few pages and handed back the comm. "When you finish, let me know if you recommend it."

"Will do." Sigmund found Kirsten had lost his place. "Jeeves, I was coming up to an eclipse reference."

Some invisible handshake between AI and his portable unit did the trick. Sigmund resumed where he had left off. What had he been reading?

A nineteenth-century time traveler fancifully thrown back to medieval England, condemned as a witch. He avoids getting burned at the stake (ugh!) by using his foreknowledge of the imminent eclipse to claim power over the sun. How very convenient, Sigmund thought—

"Finagle!" he blurted.

Kirsten looked up from her tea. "Sigmund?"

"I may need you to do some math for me." A few taps put his comm's touchpad into drawing mode. He sketched a solar eclipse: sun, moon, Earth. Free-flying worlds don't experience eclipses.

"The sun is a yellow star," he began. That was not only Sigmund's questionable memory talking; New Terran biologists concurred. Human eyes were optimized for such a sun. So were plants grown directly from seeds in *Long Pass*'s dwindling collection. Earth-evolved crops cultivated on New Terra had already begun adapting to the more orange emissions of New Terra's orbiting artificial suns. Those false stars radiated the light that Hearth's biota preferred. The best estimate was that Earth's sun had a surface temperature around ten thousand degrees—entirely ordinary. As a clue to Earth's location, that inference was all but useless.

Earth's estimated year length was also entirely normal, putting the planet well within the habitable zone for a range of candidate stellar masses. Planetary orbital parameters were a function of solar mass, so even the decent guess Sigmund had at the length of Earth's year said nothing definitive about the orbital radius.

But now factor in *A Connecticut Yankee*'s total eclipse . . .

Range of estimates for the apparent size from Earth of its sun. Twelve months—twelve orbits of a moon!—in a year. So how big is that moon to fully eclipse the sun?

It depended how close to Earth that moon orbited.

They needed a whole second set of approximations about Earth itself. New Terra had surface gravity Earth-like enough not to have seriously messed with Sigmund's reflexes. Call Earth's surface gravity New Terran, plus or minus a few percent. New Terra and the five worlds of the Fleet gave a range of densities for rocky, habitable worlds. Density and surface-gravity estimates together implied Earth's mass, and so orbital parameters for its satellites.

Jeeves collated estimates and crunched the numbers. Kirsten tweaked the program whenever Jeeves bogged down.

The moon was, in a word, big. At *least* two thousand miles in diameter. Call it a quarter the diameter of Earth itself. A real clue, at last!

"We're hardly looking for a world at all," Kirsten said in awe. "Earth and its moon are nearly a double planet."

9

Sigmund was hindmost for this mission, and the hindmost has prerogatives. Baedeker reluctantly admitted the human to his cabin.

The main furnishings were a small synthesizer and mounds of pillows. Sigmund looked about and elected to remain standing. "Baedeker, you need to make peace with Eric. We're a crew. We must all get to know each other, learn to trust each other."

Trust Eric? The man had hate in his heart. And when had a Citizen ever shared a spaceship with another species without being in charge?

Still, the hindmost had his prerogatives. "I see your point, Sigmund. The Gw'oth are a most formidable species. We will need to work together."

"And yet you remain in your cabin."

Baedeker said nothing.

Sigmund jammed his hands in his jumpsuit pockets. "At the least, share what you have concluded about the Gw'oth."

"You already know. I expressed my views at the mission briefing."

Sigmund's nostrils flared. "You're not telling me something. Finagle, you're not telling me *anything*."

Until they arrived, what more was there to tell? They could see nothing, learn nothing while in hyperspace.

Meanwhile, he was far from home, alone among humans. "There is something I have been thinking about."

"What's that?"

"A moon," Baedeker said—and Sigmund jerked. Why? "Until a few years ago, when New Terra left the Fleet, it had tides. Ten every day. Now it has no tides, and the coastal ecology has been devastated." The reek remained fresh in Baedeker's imagination.

Sigmund said, "Penny, my wife, is a biologist. She's talked about the problem. In fact, she wanted to talk to me about tidal zones, but we never got back to it." The suspicion that was always lurking peeked out of Sigmund's eyes. "But why talk now of a moon?"

"Because a moon is the answer," Baedeker said. "Give New Terra its own moon and it regains some tides."

"Give New Terra its own moon. I should have thought of that. Doubtless the Outsiders are eager to give us a planetary drive."

The sarcasm was unmistakable—long after they were dead and forgotten, the Concordance would still be paying the Outsiders the price of the Fleet's drives—but Baedeker saw something more. Sigmund truly was interested. And Sigmund's government ministry must control a *lot* of resources.

"I have been thinking," Baedeker began cautiously. "Maybe I can build such drives."

NOT EVEN A CITIZEN can wallow forever in fear.

Citizens were social creatures. Humans were not of the herd, but Baedeker had lived among humans long enough for them to have become familiar. He could talk with them. And so, with *Don Quixote* still ten days from its destination, he left the sterile confines of his tiny cabin.

Emerging during the night shift, he was typically faces to face with only one human at a time. Dealing with all at once could wait arrival at their destination. Most often he saw Kirsten. She seemed not to sleep much.

"Mothers learn to get by without much sleep," she had explained more than once.

Would he ever experience parenting? Perhaps, if he returned to Hearth. Nothing prevented him—except him. He had seen how power was wielded by those who led from behind. It was ugly and self-serving. No, it was better to take more time, to forget.

Which begged the question: How much more would he need to forget after this mad adventure?

ONCE MORE, Baedeker circled the corridors of *Don Quixote* with Kirsten. She had a quick mind and a good heart, and she had taken it upon herself to look after the interests of the Gw'oth.

The more she spoke of them, the more foolish her advocacy seemed.

Few on Hearth knew anything of the Gw'oth, and for good reason.

The sea creatures were too scary to reveal to the public. Baedeker was in the small minority, one of the technologists asked to assess the implausible findings of the *Explorer* expedition. Only everything Nessus had reported was true! The Gw'oth had, incredibly, advanced from fire to fission in two generations.

No one ever told Baedeker the Fleet had veered to give the Gw'oth a wider berth. No one had had to. The nanotech process by which General Products built its hulls was sensitive to the slightest of perturbations. Soon after *Explorer* returned, transient gravitational ripples had disrupted production in the orbiting microgravity factory. Ripples such as a planetary course change might cause.

In the few years since Kirsten last visited, the Gw'oth had added interplanetary travel to their capabilities. Who could say interstellar travel would not soon follow?

Baedeker was here, today, coerced onto this mission, because he had been immobilized by an existential question. Was it time for him to return to Hearth? Now he had his answer.

If a strike by the Fleet was not why the Gw'oth called for help, it would be—as soon as Baedeker returned to report what he now knew.

10

"Five minutes to dropout," Kirsten announced calmly.

Sigmund's eyes refused to leave the mass pointer. It was by far the largest instrument on the bridge, a transparent sphere from whose center extended blue lines of varying lengths. The direction of a line showed the direction to the corresponding astronomical object. The length was proportional to the object's gravitational influence: mass over distance squared.

He sat, transfixed, in the copilot's crash couch. The longest line, aimed right at him, nearly touched the clear surface, and that terrified him. The line seemed somehow *hungry*, ready to devour this ship, and that horrified him even more. Only a sentient mind could operate a mass pointer, which begged the question: What might be out there contemplating *him*?

Five minutes!

The math was simple. Every extra second they remained in hyperspace brought *Don Quixote* another two light-minutes closer to their destination. But a moment too late would be fatal. Sigmund gritted his teeth and said nothing. Kirsten was by far New Terra's best pilot.

"Sounds good," Eric answered from the engine room. "All ready back here."

Baedeker did not report from his cabin. Sigmund imagined the Puppeteer was a tightly rolled ball just now.

Five minutes!

After an eternity Kirsten began the final countdown. "Ten seconds, everyone. Eight, seven . . ."

"Passive sensors only," Sigmund reminded her.

She nodded. "Two, one, now."

The mass pointer went dark. Sigmund activated the forward view screen. Ahead: stars.

. . .

DON QUIXOTE DOVE into the solar system at breakneck speed.

It was a crawl compared to their moments-ago pace through hyperspace—but with the mind refusing to see hyperspace, how could you judge?

"Lots of background EM," Kirsten reported. "Data links. Video and radio chatter. It's all from the inner system. Nothing's intelligible from this far out."

"Radar?" Sigmund asked her. He raised his voice over the clatter of hooves in the corridor. Baedeker had emerged from his cabin.

"Not that I can tell, Sigmund. Nor lidar, nor deep radar, not that any of those matter in a stealthed ship." She took a deep breath. "It'll be hours before the Gw'oth can know we're here."

Because it would be hours before information from here could reach the inner system. Hyperwave radio was instantaneous where it worked—which was outside of gravitational singularities. They were almost 4.5 billion miles from the star, only a bright orange dot to the naked eye, and *Don Quixote*'s black hull would reflect little of the faint light that reached out here.

"Unless they are already out here," Baedeker chided from the hallway, before Sigmund got out the caveat. Cowardice was not a bad substitute for paranoia.

"I'm detecting interesting neutrino flux," Eric said over the intercom.

Kirsten frowned. "Check your instruments and I'll check mine. I'm still not seeing any deep radar."

"Because it's not deep radar. It looks like fusion reactors."

Sigmund glanced toward the nervous tap-tap of hoof pawing deck. Baedeker had to be thinking: fission to fusion in a few years. Sigmund knew how the Puppeteer felt. On Earth, if Sigmund remembered correctly, that transition had taken close to a century. Jeeves probably knew exactly, but Sigmund didn't ask. The details could wait. Or maybe, at some level, he didn't want to know.

Don Quixote was scarcely a minute out of hyperspace—and a third of a million miles deeper into the solar system. Einstein space (an attribution no one on New Terra but Sigmund understood) and hyperspace velocities were independent. When Sigmund had recalled *Don Quixote*, Kirsten came back as quickly as she could. It had meant a thirty-gee sprint out of the system that she had been scouting, to get where she could engage hyper-drive. *Don Quixote* still had all that Einstein-space velocity, because they hadn't spent the time to slow down before swapping crews. Relative to this solar system, *Don Quixote* traveled at about seven percent of light speed.

Well, they would have to slow down to meet the Gw'oth.

"Thrusters or gravity drag?" Kirsten had a hand poised above the thruster controls. Her preference, obviously.

Sigmund turned toward her. "Neither, just yet. Let's coast for a while and gather data."

Kirsten's hand pulled back. She used it to give Sigmund a perfunctory salute. He read disapproval.

Not so, Baedeker. From the corner of his eye Sigmund saw heads bobbing—high/low, low/high, high/low—in emphatic agreement.

Kirsten changed her tune within the hour. By then Eric had localized the neutrino readings. Fusion plants existed on every major moon of the lone gas giant and on two of the three rocky planets.

11

Intelligence was overrated.

Since time immemorial the Gw'oth had lived and died beneath the world-encompassing ice. In just three generations all that had changed. Now they built mighty structures in the vacuum above the ice, ringed the world with satellites and water-filled habitats, even colonized nearby worlds. Intelligence had made all that possible.

But intelligence required you to give up *so* much.

Er'o hovered in his meditation chamber, his tubacles rippling, seeking respite in the simple joys of motion. His hide was mostly cautious oranges and reds, shading to far red on the tips of his spines. But for an undertaste of lubricant from the pumps, he might have been below the ice. The water that endlessly circulated through this chamber was lush: rich with salts, thick with nutrients, ripe with the synthetic spoor of prey. Nothing was too good for those who made possible all the progress.

Except free will.

From tubacle tips curled downward, he gazed through the clear ice floor. Structures in every shape imaginable sprawled down the seamount slope and across the world's foundation until detail faded into a distant haze. The ancient city was built mostly in stone, of course, but here, there, everywhere jutted new steel construction. Artificial lights glowed everywhere. Cargo vessels glided about, over and among the buildings. Tn'ho Nation ruled the longest, most productive hydrothermal vent in all the ocean, and Lm'Ba was its greatest city.

But that power and wealth might vanish even more quickly than it had come.

Er'o bent and flexed, tensed and relaxed, until the stress flowed down the length of his tubacles and out of his body, until his hide recolored to more serene hues. Succulent worms and fat scuttlebugs had been delivered while he worked, and now he ate his fill. He voided his wastes. As best he could, he cleared his mind. He permitted himself a brief, timed rest period.

Food and elimination, motion and meditation: for true intelligence, one abstained from them all.

The timer rumbled, and Er'o roused himself. Somehow, he had managed to sleep. He jetted from his private meditation chamber, down the narrow access tunnel. His was one cylinder among many, arranged like spokes around the hub (wheeled vehicles above the ice being another small marvel of the age) that was the central work space. High above the clear dome, great Tl'ho, radiant, striped, roiling with storms, dominated the sky. Two cold spots—whole worlds themselves—transited the great orb.

And Gw'oth like himself crept about on their arid, rocky surfaces!

He was first among the sixteen to reach the central work space. Quickly the others arrived, emerging from their meditation spaces, most colored the same anxious reds and far reds he now showed. Their common task, unchanged for several shifts, glowed on the assignment board: Find the Others.

Er'o knew the task was urgent. Also impossible, unless the aliens responded to his people's plea.

He extended one tubacle, trembling, and then another. Both limbs were taken up. Within, ears went all but deaf, registering only the beating of hearts. Within, eyes and heat receptors went dark.

A jolt like electricity coursed through his thoughts.

More! He needed more! Switching to ventral respiration, he extended his remaining tubacles. He groped about for contact, felt probing in return. Limb found limb, aligned, conjoined . . .

Ganglia meshing!

Feedback swelling!

Heart racing!

Electricity surging!

We will take over. The thought roared in Er'o's mind. His own musings, feeble things, plodding, inconsequential, faded. . . .

Ol't'ro, the group mind, had emerged.

Intelligence was *wonderful*.

"IT AIN'T WHAT YOU DON'T know that kills you," Sigmund recited softly. "It's what you know that ain't so."

"To what do you refer, sir?" Jeeves replied.

Sigmund had been talking to himself but chose not to admit it. "Our slithery friends."

"That's why we're here," Jeeves said.

It was a neutral response, signifying nothing. An answering noise, not an answer. Sigmund missed the reasoning power—and the friend—that had been Medusa. Wishful thinking got him nowhere.

Then what about some productive thinking? "Jeeves, bring up a picture of a Gw'oth ensemble." An image shimmered over the relax-room table. "Thanks, Jeeves."

Images of the Gw'oth had become familiar. A Gw'o had five limbs arrayed about a central disc, sort of like a starfish. Spines covered the skin, again like a starfish. There the resemblance ended. A Gw'o's skin changed colors like a squid or octopus. Its appendages were flexible, like those of an octopus, and hollow like tubeworms. Tier after tier of sharp teeth ringed the inner surface of each tube. Eyes and other as-yet unidentified sensors peeked out from behind the teeth. Almost certainly Gw'oth had evolved from some type of symbiotic carnivorous worm colony. Yes, Gw'oth had become familiar, singly and in groups. Except—

Fascinated and repulsed, Sigmund examined a pile of writhing Gw'oth. The archival image was flat—in the era of *Explorer*'s visits, the Gw'oth had yet to develop holography—and for that Sigmund was grateful. Those piled, pulsing tubes, ends swallowing one another, the throbbing flesh, the occasional limb disconnecting and groping free of the twisting mass (to breathe?) came just a little too close to . . . what? A spill of loose intestines? A nest of snakes having an orgy?

No one would look Sigmund in the eye around pictures like this. Puppeteers wouldn't discuss sex with anyone but Puppeteers, and not among themselves for all Sigmund knew. They had imposed much of their prudery on New Terrans. Not that this pile of protoplasm was engaged in sex. Mature Gw'oth sprayed gametes into reefs and let nature take its course.

With a sigh, Sigmund called Kirsten's comm. "Can I pick your brain for a bit? I'm in the relax room."

"Be right up. Give me a few minutes to finish something." Faint background noises suggested she was in the engine room.

She strode into the relax room a few minutes later and suddenly noticed something interesting about her boots.

Sigmund said, "Not a pretty sight, but important." Perhaps the most important thing about the Gw'oth, if correct. "Make sure I understand this activity."

Kirsten ran a hand, the fingers splayed, through her hair. "Sure, Sigmund."

"As best I can count, that's a set of eight. Where I can see what's happening, each Gw'o has linked to three others. Just as one end of each tube links into the central mass, at the other end, the nervous system remains accessible. What you decided on the *Explorer* mission is that Gw'oth link to form group minds. Biological computers."

"An octuple like this . . ." She hesitated, not understanding his grin. She knew nothing of octopi.

Penny, bless her, had come to terms with Sigmund's apparent non sequiturs. Finagle, he missed her. "Go on," he urged.

"Right. We've seen groups of four and eight, and very rarely a group of sixteen. An octuple connected like this is suited to working 3-D simulations." Kirsten leaned against an end of the table, putting her back to the imagery. "The big mystery about these guys was how they developed tech so quickly. But these . . . linkups . . . tell us.

"I hacked Gw'oth netcams and databases to correlate these . . . episodes . . . with data growth rates in their archives. The correlation wasn't perfect, but I wouldn't expect it to be. Not all calculations produce data at the same rate. So a line of Gw'oth generates one kind of data, solving a particular class of physical problems. 2-D arrays of Gw'oth modeled another kind of problem. You're looking at a 3-D array. They even do 4-D, but like sixteen-tuples that seemed to be rare.

"Weird but true, these guys link into living computers. That makes the apparent speed of their technological spurt misleading. They had a lot of simulation to do before they ever moved above the ice to build a technological society."

Sigmund had left New Terra more or less this informed, only he had never really dwelt on it. It was hard to make time to contemplate the Gw'oth, a good ten light-years distant, when with a half-decent pair of binocs he could see the Fleet in the night sky.

Only here, now, the Gw'oth weren't distant.

"Kirsten, bear with me." It took Sigmund a while to put his misgivings into a coherent question. "How far back do their archives go?"

She shrugged. "The digital ones I hacked went back thirty years. Until then they lacked the technology to build such things."

"But the Gw'oth have other archives, much older? Pre-tech archives?" He tried to imagine how such records would be kept. Scratched into soft stone with hard stone, perhaps.

"They must, Sigmund. Unless the older records are digitized, we have no way to know."

And unless Kirsten gets back into the archives. Between her last visit and this one, the Gw'oth had deployed network security. Sigmund respected the robustness of the aliens' encryption and authentication methods, even as he cursed them for making his job more difficult.

Explorer had intercepted broadcasts in several languages, suggesting different societies, maybe distinct nations, among the Gw'oth. Rivalries could have spurred the new security measures. Or Kirsten might have brought this upon herself by leaving native-language messages with the radio beacon. It wouldn't take geniuses—though the Gw'oth were—to infer alien visitors had tapped their comm.

Most of what Kirsten had said made sense, but *must*? Her conclusion was too firm for the source data. He said, "What if the Gw'oth don't have deep archives?"

"Then they thought everything through quickly. But that can't be." She hesitated. "Can it?"

Sigmund didn't want to think so, either. Unpleasant implications hardly disproved the possibility. "Jeeves, do you have a full set of records from the *Explorer* mission?"

"I do, Sigmund."

"We're done viewing Gw'oth ensembles. Give us a map of cities versus data archives."

A black sphere popped up, with red filaments randomly zigzagging across its surface. Here and there, along the winding red threads, green dots shone. Jeeves said, "Red denotes population centers. Those stood out in *Explorer*'s deep-radar scans. Green dots are archive locations, not to scale so you can see them. Steady dots are confirmed archives, the ones Kirsten hacked into. Blinking dots are archives inferred from address directories."

Gw'oth cities hugged the ocean-floor hydrothermal vents and ringed the occasional volcano. Sunlight played little role in the ecology here; chemosynthesis around the vents drove the food chain. Tidal flexing by the gas giant kept the ice moon seismically active and its vents pumping out energy-rich nutrients. To the Gw'oth, the vast expanses of ocean between vents must be like deserts.

But the few-and-scattered archives? That Sigmund could not explain. As the holo globe turned, the distribution of archives appeared less and less even. "Why don't more cities have archives?" he wondered.

"Unknown," Jeeves said.

Kirsten raised an eyebrow. "Sigmund, you're imagining a puzzle where none exists. With worldwide comm, they can access data centers from anywhere. Not every city needs its own."

They must. They could. Kirsten was guessing.

Hacking remotely into Gw'oth data centers and netcams had been brilliant. Likewise, deducing that the Gw'oth assembled into living computers. But Kirsten's genius was technological. Divining intent, sniffing out deceit, recognizing threats . . . those tasks required different skills.

"Jeeves," Sigmund said. "Does prevalence of archives in a city correlate with anything?" That was too broad, so he clarified. "Population density, maybe. Local language. Ocean depth. Characteristics of the hydrothermal vent."

Pause. Then, "None of those, Sigmund."

Kirsten synthed a bulb of coffee for herself. "Where are you going with this, Sigmund?"

"I don't know." Sigmund trusted his intuition. A hidden truth was trying to warn him. He was sure of it.

"There *is* a correlation," Jeeves finally decided. "It's between archive sites and seismic damage."

Kirsten grinned. "Mystery solved, Sigmund. Data centers are valuable, so the Gw'oth don't put them in areas prone to quakes."

"That's not the case," Jeeves said imperturbably. "The correlation is to seismic damage, not seismic activity. There's less damage near archives because those cities use more metal construction. Differences in seismic activity aren't statistically significant."

"Similar fractions of stone buildings fallen, Jeeves?" Sigmund guessed.

"Correct, Sigmund."

Kirsten said, "Richer cities use more metal construction. Richer cities have archives. I just don't see what's bothering you, Sigmund."

"Maybe nothing." And maybe biological computers, like the digital archives the ensembles filled with data, were a recent mutation or innovation. If the latter, the Gw'oth were a bigger potential threat than Baedeker already feared.

If so—and if the call for help the Gw'oth continued to transmit wasn't bait for a trap—how scary was whatever had *them* frightened?

REAL-TIME DATA STREAMED into the main archive of Lm'Ba: high-resolution observations from a fivefold of orbiting telescopes. Faint electromagnetic waves from sources across the sky. Counts of neutrinos and cosmic rays from instruments deployed worldwide.

Ol't'ro sucked in all the data. They synthesized and integrated, deduced and projected. They drank in the stars and planets. They delighted in the fire of the sun. They tasted the faint glints of distant asteroids and the even more remote rocks and ice in the far-off cometary belt.

They gulped it all down and thirsted for more. Thirsted for one *particular* taste.

Someone had left a radio beacon and a message of hope on the back of a nearby moon. Someone had marked the position of the beacon with crossed lines lased deep, and long, across the rocky surface. Simple micrometeoroid frequency measurements and abrasion-rate calculations proved the incisions were recent.

Too recent to have been cut by whatever was headed this way.

Ol't'ro kept scanning the skies for whoever had left the beacon and the offer of help. They had to hope those Others who offered help would return in time.

12

After two days coasting and observing—during which the Gw'oth archives, despite Kirsten's best efforts, kept their secrets—Sigmund had to concede they had learned what they could from afar. That, and he was tired of rehashing what little they knew about the Gw'oth. He assembled everyone in the relax room to discuss "next steps."

Kirsten was eager to meet *her* Gw'oth. She got right to the point. "Thrusters or gravity drag?"

The answer was not obvious, at least to Sigmund. Which technology should they risk revealing to the Gw'oth? He tossed back the question. "Which do you recommend, and why?"

"Thrusters. Even if we get all the way down to the ice surface on gravity drag—which would be fancy piloting, even for me—we'll need thrusters to leave. If you hope to keep secrets, Sigmund, why show gravity drag at all?"

Sensible—given her unstated assumption. "Eric. What do you think?"

"Pilot's decision," Eric said.

"Baedeker?" Sigmund asked.

Baedeker tugged at a lock of his earnestly coiffed mane. "These Gw'oth learn so quickly. I opt for the less advanced technology, of course. But Citizens have used both technologies for so long I can't tell you which was trickiest to develop."

And *Don Quixote* didn't have a Puppeteer historical database. No New Terran ship or institution did.

The Earth Sigmund remembered, however imperfectly, knew thrusters and gravity drag. Both were fairly recent technologies. Thrusters were very new; he had flown on ships that used fusion drives instead. Fusion drives being potential weapons of mass destruction, ships reliant on them used air compressed nearly into degenerate matter for takeoffs and landings.

Sigmund did not understand thrusters well enough to make even an educated guess whether Earth's and Hearth's relied on the same physical principles. The history of technology was hardly his field. There might have been an earlier generation of thrusters he knew nothing about. "Jeeves. Have you been listening?"

"Yes, Sigmund."

"When *Long Pass* left Earth"—at least four and a half centuries earlier—"was either technology known?"

"Only gravity drag."

"Gravity drag only *drags*," Kirsten said impatiently. "It won't get us launched, so we'll reveal our thrusters anyway when we leave. We might as well slow down with thrusters."

There was that unstated assumption again. She presumed *Don Quixote* must land.

Neither Eric nor Kirsten would want to hear it, but setting down on the Gw'oth world was far from certain. The call for help that had brought them here could be part of a trap. If anything smelled wrong, Sigmund meant to go far, far away—fast.

Humans in the Fleet had had no tech to call their own, only such crumbs as the Puppeteers had let drop from their table. Then came *Explorer's* mission, discovery of the Gw'oth, and the loss of innocence. Learning to respect Gw'oth accomplishments had taught Kirsten and Eric respect for their own lost ancestors. It was the first step on the road to New Terran independence.

Gratitude to the Gw'oth was understandable. It was also his friends' blind spot.

A partial truth would serve. Sigmund said, "Braking quickly, however we do it, shows we have artificial-gravity control to offset our deceleration. Braking by gravity drag gives little else away. So: gravity drag to slow us most of the way. When"—if!—"we land, we do so with our thrusters dialed way down, disclosing little about their capability. We launch the same way." *And thrusters remain our secret if we don't land at all.* "We'll accelerate once we're out of sensor range."

"Gravity drag, full braking," Kirsten summarized. "Thirty gees."

Sigmund nodded.

She grinned. "That should be fun."

The nervous tap of Baedeker's forehoof suggested *fun* wasn't the word he would have chosen.

13

Banded and wreathed in storms—much larger and, for that reason, more luminous even than the distant sun—mighty Tl'ho commanded Er'o's attention.

It was scarcely an exaggeration to imagine that he felt the gas giant's presence. Pure, beautiful mathematics had characterized the cyclic flexing of the ocean bottom, and from that, the force of gravity, and from *that*, the enormous mass that must somehow exist, unseen, theretofore unsuspected, beyond the ice that since time immemorial had been the roof of the world.

And it was here, as real as the beauty of mathematics.

That gigantic new world, unlike anything the Gw'oth had ever known, was but one wonder. Ice was not the roof of *the* world, but only of *a* world, at that a mere moon. The universe was far vaster than anyone had imagined. And while Tl'ho had been revealed by its gravitational attraction, none had anticipated the magnificence of its appearance, or the even larger, far more distant object in whose reflected light Tl'ho glowed.

It had turned out that the sun and, by extension, the far-off stars were much hotter than Tl'ho. For a short while after first venturing up onto the ice, scientists puzzled why the fiery pinpoints in the sky had fixed locations. But as parallax measurements soon revealed, at least some of the fixed stars weren't. They were only very, *very* remote.

So Er'o had believed until the latest observations. *Something* was shooting across nearby skies. Something as hot, almost, as the surface of the sun. And that something, whatever it was, was slowing rapidly, exerting tremendous forces.

Er'o emitted a sharp tone burst. The sounds would propagate along the science-station tunnels into the farthest lab, workshop, and private chamber. "Time to assemble."

Er'o was at a loss how best to proceed.

As Ol't'ro, he would know.

OL'T'RO CONSIDERED:

A rapidly decelerating object—a ship—detectable only by the vast amount of heat it radiated. Ol't'ro contrasted the lost energy of motion with the measured radiated energy.

An approximation—the efficiency of the deceleration mechanism being unknown—of the ship's mass. Bigger by far than the largest Gw'oth ship.

The arc of the ship's course. A manipulation of space-time, Ol't'ro concluded. Interesting. Almost instantly, they began to refine their concept of gravity.

Reluctantly, they deferred the puzzle for a later time. Another inference had more urgent value to the polity. They disconnected a tubacle, to couple its mouth with a comm terminal.

The Others had arrived. Their ship would reach the ice soon.

BAEDEKER CIRCLED HIS TINY CABIN, too tense to sleep or even to sit. He had tried comforting digital-wallpaper motifs to no avail. Neither crowd scenes, not even with a double release of aerosol herd pheromones, nor tranquil meadows helped. A dollop of synthed grain mush sat in its bowl, scarcely touched.

And they had hours to go before *Don Quixote* approached the gas giant.

Over the intercom: an unfamiliar chime. Baedeker wondered if the tone was a new affectation from Jeeves.

He was wrong.

"All hands," Jeeves announced a moment later. "The Gw'oth are hailing."

Baedeker gaped at the latched door of his cabin, as though aliens were about to swim through it. His reaction was foolish, of course. This ship was stealthed. The Gw'oth hail had to be a broadcast of some sort, in the hope that someone had responded to their earlier message.

He was wrong again.

"Comm laser," Sigmund announced, surprise plain in his voice. Laser communication was directional. "The Gw'oth know we're here. Everyone to duty stations."

Duty stations meant Kirsten and Sigmund on the bridge and Eric in the engine room. And himself? Anywhere not underhoof. Sigmund had phrased it more tactfully as "on call."

The others reported in from their posts. "I'll remain in my cabin for now," Baedeker declared for completeness. "Jeeves, what is the nature of the hail?"

"I'm streaming the incoming signal, receive only," Kirsten answered for the AI.

To all appearances, rolling hills of lush purple meadowplant surrounded Baedeker for as far as the eye could see. He banished the idyllic pastoral set-ting from one cabin wall. The incoming message filled the cleared space.

A Gw'o undulated before an unseen camera. In parallel rows, cryptic squiggles and English translation straddled the image. "Thank you for responding. Once you are closer, we will talk."

14

Don Quixote plunged deep into the Gw'oth system, with every sensor straining for data.

From bases across the Gw'oth solar system, radio chatter spiked. (Perhaps laser comm spiked, too. With no way to intercept directional traffic, how could one know?) Surface vehicles massed in large formations, fanning out from the few mountain peaks that poked above the ice. Spaceships maneuvered, their fusion flames hot and unmistakable. Electromagnetic launchers stretching far across the ice flung yet more vessels into space.

So many ships! So many EM launchers! It seemed less and less likely the Puppeteers had intervened here since Kirsten's last visit.

Sigmund focused on more pressing matters: the present flurry of Gw'oth activity. Defensive measures? Factional rivalries? Preparation to attack *Don Quixote*? Knowing as little as he did about the aliens, Sigmund could rationalize any of those scenarios. Being who he was, he suspected the last.

He was sharing the bridge with Kirsten. Leaving the piloting to her, he studied the tactical summary in the main holo display. It showed far too much activity for his liking. Kirsten's certain disappointment notwithstanding, they would *not* meet soon with the Gw'oth on their home ice. That would simply be imprudent. Perhaps later, when they knew more.

"Jeeves," Sigmund said, "I assume you can also translate from English."

"Correct, Sigmund. Barring vocabulary shortfalls, of course."

"Good. Send this: We wish to meet first with those who invited us."

Kirsten squirmed in her crash couch.

"Something on your mind, Kirsten?" Sigmund finally asked.

"No. Well, yes. We know who on the ice moon contacted us. I backtracked the laser."

So why not land near there, she meant. And if that's a trap? "Who initially asked for our help and who contacted us when we arrived might not be the same."

"Besides whoever used our beacon, who knew to look for us?" she countered.

Even those Sigmund had trained seldom thought to consider spies and traitors, comm taps, or the general perversity of the universe. He couldn't *not* think of them. His gift. His curse. "It could be——"

"A reply," Jeeves interrupted. "The signal is from the same ice-moon surface peak that sent the greeting."

A holo opened in a secondary display. Sigmund couldn't decide if this Gw'o was the one they'd seen in the earlier message. Its skin tone differed, but that told Sigmund nothing. Even over short comm sessions the colors ebbed and flowed.

Gw'oth communicated in sound bursts, not unlike dolphin speech, and like a dolphin the acoustic organs were internal. Sigmund wasn't surprised that the figure in the holo didn't *look* like it was speaking. The transmission's audio subchannel sounded—the part, anyway, low-pitched enough for Sigmund to hear—like a whale crossed with a click beetle.

Sigmund read, "Greetings again, visitors. We are those who asked for your help."

Assertion was hardly proof. The mention of "help" was encouraging—Sigmund's message had said "invited"—but hardly conclusive. "Respectfully," Sigmund began. How should he phrase this?

"Sorry. I can't translate 'respectfully,' " Jeeves said.

The Gw'o had not finished speaking. New text appeared in the holo. "But I ask myself, how can you know that?" (Sigmund had an answer for that—not foolproof, but an answer. He waited to see what the Gw'o would say.) "We should meet where you left your beacon, although the radio itself has since been moved to a more convenient location. You will know that we know the spot."

At the beacon: That was the solution Sigmund had envisioned. Tanj, but these Gw'oth were fast.

Baedeker was monitoring from his cabin. "Sigmund, tell these Gw'oth to arrive first. If they follow us or extrapolate our course, their arrival near the beacon would prove nothing."

"Agreed, Baedeker. I'll give it a minute to be sure our new friend is done."

It wasn't. "We will launch from this location, arriving before you. When we meet, you will also know that we control the beacon area."

Anticipating another possible objection. Implying, if not proving, that these Gw'oth were those who first found the beacon. "Acknowledged," Sigmund said.

Very tanj fast.

THE GAS GIANT HAD FOUR MOONS, all tidally locked to their primary. *Explorer* had left its beacon on the outermost moon, on the outermost side, on an airless, stony plain forever invisible from the ice moon. From space, however, the laser-carved X could not be missed.

A ship sat near the crossed lines, in a shallow depression seared by fusion flame. Spectral analysis of the dim sunlight reflecting from the hull suggested steel and ceramics. *Don Quixote*'s instruments had tracked the Gw'oth vessel from an electromagnetic launcher on the third moon to its landing here.

A low dome rose from the plain half a mile from where the alien vessel now sat. Electromagnetic railguns around the dome made a point: The Gw'oth in the ship had come with the consent of those who controlled this area. Probably additional railguns remained hidden in camouflaged emplacements.

Don Quixote was in a high orbit around the moon, where it would remain until Sigmund decided a landing was safe. The Gw'oth ship would disappear soon below the horizon.

Those on the ground saw that, too. A Gw'o appeared in the main bridge comm display. "Again, we thank you for coming. We have much to discuss. Will you join us?"

Sigmund studied the tactical display. The railguns did not represent any threat to a General Products hull. At worst a volley from the surface might rock *Don Quixote* a bit. Nothing else nearby seemed threatening.

He polled his crew. Eric and Kirsten wanted to land immediately. Baedeker proposed they continue by radio, now that they had eliminated any appreciable light-speed delay. And Sigmund considered the message that had summoned them: "Friends, come at once. Something is rushing our way. Something very dangerous."

Perhaps not to meet was more dangerous than meeting.

"We'll be right down," Sigmund said.

. . .

THE AIR LOCKS OF THE GW'OTH SHIP and dome stood no taller than Baedeker's knee. No one from *Don Quixote* could enter even if they wanted to—which he certainly did not. The humans, though, were clearly disappointed.

But neither did Baedeker want to see any Gw'oth aboard *Don Quixote*.

"We cannot permit them aboard this ship!" he shouted. He and the humans had crowded into the relax room. "They will see things. They will ask questions. Who knows what they will discover about our technology."

Eric and Kirsten exchanged glances. Recalling their first and only visit to the General Products orbital facility and the secrets Nessus had carelessly let slip? A deflated minor chord escaped Baedeker at the memory.

"We haven't much of a choice," Sigmund said. "We wouldn't fit inside their facilities, even if we felt like swimming, nor do I care to give them potential hostages. We can't stay on the surface for any length of time because of the radiation. That leaves *Don Quixote*."

"And radio," Baedeker reminded.

"We'll take precautions," Sigmund said. Tone of voice declared the subject closed.

Baedeker pawed nervously at the deck. A paranoid's precautions might keep them physically safe, but that was not enough. "Then we must control what any visitor can learn. We have seen no evidence that the Gw'oth know about hyperwave radio or hyperdrive shunts, or of deep radar." Of course, within his lifetime they had not known fire. These aliens were very quick. Too quick. "We cannot even allude to the existence of such technology."

Sigmund nodded. "Fair enough. They're small; some of them and a couple of us can meet in this room. We'll move or cover the few stepping discs between the main lock and here. No access to the engine room, so they won't see the hyperdrive shunt. What else?"

"No bridge access," Eric suggested. "A glimpse of the controls might imply things about all sorts of systems, from propulsion to the emergency protective force fields for the crash couches."

Baedeker made an unfamiliar sound, part whinny and part whistle. Nerves? "We cannot hide the hull, but we do not mention its properties or how it is made."

"We paint over the few clear areas of the hull," Kirsten contributed. "And we don't show or allude to our computers. Given that the Gw'oth compute biologically, they may not suspect what can be done with hardware."

Sigmund nodded. "Jeeves, when our friends come aboard, don't speak unless spoken to. You're a crewman. We can say you're on watch on the bridge."

"Yes, Sigmund."

"Good," Sigmund said. "What else?"

Baedeker had a stasis-field generator in his luggage for medical emergencies. It was locked in his cabin, secured behind a biometrically controlled lock he had installed. He had not admitted to having it, and he would not now, but—"We should not mention stasis technology."

The length of the eventual list did nothing to assuage Baedeker's doubts.

PARANOIA HAD ITS USES, Baedeker had to admit.

It did not matter that a Gw'o was only two feet across, or that only one would come aboard for this first meeting. Sigmund saw no certain way to distinguish between a pressure suit and battle armor, or between instrumentation and weapons.

And so, before they opened the outer air-lock hatch for the tiny figure scuttling across the arid plain, Sigmund set into place a final safeguard.

Unless one of *Don Quixote*'s crew periodically reset the failsafe, the hyperdrive shunt would activate. If Jeeves decided the crew was acting under duress, *it* would activate the shunt. Either way, the ship would be forever beyond the reach of the Gw'oth.

The precaution was Eric's idea, and he had the decency to look embarrassed when he suggested it.

15

Despite the motorized exoskeleton of his pressure suit, the trek to the alien ship left Er'o exhausted. A trace of memory from Ol't'ro condescended about how easy Er'o had it. Early pressure suits had been only garments made from the tough hide of deep-sea creatures, trailing hoses to leather-bag "pumps" kneaded by helpers who remained beneath the ice.

The echo of memory did not dwell on how many had died in their explorations.

The alien hatch controls were intuitive enough but above Er'o's reach, and he waited for those inside to cycle the access mechanisms. The outer hatch shut and he got his first surprise. Gas, not water, gushed in. The pressure leveled off at a very low value. Without his protective gear, he would burst before he could suffocate.

Soon enough, the inner hatch opened into a long, dim, curving corridor. Two immense creatures, disturbingly asymmetrical in all but one plane, waited within. They towered over him. Somehow they balanced on two limbs. Loose coverings obscured most of their bodies, which glowed in far-red.

One of the humans stepped forward. A slit opened and closed in its top/central mass (some sort of sensory pod?). Er'o felt low-pitched, unintelligible sound. With his amplifiers set at maximum, he heard without understanding what the alien was saying.

Sound rumbled from a device grasped by an alien limb. "Welcome. I am . . ."

A translation device of some sort. No wonder they spoke so poorly. Er'o knew seven languages and was about to learn an eighth. He wondered why anyone would bother with a translator. The untranslated noise burst, Sigmund, might be a name.

So: introductions. Er'o modulated his voice to the frequency range

Sigmund had used. The sound would not carry far through water, but it did not need to: A transducer in his suit captured his speech and an external transducer repeated it. If need be, the speech would be routed to his suit radio.

"I am Er'o. Welcome." For now that exhausted his vocabulary of humanish, so he let the humans' translator deal with, "Thank you for answering our call."

The other, Eric, introduced itself. Together they moved deeper into the ship. Er'o chose a tripedal gait, bearing two tubacle tips aloft, the better to observe ahead and behind. Somehow the humans managed to move on two curiously rigid lower limbs.

They came to a large interior chamber. At Eric's self-explanatory upper-limb gesticulation, Er'o climbed onto a four-limbed structure (another untranslatable term, chair) and from there up to the table. The humans folded onto chairs and Er'o did not feel quite so tiny.

And so it began.

BEHIND THE LOCKED DOOR OF HIS CABIN, Baedeker listened over the intercom. He observed via security cameras. Through Jeeves, he monitored life-support sensors for subtle treachery. And he trembled, plucking at his mane.

The procession finally reached the relax room. Er'o, wearing a transparent, mechanically assistive suit, sprawled across the table. Inexplicable instruments hung from its harness. Eric and Sigmund, seemingly without a care in the universe, took seats on either side of the table, inches from the Gw'o.

How did they do it? How could they bear it?

Baedeker permitted himself for the first time to marvel: How did Nessus and the very few like him bear to scout for Hearth?

HALF AN HOUR WITH ER'O and Sigmund had begun to feel dim-witted.

Within a day Er'o could be speaking English like a native. The Gw'o never needed to hear a word or a conjugation more than once. It caught on immediately to grammar rules. Every so often it would get into a heated argument with Jeeves, speaking through Sigmund's comm, about fine points of translation. Within minutes Er'o had been teaching Jeeves more than the other way around.

"We can begin," Er'o said abruptly.

Sigmund had just been thinking that. "All right. Why did you contact us?"

"For most of our history, the roof of the world was ice. Then we discovered that the universe is a much bigger place. Ever since, the sky has fascinated us, and we have put considerable effort and resources into"—quick consultation with Jeeves in Tn'hoth—"astronomy. Perhaps we would watch less if, like you, we could travel faster than light."

Eric blinked. Sigmund hoped with little conviction that Er'o would be slower to master body language than the spoken variety.

"How do they know?" Baedeker yelled from the safety of his cabin. "We must find out!"

The howl went straight to Sigmund's earplug speaker. He put a finger up to his ear, pretending to scratch. The pressure cranked down the amplification.

How was a good question, and Sigmund would follow up. First, though, he wanted an answer to his own question. "And what have your astronomers seen?"

"Something unusual moving through space, more or less toward us. At sublight speeds, but fast."

"The Fleet?" Baedeker asked, loud despite the lowered setting of Sigmund's earplug.

Maybe, Sigmund thought. Five worlds accelerating through space looked scary enough to him. "Can you describe it, Er'o? Better, are there images we can see?"

"Images would be best," Er'o said. It unclipped one of the devices that dangled from its harness. "This is at the limits of resolution of our instruments." A hologram appeared, ghostly faint. "My apologies. This projector is designed for use under water, not in air."

Sigmund dimmed the relax-room lights nearly to off. His eyes adapted and details emerged. Stars, all in shades of red. Lurid dust clouds. Here and there, momentary sparkles. The projection was some sort of time-lapse graphic, because the clouds seemed to change.

Whatever this was, it wasn't the Fleet. It wasn't New Terra.

"I don't recognize the starscape." Eric rapped once on a leg of his chair, addressing his comment to Jeeves, then twice more in quick succession.

The double tap signified Kirsten, sitting unhappily on the bridge at the launch controls. And at the weapons console. Sigmund didn't trust Baedeker to use the laser if a reason arose—or not to run for home without reason.

"Me, either," Kirsten said, sounding embarrassed by the admission.

"I'll see if I can match it," Jeeves said into Sigmund's earplugs. "It may take a while."

Meanwhile, Sigmund thought, there were other things to clarify. "Er'o, you said, fast. How fast?"

The Gw'o had flattened itself on the table, and Sigmund guessed it must miss the effective weightlessness of the ocean. It raised a limb tip and wiggled it about. "There is no single answer, Sigmund. Local variations span the range from rest to four-fifths light speed."

"What about overall?" Baedeker asked in Sigmund's earplugs.

Sigmund repeated the question.

The Gw'o waved the tentacle tip again. "In the short time we have been watching, the overall phenomenon has been propagating at about two-fifths light speed. Modeling of the turbulence is inconclusive."

Sigmund was feeling dim-witted again, like Dr. Watson to an alien Sherlock Holmes, when Jeeves interrupted.

"I've matched stellar configurations," Jeeves announced via earplug. "As for why the image looks so odd, Gw'oth appear to be blind across most of what humans consider the visible spectrum. I'll send an adjusted version."

Gw'oth cities hugged the hydrothermal vents. Life on their world sought heat, not light. Sigmund guessed the aliens were sensitive mostly to infrared.

An image formed on his contact lenses. Stars shifted color. Dust clouds, and the turbulence within them, took clearer shape. The phenomenon, whatever it was, loosely suggested a rippled, steep-sided cone. The tip of that cone was truncated, lost in the distance.

Jeeves, helpfully, had superimposed grid lines in the coordinate system learned by Puppeteer and New Terran pilots.

Baedeker made no comment. Rolled into a tight ball, comatose, Sigmund guessed.

Something was erupting from the galactic center. The disturbance was light-years deep, light-years across, and spreading.

Before reaching the Gw'oth, it—whatever *it* was—would overtake the Fleet of Worlds and New Terra.

16

Sealing his pressure suit, preparing to exit the dubious protection of an inflatable emergency habitat, Baedeker groped for reasons to venture onto the ice. He tried logic: The Gw'oth had no reason to harm him. And the greater good: What he might accomplish here could safeguard the herd. Even cowardice, after a fashion, helped: He would die painlessly, his hearts stopped by autonomic conditioning, if the Gw'oth used coercion to obtain Concordance secrets.

Mostly, though, an epiphany propelled him forward. He finally understood how Nessus, and other scouts like him, did it. One quivering step at a time.

Kirsten exhibited neither doubts nor rational prudence. She was fairly bouncing with impatience. Of course bouncing took little effort here. The Gw'oth home world—Jm'ho, Er'o had called it—massed less than a quarter what Hearth or New Terra did.

Bending his necks this way and that, Baedeker gave his pressure suit a final front-to-back, top-to-bottom inspection. Everything looked proper. A small, flickering light reported that the suit's sensors were active and recording. He tongued an electronics self-test. *All systems functional*, his heads-up displays declared. Clearing the HUDs brought up *Me, too.* As uneasy as artificial intelligence made Baedeker, he would not forgo an onboard translator. That had meant downloading a Jeeves subset into his suit computer.

Finally, Baedeker checked the shelter's external radiation sensor. It barely registered. This moon generated enough of a magnetic field to shield against the radiation belts of the nearby planet. The local field originated in the currents in the salty ocean just beneath his hooves.

"Ready," Baedeker declared reluctantly.

"About time," Kirsten said. "They're waiting for us."

As though he had not known. What Citizen on an unknown world would *not* monitor all available surveillance sensors? He tongued a mike control. "We're coming out."

"Excellent," a Gw'o responded. "We have much to do."

Er'o, Baedeker read. So the AI, too, could identify Gw'oth from auditory cues. That made sense. Clearly Jeeves recognized humans and Citizens from their speech.

The Gw'oth who spoke English—more by the hour—had personalized their voices. Baedeker had noticed emphases on different harmonics and slight variations in pitch. Whether he could rely on the Gw'oth to maintain consistent auditory cues remained to be seen.

The shelter air lock accommodated only one person at a time. Baedeker let Kirsten precede him, as a favor more than from caution. He activated intrusion alarms. Then his turn came and he stepped onto the icy, vacuum-cloaked surface.

Eight Gw'oth waited in a semicircle beyond the air lock. Despite their transparent protective suits Baedeker could not tell them apart. One stood on all five limbs, the rest on three. The freed limbs coiled around unfamiliar devices or were merely held aloft (for a better view, perhaps).

The gas giant hung overhead, at nearly full phase, luminous with an eerie blue light. Blue because methane in its upper atmosphere absorbed red. The distant sun could not compete. Baedeker raised his suit heater against a chill he knew was psychological.

Most directions offered only rippled ice out to the unnaturally close horizon, but a mountain stood a short walk away. Tall structures all but hid its slopes. Solid, aboveground land was exceedingly scarce on this world. Baedeker looked at the peak in vain for a flat, unused expanse where he and Kirsten might relocate their shelter.

The Gw'o standing on all fives scuttled closer. "Hello again," it said. "Shall we proceed to the observatory?"

Er'o, Jeeves commented unnecessarily.

Baedeker gestured at the shelter. "If used improperly, our equipment can be dangerous." Such as the self-destruct charge rigged to the intrusion sensors. "For your safety, no one should attempt to enter when we are away."

Er'o waggled a limb side to side. (An acknowledgment? A dismissal?) "Thank you for the warning."

"Er'o, would you introduce us to your companions?" Kirsten looked unhappy, and Baedeker supposed she was changing the subject.

"They are not important," Er'o answered, repeating that side-to-side limb gesture. He started toward the mountain without turning; the two closest of the unnamed Gw'oth accompanied him. The rest took up positions around Kirsten and Baedeker.

Guards, Baedeker decided: They grasped weapons. Protecting Er'o from Kirsten and Baedeker, or protecting all of them from some external enemy? With a mind of its own one of Baedeker's forehoofs pawed the ice, spraying ice slivers.

An escort edged closer, and Baedeker's radio offered a burst of hums and chirps. *Come with me,* Jeeves translated on the HUDs.

They set off together after Er'o.

An elevated tram went up the mountainside. Its cars were far too small for Baedeker or Kirsten. They proceeded on foot, single file, up a narrow switchback road apparently vacated for their use. Tall buildings to both sides closed off Baedeker's view. Bare limb tips—thousands of them!—pressed against the windows. Gawkers? Bubbles behind the glass proved what logic had foreseen: water-filled habitats.

Baedeker peered down cross streets as they passed. Everywhere, Gw'oth in protective suits rushed about on their unknowable business. Some stopped and raised a limb or two, staring, as the entourage passed. He and Kirsten might even have inspired a vehicle crash.

He was winded as they approached the summit, but also oddly comforted. It was the gapers, he decided. Water dwellers living above the ice were probably the elite, but they gave no evidence of dangerous genius. Er'o was dangerously perceptive, but you *would* send your best mind to a first contact.

"This is a fascinating city," Kirsten was saying. "How many Gw'oth live here?"

"This is more a research center than a regular city," Er'o said.

Not an answer, Baedeker noticed. Was the population a secret?

"A *large* research center," Kirsten persisted. "What types of research?"

"Many kinds," Er'o answered vaguely. "But I see we have arrived. For now we will concentrate on astronomy."

They rounded a corner and their way forward was in shadow. Baedeker looked upward at the metal dish of a radio observatory. Behind a sturdy (but only knee-high) fence, a squat building served as the antenna's base.

"We are here," Er'o announced, adding something unintelligible in his own language. (*A security code,* Jeeves guessed.)

The gates opened, and Er'o passed through. Kirsten and Baedeker stepped over the wall. The guards remained outside.

Now their work began.

BAEDEKER WAS HAPPY TO LEAVE their escorts at the barricade. Tiny though Gw'oth were, small weapons could make large holes.

More Gw'oth met them in the courtyard. These were introduced. In order of ascending pitch, their new acquaintances were Kl'o, Ng'o, and Th'o. They looked as interchangeable as everyone else on this world. (Like three more peas in a pod, Kirsten offered without explanation.) All were mathematical physicists. From the intimacy in which they gathered, with Er'o joining the cluster, Baedeker knew they were close. He guessed they were part of an ensemble mind.

"We will begin with the radio observatory," Kl'o said.

"Excellent," Kirsten said. She peered up at the enormous dish. It was tipped toward the horizon, providing her an edge-on view.

Baedeker inspected the antenna, too—more surreptitiously, he hoped—with the ambient-neutrino scanner clipped to a utility loop of his pressure suit. The steel was surprisingly thick and the ghostly image on the instrument screen showed why. All that metal was rife with flaws and microfissures. Here was another example that the Gw'oth had much to learn—in this instance, how to manufacture with atomic-level precision. Baedeker added nanotech to his mental list of the topics to be withheld from the Gw'oth.

"Putting the antenna here was a compromise," Er'o volunteered. "Someplace far out on the ice would have reduced the electromagnetic noise, but"—he pointed at the blue orb looming overhead—"the tides pull at the ocean and flex the ice more than they move the rock. The ice surface seldom fractures, but ruptures do occur. So we built on the mountain instead and correct for interference as best we can."

"We thought you might look at our filtering algorithms," Kl'o added. "Perhaps you can suggest improvements."

The Gw'oth had set up several electronic slates in the courtyard, and Kirsten crouched over one. Kl'o and Kirsten (and surely Jeeves, in the privacy of her helmet) began a dialogue to learn each other's mathematical notations. Er'o joined in with them.

The last two Gw'oth approached Baedeker. Th'o said, "Another matter we hope you might comment upon is combining measurements across observatories. In theory, readouts can be integrated across a collection of instruments. Such a combination should offer the angular resolution of an apparatus as large as the distance between instruments. We have yet to achieve that result."

Aperture synthesis, Jeeves offered unnecessarily.

The AI knew mostly centuries-old Earth technology. If Jeeves knew this technique, why had the Gw'oth not mastered it?

Ah. The math was not difficult, but the data volumes were significant. Perhaps the Gw'oth ensembles could not process so much data. Baedeker felt more and more relieved. After a point, biological computing surely became more limitation than asset. He plunged a head into an outside pocket to tap out and encrypt a private reminder to Kirsten: *Disclose nothing about computers.*

Still, the Gw'oth were wise to ask about aperture synthesis. Baedeker said, "An instrument to span the world. That would give much more detail."

Th'o and Ng'o consulted among themselves, an extended dialogue of clicks and whistles. "There are some practical obstacles to an instrument that large," Ng'o finally offered cryptically.

Rivalries among political entities, Jeeves wrote, *although I do not understand the details. They spoke in an unfamiliar dialect, one Kirsten never tapped on her earlier visits. I am confident of this much: These Gw'oth doubt they could link to distant observatories without revealing more to local authorities than they care to.*

Baedeker felt better and better. Political entities sharing this little moon? How absurdly primitive! Citizens had been cohesive within one Concordance for millions of years. And a single world government had been a gift to their human Colonists, whether the New Terrans recognized their unity as such, or not.

But he and Kirsten were here—even as Sigmund and Eric, aboard *Don Quixote,* sped from the singularity to report to their government—to get better data. He urgently needed to learn what was rushing at the Fleet. Revealing a little might be the lesser among imprudences.

Baedeker said, "Kirsten and I can work more productively in our shelter, without our pressure suits. If you provide time-stamped data from several observatories and the exact locations of those observatories, maybe we can do something." The math was straightforward enough; aperture synthesis merely took computing power. His pocket computer, away from prying eyes, would suffice.

"I will make arrangements for a copy of the information," Th'o offered.

In small groups that formed and scattered and reassembled at dizzying speed, they discussed observations made across the spectrum. They reviewed the theoretical and practical limitations of various instruments. There was *much* the Gw'oth had yet to learn. Baedeker was resisting complacency when Er'o revealed, almost in passing, that consideration was being given to the subtle repositioning of several orbiting telescopes—

To use stars between here and the oncoming phenomenon as gravitational lenses.

Baedeker's manic complacency vanished. It was all that he could do not to leap the fence and gallop to the shelter.

In the short while since *Don Quixote*'s arrival, the Gw'oth had developed a theory of general relativity.

17

Hyperwave radio was a wonderful thing.

Don Quixote was once more 4.5 billion miles from the star the Gw'oth knew as their sun, the separation increasing by fifteen thousand miles every second. It had been a ten-day trek to the edge of the gravitational singularity. *Don Quixote* could have crossed that distance in three days—if its tanks were fuller. Sigmund was not ready to depend on the Gw'oth for fuel for the trip home.

Facing Sigmund and Eric in the main bridge display—from ten light-years away—was the New Terran security cabinet. *They* met in the relative comfort of a secure conference room in the Ministry of Defense. For a small, free-flying planet like New Terra, the singularity began a mere twelve million miles away. Call it a light-minute. The round-trip comm lag between the surface and an orbiting hyperwave relay was tolerable.

"Thanks for fitting us in, Sabrina," Sigmund began.

She smiled humorlessly. "Your message didn't leave me much choice. Now would you care to elaborate upon 'Something scary is rushing your way'?"

That was all Sigmund had known at first. The radioed updates from Baedeker and Kirsten kept adding detail—and with every report the situation grew scarier. "With our help, the Gw'oth have significantly refined their long-range imagery. At first, we knew only that something was heating and disrupting the interstellar medium, something in a cone aimed right at you. Something light-years across." He paused for them to contemplate the scale of the phenomenon. "We now know what's causing it. Wave after wave of ramscoops."

Two minutes later, everyone was shouting at once. Sigmund waited for Sabrina to impose order.

She said, "One at a time, people. Governor's prerogative, I'll go first. Sigmund, might these be human ships, like *Long Pass*?"

Sigmund shook his head. "Unlikely. The human worlds I knew replaced ramscoops with hyperdrive centuries ago."

Juan Royce-Hernandez was Sigmund's deputy at the defense ministry. Juan's open, honest face belied the insightful mind beneath. He asked, "What exactly are your new friends seeing, Sigmund?"

Eric leaned toward the bridge camera. "It's a bit esoteric. Decelerating ramscoops headed this way would show their exhausts. Exhausts pointed this way would be unmistakably hot, and the Gw'oth don't detect that.

"What they see is less dramatic but equally compelling. Helium concentrations in the disrupted region are unnaturally high. The obvious explanation is that the excess helium is a fusion byproduct. Think of it as exhaust streaming away from us, cooled and diffused. The Gw'oth astronomers also see turbulence patterns in the interstellar gases that are consistent with magnetic scoops."

Another interminable pause. "Thank you," Juan said. "I have to agree, that sounds like ramscoops. Whoever is on them may be fleeing from the core explosion, just as we are, without benefit of hyperdrive or a planetary drive.

"The good news, it seems to me, is that these ships are accelerating. Why think they'll suddenly brake for New Terra, or the Fleet, or the Gw'oth?"

Sigmund had had the same hope—for maybe a nanosecond. When your only chance of escape from the core explosion was aboard ramscoops, how crowded must those ships be? How intolerable were the conditions aboard? Why *wouldn't* you investigate the possibility of using a whole world as your escape craft?

He would. He could hardly expect those commanding the ramscoops to act differently.

Neither the Fleet nor New Terra had a spare planetary drive, or the knowledge to make more, or the wealth to acquire more. Only the Outsiders built such drives. Sigmund kept to himself Baedeker's speculation that he might learn to make one. *That* hope was an even thinner reed on which to base policy than the wish that the ramscoops might pass by without stopping.

Centuries of benign servitude had left New Terrans deficient in judging intent. One paranoid's example could not begin to reeducate them. It was, ironically, for the best that they had bigger causes to worry.

"There's more," Sigmund began cautiously. "True, we believe the ram-scoops are accelerating. The turbulence in their wake reveals deceleration episodes. Sometimes elements of their fleet accelerate while others decelerate. I can't claim to understand the pattern.

"The leading wave as we see it—which, remember, is from light fifty years on its way—is approaching at about four-tenths light speed. The analysis further suggests that the fleet has often moved faster, up to nine-tenths light speed.

"With Baedeker's expert assistance, the Gw'oth have begun surveying solar systems recently passed by the ramscoops." This was the breaking news, from an urgent message uploaded from the ice moon less than an hour earlier. "I'm sending you a short vid."

"Got it," a technician declared from New Terra. "Projecting it now."

Eric brought up a copy for himself in an auxiliary display. "This doesn't look like much. Bear with me. First, see the dots: the spark of a distant star and the much dimmer glints of sunlight reflecting from its planets. Now"—software improved the contrast—"the enhanced image emphasizes dust rings in the same solar system."

Juan frowned. "I thought planets formed from such dust."

"That's right," Eric answered. "The dust should be long gone, swept up by the planets. So why do selected solar systems in the ramscoops' wake show planets *and* dust clouds?"

"Mining?" Sabrina guessed. "Replenishing their supplies?"

"That's one possibility," Sigmund said. "Here's a final observation." He waited for it to be transmitted and opened. This image showed another solar system, but with *two* brilliant sparks. "Contrary to appearances, that's not a binary star. One bright spot is a sun, with a perfectly normal spectrum. The second has a completely different, very unique spectrum.

"That's the signature of a kinetic planet-killer."

MUCH TALK FOLLOWED, all unnecessary, since there could be only one practical decision. Someone must go investigate.

Who better than Sigmund and his handpicked crew?

It would not be easy. They had only fifty-year-old data from which to make plans. If the ramscoops had maintained their last observed speed, the fleet was already twenty light-years closer.

Or, at top speed, the ramscoops might already have advanced to within five light-years of the Fleet of Worlds and New Terra.

Which led to the topic Sigmund most dreaded: notifying the Concordance.

"Sabrina, we don't dare just sit here waiting. Let me see how close the ramscoops have gotten before we involve the Fleet." Not that Sigmund would limit his intel gathering to that one question. The less specific he got, the less well-intentioned guidance he would need to ignore.

His recommendation prompted *more* discussion, much of it unproductive finger-pointing about New Terra's lack of high-precision observatories. Sabrina, looking grim, finally put a halt to it. "All right, Sigmund," she said. "You're our expert. Call in when you know more." She left up to him if and how to further involve the Gw'oth. "And be careful."

On the trip in-system to retrieve Kirsten and Baedeker, Sigmund recorded and relayed personal messages for Penny and the kids. It might be a *long* time before he saw them again.

18

Their sixteen parts integrated, Ol't'ro considered:

Humans, Citizens, and whoever rode the onrushing ramscoops. The universe above the ice was vast—and crowded.

Competition among species. Human and Citizen efforts to keep secrets showed an unwillingness to share. Anything else would have been the surprise. Tn'ho Nation was but one of many polities on this world. Tn'ho was rich *because* it was powerful. None but the powerful could retain their wealth.

Hence: the wealth of humans and Citizens. Ol't'ro would learn all that the newcomers had to teach—not merely what they chose to offer.

Hence: faster-than-light technology. The visitors could survive unprotected nowhere in this solar system, and yet they had appeared in response to a radio summons long before the message could have reached the nearest star.

And: unknown means of calculation. In the privacy of their shelter, Baedeker and Kirsten had combined observations from widely spaced instruments. *No* Gw'otesht could assimilate the quantities of data necessary for the practical application of that algorithm, neither small groups who merely computed cooperatively, nor even fully emergent group minds like Ol't'ro themselves. Yet somehow the calculation had been done.

And cooperation among species: The strangers in the ramscoops were a danger to all. To learn more about the strangers would benefit all. Surely *Don Quixote* would leave soon to investigate. And if Ol't'ro was to join its crew . . .

Er'o, they signaled to their most capable component. *You will get us into the coming mission.*

ER'O HALF SWAM, half crawled, from him/themselves. Separation was always disorienting. To disconnect from an ongoing meld staggered him.

The confusion abated and he jetted into his meditation chamber, only without time to meditate, or even to feed the gnawing hunger a meld always produced. Wriggling into a surface suit, he summoned a servant to independently check his seals. "I am ready," he radioed, trying to ignore the feeling that he spoke with himself—which, in a way, he did.

Ol't'ro had interfaced themselves to a comm terminal. "Good," they responded. "Proceed."

From the nearest water lock Er'o made his way to a tram terminal. As his car sped down the cable to the ice, he consulted with Ol't'ro. There were many factors, practical and tactical, to consider.

He struggled to concentrate, his thoughts, and those of Ol't'ro, roiling. A sustained meld among fewer than sixteen was abnormal and sad. Such things only happened after a member died, while they wondered and worried whether they could find a compatible mind to heal them. But for a healthy member to decouple, to *talk* with an impaired Gw'otesht . . .

"We share your doubts," Ol't'ro said. "Best for you and us that you hurry."

"I UNDERSTAND," BAEDEKER SAID.

To understand neither agreed nor disagreed. It did little to encourage further discussion. The artful evasion reminded Baedeker of his life before exile, and of too many Concordance officials he had known. The comparison rankled.

He saw no other choice.

To refuse Er'o's request put at risk further cooperation with the Gw'oth. That might put him and Kirsten in immediate, personal danger.

And to accept? Baedeker managed not to shudder. If he had any say in the matter, no Gw'o would ever again board *Don Quixote*. Just allowing Er'o into the emergency shelter had Baedeker's hide itching. It was unnerving that the aliens had intuited *Don Quixote*'s upcoming mission. Or cracked the Fleet's most robust encryption algorithm to learn Sigmund's intentions, which would be even more unsettling.

Of all those doubts and fears, Baedeker hoped sincerely, his visitor was unaware.

Er'o had one limb held aloft, arched, its tip directed at Baedeker. Eyes glinted behind circles of sharp white teeth. Er'o swiveled the limb. "Kirsten.

What is your opinion? Might some of my people accompany your expedition?"

Kirsten laughed uneasily. "What I think doesn't matter, Er'o. I only fly the ship where I'm told."

Interesting, Baedeker thought. Was she also reticent about allowing Gw'oth on the ship? Baedeker felt he could trust Sigmund's habitual paranoia to keep the little aliens off *Don Quixote*—if Kirsten and Eric did not press too hard on the other side.

Er'o waggled the elevated limb. "Not to toot my own horn, but Gw'oth participation could be useful on this mission."

Toot my own horn? Baedeker puzzled over the expression at which Kirsten grinned. The Gw'oth were already mastering idiom? Bonding with the New Terrans? He had to discourage this relationship!

"Without speaking for our hindmost," Baedeker said, "I do not see how Gw'oth could come along. You and we live in very different environments." You learn fast, but have you learned yet to breathe air?

Er'o raised a second limb. (For a moment, the two elevated limbs peered at each other: a Citizen's ironic laugh. So now the Gw'o mimicked Citizen body language! Er'o might think to seem familiar and friendly, but such quickness rattled Baedeker.) "Of course, my friend Baedeker, we would provide our own shipboard environment. Any of our standard above-ice habitat modules will serve. They are self-powered and recycle quite effectively. Each has a water lock, should it become necessary to bring in supplies. Many of our modules would fit through your air lock, as long as you open inner and outer hatches at once."

"We can do that," Kirsten agreed all too quickly. "And we can . . ."

"Can what?" Er'o prompted.

"Nothing." Kirsten suddenly bore a guilty look. (Baedeker had a good guess what she had nearly blurted out: That a force-field curtain over the wide-open lock would hold the ship's air. The Gw'oth had shown no signs of having force-field technology.) "Just that we can refill the ship with air after that."

Er'o resumed a five-footed stance. "Good. We will be happy to replenish your gas supply. Oxygen from the hydrolysis of water is easy. Nitrogen is less common, but we extract it from minerals."

"I understand," Baedeker answered again.

Er'o paused for a long while: consulting by radio, the link encrypted.

The Gw'o finally continued. "Baedeker, Kirsten, there is another logistical topic we thought to raise. You plan to travel a great distance. Will you need additional fuel?"

"It never hurts to supplement our supplies," Baedeker conceded.

In fact, they would have to fill *Don Quixote*'s tanks before the long flight to the ramscoop fleet. Either *Don Quixote* refueled here, or they would detour to New Terra. The irony was that *Don Quixote* carried refueling probes: hydrojet-propelled submersibles for autonomous operation in any convenient water ocean. The probe's active filter separated deuterium and the tiny traces of tritium from seawater; its stepping disc then transferred the fuels directly into *Don Quixote*'s tanks. But to deploy probes in this ocean risked losing teleportation technology to the Gw'oth. . . .

Er'o said, "Naturally we observed the neutrino flux from *Don Quixote*. If some colleagues and I are permitted to join your expedition, we will arrange for supplies of deuterium, tritium, or helium-3. Whatever you prefer."

Naturally? Hardly. The hull itself *blocked* neutrinos, disguising the fusion reactor. But as weakly as neutrinos interacted with most matter, trapped neutrinos ricocheting indefinitely inside a ship could eventually become a radiation hazard. Only a small patch of the hull, near the engine room, permitted neutrinos to escape—and the Gw'oth had detected them.

As for fuel, Concordance ships used deuterium/deuterium reactions and New Terra had retained the practice. For all its shortcomings, D/D fusion was optimal in the way that most mattered: safety. In an emergency, any ocean or cometary-belt snowball would provide fuel. Ships could *add* tritium to the mix—D/T reactions released more energy than D/D reactions—but never relied on tritium. That isotope had a brief half-life. Away from civilization, where only cosmic rays produced new tritium, the availability was too limited.

None of which had been discussed with the Gw'oth.

Why did Er'o offer helium-3? Because the Gw'oth used it, perhaps. Or because, absent force-field technology, D/D and D/T fusion required bulky, massive shielding against the neutrons produced by the fusion reactions. Er'o could be subtly probing whether *Don Quixote* used force fields, or if the ship carried unproductive mass as internal shielding. He might be snooping for vulnerabilities, or assessing a commercial opportunity, or engaging in industrial espionage.

Physics, Baedeker understood. The motives of other Citizens? Only sometimes did those make sense. What, then, could he know of the hidden agendas of the Gw'oth?

So much ambiguity! It made Baedeker's hump hurt.

Suddenly, he was eager for Sigmund's return. There were worse circumstances than that another be hindmost.

THE LAST THING SIGMUND wanted—on the ice, at last, to reunite his crew—was an argument. He got one anyway.

"It is unacceptable to bring any Gw'oth," Baedeker insisted. "Merely by observing *Don Quixote* decelerate, they were led to deduce general relativity. Permitted aboard *Don Quixote*, who can know what they will see, what else they will infer? Why risk them acquiring technologies we would rather they not wield?"

Known hostiles were careening toward New Terra and the Fleet. They used kinetic planet-busters, for Finagle's sake! Careening toward Penny and the children! Worry about long-term risks was an unaffordable luxury when delay was surely the biggest danger of all. Sigmund focused on nuts-and-bolts practicality. "Full tanks are a big incentive, Baedeker. So unless you would rather use refueling probes while the Gw'oth watch?"

Baedeker plucked at his mane. "Reveal stepping-disc technology? I think not. But, Sigmund, you present a false dichotomy. *Don Quixote* brought ample fuel for a round trip. Our best option is simply to resupply at home."

Delay for a detour to New Terra. More delay when, inevitably, Sabrina, or someone in her cabinet, saw Sigmund's stopover as an opportunity to plan, or run through scenarios, or give advice—to "help." Or a Puppeteer spy would learn about the mission—presuming, for the moment, that Baedeker resisted notifying Hearth's authorities himself—and then they would be delayed longer still to coordinate with the Concordance.

No way. Sigmund took a deep breath. It was time to pull rank.

But Kirsten jumped in first, her eyes ablaze. "We wouldn't even *know* about the present danger but for the Gw'oth. For me, that alone earned them a spot on the mission. But if gratitude and common decency are insufficient, consider this: *Don Quixote* will be one ship among . . . what, hundreds? Thousands?

"Almost certainly, the Gw'oth are more skilled than we at astronomy. They're probably better at wringing inferences from observations. Good!

We *need* those skills now! With Er'o and his colleagues aboard, maybe we can surveil without approaching quite so close. Wouldn't that make us safer?"

"Perhaps," Baedeker allowed. (That was sufficient concession for Sigmund, only Baedeker had not finished.) "But, Kirsten, they propose to bring *sixteen*. One of their biological computers, obviously, although Er'o has not volunteered that fact."

"It's settled," Sigmund said firmly. "Er'o and the others will join us. Why accept their help if we're not willing to welcome their best minds?"

We're going to need all the help we can get.

THSSTHFOK

19

As sunlight to a drowning Pak, so did consciousness beckon. Thssthfok struggled upward, if not into awareness itself, at least into the concept of the possibility of awareness. Memories stirred, disordered and ill-formed.

With a shudder Thssthfok regained control of mind and body. His eyes flew open. His right hand, trembling, released the latch of the cold-sleep pod. The dome receded.

He checked the chronometer, even as he recognized the absurdity of the habit. The years whose passage the clock marked were real—and without significance. Life on Pakhome had been extinguished thousands of years earlier.

As life here, too, would be obliterated. It was not supposed to end this way. . . .

THE COMET DWELLERS HAD HONORED their commitments. Why not, since numerical superiority worked in their favor? Natural attrition served their interests without the risks attendant to betrayal and open warfare. They respected their agreement with clan Rilchuk, but they had chosen not to risk rescuing a lost one of that clan.

And so Thssthfok had been abandoned.

He remembered, as though it were yesterday, the raid on a world then nameless. Its natives had vast granaries ripe for the plundering. All that conveniently gathered biomass would supply the fleet's synthesizers for years. The aliens were primitive, without the technology to offer any meaningful defense. They were physically fragile.

They were not without courage.

The shuttles struck in waves, strafing with their railguns before landing to disgorge troops. Thssthfok was but one of hundreds of Pak in the assault.

He took no pride in slaughtering the gaunt creatures, guilty only of the poor judgment to try to defend their pathetic wood and stone houses.

Lasers, railguns, and grenades against swords and spears: The contest could not last, and it had not. The natives scattered, with much of their town burning. The raiders broke into the granaries and began loading their vessels.

Thssthfok was at the controls of his shuttle, its cargo hold packed, his squad of Rilchuk warriors strapping into their acceleration couches, when the natives tripped a crude but effective rock-fall trap. If they could not have their crops, the raiders would go hungry, too.

The first boulders struck the shuttle's stern, and fail-safes disabled the engines. Alarms flared across Thssthfok's instrument panel. For a moment, before external sensors gave out, there was a victorious ululation from the natives. Then the only sounds were the pounding of boulders and the sickening crunches of the hull. The only sensation was an end-of-the-world rumbling, until awareness ceased.

THSSTHFOK CAME TO IN HIS ACCELERATION COUCH, battered but not seriously injured. His instrument panel crackled and spewed acrid fumes; this ship would never fly again. His radio died in a shower of sparks when he tried to call for help. They had to get out before the other shuttles launched.

Only there was no *they*. Boulders had crushed the midship passenger compartment. Everyone else aboard, clanmates all, were dead.

He feared he had been buried alive, but one small porthole remained uncovered. He should be able to get out. And then be torn apart?

How long had he been unconscious? A considerable time, to judge by the scene beyond the porthole.

By the thousands, natives in bucket brigades battled the conflagration. Flames now extended to the wooden piers that lined the riverbanks. Boats burned at the wharfs; other vessels, powered only by sails and oars and desperation, struggled for the safety of the river.

If the inferno spread, he would roast to death inside the wrecked shuttle—unless the fuel tanks ruptured first and an explosion killed him. If the natives contained the fire, they would then surely turn their attention to their hard-won trophy. Either way, to wait here was to die.

Atop a low stone pyramid, he spotted a cluster of the natives. A few, gesturing, stood apart at the very apex, ringed by others who held swords.

Thssthfok decided that the few in the center were rulers, directing the fight against the blaze.

Both air locks refused to open. No matter. Hatches—when they worked—offered the fastest ways out, best for combat situations. They were not the only way.

Thssthfok rummaged through equipment lockers until he found a structural modulator. Working methodically he traced closely spaced parallel strips with the modulator. More and more of the hull *twing* turned clear. Eventually he found a hull section not buried under rock, the exposed area just large enough to squeeze through. Reconfiguring the modulator, he turned that section of *twing* permeable. He forced an arm through the softened hull, got a solid handhold on a boulder, and oozed out of the ruined shuttle. The *twing* resealed behind him.

Only scorched ground and long, wedge-shaped indentations showed that additional shuttles had once landed here. And high in the sky—

Blinding blue-white streaks: fusion fire. The ships were leaving. Forsaking him.

He rigidified the exposed hull section before dashing from shadow to shadow, from wreckage to ruin, to the rear of the pyramid. The local gravity was oppressive, about half again what he was used to, and the air felt thick as syrup. Silently, he climbed the steep steps. Intent on the battle against the flames, no one noticed Thssthfok until he approached the summit.

The natives were as tall as he but only a fourth or fifth of his mass, with gossamer webbing between arms and legs. Their bones were hollow, judging from how they had snapped in battle. He guessed they had evolved from some sort of arboreal gliding creature.

To make a point, Thssthfok let the bodyguards whack futilely at his battle armor before scything down several with his laser pistol. Then he aimed his gun at the most garishly clad alien—and paused. "You're next," he said.

The native gabbled, as unintelligible to Thssthfok as Thssthfok must be to it. The surviving bodyguards, quaking, lowered their swords.

The ruler was smarter than a breeder. He might be smart enough to serve.

A plan took shape in Thssthfok's mind. With his empty hand, he thumped his chest. "Thssthfok."

"S'fok," the ruler tried, tentatively.

Close enough. Thssthfok waggled the gun: Come this way. They went down the pyramid and toward a nearby stone building. The ruler's domicile, perhaps. One of the guards there unsheathed its sword and Thssthfok lased it in two. "Thssthfok kills," he instructed.

Gabble, gabble. The remaining guards backed away.

Thssthfok did not dare rest—nor did he let his royal prisoner rest—for much of a Pakhome day. By then, he had absorbed much of the local language. He knew that the "empire"—the fertile banks of one long, meandering river—was called Roshala. He knew that Roshala dominated this continent of Taba, and that the world was called Mala. He knew that a native was a Dra, collectively the Drar. He knew that his prisoner was Noblala, the empress.

She knew that he was a potent wizard and a warrior of extremely limited patience. She would prosper or perish at his whim.

Whether because of Thssthfok's teaching, or some as-yet-unappreciated subtlety among the Drar, he woke unharmed the next morning. Noblala had grasped the concept of a power behind the throne.

IGNORING BASKETS OF FOODSTUFFS—though cold sleep left one ravenous—Thssthfok disarmed the sensors and explosives that had guarded his hibernation. He put on his battle armor. He checked the charge on his laser pistol. After the first-aid/cold-sleep pod and the emergency stock of tree-of-life root, weapons were the most valuable items of salvage from the wrecked shuttle.

Only then, from habit more than interest, did he break his fast. Most of what waited for him was native food, smoked or salted or air-dried, uniformly desiccated into a leathery consistency. Tree-of-life scarcely grew here; the unsuitable sunlight, he surmised. He only occasionally needed to eat the roots—or, more precisely, the virus that reproduced nowhere but inside the roots—and he scarcely got that. The dearth of the tubers, more than the plodding pace of his slaves' progress, prompted many of his hibernations. His enemies among the Drar still had not realized that the root was a necessity rather than a luxury. If they ever did, they need only burn down the tree-of-life grove as he slept.

The attempts on his life, fortunately, had all been very direct. Even those were ebbing. This awakening marked twice in a row that a timer, not the triggering of a booby trap, had roused him. Were it otherwise, he would have, yet again, killed anyone near enough to have been involved. And whoever ruled at the time of an attack. The ruler would have been responsible, by definition, whether for the attack itself or for failing to prevent it. And for good measure, several nobles (randomly chosen, but that was his secret) for *their* scheming. Who could say the dead had *not* also plotted against him? Anyone in the ruling class almost certainly had.

Very pedagogical, the death of others. And it was not as though these were Pak.

Thssthfok filled his pockets with grenades. Laser pistol in hand, he unlatched the massive door, almost too heavy for any Dra to open, then withdrew deep into the chamber. He smote the large brass gong and waited.

Soon enough, the door slowly swung inward in response to the gong. A Dra appeared, trembling, dressed in the lavishly feathered garb of the court scientist. The usual small honor guard waited behind her in the hallway.

During past cold sleeps, swords had changed from bronze to iron to steel. Now each soldier wore a holstered sidearm. These Drar stank of charcoal, sulfur, and saltpeter. A crude chemical explosive, then, to propel projectiles.

The superiority of Thssthfok's weapons diminished each time he emerged.

"Excellency," the Dra scientist said, her voice soft with fear. "The emperor bids you welcome."

The emperor, whoever it was this time, could have offered his welcome in person. No matter. Emperors served only to channel resources to research and development. This latest emperor would make an appearance once his spies, usually found among the guards, assessed the state of Thssthfok's mood.

"And you are?" It galled Thssthfok to ask such obvious questions.

"Koshbara, Excellency." Her vestigial wings fluttered nervously. "We have many advances to show you."

"Proceed," he told her.

Thssthfok recognized progress in their course through the palace, whose walls for the first time were brightly lit. Mass production of identical fixtures. Electric lamps, using some sort of incandescent filament. Power generation and distribution. "Alternating or direct?" he asked. "How do you generate it?"

Koshbara blinked. She would adapt soon enough to the pace of his thinking, or be replaced. "Alternating current, Excellency. Braf-fired steam engines drive the generators."

Braf? He had not encountered the word but let it pass. Something that burned, probably peat or coal. The forest that once abutted the city was all but gone, sacrificed, he presumed, to the wood-fired steam engines he had introduced at his last awakening.

Outside the palace, the sun beat down: huge, mottled, the sullen red of dying embers. In absolute terms it was a tiny star, an unexceptional red dwarf. Only because Mala orbited its sun so closely was this world habitable at all. As a consequence of that tight orbit it was tidally locked. One hemisphere baked unrelentingly, the other lay shrouded in permanent dark and cold. Fierce circulation patterns mixed day- and night-side atmosphere enough to moderate both.

The climate was unique to Thssthfok's experience; he ought to be fascinated. But to what purpose? The core explosion would sterilize Mala, too, soon enough.

They climbed the ceremonial pyramid for a panoramic view. The city had doubled in size while he slept. The skies were disappointingly empty of aircraft, but self-propelled vehicles had all but replaced beast-drawn carts. Along several corridors into the city, parallel steel tracks glinted in the sun and great engines, belching black smoke, pulled long chains of cars. Large, paddlewheel ships had replaced small sailboats. At the limits of his vision, ships anchored in the river delta awaited their turns to unload.

The air stank of complex hydrocarbons and their combustion byproducts. More of this braf, or something like it, he inferred.

Thssthfok let Koshbara lead him through the newest factories and research labs. He observed simple chemical plants, blast furnaces, and production lines. He saw crude experimentation with electricity and machinery for grinding lenses. They had produced lenses as wide as Thssthfok's forearm was long. For an observatory the empire planned to erect on Darkside, Koshbara explained eagerly, her pride finally overcoming her fear.

The chemistry was all empirical. The physics was quaint. The machinery wheezed and squeaked and groaned, every tortured sound a cry for optimization. The reek of chemicals and sewage—the very stench of the Drar themselves—oppressed Thssthfok. Still, what had begun in desperation had developed a veneer of plausibility: The Drar might be led to build an interstellar ramscoop within his lifetime. He could yet escape.

If he could manage to care.

THE LONGER IT TOOK to build a starship, the less it mattered. What remained of his family, what remained of clan Rilchuk, were beyond all hope or pretense of reuniting. Of what conceivable use, then, was his life?

What use was a protector with no one to protect?

The growling of his stomach, the more and more frequent pangs, seemed to belong to someone else. He had no appetite. It would be easy to stop eating, to waste away, to die. It would be easy, and faster, to let slip the precautions that kept assassins at bay.

The Drar meant nothing to him. Let them survive, or not, as they chose. Perhaps a laggard clan, taking note of their emergent technology, would make the decision for them.

"Excellency?" Koshbara had noticed his distraction. "Shall we go on to the repository?"

He would rather lie down and starve in his room, in familiar surroundings. To express the thought took more effort than it was worth. He followed her and their escort onto a noisy, self-propelled conveyance and then into another building. The repository turned out to be—a library.

A memory stirred, and with it a twinge of appetite.

It had been easy in his youth, in the vigor of his family, to be ambivalent about *the* Library, the great epochal archive on Pakhome. He remembered disparaging the childless protectors for claiming to have made the Library their cause, and the welfare of *all* Pak their purpose in life. He remembered how abstract—how unnatural—their service had seemed.

"Show me," he ordered Koshbara.

They wound through aisles lined with tall shelves filled with books and scrolls. She pointed out sections on hydraulics, architecture, optics, and orbital mechanics. Idly, he unrolled scrolls and flipped through bound books. The storage medium was primitive; a few centuries would turn everything here to dust. It was nothing like the metal pages on which *the* Library scribed its knowledge.

They sampled the files in which an army of Drar labored to maintain an index to their arduously acquired new knowledge. He saw dread in the posture of these librarians, but also satisfaction in their accomplishments, and even gratitude for Thssthfok's guidance.

Curious, he thought.

Transfer these catalogue cards to metal, and the Drar system would little differ from the Library index on Pakhome. One group of librarians had scarcely discovered electricity; the other group planned for the interregnums when all knowledge of electricity had been lost.

Now the Library itself was lost. Its store of knowledge was too bulky to move even when—if the radioed messages of laggard fleets could be believed—the Librarians built or stole their own starships.

Knowledge abandoned left childless protectors without a reason to live. If the stories were true, the Librarians must pursue the surviving clans, with elements of the ancient archives somehow made portable. They must convince themselves that, in time, sometime, those clans would value what had been preserved.

Preserved how? In such circumstances, Thssthfok would transfer the old, scribed records to electronic or optical form—so that must be what the Librarians did. The logic was clear.

The chain of logic reminded Thssthfok of an idea he had had just as cold sleep last took him. The Drar outthought breeders, but never protectors. The technology *he* needed must soon outstrip their feeble minds, if it had not already done that.

"Koshbara," he said, interrupting a lengthy and unnecessary description from one of the librarians. "Show me your mechanical calculators."

Her ears bobbed in confusion. "Our what, Excellency?"

"Machines that calculate for you, that efficiently sort and search large collections of data."

She backed away, unease in her eyes, afraid to disappoint him. "Excellency, I am not familiar with such devices."

Nor was he, beyond the concept. Protectors had no need for such prostheses. He could initiate a new line of research, directing an army of Drar to develop—call them computers.

He felt renewed stirrings of appetite. Why?

Leading the Drar to build mental prostheses? Surely not.

An earlier thought, then. Not the Library. Age and personal disaster had brought Thssthfok a bit of empathy for others bereft of their children and breeders, but the Library itself still left him cold.

A few hundred years before Thssthfok's time, a bit of insanity birthed in the Library had plunged all of Pakhome into war. Librarians, those who claimed they lived to serve, to protect knowledge against the ravages of war, had instead *launched* a great war. Childless protectors across the planet had rallied to their cause.

And for what? A single message, garbled and attenuated, translated and retranslated hundreds of times as languages evolved and died. If the chain of inferences was correct, if the many translations had not erased all meaning, then a plea for help had been transmitted, eons earlier, from a long-forgotten Pak colony somewhere far across the galaxy. And though nothing had been heard since, *that* was enough. A rescue expedition was launched.

Thousands more from Thssthfok's era would have escaped the core explosion if the Librarians' War had not earlier stripped Pakhome of its ramscoops—all to chase an ephemeral wisp of an illusion of a pretext. All for a purpose in life. For a reason to live.

Another rumble from Thssthfok's gut. Suddenly he *wanted* to eat, yet the reason eluded him. Not for the Drar, but something about them. Not anything to do with the Library. Not the Librarians' War.

For a fleet of his own!

The galaxy teemed with life. It was richly strewn with intelligent species. The Pak evacuation must eventually encounter species with similar, perhaps even greater, technology. Preemptive strikes might fail to eliminate some threats.

His family and clan were beyond his reach; he could not protect them. Then the protection of the race would be his goal!

He would build an armada of ramscoops. He would fill those ships with Drar crews. Together they would defend Pak fleets against any that might try to overtake the Pak from behind.

And his Drar pilots would need computers to guide them across the light-years.

Thssthfok's mind suddenly brimmed with the mathematics of sets and the algebra of logic. Hints of circuit design tantalized him. Computing would be a whole new science, and a whole new engineering discipline. He would see its development well under way before he next hibernated.

Then why not start immediately? Thssthfok sought out a slate and chalk. "Observe, Koshbara. All data can be represented in just zeroes and ones. . . ."

20

The closer Sigmund looked, the more helpless he felt.

He excelled at ferreting out plots and danger—even, occasionally, where none existed. That well-practiced paranoia was why Nessus had kidnapped him to New Terra. But to find the threat *here* required no skill. What New Terra needed was a gigantic navy and a military genius to wield it.

He flipped through some favorite family holos. Athena frowning in concentration, forehead furrowed, tongue peeking out a side of her mouth, one hand poised above a jigsaw puzzle. Hermes beaming, his grin crooked and mostly toothless and totally charming. Both kids playing in the park. An image of Sigmund and Penelope just before the governor's last Independence Day ball. Penny was dressed to kill and achingly beautiful, with a coy twinkle in her eyes. That picture always made him feel like the luckiest man on several planets. A formal pose of the four of them. A candid shot of the four of them amid Penny's entire extended family.

He had to focus. If anyone could save his family and friends—save his *world*—it was him.

And he didn't have a clue how. Old thought patterns seemed to have faded from disuse. Success and happiness might have doomed them all.

He was alone in his cabin, struggling to come to grips with the enormity of the situation, just as the rest of the crew seemed to be. It was the crew's mood he speculated about, not their location: *Don Quixote*'s surveillance systems left no doubt to anyone's position.

(Unless Kirsten or Eric had hacked the security system, a small inner voice corrected, offering no reason. Sigmund brushed aside that whisper of suspicion. As for the others, those whose loyalties were surely divided, the opportunity did not arise. No Puppeteer or Gw'o could fool the retinal scanners to gain privileged-level system access. Old habits had not deserted Sigmund entirely.)

Behind closed doors, where Sigmund's crew could not see him, why not brood? Even more fundamentally, *how* not brood?

Glimpsed from afar, the evidence of oncoming ramscoops had been subtle and indirect. Viewed, finally, from close behind, after months of hyperspace travel, any ambiguity vanished. Fusion flames hotter than the surfaces of stars shouted the presence of ramscoops. Hundreds of them. Many exhibited accelerations high enough to imply gravity control.

And peering toward the galactic core, yet worse news. Subtle clues of the type that had brought *Don Quixote* this far revealed wave after wave of more ramscoops for as far as instruments could reach. Also headed this way—toward New Terra and everyone Sigmund held dear.

With hyperdrive and sufficient patience, *Don Quixote* could reach any part of the armada. With their stealthy hull and thrusters for unobtrusive maneuvering in Einstein space, they had avoided unwelcome notice. Barring bad luck, they could continue to scout unobserved. And when their luck failed, as it inevitably must, they were in an all-but-invulnerable hull and they could escape instantly to hyperspace.

What they could not do was fight, not against opponents so numerous and well armed—and so *vicious*—as these. For lack of a better name: the enemy.

Compared to the enemy, even Kzinti were restrained. The ratcats ate only those who resisted and enslaved the rest. The enemy took no prisoners. Fresh impact craters on a dozen worlds—always on ocean floors, to compound shock, blast, and seismic destruction with monstrous tsunamis—showed that the enemy had used kinetic planet-busters. Preemptively obliterating any possible rival. . . .

New Terra needed powerful allies to survive. It needed great navies and vast resources. It needed *Earth*. Sigmund had dared to hope that this voyage deep into unexplored regions would provide some clue. Alas, for as far as *Don Quixote*'s instruments could see, nothing began to match his incomplete and painfully reconstructed description.

Tanj it!

Sigmund stared for a while at the family holo. Were planet-busters even now hurtling toward them?

The most certain path to defeat is apathy.

He took a deep breath and activated the intercom. "We need to re-group, people. Meet in the relax room in ten minutes."

THE CLOSER BAEDEKER LOOKED, the more terrified he grew.

Throughout *Don Quixote*'s long flight he had distracted himself with analyses and simulations of the planetary drive. Bringing a moon to New Terra had become the least of his motivations. Just maybe, if he sufficiently understood the technology, extra drives could be used to speed Hearth and New Terra from harm's way.

He made limited progress at best, intimidated by the vast energies involved.

Then *Don Quixote* had emerged into the midst of the enemy and distraction became impossible.

The nameless, faceless enemy was ruthless. Devastated worlds littered their trail. Sigmund had led them on a hasty surveillance of several planetary systems passed by the enemy vanguard, and the images haunted Baedeker. Not in sleep, not even rolled tightly into a near catatonic ball of trembling flesh could he put from his thoughts the horrors they had seen. Ecosystems reduced to ashes. Atmospheres choked with dust, smoke, and volcanic fumes. Continents swept by floods, the trappings of civilization washed out to sea.

Wreckage made it plain that on the devastated worlds there *had* been civilizations. Ruins suggested road networks, factories, dams, airfields, sometimes even the beginnings of spaceflight. Most were shattered and abandoned.

And just ahead of the enemy, more advanced than any culture they had preemptively destroyed: the Fleet of Worlds.

Here and there survivors struggled to put things back together. The natives of those violated worlds either hid or attacked on sight—in the latter case, futilely, to be sure—wherever *Don Quixote* had landed in pursuit of information.

All that prevented Baedeker from retreating into catatonia was the threat much nearer. The Gw'oth had done exactly what they promised, and therein loomed a new horror. They *did* glean more information from astronomical clues, from the outputs of *Don Quixote*'s sensor suite, than the humans or even Baedeker himself. Day by day, Er'o and his cohorts wrung new insights from the ship's sensors, intuited infinitesimal drifts from calibration, invented novel means of data collection, and made intriguing new correlations.

And as though making sense of the enemy onslaught was insufficiently challenging, the Gw'oth also mapped nearby dark-matter concentrations and discovered for themselves the concept of black holes. If, miraculously, the Fleet survived the onrushing threat, Citizens would confront another fearsome rival soon enough.

Unless the Concordance learned a lesson about ruthless preemption from the enemy.

Turning away from a hoof's ceaseless pawing, Baedeker found himself staring himself in the eyes. He forced his gazes apart. The action he contemplated was bitterly ironic, but he saw no humor in it.

He had once stopped a genocidal attack on newly independent New Terra, and then, disgusted at what his government had sanctioned, settled among the humans. Now New Terra might be the Concordance's best hope, for Citizens had no aptitude for war. Meanwhile *he* contemplated his own atrocity, and for no more reason than that the Gw'oth might be too smart.

Sigmund's voice over the intercom interrupted Baedeker's dark thoughts. "We need to regroup, people. Meet in the relax room in ten minutes."

THE CLOSER ER'O LOOKED, the more wondrous things grew.

Not the nameless enemy, of course, but everything—even danger—existed within a broader context. Such as the means of study . . .

Don Quixote carried extraordinary instruments. Er'o eagerly drank in everything that the ship's sensors had to offer, but while he and his companions extracted meaning where their giant shipmates did not, those new eyes on the universe were only a part of the wonder.

The true marvel was *Don Quixote* itself, and the technology it embodied, and the secrets its crew hoped to keep. Such as the never-seen Jeeves.

The network that interfaced the Gw'oth habitat with *Don Quixote*'s sensors also gave access to shipboard archives. Er'o—and more so, Ol't'ro—was increasingly certain their shipmates must control artificial computing devices of some kind. Those might be electrical, optical, or even quantum mechanical, for direct access to the hypothesized devices was blocked. All questions about such technology were turned away.

But as Ol't'ro characterized the shipboard comm network, many things became clearer. The ship's sensors were under real-time control. Ol't'ro felt certain that that control operated too quickly to be biological and natural. Like the synthetic-aperture calculations preceding this mission, some of the data consolidations embodied algorithms requiring *prodigious* computations. Data retrievals from shipboard archives exhibited responses that correlated with the behavior of one—and only one—member of the crew.

And so, even as Er'o analyzed the latest sensor data, his speculations returned to the unseen shipmate. Er'o spoke into a comm terminal that interfaced wirelessly through the opaque habitat wall to a network node Eric had mounted to a wall of the cargo hold. "Jeeves."

"Yes, Er'o," the familiar voice replied.

That Jeeves *never* appeared in person was surely significant. Even the timorous one, Baedeker, visited the cargo hold. From time to time Er'o invented a reason to put on a pressure suit and walk around. He never encountered anyone that might be Jeeves, only a hatch marked Jeeves in the curiously blocky script of the humans. That hatch was always locked.

But Er'o's wandering about the ship (except onto the bridge and into the engine room—his shipmates had countless reasons why he should not visit those compartments) revealed internal dimensions. Trivial geometry showed that the "cabin" behind that hatch must be compact even by Gw'oth standards, no larger than nooks elsewhere labeled as wiring closets.

So what secret did the mysterious crewman embody? That was one of many topics Er'o chose never to raise explicitly. "Jeeves, I am interested in readings of the electric constant."

"That's not something measured by ship's sensors," Jeeves answered.

Theory related the speed of light to the electric constant, a measure of electric-field penetration. Theory decreed that the speed of light in vacuum was everywhere the same. Here, on *Don Quixote*, Er'o could test those theories. He and his companions measured, with instruments that probed beyond habitat, cargo hold, and hull, many properties of the vacuum.

When *Don Quixote* traveled between stars, those readings were—odd. A clue to the nature of faster-than-light travel, Er'o surmised.

Inferences and clues were all he had. The humans and Baedeker steadfastly declined to discuss faster-than-light travel, even if or when the drive operated. "Whether to transfer technologies is not for any of us to decide," Sigmund had declared. "Perhaps after this mission."

Doubtless *Don Quixote*'s digital archives contained relevant data, but cautious probing of the network had yet to find it. In an incautious moment, Kirsten had made mention of a firewall.

Fire was unnatural, chaotic, and transformative. Fire was fearsome. Early in the great breakout above the ice, fires had killed and hideously maimed many. As Er'o, he had never experienced a wildfire, but a mountaintop foundry consumed by flames was etched deep into Ol't'ro's memory. The Gw'otesht had lost two members to that terrible conflagration. Two dead! That accident had almost extinguished Ol't'ro themselves, long before Er'o's birth.

Firewall! Er'o wriggled in revulsion at an almost-remembered wall of flame: hypnotic, searing, alien. Surely Kirsten had used a metaphor—a distinctly human notion—but the evoked image horrified nonetheless.

It was better to imagine other things, even the cataclysms on the worlds *Don Quixote* surveyed.

To make a planet-killer required no imagination. Anything moving fast enough would do. The enemy ships certainly moved fast enough. And when, soon enough, enemy ships came upon Jm'ho?

Then the ice would shatter and much of the ocean would flash to steam. Death would come in a race between boiling and exploding. Around the point of impact the crust itself would shatter. Waves of magma—walls of fire, indeed!—would spew forth.

Millions would die. Everything Ol't'ro had accomplished would be lost. Civilization itself might fall. And the Gw'oth were defenseless.

Er'o forced himself to focus. This ship held secrets that might give the Gw'oth a chance to survive. Secrets that Ol't'ro, better than anyone, could exploit in the defense of Gw'oth and Citizens and New Terrans alike. Secrets that he *must* acquire.

The secret of faster-than-light travel would surely be a start.

Er'o said, "Jeeves, perhaps the archives have surveys of electric-constant measurements from other interstellar journeys."

"I'm afraid not," Jeeves answered, sounding apologetic.

Did Jeeves dissemble? Almost certainly, but confirmation would need eight separate metrics, each a multispectral correlation in several frequency bands across a series of speech samples. The calculations were far beyond Er'o's capacity.

Even Ol't'ro had needed much of the flight to fully master alien voice inflections. Aural qualities and nonverbal cues correlated imprecisely, varying slightly from person to person. The correlations even drifted over time for an individual—except for Jeeves. Jeeves always inflected the same way. And his spoken mannerisms correlated exactly with the translator used at Er'o's first encounter with his shipmates. He no longer needed a translator, of course.

All around Er'o, throughout the habitat tank, his companions analyzed observations, tended to the recycling apparatus, and considered various open questions. Everything that they did was important, but it could all wait. Er'o gestured to the group: We must meld.

Human computing technology, its specifics well hidden (firewall!), seemed to be even more capable than first surmised. Any artificial computation was a mind-expanding notion, but what Er'o most recently inferred greatly surpassed computation. How could intelligent, aware behavior happen on machines? Perhaps Jeeves was something like Ol't'ro themselves, arising from grouped minds.

The Gw'otesht gathered. Tubacles quested. Memories merged. Egos meshed. Overmind began to emerge. What remained of Er'o began to offer his latest suspicions—

"We need to regroup, people," Sigmund announced over the intercom. "Meet in the relax room in ten minutes."

Er'o projected his speculations into the group mind. Reluctantly, he disconnected. It must be another meld without him.

To the comm terminal Er'o said, "That gives me time to suit up." And the others enough time, barely, while he wriggled into his pressure suit, to evacuate the equipment from the water lock. The tiny out-of-water machine shop and laboratory remained a Gw'oth secret.

"That's why ten minutes," Sigmund said.

21

Sigmund paced the confines of the relax room, a bulb of untasted coffee warm in his hand. The digital wallpaper suggested that lush forest surrounded him. Eyes might have accepted the illusion, but his other senses refused to be fooled. The whir and clatter of the ventilation system intruded, and the unyielding plasteel deck beneath his feet, and the taint of air too long recycled.

Tanj, but he was sick of this ship!

Quickly enough the crew assembled. Er'o, clad in pressure suit and exoskeleton, assumed his usual position on the table. Kirsten and Eric sat side by side along one edge of the table. Baedeker, predictably, occupied the table edge nearest the hatch, twitching whenever Sigmund's meandering blocked the way to the exit. The Puppeteer crept closer every day to collapse.

Jeeves, as always, "would participate from the bridge." His absence should be no more noteworthy than that few of the Gw'oth, and typically only Er'o, ever ventured from the opaque water tank/habitat that largely filled the largest cargo hold.

For that real mystery, Sigmund had a theory. The Gw'oth recognized that their protective gear and exoskeletons looked a lot like battle armor. Too many of them roaming the ship would look like a boarding party.

Ordering the Gw'oth to limit their excursions would imply distrust, so Sigmund only took precautions. The ill-concealed stunner he carried was the least of them.

"We've seen the same data about the enemy. We agree on the facts," Sigmund said abruptly. "We need options. Ideas, anyone?"

Eric and Kirsten exchanged weary looks. Eric said, "We've talked about it endlessly. Neither of us sees what else we can learn out here."

Meaning they wanted to go home. "And then what?" Sigmund asked gently.

Silence greeted the question. Kirsten could not meet Sigmund's eyes. "Baedeker, what do you think?"

The Puppeteer plucked at his mane. "Reluctantly, Sigmund, I agree. It is time to go."

For appearance's sake, Sigmund called, "Jeeves, anything to add?"

"No, Sigmund," they heard over the intercom.

Sigmund paused for a sip of coffee. "Er'o, can you speak for your colleagues?"

The Gw'o raised and waggled a limb sinuously, in the gesture Sigmund had come to interpret—never mind that the alien had no head—as a nod. "I am in radio contact. We all recommend continued study."

"To what end?" Baedeker asked. All the grace notes, the richness, the harmonic depth, were gone from his voice, as though even to speak English had become too much to bear. Perhaps it had.

"We're still learning." With a clink, Er'o settled the raised limb back onto the table.

Baedeker dipped a head into a pocket of his belt. Moments later a text from Baedeker popped onto Sigmund's contact-lens display: "Yes, and it is clear why. They continue to learn the secrets of this ship. Er'o is still spying on us."

Of *course* the Gw'oth spied on them, Sigmund thought. Why wouldn't they? It seemed an acceptable price for their aid in characterizing the bigger threat.

"What's your opinion, Sigmund?" Kirsten asked. She had dark bags beneath her eyes, as though she had not slept in days.

Sigmund knew how that felt. "I lean toward heading back." He didn't explain. Here or there, what could they do? Fighting for real estate set limits: Your adversary did not destroy the worlds he hoped to occupy. But when your enemy only wanted to destroy . . .

Eric reached for his wife's hand. "New Terra has few pilots. It has very few ships to match *Don Quixote*. The Concordance can build endless ships, but how does that matter? Not one in a billion Citizens will leave Hearth.

"Sigmund, for the sake of our loved ones, perhaps we need to sacrifice ourselves. Help us. Tell us how we can make a difference."

A diversion, in other words. That would be heroic and selfless—Kirsten and Eric also had children on New Terra—and entirely futile.

Sigmund kept his voice level. "It's a noble offer. Who knows? In a few years, it may come to that. But for now, I see no way one ship can deter so many."

"So we go home and wait for the end?" Kirsten asked sadly.

Baedeker took the head from his pocket to pluck again at his mane.

Home it was, then, Sigmund thought. He stood to make the announcement and never got out the words.

"WE MUST STAY! Make it happen."

The command reverberated in Er'o's earplugs. He fully agreed—how could he not?—but that hardly mattered.

Melds were subtle things. Every Gw'otesht delicately balanced minds and temperaments, blending many personalities into one superordinate distinctiveness. Partial melds, their customary symmetries broken, were always volatile. Many, like this meld, were a bit petulant.

Er'o understood; he also felt incomplete. He replied on an encrypted link, using a microphone inserted well down into a tubacle, "Ol't'ro, the others want to go home."

"That is unacceptable!" Ol't'ro insisted. "Our studies are unfinished."

Er'o felt like he debated with himself. With each interstellar journey he learned a little, came that much closer to insight. In the course of this mission, Rj'o had twice rebuilt their long-range sensors. The data suggested, so far inconclusively, that faster-than-light flight involved extra or other dimensions. Either theory would explain the electric-constant anomalies. Call it travel through a hyperspace.

It seemed Jm'ho must suffer the same doom as the worlds *Don Quixote* had surveyed. Ramscoops, the implementation of which had become obvious, might save a few Gw'oth—for as long as they could maintain a precarious lead. If they stopped for supplies, or fell short of the efficiency of the enemy ships . . .

And launching ramscoops might draw that much *more* death and destruction upon the world that dispatched them.

In past melds, Ol't'ro had considered taking control of this ship, for the Gw'oth aboard outnumbered the original crew four to one. Mastering the secrets of faster-than-light travel would surely be simpler with a working mechanism to study.

Overwhelming uncertainties always stopped them. Merely opening the cargo hold's outer door with artificial gravity turned off would blow the habitat into space. Or Sigmund might (in Er'o's opinion, *would*) have set booby traps. And even a successful takeover, if they incurred only two or three casualties, might mean the end of Ol't'ro.

Seizure was too risky. Their current state of ignorance was intolerable. They must extend the mission long enough to solve the hyperspace puzzle.

Er'o radioed, "Ol't'ro, they mean to leave. Give me a reason for Sigmund to stay."

"The mission files are rife with observational anomalies. We will find something intriguing. Can you postpone Sigmund's decision?"

What alternative did he have? "Somehow."

As Sigmund stood, Er'o switched to English. "We may have found something worth a closer look." He waited anxiously for Ol't'ro to disclose that *something*.

"What?" Kirsten finally prompted.

"I am sorry. I need a moment to put this into English," Er'o lied. To Ol't'ro, using the deep-in-the-tubacle mike, Er'o added, "I need something *now*."

A moment later: "Done. Check ship comm channel three. We will talk you through it."

"I apologize again for the delay," Er'o told the gathering in the relax room. "My colleagues suggest we look at channel three."

Eric set his pocket communicator on the table. He tapped the touch screen and a hologram shone up from it. "Another tanj stellar map! What now?"

Ol't'ro explained on a secure channel.

Er'o said, "This is a view from our present coordinates toward the galactic center. Away from the enemy vanguard. The blinking dot marks a world our research has recently noticed."

"What kind of research?" Baedeker asked.

Er'o flexed several tubacles. His exoskeleton amplified the effort, raising him from the table—though no one here would recognize the confident stance. "We looked for radio signals, something to indicate a possibly better source of information."

"And you *found* something?" Eric replied. "A technological civilization the enemy failed to destroy?"

"We found something." Er'o paused for them to digest the simple statement. "A very weak signal that took a great deal of signal processing to separate from the background noise. Perhaps the transmissions are shielded, or very directional, and the enemy did not notice." The modest level of atmospheric dust made it almost certain the enemy had left this world unmolested.

Baedeker stopped tugging at his mane. "How long to get there?"

Er'o hesitated. Astronomical skills had earned him and his companions their place on *Don Quixote*. Merely a clock and before-and-after navigational fixes revealed the ship's rate of travel. It should come as no surprise he could answer the question. Still, he hesitated to show any attention paid to the interstellar drive. "About ten of your light-years." Meaning thirty days, had Er'o cared to answer fully.

"Far out of our way," Baedeker said. "Sigmund, it is past time that we return home. If planet-killers are on the way, every ship will be needed for evacuation."

And where, Er'o wondered, does that leave my people? We start with *no* starships. He tried to reclaim the initiative. "But the survivors on that distant world may have much to tell us."

"Let me check something." Kirsten took a device from her pocket. Her fingers moved quickly over the touchpad. "As I thought. Baedeker, it's safe to check this out before heading home. The planet-killers hit half a year or less before the enemy's leading edge passes."

"You cannot know that," Baedeker challenged. "Yes, we saw one world just ahead of the vanguard that was already attacked. One instance proves nothing."

Kirsten shook her head. "Turbulence models of the interstellar medium reveal how long ago each wave of ramscoops passed. To the first approximation, I assume all impacts eject similar amounts of vaporized crust. Then atmospheric models show when the impacter hit, estimated from the amount of dust that has since rained out. The answer isn't exact, because volcanism must differ from world to world. Still, the regression has pretty high confidence bounds. Call it ninety-nine percent."

Er'o marveled at the calculation Kirsten so casually offered. To have such tool at one's tubacle mouths! How much faster progress would come then. One more secret to discover—if they had the opportunity. "Sigmund, can we afford the time to visit this world?"

Sigmund tipped back his head, staring silently for a long while at nothing. "All right," he finally said, "We'll go see whoever is transmitting."

22

Dizzy and confused, Thssthfok struggled into awareness. Curious—he was not hungry. How long had he slept? Not long, obviously.

By the cold-sleep pod's chronometer, scarcely three Pakhome months.

Across the room, a red light flickered: his comm unit. A fiber-optic cable salvaged from his shuttle connected the comm to the cold-sleep reactivation circuit. When the Drar mastered primitive radios, it became possible to reach him safely during hibernation. Until now, no one ever had.

Wondering who dared, he put on his battle armor and checked his weapons. He ate a tree-of-life root before activating the intercom. "Who presumes to interrupt me?" he thundered.

"Koshbara, Your Excellency," came the answer, tremulous. "Something unusual has happened."

It had better be important. "Explain."

"May I enter, Excellency?"

Sensors showed only one Dra, shivering, beyond the massive steel door. Thssthfok disarmed his defensive systems and slid aside the sturdy steel latch. He recognized Koshbara despite her lack of ceremonial garb. He pulled her inside by a slender limb and resealed the entrance. "What has occurred?"

"A . . . a vessel, Excellency." She shivered, her vestigial wings rippling. "From the sky."

A scout ship, Thssthfok guessed, surprised the last wave of evacuees had not already passed him. Looking for biomass, surely. Landed here, specifically, because this dirty, pathetic city was its world's sole source of radio signals. Had he somehow pushed the Drar ahead only a little faster, a planet-buster, not a scout, would have come.

His own clan long gone, Thssthfok was, by definition, a threat to the newcomers. They would kill him without a second thought.

Unless he killed them first.

"You did well to awaken me," Thssthfok said. "Go. Tell the emperor that the visitors are to be welcomed and my presence kept secret. And inform her that I will require the army."

FLYING SQUIRRELS.

Sigmund had to shake his head. More than anything, the aliens he had come so far to meet looked like flying squirrels. Not that there weren't differences. . . .

The creatures were hairless, skeletally thin, and walked upright. They were much larger than any earthly rodent, about five feet tall and—when they spread their arms—ten feet in wingspan. They had an extra arm in the middle of each wing. When they got down on all sixes and ran they were as fast as cheetahs. Hull sensors revealed that much of the sound they made was ultrasonic, well above the human audible range.

Local gravity was forty percent above New Terran standard; the atmosphere was thick as soup. With those great wings and gaunt builds, it was easy to picture them soaring among the local version of trees.

Don Quixote sat in an open field near this world's only radio transmitters. Nearby, paddlewheel steamers, their pipes belching black smoke, plied a broad river. The boats, apart from their oddly bulbous, backward tilted smokestacks, looked like something Mark Twain might have piloted. Across the river stood a city like nothing Sigmund had ever seen, part adobe and stone, part steel and glass. Pyramids and turreted castles rubbed shoulders with squat offices and warehouses, a bit like nineteenth-century London and ancient Egypt brought together.

Outside *Don Quixote*'s main hatch waited a delegation of the natives, ornately garbed. They talked and gestured a lot, to the point that Jeeves made steady progress translating. The invitation to a palace came through clearly enough.

Eric paced outside the bridge. "Sigmund, Jeeves will learn the language faster once some of us go outside. Then *we* can point and gesture, too, and maybe teach them some English."

From the pilot's seat, Kirsten nodded. "We're here to talk, Sigmund. Let's do it."

The natives seemed surprisingly calm. You would think a spaceship landed every day, setting aside that the planet was tidally locked to its sun so that this city experienced only day. But Sigmund knew Eric was right. They *had* come to talk.

Sigmund said, "All right, everyone, it's time to meet the natives. For now we'll stay near the ship, in range of the external stunners." And in reach of every precaution he had been able to devise. "*No* excursions yet, not even to the palace."

Kirsten stood. "Finally. I'll get my—"

"No, you won't," Sigmund insisted. "You're pilot and navigator, and we're far from home. I'll go with Eric. While I'm outside, you are in command."

She sat, disappointment plain on her face.

"Baedeker," Sigmund called. The Puppeteer was in his cabin. Cowering, no doubt.

"Yes, Sigmund?"

"Please come to the bridge. I need someone cautious at the weapons console."

"How can we help?" a Gw'o sent from their tank. Sigmund recognized Er'o's voice.

"Keep watch through the external sensors," Sigmund answered. "And stay put. We may need to leave fast. If so, it would be better that you all be in the tank."

The Gw'oth had been valuable assets for the entire trip. Sigmund had no reason to believe they might try to capture this ship—and no confidence that they wouldn't. If they meant to try, the ideal moment was when he and Eric went outside.

"Eric, meet me at the air lock," Sigmund said. "No armor. We don't want to look hostile."

"I'm on my way."

Sigmund had one stop to make first: his cabin, for a welder. Standing so that the corridor security camera saw only his back, Sigmund spot-welded shut the interior hatch from the main cargo hold. If the Gw'oth tried to come out, he would have some warning.

"Where *are* you?" Eric radioed impatiently.

"On my way," Sigmund replied. *Now* I've taken every precaution I can think of.

THE CRAFT WAS OF AN UNFAMILIAR CONFIGURATION, larger than Thssth-fok's ruined shuttle, without visible exhausts. He had not seen it land; he inferred its nozzles were out of sight beneath. The absence of scorch marks puzzled him.

His handpicked team took up positions near the obvious air lock and made welcoming speeches. Finally the air lock opened and Thssthfok's eyes bulged. Those two were no Pak!

"Now!" he radioed. Capture the ship!

The commandos flung off their cloaks, dropped to all sixes, and swarmed.

FINAGLE, THOSE THINGS WERE FAST!

The aliens were halfway to the air lock before Sigmund's mind even registered the holsters that had been concealed by billowy cloaks. "Back inside!" he shouted to Eric.

Too slow. Eric vanished from sight beneath a pile of the natives. More grabbed at Sigmund. They weighed next to nothing and he flung them off—only they swarmed even faster. The weapons remained holstered; the aliens wanted prisoners.

Why did Baedeker not open fire?

Two aliens hit Sigmund's knees from behind. He toppled like a rag doll, glimpsing as he fell more of the rail-thin aliens at the controls at the inner hatch. The safety override had intuitive controls illustrated with a bold graphic. Any child could understand it.

Or any industrial-age alien.

The inner hatch began to cycle. *Now* weapons appeared in alien hands. "Launch, Kirsten!" Sigmund ordered. "Shake them off!"

The air, already thick, turned almost solid. He had stripped the crash couches of their emergency protective force-field generators. Within the air lock and for a short distance outside, they reasonably approximated a police restraint field.

Sigmund knew to lie still, and the field around him eased enough to allow him to breathe. "Don't fight it," he hissed to Eric.

The aliens panicked. The more they struggled, the more the field restricted them. Those distant enough to break free of the force field ran.

From the inner hatch, still opening, the frying-bacon sizzle of sonic stunners. Sigmund cautiously craned his neck to see Kirsten with a gun in each fist. She was methodically stunning every immobilized alien. Finally, the weapons turrets let loose, stunning anything that moved.

Best guess, thirty seconds had passed since the ambush.

The force field vanished. Sigmund struggled to his feet and helped Kirsten clear the air lock and pry stunned natives off Eric. Eric limped a bit and bled from lots of superficial cuts but made it into the ship under his own power.

Sigmund punched the emergency-close button. The hatch slammed shut. "I ordered you to take off!"

Kirsten shrugged. "Yes, but first you put me in charge."

BOARDERS! WAVES OF ALIENS inrushing from nearby buildings. On the river, ships opening hatches in their sides to reveal large metal tubes. The ships were coming about, bringing to bear what must be weapons.

Baedeker's heads whipped from display to display. "Take off!" he shrieked at Kirsten.

Instead she keyboarded feverishly at her console before standing. "You have the weapons console. Use it." She dashed from the bridge.

This was madness! He must flee!

Even Sigmund agreed. "Launch, Kirsten! Shake them off!" But Kirsten was not here to obey.

Baedeker grabbed the copilot controls. They had been designed for hands and were awkward in his mouths. Nothing happened. "Jeeves!" Baedeker screamed. "Get us out of here! Shake off the intruders and close the air lock."

"I'm afraid I can't do that, Baedeker," the AI said calmly.

In the corridor, the sound of handheld stunners. They had to get away! "Why not?"

"Kirsten's orders. Only human crew may fly the ship."

Her last-minute typing. And in the tactical display, *more* aliens swarmed. A second wave of attackers.

Because they could not flee, the only option was to fight. Baedeker shook off the paralysis of fear. He put his mouths to the weapons console and began zapping anything nearby that moved.

On the river, out of range of Baedeker's stunners, ships continued turning into firing position.

IMAGERY STREAMED OVER THE SHIPBOARD network into the Gw'oth habitat. Eric disappearing under a pile of aliens. Sigmund falling.

The primitive natives had sprung a trap.

The humans needed help, but the battle would have ended, for good or ill, before Er'o or his mates could even get into pressure suits.

Keep watch through the external sensors, Sigmund had directed. Very well. Er'o scanned the last few minutes in the sensor logs. There! A radio burst. Seconds later, the welcoming party attacked. More comm bursts and correlated maneuvering by troops and the forces on the river.

Someone commanded these attackers. Where?

Er'o had a rough bearing on the signal source, no more. The enemy headquarters could be almost anywhere in the native city.

Events were coming too fast for him—but maybe not too fast for Ol't'ro. "We need to meld," Er'o called. "Quickly."

23

So close.

Thssthfok put from his mind what might have been. His troops—the empire's finest commandos—had failed to seize the spaceship.

The strangers' vessel had yet to emit any recognizable long-range signal. If they could be destroyed quickly, perhaps no others would come. He might be left unmolested here to complete his fleet.

The aliens had broken free of the Drar and retreated into their ship. They would do *something* soon, whether lashing out with more destructive shipboard weapons or taking off. The reaction engines Thssthfok had yet to see could easily put the whole city to flame—with him deep in the urban center.

To the infantry reserves, he radioed, "Break into that ship or face the emperor's wrath." To the engineering squads, he ordered, "Deploy at bow, rear, and cargo hatch." The engineers ran toward the spaceship dragging long iron tubes filled with primitive explosives. And to the naval artillery, he commanded, "Prepare to open fire."

The foot soldiers were as good as dead, but their charge might divert attention from the more serious attacks.

BY SCANT SECONDS SIGMUND BEAT Kirsten to the bridge. Baedeker took one look at their grim faces and ran.

"I'm surprised he didn't fly away and strand us," Sigmund said.

"I didn't leave him that option," Kirsten answered cryptically. She switched on the intercom even as she dropped into her crash couch. "All hands, takeoff in five seconds."

Sigmund grabbed the weapons joysticks, sticky with Puppeteer saliva, and blasted all around. Better to be stunned at a safe distance than crushed by the fringes of the thruster field when *Don Quixote* lifted. Despite everything, he wished the flying squirrels no harm. They obviously had met the enemy, too. He respected their self-control, if not the trap they had set.

"Anytime, Kirsten," he said.

Blam! An explosion at the bow rocked the ship. The hull, unharmed, rang like a gong. The concussion threw Sigmund and Kirsten from their seats. A second later, from the stern: *blam!* A third explosion toppled Sigmund as he tried to regain his feet. The emergency protective field generators that should have held them in their crash couches were still installed at the air lock. The hull was nearly impregnable. The crew wasn't.

"Jeeves," Kirsten called—hissed?—from the floor. (Sigmund craned his neck at something in her voice. Her left arm flopped at her side. Dislocated, he thought.) "Jeeves. Take us up to one hundred feet."

The ship lurched and slewed: another explosion just as they lifted off.

"Sigmund," came a call over the intercom. Er'o. "I've been watching external sensors. We need to get away from those gunboats."

Sigmund helped Kirsten up before settling into his seat. In his tactical display, the river fleet had come about. Hundreds of cannon pointed this way. Artillery crews worked feverishly to raise their aim.

"Evasive maneuvers, Jeeves," Er'o shouted.

"I am afraid I can't—" Jeeves began.

Blam! Blam! Blam!

Sigmund wasn't much of a pilot, but anything beat being a stationary target. He took the controls and *Don Quixote* darted toward the crowded wharfs. A cool corner of his mind analyzed Er'o's practical advice, one more suggestion that Gw'oth city-states sometimes warred.

The ragged broadside volley passed where *Don Quixote* had just been. A dense cloud of smoke all but hid the riverboats.

Sigmund put *Don Quixote* into a steep climb. The tanjed squirrels couldn't possibly shoot very high, not with only chemical explosives. Something crude like gunpowder, he surmised from the thick smoke.

"Sigmund," Er'o called. "Go down within range for a bit. Pretend we're damaged. I want to see something."

A cannonball strike or two, if it came to that, wouldn't hurt anything, and the Gw'oth had been pretty perceptive so far. Sigmund sent his ship into a shallow dive.

"Come to bearing 225," Er'o said. "Good. Now turn to 112."

The riverboats could not turn fast enough to use their main batteries again, but a few boats fired off rounds from their bow guns. Compared to space junk, cannonballs were trivial to track and destroy. Nothing made it through to *Don Quixote*.

"Got you!" Er'o shouted.

RADIO BURSTS CAME MORE and more frequently: from the riverboats, the clusters of ground troops, and the city. The messages meant little to Ol't'ro, but the signals themselves . . .

Ol't'ro ignored the messages from the battlefield—those would be reports, or pleas for reinforcement, or excuses—to concentrate on comm *to* the warriors. *Those* messages might reveal who commanded the attack.

Don Quixote's zigzag course did more than evade the primitive projectile weapons. Ol't'ro now had three separate bearings on the source, from deep within the city, of the radio bursts. The bearings intersected at an imposing stone edifice near several pyramids. The rooftop antenna, now that Ol't'ro knew where to direct a telescope, was decidedly out of place.

Each of *Don Quixote*'s sensors told a story. What tale would they tell speaking together?

Ol't'ro decoupled tubacles, one for each external sensor. Data from across the spectrum streamed into their consciousness, but not without cost—all those dropped inter-mind connections slowed and muddled their thoughts. It was only with great concentration that Ol't'ro rescaled, aligned, superimposed, and synthesized all the imagery. He directed Jeeves to alter the ship's scanning patterns.

A clearer picture emerged. The suspected headquarters building teemed with frail six-limbed creatures—

And one figure, far more massive than the rest, with *four* limbs.

Using Er'o's voice, Ol't'ro shouted to the bridge, "Got you!"

IN THSSTHFOK'S HELMET, an alarm flared red. His battle armor had detected an unexpected electromagnetic signature. The beam was low energy and ultra-wideband: wall-penetrating radar.

The aliens had found him.

He dashed from his command post, headed for the escape tunnels beneath the palace.

"GOT *WHO?*" Sigmund called.

"Check channel six," Er'o answered.

Sigmund switched the tactical holo. A human running! About as tall as the flying squirrels: five feet.

No, not quite human. The arms were too long. The head shape was wrong. Or was that a hat or helmet? Even at max resolution, Sigmund could not distinguish clothing from body. Still studying the image, he said, "How did you find—no, don't answer. Just keep tracking it."

Kirsten settled into her crash couch, wincing with pain. Her good hand hovered above her controls. "Sort of like flying with one arm tied behind my back," she said. "I'll manage."

The humanoid in the tactical display sped through corridors, the image jerky as Er'o struggled to follow. Sigmund said, "Can you add a distance scale?"

Grid lines appeared and Sigmund blinked. One question answered; no human moved that fast. Then who or what?

Sigmund turned to Kirsten. "*Can* you fly this?"

She put *Don Quixote* through a sharp curve, then veered back toward the building with the mysterious stranger. Through gritted teeth, she said, "Looks like yes."

They had to know who that was running. "Eric," Sigmund called. "Bring battle gear for the two of us to the main lock. And stepping discs. We're going in."

"Stepping discs?"

OL'T'RO KEPT WATCH on the humanoid racing through the headquarters building. "It's headed deeper into the building. How are you going to get at it?"

"Comm laser," Sigmund answered. "At this range, we can drill right through the building. Jeeves, that's your job. Avoid the natives if you can."

A long silence before Jeeves answered. "I don't think I can, Sig—"

"Sigmund, permit me to control the laser." Ol't'ro hated to reveal one of the secrets they had uncovered, but the mission took precedence. The running figure might be one of the enemy, perhaps a straggler or deserter. "Combat evidently exceeds the device's design parameters."

Over the intercom, a sharp intake of breath. Ol't'ro could not identify the source. Then they were correct—about Jeeves *and* that its artificial nature was meant to remain hidden. "Sigmund, we do not have time to waste."

"Right," Sigmund decided. A channel appeared through the firewall. "Don't harm the natives unnecessarily."

ERIC WAS STRUGGLING into his combat gear when Sigmund reached the main air lock. Sigmund did a quick inventory of what the engineer had chosen: handheld stunners and lasers, two sacks of grenades, and four stepping discs. He closed the inner hatch behind them.

Well, Sigmund thought, I was *almost* prepared. It would have been nice to have police restraint fields. The emergency protective force-field generators from the crash couches were still hot-wired into an air-lock circuit. He unplugged one field generator and put it into an outside pocket of his battle armor.

"Over the target," Kirsten called.

"Ready when you are," Er'o added.

Sigmund had an image of the big native building on his heads-up display. His quarry was deep inside, apparently headed for the warren of tunnels beneath the structure. Some of the passageways went far below the surface, beyond the penetration range of *Don Quixote*'s sensors.

The streets were too narrow to set down the ship. How could they head off their target? Once the humanoid got into the maze, it would take an army to drive it out. Sigmund didn't have an army.

Sigmund asked, "How tall is that building, Kirsten?"

"About three hundred feet."

Sigmund stuffed his pockets with grenades and picked up a stepping disc. "Good. Hover over the street, as close as you dare. Er'o, be ready to burn a street-level entrance for us."

Eric's eyes went round. "Armor or no, we can't jump three hundred feet!"

"I don't plan to." Sigmund smacked the emergency override on the air lock. The outer hatch opened—and snipers opened fire.

The nanofabric of the armor stiffened, distributing the impact of the tiny bullets. Sigmund hardly felt them, but it didn't keep him from cursing. He dropped the stepping disc into the street hundreds of feet below. It landed with a crash, dark side up. Upside down. So did the second disc. He grabbed and dropped a third. It landed right side up.

Time to see how well Puppeteers built these things.

One more stepping disc remained on the air-lock deck. Transport controller in hand, he stepped onto the disc—

And reappeared on the street.

He jammed a stepping disc into a sling across his back and plunged through a ragged, smoking hole into the building.

EXPLOSIONS BOOMED ALL AROUND, the closer ones shaking the palace. Between explosions Thssthfok heard the ululations of Drar, and small-arms fire, and masonry creaking. And there was a whooshing sound he did not understand.

The comm gear in his armor sensed signals at frequencies beyond the capability of Drar radios. The signal sources changed bearing steadily.

He could not see his pursuers, but he knew he was being chased.

Thssthfok raced down the stairs, for once wishing he were more like his servants. If he had wings, he would have leapt the banister and glided down in an instant.

Still, he had almost reached the catacombs.

TANJ! THE HUMANOID had almost reached the basement.

"Er'o," Sigmund called, "we can't head it off."

Sigmund lobbed a flash-bang grenade into the upcoming hallway intersection. He dashed through, ignoring the dazed natives staggering in the cross-corridor. Shots came from far behind them, and he heard Eric's stunner.

"It is still in sensor view," Er'o reported. "I will drive it toward you."

Drive how? Sigmund wondered—and then a deafening roar answered his unarticulated question. Laser fire turning stone, wood, and metal to vapors and powder. Combustible dust and fumes exploding. Dust and gravel pinged off the stepping disc slung across his back.

Some of the building collapsed, the floor shaking beneath Sigmund's boots. "Try not to bring the whole building down on him." Or on Eric and me.

CRACKED BEAMS AND STONE SLABS RAINED down the stairwell. In an instant, the path to the tunnels was gone. The palace groaned.

A chunk of granite as big as Thssthfok's head ricocheted off the stairwell wall into his helmet. He stopped, stunned. When he shook off the paralysis, the two mobile radio sources were much stronger. Closer.

Too close.

A BATTLE-ARMORED BIPED DISAPPEARED around a corner.

"I see it," Sigmund shouted. "Er'o, drive it toward us."

A roar of exploding masonry served as answer. Ruby-red glare, dazzling, shone from the stone walls.

Sigmund's visor turned nearly opaque against the blazing light, and his eyes brimmed with tears. He couldn't see a thing!

Something hit him, the impact staggering. Without armor, that blow would have snapped him in two. He heard the frying-bacon crackle of Eric's stunner—stunners don't work through armor, tanj it!—and the pop of grenades.

"Kill the laser!" Sigmund shrieked. The lurid light vanished and his visor cleared. Blinking away the tears he saw the alien bearing down on Eric. And behind Eric, tens of armed natives racing closer.

Sigmund took the force-field generator from his pocket, switched it on, and hurled it with all his strength. If he had thrown it fast enough, and that armor was hard enough . . .

THSSTHFOK'S VISOR TURNED BLACK against the sudden glare. He turned and ran back the way he had come, the path he had taken clear in his mind's eye.

The glare eased as he rounded the corner. His visor cleared a bit to reveal two armored bipeds taller than any Pak.

Thssthfok charged at top speed, flinging aside the first. He had almost reached the other when, with a clang, something smacked the back of his helmet. The air around him turned rigid.

He toppled forward, helpless, coming to a halt floating a handspan above the floor.

"KIRSTEN!" SIGMUND CALLED. "Is the stepping disc still in the main air lock?" Surveillance cameras would tell her—unless an unlucky shot had taken out the camera.

For once their luck was good. "It's still there, Sigmund."

He lased the ceiling ahead of the charging natives. Stone crashed down, and the natives turned and ran. "Make sure both inner and outer hatches are closed."

"Done."

The alien hovered above the floor, trapped like a bug in amber. The force field suspended its own generator just above the prisoner.

Force fields were power hogs. Maintaining the restraint would drain the generator's battery within thirty minutes. Sooner, if the prisoner struggled.

Some half memory from a life before New Terra raised the hairs on the back of Sigmund's neck. What was this creature? One of the enemy? Even in its armor, it looked like a goblin, some perversion of the human shape.

Tanj it, Sigmund wanted *answers*. This creature was going to provide them. "Eric, find some boards or poles. Clothes rods, broken furniture, I don't care what. Make sure they're sturdy and at least six feet long."

Eric nodded and went to search.

Sigmund took the stepping disc from its sling. He set it on the floor near the immobilized alien. His toes tingled through his armored boots as he slid the disc to the edge of the force field. "Kirsten, lift the ship to fifty miles, then maintain a velocity match with the ground."

Only a momentary pause betrayed the questions she resisted asking. "Lifting, lifting"—at max acceleration, it would take only about a minute— "decelerating now, still rising. Fifty miles, mark. Hovering on thrusters directly over the city."

"I'll be sending through a prisoner. In theory, it's immobilized. If it moves—blow it out the air lock. Do *not* hesitate."

"My finger's on the switch," she said.

Rasping sounds heralded Eric's return. He reappeared, his gloves around two solid planks. The other ends scraped along the stone floor.

Sigmund grabbed a board. "We're going to move our prisoner against a wall. Then, while you keep it there, I'll slide the stepping disc beneath."

"Got it." Eric lifted his plank into the force field. The field grabbed the end and held it.

Sigmund followed suit. Amid ominous groaning and the ever heavier rain of dust and debris, they shoved the alien into place.

To slide the stepping disc beneath involved lifting alien and armor. The disc was little thicker than the planks, which kept slipping off.

Eric dropped his plank. He needed both hands to roll a basketball-sized lump of rubble to the force field's edge. With the masonry chunk as his fulcrum and his board as a lever, huffing mightily, Eric raised the alien about an inch. "Now," he grunted.

With his board, Sigmund forced the stepping disc beneath—just as Eric's board snapped. The prisoner dropped, pinning the stepping disc, not *quite* centered beneath.

With a sickening moan, part of the corridor ceiling gave way.

"We're ready to send," Sigmund radioed. If their prisoner was unlucky, an arm or a leg might be left behind. "What about your end?"

"It goes out the air lock if it moves," Kirsten confirmed.

"Your decision whether that's necessary, no questions asked. Err on the side of safety." Sigmund paused for any objection. There wasn't one.

"On the count of three," Sigmund said. He had a transport controller in his gloved hands, a thumb poised above the TRANSMIT button. "Kirsten, be alert."

"Copy that," she replied.

"One, two, three." The alien—all of him—disappeared.

"Got it!" Kirsten called out. "Frozen stiff. Now how about you two?"

Cargo holds had stepping discs inlaid in their decks for ease of loading and unloading. Sigmund used his transport controller to retarget the disc here to a disc in *Don Quixote*'s auxiliary cargo hold. "After you, Eric."

Eric stepped away.

In twenty minutes, no more, the battery would be drained and the restraint field would vanish. They had that long to somehow get the prisoner into a more secure environment. Or to chuck it, and any hope for answers, out the air lock.

"Sigmund!" Eric yelled. "Get out of there."

Sigmund stepped onto the disc. His impression, in the instant that the stepping disc activated for him, was of the whole stone structure crumbling.

24

Frozen in midair, helpless, Thssthfok considered.

Non-Pak spacefaring aliens. Either Koshbara had been slow to awaken him, or the spaceship had approached Mala unnoticed. If the latter, the aliens had a means of propulsion other than fusion drive.

There had been no time to ask for details; now Thssthfok could not. As mightily as he struggled, the force field did not permit him to speak, or even to tongue the radio controls. He could hardly breathe against the invisible restraint.

He remembered the dank stone basement of the Drar palace, and confronting the aliens, and getting snared by a restraint field. That was only a moment ago, his senses insisted. How had he gotten here, wherever here was?

He listed the possibilities. He might have been stunned by an alien weapon. For that or some other reason, he might have lost consciousness. But no: His helmet clock insisted only a moment had passed. Then somehow he had been moved instantaneously. The aliens had a means of teleportation! He must acquire the technology.

Those who had captured him were not without skill. They also had failings, to carelessly reveal so much about their technology. Or they were confident he would not survive to use what he learned. . . .

He floated facedown, a surface with a not-quite-metallic sheen a handspan beneath his visor. His peripheral vision hinted at barriers on every side. Featureless walls to his left and right. In the wall in front of him, hard to see, the lower rim of a hatch and a control panel. He guessed he was in an air lock.

A thin disc lay atop the decking, beneath his belly. What purpose did the disc serve? His neck refused to bend, but with effort he shifted his eyes and—

Discontinuity!

He hung in midair above more quasi-metallic decking and a thin disc, but the confining walls had receded. A new room, then, perhaps a cargo hold—and certain proof that the aliens had instantaneous transportation.

The force field vanished.

The crash of his battle armor against the deck suggested a metal/plastic composite. Something banged off his oxy tank on its way to the floor. He recovered the fist-sized artifact and stowed it in a pocket of his armor for later study.

Thssthfok stood, the burden of his armor noticeably lightened here. Was this gravity weaker than that of Pakhome? He could not decide. His muscles had acclimated to Mala.

He began surveying his cell. The room held only empty cabinets and shelves, a sturdy but empty metal box, and the disc.

One side of his cell was curved, its area mostly taken up by a single large hatch. He was in a cargo hold. The clear rectangular expanse in that hatch revealed featureless black. In space, perhaps, the ceiling's glow over-whelming the stars. Perhaps only night.

As he approached the hatch a sullen red sun came into view. Closer still to the window he saw the curved surface of a planet, its atmosphere dappled with cloud. Mala. At this altitude the works of the Drar were in-visible to the unaided eye.

His tongue flicked out to the helmet radio controls, hoping that Koshbara might have observed something useful. He heard only static. Jamming.

A sudden tap-tap.

Thssthfok's head swiveled sharply, toward the small hatch that would give access into the ship. A metal plate had been welded to the hatch where a latch, knob, or keypad belonged.

Through the small, inset window Thssthfok saw a pale oval. A face. The eyes were eerily breederlike, but everything else was *wrong*. The forehead was vertical when it should be sloped. The nose was too pronounced. The receding jaw was disturbingly short.

Drar varied enough from Pak to seem exotic. This alien was only Pak-like enough to be . . . repulsive.

More rapping, impatient. Something rectangular replaced the face in the window.

Thssthfok moved closer. The object held against the window was a display device. Imagery moved: most performed by one of the not-quite-breeders, the rest in animation.

The demonstration was clear. Thssthfok was to remove his protective gear and clothing. (Beneath his armor, he had only a many-pocketed utility vest. His captors, like the Drar, evidently wore more.) He was to stow in the box all his things, the disc, and the fist-sized object he had recovered. Then he was to sit on his hands, heels drawn tight against his buttocks, knees spread, head between his knees, with his back against the main hatch. Once he was vulnerable, armored and armed aliens would enter and remove the box.

Helmet sensors reported nitrogen, oxygen, and a bit of carbon dioxide, easily breathable. Enough like Mala that his captors would conclude—correctly—that he could breathe it.

The main hatch, if opened, would vent the hold's atmosphere. Without his armor's magnetic boots, he would be blown into space.

And if he defied his captors and remained inside his suit? The animated instructions addressed that, too. The force field would return for a while and then he would get another chance to comply. Until, Thssthfok surmised, he cooperated—or his suit ran out of oxygen.

He needed a third option. He lifted the disc to study it. It must be important or the aliens would not want it packed for removal. A disc in the air lock and another disc—or was it the same one?—here. Either way, the disc seemed implicated in the alien teleportation technol—

Thssthfok gasped. His weight had tripled in an instant. Artificial cabin gravity, as in a Pak ramscoop—but used to punish, not to offset acceleration.

Servomotors adjusted, but within the armor his muscles strained. The apparent gravity increased further. Further. Further . . .

Thssthfok released the disc and it shot to the deck. His ears rang from the clang. After a moment the gravity eased, and he again weighed something close to normal.

Be crushed now, suffocate soon, or be seen to cooperate. It was not a hard decision. Thssthfok removed his helmet.

The stench! Horrible things, bestial things, inhabited this ship. With one sniff, Thssthfok divided the odors into two types. The first were wholly strange, as foreign as the Drar. He had learned to coexist with those.

But at the remaining stench, not *entirely* alien, Thssthfok's hands ached to rend flesh asunder. At the faint limit of sensitivity, that dominant reek evoked defective Pak infants. For millions of years, such not-quite-right smells had triggered the reflex to destroy any mutant birth.

Somehow, these were Pak mutants.

Willing his fists to relax, Thssthfok set down the helmet and finished removing his armor. The opportunity to resist would come.

SIGMUND TWITCHED AS THE PRISONER removed his helmet. Those eyes! They were so *human*. But by human standards the head was grotesque: misshapen, topped by a bony crest, totally hairless, and too large for its body. The skin looked leathery. The face had neither lips nor gums, only a hard, nearly flat, toothless beak.

Sigmund watched a holo, not the prisoner himself. Only a few fiber-optic cables penetrated into the improvised cell. There had scarcely been time, before the improvised restraint-field generator drained its battery, to empty the auxiliary cargo hold and run cables for monitoring. No active bugs, whose electronics might somehow be co-opted.

"Are you all right, Sigmund?" Kirsten asked. She shared the corridor with him, standing on the other side of the holo. The rest of the crew watched from their posts. "You look upset."

Sigmund shivered, in the grip of déjà vu. He hoped his suspicions were misplaced. "I'm not sure."

Within his cell the prisoner began stripping off battle gear. Inside the pressure suit he had looked humanoid, but that was only a matter of over-all shape. Briskly now, having taken to heart the gravity-field lesson, he worked his way out of the suit.

His chest, like his face, was flat and leathery. The more of that body emerged, the more clearly humanoid he was. He had joints where a human had them—only the prisoner's joints were grossly enlarged. His elbows were as large as softballs. His hands were knobby, his fingers like strings of walnuts. The fingers lacked nails but the tips suggested retractable talons.

Not he. Not she, either. It. The prisoner's crotch lacked sex organs.

Sigmund's hands trembled. He willed them to stop.

"What's happening?" Baedeker demanded over the intercom. From the safety of his locked cabin, no doubt.

Only Sigmund did not believe any of them was safe. He managed *not* to order Jeeves to open the cargo-hold hatch and vent the air. He needed to know what the prisoner could tell them.

Sigmund had once seen such a creature, or at least its mummified remains. In an earlier life. In Washington, at the Smithsonian Institute, of all places.

He took a deep breath. "I know who our enemies are. It is *not* good."

25

"The intruder entered Sol system in 2125," Sigmund said, although Earth's calendar had meaning only to Jeeves and himself. "More than half a millennium ago."

To be precise, a good 550 Earth years earlier. Only any claim to precision was laughable, given the gaping holes in Sigmund's and the AI's memories. By Sigmund's best approximation, the present Earth date was 2675.

From their customary seats around the relax-room table, Kirsten, Eric, and Baedeker waited for Sigmund to continue. Jeeves listened in while keeping watch on the prisoner, no longer pretending that he was on the bridge.

The Gw'oth participated from their habitat. By choice, Sigmund wondered guiltily, or because the path was blocked? Without Er'o's help, Sigmund would never have captured the prisoner—and Sigmund had welded the Gw'oth into the cargo hold.

Did they know that they were trapped? He should know, but didn't. With equal delicacy, no one ever mentioned hiding sensors in the cargo hold, or finding and neutralizing them. It was a game of cat and mouse like Sigmund had played with Puppeteer agents back on New Terra. Aboard *Don Quixote*, the mice—that was to say, the Gw'oth—appeared to hold the advantage.

Sigmund clutched a drink bulb, more to steady his hands than from any interest in the coffee. So: 2125. Only the saga began long before that.

He started over. "Humans aren't native to New Terra. You've *always* known that. Well, it turns out humans aren't native to Earth, either."

"What?" Kirsten and Eric shouted, nearly in unison. Baedeker's comment, orchestral and discordant, sounded equally surprised.

"The year 2125. That's when a few learned otherwise." Sigmund's mind's eye offered up the mummified alien he had once seen. Far away. Long ago. "Jeeves, what records do you have on the incident?"

"Very little, Sigmund, assuming I'm correct to what incident you refer." A hologram formed over the relax-room table, a museum display of a spacesuit with great ball joints at the knees and elbows. The gear closely matched the suit worn by their captive.

Jeeves went on. "As you say, in 2125 an alien ship appeared from deep space. A ramscoop. Belter and United Nations authorities found one alien aboard: the pilot, long dead. His equipment was eventually donated to the Smithsonian. The body carried a pathogen—it killed some of those who intercepted the ship—and was destroyed. The authorities kept the derelict itself for study."

"Thank you, Jeeves," Sigmund said.

That, until well after *Long Pass* and Jeeves departed Earth, had been the entire story for public consumption. There had been no choice but to tell the public something. The alien ship used magnetic monopoles; its approach had triggered monopole detectors across Sol system.

After centuries passed without similar visitors, the authorities had relaxed a bit. They admitted they had quarantined the alien corpse, not incinerated it. The Smithsonian exhibit now included the dead pilot's body.

Even in Sigmund's day, that was all Sol system's public knew, but he wasn't from the clueless majority. He had been in the Amalgamated Regional Militia, the UN's unassumingly named police/military/intelligence organization. Kirsten and Eric knew that bit about Sigmund's past—and that he was loath to discuss his former life. He had told even Penny little more than that. It dredged up too many painful memories.

He had to discuss it now.

Sigmund hadn't been just any ARM, but a high-ranking member of the Bureau of Alien Affairs. That was how he wound up spending so much of his time stalking Puppeteers. That was why Nessus had stalked *him*.

And Alien Affairs had had extensive files, still heavily classified, about the 2125 incident.

Sigmund remembered checking out the archives when his clearance finally allowed him to. Interesting stuff, but—so it had seemed—ancient history. *Very* ancient.

He wished now he had studied them more thoroughly.

Sigmund said, "About three million years ago, a generation ship left a planet somewhere near the galactic core. That vessel traveled deep into one of the spiral arms before the crew, from a species calling itself the Pak, found a world to colonize. Only their colony failed."

He brought up a second holo, of the improvised cell in which their prisoner moved ceaselessly. The match between their captive and the museum's spacesuit was undeniable.

A pacing human tends to retrace his steps, but the prisoner slightly altered its route with every circuit. Each lap would offer a slightly different perspective on its cell, the opportunity to glimpse something overlooked on previous perambulations.

So what, in their haste to empty the room, had Sigmund and Eric carelessly left behind? (Baedeker had been too terrified to help. Kirsten, her arm just put back into its socket, had been unable to help. After hours in the autodoc she looked much better.) If anything at all had been overlooked, this prisoner would find it. And use it against them.

"And Earth has records of ancient Pak," Kirsten said dubiously.

Paleontology was surely obscure to her, if she could even articulate the concept. All life on New Terra had a recent and well-documented beginning. Whether of Hearth or Earth origin, *everything* had been transplanted by Puppeteers. The primitive life that had gone before, source of the oxygen-rich atmosphere that had made the world ripe for exploitation, had perished in the interstellar deep freeze while Puppeteers moved the future Nature Preserve Four to their Fleet.

Puppeteers not only lacked curiosity, they discouraged it. They cared nothing about the primordial ecosystem they had obliterated, nor did they allow their servants to waste time on anything as useless as the dead past. New Terran scientists were as curious as anyone Sigmund had ever met. Still, since independence, concerns far more urgent than ocean-floor microfossils from pre-NP4 days had occupied them. Like keeping the present ecology healthy, despite the disappearance of tides. . . .

Yearning for Penelope—her smile, her grace, her touch, everything—burst out of Sigmund. Burst over Sigmund. They had been apart *so* long.

He struggled to set aside the hunger, to focus. For Penny more than anyone.

Fossils. Ecology. Pak. Something nagged at Sigmund. "Nature, red in tooth and claw," he muttered.

Kirsten eyed him strangely. Baedeker shuddered.

Where was that phrase from? Sigmund couldn't remember, whether from Nessus' meddling or the passage of time.

"Tennyson," Jeeves said. "From—"

The poem hardly mattered. Sigmund, finally, had grasped the deeper issue.

Even the brightest New Terran scientists failed to get evolution. Oh, they understood it intellectually, but they did not *feel* it. Not at a visceral level. How could they? Their biosphere was simply too young. Except on the tiniest of scales, in slight variations of crops and insect populations, they had yet to see natural selection in action.

They could not understand the terrible evolutionary imperatives that drove the Pak.

So to Kirsten's implied question. Yes, Earth had skeletal remains. They had been short, the adults typically about five feet in height. They had disproportionately long arms and receding foreheads. With a brain capacity at best half that of modern humans, the creatures could have been at best marginally sapient. Paleontologists called them Homo habilis, and over a couple million years they had evolved into Homo sapiens.

And no, because Earth failed to nurture a plant on which the colonists had depended. Pak like their prisoner—with its backward-bulging cranium, and Finagle alone knew how smart it was—had been rare in the colony. Nothing like it had been found in the fossil record.

All that detail could wait. Sigmund answered Kirsten with a nod. "The colony transmitted a distress call. Long after, a starship responded, loaded with supplies. A one-person ship whose pilot looked"—Sigmund gestured at their prisoner—"just like him."

"The ship reaching Sol system in your year 2125," Baedeker prompted. "And yet no one knows."

Sigmund nodded again. "Luckily for us all, a Belter prospector named Jack Brennan, a singleship pilot, was first to reach the incoming ramscoop. Everything we know"—or believe we know—"about the Pak, we learned from Brennan.

"Contrary to what the public was told, the ramscoop pilot was very much alive. He took Brennan captive." The Pak's name was almost all consonants. Phssthpok, Sigmund recalled, or something similar. A transliteration, obviously. Probably it took a beak and hardened palate to enunciate correctly. "Aboard the Pak ship, Brennan got a whiff of an alien vegetable.

"To a Pak or human of suitable age, the smell of tree-of-life root is irresistible. Brennan gorged on the tubers. The symbiotic virus in the roots turned him into"—Sigmund gestured at the holo—"something like that. Because *that* is meant to be a human's final life stage."

Eric froze the holo, rotating it slowly, examining their prisoner from every side. "Those huge joints. They're like the world's worst case of arthritis, gone untreated. The toughened, wrinkled skin. The lack of teeth and hair. It's almost like old age."

"Exactly." Sigmund sipped from his drink bulb, gathering his thoughts. "What we know as old age is the body's abortive attempt to transform. Changing successfully takes the retrovirus insinuated into the host's genetic code. Then you get skin like armor, increased muscle mass and the enlarged bones and joints to handle it, and other modifications. At the top of the list is a greatly enlarged brain.

"That ancient colony failed because tree-of-life didn't grow properly on Earth. The plant grew, but it didn't support the symbiotic virus. Without the virus, the adult colonists never reached the third stage of life, which is"—again, Sigmund pointed at the holo—"that. The cargo Brennan found was mostly tree-of-life seeds and trace elements critical to proper tree-of-life growth. If Brennan was correct, that final stage can live for fifteen hundred years."

Only few Pak did, and therein was the problem. Evolutionary pressures, tanj it! Sigmund wondered if he could make his crew understand. Make them believe.

"And Brennan became . . . like that," Eric repeated skeptically.

"That's the point," Sigmund said. That Brennan *could* transform was compelling evidence, if you understood evolution, of the close kinship between humans and Pak. Still, just as Homo sapiens varied from its Homo habilis ancestors—a brain twice as large, for starters—the respective next-stage forms had their differences. "Then they talked. Brennan said the Pak was far smarter than any human."

Transformed, Brennan himself had become smarter still.

Sigmund kept *that* detail to himself. It hinted at a way to outthink the enemy, but with a terrible sacrifice. Wherever a Pak lived, tree-of-life root must be available nearby. Certainly on the world of the flying squirrels. Perhaps even a few tubers, emergency rations, inside the sealed box of the prisoner's gear.

The ARM might have kept Phssthpok's cargo as insurance against future emergencies. They chose, instead, to destroy it. Things did not look *quite* so desperate that Sigmund wanted to plant in the mind of anyone here the possibility of exposing themselves to tree-of-life.

Eric had a guarded expression on his face. Did he suspect?

Best to change the subject. Sigmund took a deep breath. "When Brennan got the chance, he killed the Pak."

Baedeker pawed spasmodically at the deck. "This Pak crossed much of the galaxy to help your people, to extend their lives, to enhance their minds, and the first human it met killed it?"

Yes, because that was the right thing to do! The *only* thing!

Brennan had explained his actions all those years ago to ARM and Belter authorities—before escaping with contemptuous ease from their custody and disappearing from history. Sigmund summarized Brennan's argument. "The final life stage is called protector. Protecting their bloodline: That's what they're about. That's *all* they're about. They themselves are sterile.

"Protectors battle instinctively, incessantly, single-mindedly, for their families. They exterminate rival clans without qualm or hesitation. *That* is what would have become of Earth had Phssthpok survived. And such will be the fate of any human world on which tree-of-life ever gets loose."

Yet Brennan had abandoned his children. Belter authorities told Brennan's family only that contagion from food in the alien ship had taken him—truth of a sort—and that for safety the body had been incinerated into atoms. Maybe Brennan's above-Pak intelligence let him resist his protector instincts. Or—a flash of weird insight—maybe Brennan disappeared *for* his children.

Could Brennan's absence have helped his family? If not his absence, then something he intended to—

Baedeker erupted into noise: a frenzied and arrhythmic bleating, jarringly atonal. Sigmund's concentration faltered. The rickety structure of inference and conjecture collapsed.

With a shudder, Baedeker regained control of himself. His flanks trembled. His heads twitched, stealing peeks at the exit.

"Unending conflict among the Pak clans," Kirsten said wonderingly. "That's why eons passed between the colony ship and the rescue attempt. Resources gathered to prepare for such an epic journey would tempt every other clan. It's probably why, in millions of years, the Pak have not advanced beyond fusion-powered ships. That's the first good news we've had."

Good news? No, Sigmund thought sadly, she doesn't get it. Millions of years in ceaseless warfare, clan against clan. Millions of years of natural selection: for tactical brilliance, combat prowess, and utter ruthlessness. Millions of years evolving into the galaxy's consummate warriors.

That was who, in hundreds upon hundreds of ships, killing every civilization in sight, was rushing down New Terra's throat. . . .

What good could come of burdening everyone with Sigmund's own sense of doom? It was time, yet again, to change the subject. "That's enough for now. I need to talk to the prisoner."

26

Thssthfok strode about his cell, his eyes in constant motion.

His only value to his captors was the information he might give them—and he was determined to give them nothing useful. He could serve the Pak by escaping. Or by dying.

That he continued to study the cell was misdirection, for surely his captors watched through hidden sensors. He had long ago completed an inventory of useful materials. For sophisticated parts, the repair kit he had palmed from a pocket of his armor. To fashion into structural elements, bolts and brackets from the empty shelving units, and parts from the latching mechanisms within the empty cabinets. From the corners and recesses of the room, scraps in endless variety, all individually innocuous, the sign of a room hastily emptied. To run what he would build, the magnetically coupled wireless power transmitters recessed into the walls. And for the privacy in which to construct—whatever—the empty storage units themselves, their interiors invisible to watchers.

Like the briefly glimpsed air lock, every mechanism in this prison was straightforward in function, designed for a single obvious purpose, and profligate in its use of materials. His captors, like the Drar, must be a young race, their worlds all but unexploited. He could fashion many things from the components at his disposal, and what he would make—multipurpose, tiny, frugal in its use of resources—might go unnoticed among such primitives.

The situation was clear. He would escape and take charge of the ship. He would, if possible, take prisoners for the information they might provide. If their capture proved impractical, the ship itself would reveal much—

An eruption of noise: complexly modulated, unintelligible, not altogether unpleasant. Speech. It came from a tiny grille high on an interior wall, and Thssthfok added an audio transducer of unknown type to his list of building materials.

He saw flashes, roughly synchronized to the sounds, at the entrance into his cell. From the rectangular display device still attached to the inset window of the hatch. An image of his battle armor and a sound burst. An image of his captor's spaceship and another sound burst. An image of Thssthfok himself—and silence.

"Thssthfok," he offered.

And so the language lessons began.

IN THE PRIVACY OF HIS CABIN and inadequate comfort of his own rolled-up body, Baedeker trembled. The wonder was that he had made it to his cabin before collapsing. Sigmund's revelations had left him teetering on the brink of catatonia.

Pak fought other clans to extinction! Valuing their own kind so little, of course Pak attacked any other possible threat without hesitation. And so they had, with all those kinetic-kill genocides. And Hearth was in their path.

Would the New Terrans make common cause with their Pak cousins, abandoning—or betraying—Hearth? The humans had given no reason to expect that, but why wouldn't they? How else *could* they save themselves?

With an inner strength Baedeker had not known was in him, he unclenched and climbed shakily to his hooves. He activated a holo display to follow the interrogation.

He must study Sigmund as closely as the Pak.

WITH BUT ONE THREAD OF CONSCIOUSNESS, Ol't'ro monitored the interrogation. What the Pak might reveal mattered.

Right now, other things mattered more.

Thssthfok's capture had involved instant-transport devices, what Sigmund had called stepping discs. Like hyperdrive and nonbiological computing, instantaneous transport was a wondrous technology Ol't'ro's "allies" had failed to mention.

So that the technology could be deployed against the Gw'oth?

The auxiliary cargo hold become Pak prison had had a stepping disc in its deck. It took no imagination to suppose another such disc sat beneath their habitat. Activating such a disc would carve a hole in the tank, release the water, and deliver them to a slow and agonizing death.

But now they had seen a stepping disc.

An active acoustic sensor would probe *through* the tank to the deck beneath, and show whether a stepping disc in fact lurked there. They could easily fabricate such a sensor in the habitat water lock/workshop. Ol't'ro repurposed a thread of consciousness to develop the sonar design and choose its means of fabrication. They assigned yet another thread to mining their archives for hints to how teleportation might work.

Clearly the Gw'oth had been allowed aboard solely for the help they could provide. If that was the rule, they would help themselves, too.

Beginning with *Don Quixote*'s technologies . . .

SIGMUND STRODE DOWN a curving corridor, clad in battle armor, his massive boots clomping. The world dimmed and shrank and receded in his vision until all that he saw, as though at the end of a long tunnel, was a simple hatch.

Behind that door, the prisoner waited.

Thssthfok was smarter than Sigmund. Much smarter. If that wasn't bad enough, Brennan's testimony made clear that protectors were also stronger, faster, and more agile than any human.

Superior paranoia would have to compensate.

For hours, as Sigmund had mentally prepared for this confrontation, a trace of memory had tantalized. It hung out there still, just beyond his grasp. Not Brennan-as-protector leaving behind his family, the puzzle that Baedeker had chased from Sigmund's thoughts, but something related. Like a chipped tooth, it nagged at him. Everything Sigmund knew, or wondered, or feared about the Pak ran about in his brain like cats chasing their tails. Until—

To reach Sol system, Phssthpok had spent most of a millennium, most of his life, alone in a glorified singleship. Would a protector with a family do that?

Sigmund stopped short. Finally, the right question.

A voice crackled in his headset—Kirsten asking worriedly, "Are you all right?"—and Sigmund shushed her. He had the elusive memory!

It was a snippet from the classified files of the 2125 incident. An ancient vid of Lucas Garner, the only ARM to have met the Brennan-monster, dictating his memoirs. The recording included hearsay about Phssthpok: "He had no children, so he had to find a Cause"—proper-noun status echoed in Garner's voice—"quick, before the urge to eat left him. Brennan's words. That's what happens to a protector when his bloodline is dead."

Phssthpok was childless. Finding and saving the lost colony had been his Cause.

What of Thssthfok? Stranded, obviously, on the flying-squirrel planet, how could he hope to protect his family? So he, too, had committed to some Cause.

Phssthpok had committed a lifetime to crossing the galaxy. Thssthfok would be just as fanatically determined to accomplish *his* Cause, whatever that was.

Well, Sigmund had a Cause, too: Penny, and Athena and Hermes, and the millions on New Terra. They were depending on him.

And so was his crew. Sigmund responded, belatedly, to Kirsten's worried question. "I'm fine. Just thinking."

Outside the makeshift prison he did a final inspection. Battle armor: sealed. Pressure suit, exoskeleton functionality, and comm: all status lights green. Dampers repositioned in the air ducts, isolating this deck from the rest of *Don Quixote*: check. Back-to-back emergency hatches cutting off the corridor behind him: double check. Holsters: empty. Better to forego weapons than have Thssthfok grab them. The alien moved too tanj *fast*.

Gravity in the hold could change in an instant to micro-gee, or thirty gees, or any intensity between. Worst case, Jeeves would kill artificial gravity, open the exterior hatch, and blow Sigmund and their captive into space. Sigmund would live to be retrieved. The Pak would not.

The decision was delegated to Jeeves. Electrons and photons beat neurons every time.

"Arm the hold's outer hatch," Sigmund ordered. Across the ship an alarm began to wail. A red light strobed in his heads-up display. "Suppress the audible." A few eye flicks to the HUD virtual keypad set his visor reflective and blocked the flashing.

In the HUD, the alien continued his pacing, unperturbed. "Jeeves, tell it to move away from the interior hatch."

"I've connected you to the speaker. You can tell Thssthfok yourself," Jeeves said. "He speaks excellent English."

Sigmund sensed pique in that answer, as though Jeeves resented its struggle to master the Pak's language. Or maybe Sigmund only projected his own insecurities. Did *everyone* learn languages faster than he? "Go to the other end of the room," he ordered Thssthfok.

In the HUD view, Thssthfok complied.

Sigmund activated his boot electromagnets, just to play safe, and let himself into the hold.

27

Thssthfok stood at ease with hands clasped behind his back.

The casual stance failed to disguise an aura of power and speed. Like a cat, Sigmund thought, and then, unavoidably, of a cheetah about to pounce. Thssthfok had claws, too.

"Go to the curved wall and sit," Sigmund ordered.

Thssthfok complied. Seated, he looked no less ready to spring.

Letting the silence stretch, Sigmund studied the Pak. Leathery and gaunt, with eerily human eyes peering with superhuman intelligence from that expressionless face. Sigmund thought of jack-o'-lanterns, and gargoyles, and things that go bump in the night.

He told himself to get a grip.

He towered over Thssthfok. He would have done so even had the alien stood. Sigmund was massive in his armor, mysterious behind his silvered visor. Ominous. In control. Intimidating.

But how intimidating could he be, girded in his battle armor, while Thssthfok, naked, sat impassively studying *him*? Sigmund could not shake the feeling the Pak was one step ahead.

How do you question someone much smarter than yourself? You keep them off balance. You give them no time to regroup. Interrogation 101.

Sigmund leaned forward belligerently. "You attacked our ship. Now tell me why."

"I need it," Thssthfok answered emotionlessly. Clicks and pops punctuated the short sentence. English must be an unfriendly language for that hard beak.

"To catch up with your family," Sigmund said.

No comment.

More Interrogation 101: Pretend to know more than you do. "The galactic core isn't a good place to be, is it?"

No comment this time, either.

"Yes, I understand why the Pak"—the word earned Sigmund a twitch—"needed to move."

New Terra was too peaceful. Interrogation was yet another skill Sigmund had found neither the time nor any reason to teach. Now he had every reason and no time. He had to be good cop and bad cop both. "It was stupid to try to take our ship. I had expected a protector to know better."

Silent but preternaturally alert, Thssthfok watched. From a single unexpected word he knew that Sigmund had other sources of information; he wasn't going to react again.

Lucas Garner, in his memoir, had spoken of free will—and that the Brennan-monster had claimed to have none. Sigmund had forgotten the specifics. Something about when the best course of action was instantly obvious, one had no choices to make.

How, Sigmund wondered, do I make a protector see cooperation as his only choice?

"Here's the thing, Thiss-the-fok." The extra vowels made the word more manageable, but that wasn't why Sigmund inserted them or stretched out the name. Mispronounced names annoyed subjects, at least the human kind. Annoyed subjects sometimes let important stuff slip. "We have a problem."

Thssthfok rapped the exterior hatch behind him. "One you can easily solve."

"And some of us"—Sigmund playing bad cop—"see no reason not to pitch you out the hatch. I assume you would rather we didn't."

Thssthfok made a gesture that, making allowances for his stooped posture, enormous shoulder joints, and wrinkled leathery skin, might have been a shrug.

Sigmund said, "We can open the hatch anytime. Whether we land the ship first is up to you. Given the death and destruction brought on by your unprovoked attack"—he had to pause for Thssthfok and Jeeves to reach an understanding of *provocation*—"I would have no problem blowing the hatch here in orbit."

Sigmund wouldn't, of course. Not unless jettisoning the Pak was necessary to protect the crew. But Thssthfok could not know that.

Or did he? Thssthfok sat motionless, sphinxlike, serene. To a protector, any mere human must be an open book.

No, tanj it! Sigmund defied his insecurities. "You see, Thssthfok, handling you is quite simple. You aren't the problem. Would you like to know what is? The Pak fleet now destroying everything in its path. They can run from the core explosion. There's no need to attack those you'll be leaving behind."

Thssthfok stared impassively. "Why?"

"Why what?"

Thssthfok opened and snapped shut his beak with a loud clack. Resignation, bravado, disdain . . . the mannerism could mean anything or nothing. Sigmund, pretending to knowledge he did not have, was left to guess at any significance. Disdain, Sigmund intuited. For him personally, or anyone in the enemy's path?

The epiphany, when it struck, was blinding. And humbling. He felt like a child badgering an adult—and in a manner of speaking, that was exactly the case.

Sigmund pictured, suddenly, how Thssthfok saw his circumstances. He lived because his captors wanted him alive. Hence threats were hollow. Hence Sigmund had only proven himself flawed and weak.

He trembled with the need to order the hatch blown, if only to dent Thssthfok's smug complacency. No matter that the ground attack on *Don Quixote* justified it, to execute the Pak now would be self-indulgent, pointless, and counterproductive. Sigmund would not do it.

As, maddeningly, Thssthfok had realized long before.

THE VISITOR WAS AN ENIGMA.

English lessons had been straightforward enough. Thssthfok quickly found Jeeves's conversation stilted and formulaic. Testing a theory, Thssthfok experimented with ambiguities and incongruities. He concluded that the disembodied voice *had* no body. Jeeves was a symbolic processing entity, an impressive—but by no means final—extrapolation of the computing technology Thssthfok had begun for the Drar.

He found humans much more interesting.

Worlds showing evidence of spaceflight were dangerous and were preemptively destroyed. A few ships might survive such attacks, but survivors would have more urgent tasks than hunting down stragglers like himself to question. Ergo humans almost certainly did not come from anywhere within the wake of the Pak fleets.

Nor did it seem plausible that the humans came from regions alongside the ever-expanding zone of preemption. No species from outside the zone, having detected the nearby obliteration of worlds, would so foolishly draw attention to themselves.

That left the humans originating somewhere in front of the fleets, on a world or worlds the vanguard had yet to overrun. But for the humans to explore deep within the wake of the Pak fleets and return home before the vanguard struck—

Almost certainly the humans had a means of faster-than-light travel.

As an act of will Thssthfok had fast-forwarded the Drar's technological development. A possible fleet of Drar servant-warriors was a reason to keep eating. A rationale, anyway, he could now admit, like the mad project for which Phssthpok and his legions had once perverted the Library and plunged Pakhome into war. (Well, somewhat better than that. Thssthfok's selfish clinging to life only affected Drar. *They* scarcely mattered.)

A faster-than-light ship changed everything.

He could reunite with his sleeping breeders. He could lead clan Rilchuk to safety in some secluded hinterland of the outer galaxy. Now, Thssthfok wanted to live. He ached to live. He *must* live. Suddenly he craved food, in a way he had not since being abandoned.

He must seize the humans' ship. To take the ship, he needed to stay aboard. To remain aboard, he must seem to offer value to the humans. He must speak.

Thssthfok told his visitor, "You asked why Pak attack. You have many more questions. Answer my questions and I will answer yours."

"There are questions I won't answer," the human answered. "But here is one fact, for free. I am called Sigmund."

As there are questions I will not answer. "Very well, Sigmund. We eliminate from our path those who pose a danger to our safety."

"Have any of those worlds done anything hostile?" Sigmund asked.

English was verbose, its words ill-suited to Thssthfok's mouth. Vs and Ws came out entirely wrong. Still he explained patiently, slowly, almost as though to a breeder. "To wait for an enemy to attack is to sustain unnecessary losses." And is a breeder-stupid error in tactics.

"How are they your enemy?" Sigmund bellowed. "You talk of civilizations struck down before you even meet."

Sigmund knew of Pak by name. From other Pak prisoners was the obvious explanation. Even the prospect of another Pak prisoner made Thssthfok himself less valuable. He must seem to offer more information. And he must act quickly. Another prisoner would also covet the FTL ship. "They are not Pak, so they are enemies."

"Expendable, then."

By definition. Thssthfok snapped his beak in answer.

His turn to ask a question. Any question about technology or the humans' home would be wasted. Useful information would come only when he could seize it. Until then he must bide his time.

A carafe of water and a tray of unfamiliar foods had been provided hours earlier. Nothing smelled inedible, but Thssthfok had yet to touch it. Of course, he had had little appetite. Now the newly awakened hunger gnawed at him. "Sigmund, is this the best food you have for me?"

"You can eat it," Sigmund said bluntly. "I know."

Because, presumably, other prisoners had eaten such fare. "I cannot live on this indefinitely."

"No, I suppose not." Sigmund crossed his arms across his chest. "Not without tree-of-life, too."

Other prisoners, clearly.

Thssthfok turned to look behind him and point to the world below. "In the city from which I was taken, there is an orchard. I will need a supply of the root."

"You got tree-of-life to grow out here?"

Sigmund sounded surprised. Why? And what was the context of "out here"? Then Sigmund continued, shocking Thssthfok speechless.

Sigmund said, "Phssthpok thought he had the solution. Did you get the cultivation technique from him?"

28

"Go down fighting" was not a plan.

Oh, Sabrina and her senior ministers, consulting over hyperwave radio, entertained other options. Volunteers would be shuttled to other worlds, yet to be identified, to live lives hopefully primitive enough to escape Pak notice. On New Terra itself the government would dig deep shelters, in the unlikely event sensors spotted the inward plunging planet-buster with enough warning for an evacuation.

Neither precaution could save more than a few thousand lives.

No one had liked the idea of exposing childless volunteers to tree-of-life root, and that made Sigmund proud. Human protectors would be scary smart. If anyone could find a way to defeat the Pak, *they* would. But afterward, would New Terra be a human world? Better to rebuild a shattered world as humans than to become the enemy.

So going down fighting was the best anyone could offer. Sigmund stood in awe of the courage to confront such overwhelming odds. To fight at all was to triumph over centuries of Puppeteer conditioning.

It was all so futile.

Sigmund shook off the depression that threatened to overwhelm him. He squared his shoulders, took a deep breath, and looked straight into the camera. "Sabrina, you and I need to speak alone." He sat in stubborn silence until her advisors, looking grim and relieved at the same time, shuffled from her cabinet room. The *secure* cabinet room, in the undisclosed location in which Sigmund's people did not allow bugs.

"*We* can't defeat the Pak, Sabrina. We don't begin to have the resources. The Puppeteers might have the resources, but they don't have the will." Baedeker, the last time he had emerged from his cabin, was a twitchy mass of reflexes, his mane long collapsed into the tangle at which he had plucked compulsively. Yet for a Puppeteer, Baedeker was crazy/brave. He could not otherwise have left home and herd. "If we have *any* chance, it's by our worlds working together. It's time we bring Concordance authorities into the loop."

"Do you believe we can convince them to provide ships?" Sabrina asked. "From past dealings, I fear this news will be more than they can handle. I picture them going catatonic."

"They might rise to the occasion," Sigmund said.

And pigs might fly. The slightly more hopeful scenario was that enough Puppeteer ships could be stolen for use by New Terran pilots. For that gambit, Sigmund needed *lots* of intel. It could only be gathered on the ground, among the worlds of the Fleet.

He respected Sabrina too much to involve her in such a harebrained scheme.

"You were right to want everyone to leave, Sigmund. We'll have to get an audience with the Hindmost himself, and that's always a most sensitive matter." Lost in thought, Sabrina brushed a strand of loose gray hair from her forehead. "Maybe Nessus can help us."

The last time Nessus wanted to help New Terra, he had kidnapped Sigmund and poked holes in his memory.

Sigmund shook his head. "I need to do this in person, Sabrina. It's best the Puppeteers not speculate uselessly until I get there."

That meant appearing with little warning. Hearth's safety had long lain in stealth and secrecy, but the home world's location was hardly a secret from its former colony. In the years since New Terra won its freedom, the Concordance had surrounded Hearth with conventional planetary defenses. Not nearly enough to inconvenience the hordes of Pak, but *Don Quixote* alone? Despite an "invulnerable" hull, they would not stand a chance.

"On second thought, Sabrina, once we're back to the Fleet"—months from now—"maybe you should give Nessus a heads-up. You can hint that we're all in danger and I need an audience with the Hindmost."

HATING THE TOO-FAMILIAR RELAX ROOM, hating the too-familiar *ship*, hating—impersonally and without reservation—everyone else aboard, Baedeker waited. And waited some more. His mane, unattended, had long ago dissolved into the snarl at which he now plucked listlessly. All the herd pheromone in the world could no longer comfort him.

Those with whom he waited were as despairing. Kirsten clearly had not slept in days. Eric's cheeks were hollow and his eyes dull; he had stopped shaving days ago. The Gw'oth participated by comm link and did their waiting remotely. Baedeker could not read their body language, anyway, assuming they had any.

A holo of the improvised prison hung over the relax-room table. Thssthfok was in one of his accustomed places: amid the empty storage units of the repurposed cargo hold. Privacy mattered to him, Baedeker presumed, as it did for his distant human cousins. Not that Thssthfok had privacy. Even seated as he was, on the deck between rows of empty shelves, two of the fiber-optic cables that penetrated the cell ceiling caught glimpses of his head and neck.

Sigmund, when he arrived, quite late, was as desperate as anyone. Oh, not outwardly: He was too proud, too duty bound, to project anything but serene assurance.

But after so many months together, Baedeker knew the stoic exterior for the facade that it was. That confident attitude must be harder and harder to maintain. Almost certainly, that was why Sigmund came late. He was as close to the edge as any of them. If *he* cracked, it was hard to imagine how any of them would ever get home.

Not that Hearth would be a haven much longer.

"You know why we're here," Sigmund began abruptly. No one commented, nor even met his gaze. "There's one bit of unfinished business before we can head home."

Everyone turned to the holo that floated over the table. The unfinished business they kept putting off: what to do with Thssthfok.

Sigmund was hindmost of the mission. What he decided would happen. To give credit, Sigmund solicited opinions before he chose. A hindmost could do worse.

"Thssthfok goes," Baedeker said. "We all know that he must."

Kirsten cleared her throat. "Goes where? Back to the flying squirrels?"

With a mind of its own, one of Baedeker's paws began scraping at the deck. "The prisoner knows about us. Maybe not much, but some things. That we have starships. He knows enough to make our worlds prime targets."

"So kill him, you mean," Kirsten snapped. "At least admit it."

Yes! Killing the Pak was the only safe option. But Baedeker had not said it, had he? Even a Citizen found it hard to kill in—what was the human expression?—cold blood. "Regrettably, I see no option," Baedeker finally said.

Sigmund looked at Eric. "What do you think?"

"If a Pak ship rescued Thssthfok today, it wouldn't matter. We're too many light-years behind the vanguard here. The lead ships will have attacked our various home worlds, or passed them by, long before any light-speed signal from here could reach them."

As Sigmund nodded agreement, Baedeker's paw ceased its scratching. This was insanity! "Suppose that, for some reason, the front wave does pass by our homes. However unlikely, it is possible. We must do nothing to risk the attention of later waves."

Kirsten stood to pace, fists jammed in her jumpsuit pockets. "Thssthfok's clan is near the front of the pack, among the first to escape Pakhome. Clans are bitter enemies. Why would he signal another—"

"He *says* his clan is near the front," Baedeker interrupted. "Assume it was. He cannot know what happened since he was marooned. He has to allow for the possibility his clan lost a skirmish and fell back, or delayed to gather supplies. You cannot know Thssthfok *won't* signal ahead if he can."

And of course the prisoner lied! Only naïveté could say otherwise. The only mystery was on which topics.

Conflict among clans was the only disclosure Baedeker truly believed— not for the stubborn skill of Sigmund's interrogation, or anything about how or why Thssthfok revealed the detail, but because, for once, they had corroborating data. The cone of destruction that marked the Pak incursion grew wider the farther the aliens traveled from home. Such dispersal was only logical as a consequence of battles among the Pak. Some would break away from the rest to replenish supplies, or scatter after a defeat, or to find shelter behind a convenient dust cloud. They fled from each other as much as from the deadly radiation that pursued them.

Holo Thssthfok stood abruptly and stalked across his cell. He settled again, seated, with his back against a bulkhead. That was another of his preferred spots, although Baedeker could discern no pattern to where along the long bulkhead the Pak chose to sit.

Thssthfok *must* go, and not back to where they found him. Blowing the hatch was the safest way to do it. And as even the youngest Citizen knew, the safest way is the only way.

Still.

To die with one's blood boiling, screaming silently into the void to relieve the pressure and keep one's lungs from bursting . . . Baedeker shivered. "We can leave the Pak on another habitable planet. Someplace no one can know to look for him."

"Where he would starve to death, slowly, for lack of tree-of-life," Kirsten said. "Even if we leave him with a supply, we won't know if a new crop will grow. Any planet we pick might turn out like Earth, where the crop failed."

"Return him to where we found him," Eric said firmly. "It's the humane thing to do."

"Er'o?" Sigmund called. "What do you and your friends think?"

Silence.

"Er'o," Sigmund said again. "Are you there?"

"Yes, Sigmund," a voice answered over the intercom.

But that voice did not belong to Er'o, nor could Baedeker match it to any of the Gw'oth. The unfamiliar voice was deeper than a Gw'o, resonant, commanding. Of course all Gw'oth "voices" were synthesized; they could be changed on a whim. Maybe Baedeker's failure to recognize it meant nothing.

The quaver in his gut told him otherwise.

HANDS BEHIND HIS BACK, back against a bulkhead, Thssthfok activated the makeshift sensor in his fist. Hiding the device with his body, he characterized one more handspan of the cable bundle that led to the hatch.

Tracing cables and analyzing control logic were standard uses of his multi-scanner—but like most items in his utility kit, the instrument made no provision for surreptitious readout. Designing a tactile-feedback mode was straightforward. Making the modifications with the few resources at his disposal, working by touch within the unobservable regions between and inside empty storage units—that had been difficult.

To live long enough to capture this ship, he had to keep up the interest of the humans. Ancient history was curiously fascinating to Sigmund, and it would not disadvantage clan Rilchuk, so Thssthfok doled out what he knew about Phssthpok. Time spent discussing the mad Librarian was time not being questioned about far more dangerous topics.

And Sigmund talked, too. How strange to know the lost colony had actually existed. How strange that Phssthpok had found it! Alone. Without even a hibernation pod. Just twelve hundred subjective years in a tiny cabin, in a ramscoop accelerated to near light speed to prolong his life.

Was Phssthpok sane even at the beginning of his quest? Thssthfok had his doubts. Regardless, Phssthpok was surely insane when he reached the lost colony—

There to be killed.

Sigmund would not discuss Phssthpok's fate, but a quick death was the obvious answer. Only death could stop Phssthpok from striving to exterminate the humans. *They* were what remained of the lost colony. And they had spread—far—or Thssthfok could not have encountered them here.

Mutants! Abominations! Their stench was unavoidable. Thssthfok's nostrils wrinkled.

He edged his modified multi-scanner a handspan closer to the hatch. Underneath his fingers, the prickling changed subtly. Another spot along the unseen wire where insulation had degraded from friction or age. Another vulnerability.

Sigmund did not know everything.

The launch of Phssthpok's ramscoop had left his legions of childless protectors on Pakhome without a reason to eat—so they found one. And so whole fleets had followed in Phssthpok's wake. Lest Phssthpok failed to survive his trek. Lest inferences about the colony's location had been imprecise, and Phssthpok's chosen course misguided. Lest the reborn colony need succor before it could build an industrial base. The reasons did not matter.

Thssthfok told himself *his* clinging to life was no such delusional rationalization—and wondered if it was true.

On the one hand: a new Pak world in the galactic hinterlands. It would battle other Pak clans to the death. On the other hand: aliens who destroyed whole Pak fleets. Those were the only possibilities. Whichever doom had befallen the Librarian armadas following in Phssthpok's wake, *something* barred the only marginally explored path into the spiral arm.

And so the evacuation from Pakhome in Thssthfok's time had had to chart a different course. Thssthfok cursed Phssthpok, and his hordes of followers, and the Library yet again.

His fingers moved infinitesimally, taking yet another measurement, as he pictured the device that would wirelessly usurp the hatch controls. He did not mean to open the exterior hatch. In its porthole Mala was long gone from view, and even its red-dwarf sun had receded into a mere spark. That was why he studied here, where the humans were least likely to suspect his purpose.

Because within the bulkhead around the hatch into the ship were similar circuits.

"ER'O?" SIGMUND CALLED. "What do you and your friends think?"

Ol't'ro considered. This Pak must die. Its death was the only prudent choice, and yet the humans hesitated. Er'o's advocacy would not convince them. No Gw'o could—by reason of deficiencies in human nature, not any flaw in the Gw'oth analysis.

Wishful thinking wasn't.

To make humans see reason, Ol't'ro would have to reveal truths kept hidden for this entire voyage.

"Er'o," Sigmund said again. "Are you there?"

Failure to convince Sigmund carried worse risks than disclosure.

Extending a tubacle, Ol't'ro reconfigured a comm terminal to transmit human-authoritative acoustical properties. "Yes, Sigmund."

"Who *is* this?" Baedeker asked.

"We are Ol't'ro." Ol't'ro paused for the humans and Citizen to ponder the pronoun. "We are Er'o and Ng'o and Th'o. We are *all* the Gw'oth aboard, and we are many become one."

"One of their biological computer groupings," Eric whispered.

"More than that, I think," Kirsten whispered back.

Sigmund, in an even softer undertone, wondered, "Why reveal . . . themselves now?"

The human murmuring was scarcely detectable. By correlating these acoustic scraps with months of phonetic templates and syntactical patterns, Ol't'ro recovered the conversation.

"Let us explain," Ol't'ro said. They remodulated the voice in the manner calculated to be soothing. "Together we form a biological computer. In our language, we are a Gw'otesht. We thought you were aware."

"Not from anything a Gw'o ever said." Sigmund's voice was now firm, even loud. Accusing. "I did not anticipate a collective mind."

For *Sigmund* not to suspect—they had kept their secret well, indeed. Or Sigmund lied. No matter. "Let us explain. Even Gw'oth seldom speak of this capability." And then, mostly, in condemnation.

Since time immemorial, a few had had the ability to link—and been shunned for it. Ensembles were inherently vulnerable, a tangle of limbs lost in contemplation. Across eons of hunting and gathering, of endless primitive tribal warfare, to link was a selfish indulgence that endangered the tribe. A corruption of nature . . .

And across the ages, some had succumbed to the addiction of deeper thought.

With the rise of great cities, ensembles became practical. Traditionalists still abhorred them. Society recoiled from them. Governments exploited them. Government biologists found ways to expand, and strengthen, and deepen the couplings.

And awareness happened.

Technology exploded. City-states with the most gifted ensembles raised empires, spread over the ice, even leapt to new worlds. And Gw'otesht, become indispensable to the rulers, became partners rather than servants—

Even as ensembles remained repugnant to all but the most progressive Gw'oth.

That was more than Ol't'ro cared to share. "Those like us are a recent development, Sigmund. Some of our own kind . . . disapprove. We did not know how you would feel."

"Then why reveal yourself at all? And why now?" Sigmund asked.

"We have a unique perspective." Ol't'ro chose their next words carefully. "It relates to whether Thssthfok returns to the planet below."

Baedeker whistled skeptically. "How does secretiveness bestow unique knowledge?"

"Our apologies." But no explanations. "We claim no special wisdom, Baedeker, only relevant experience. It is from the efforts of ensembles like us that the Gw'oth have recently developed much new technology."

"Connecticut Yankee!" Kirsten blurted. "Oh, crap."

For once, Ol't'ro was without a clue. They disliked the feeling.

CONNECTICUT YANKEE?

Sigmund's brief interest in *A Connecticut Yankee in King Arthur's Court* began with insomnia and ended that same night with the discovery of the eclipse scene. He never went back to the story, never gave Kirsten the recommendation she had requested. Apparently she had proceeded on her own.

He scarcely remembered the 3-V adaptation he had watched so long ago, but one scene had stuck with him: medieval knights slaughtered with Gatling guns. The Yankee had introduced guns and gunpowder, dynamite, electricity. In short order, he had remade society.

"Finagle, yes!" To Baedeker, who looked even more troubled than usual, Sigmund explained, "Thssthfok will push ahead the flying squirrels' technology. How quickly, and how big a threat could he create? I don't know. I don't see how we can know."

"*We* know," Ol't'ro boomed in that gravelly, resonant voice. "We know because we accelerated the rate of progress of our home city. That is why, against all our instincts, we now reveal ourselves. Because you *must* believe us.

"With *Don Quixote*'s instruments, we have inferred a great deal about the beings that Thssthfok calls the Drar. Technology falls off very quickly with distance from the city where we found him. We have assessed alternative development paths and done the simulations. The results are clear. Within fifty New Terra years, probably fewer, Thssthfok's servants can build him ramscoops."

Something in that warning rang false. Sigmund's gut told him Ol't'ro was holding back, making a point without telling the whole truth. They, it, whatever pronoun applied, could advance the Drar—and the Gw'oth themselves—even faster.

Gw'oth progress, like the existence of Ol't'ro, could await another day. They should live long enough to worry.

Ol't'ro's warning had set Baedeker to burrowing into his mane, and launched Eric and Kirsten into intense whispers. Sigmund stopped them all with a stern look. Almost, the puzzle pieces had fallen into place. He had to think this through.

Pakhome was sterilized, its history over. Thssthfok surely thought those safe topics, and Sigmund a fool to be distracted by them. But in describing lost lands, and clan rivalries, and vanished institutions like the Library—anything but the weapons and tactics in which Sigmund professed interest, certain Thssthfok would divulge nothing useful about them—the prisoner had conveyed something more precious. Psychological and sociological insight.

Thssthfok had lost his family and any hope of recovering them. Still he ate. Everything Sigmund knew about protectors said that Thssthfok had rededicated his life to serving all Pak. Like Phssthpok in an earlier age, Thssthfok had found his Cause.

Now, thanks to Ol't'ro, Sigmund knew that purpose.

Thssthfok would raise a great host. He would command a rearguard fleet to protect all Pak. He would smash any technological civilization missed by the Pak fleets, and smite anew any world recovering too quickly in their wake.

Decision time, Sigmund thought. He would not allow Thssthfok to raise a battle fleet.

That left two choices. They could kill Thssthfok—to strand him anywhere but where they found him meant only a slow and lingering death—or they could keep him aboard this ship.

Only there was no *they*. This was Sigmund's mission. His ship. His responsibility.

He would kill to protect New Terra—if killing was necessary. It wasn't.

So: They would return to the planet of the flying squirrels and grab a supply of tree-of-life root. They would head, with Thssthfok, to the Fleet of Worlds.

Sigmund made a final mental note. While on the ground to collect tree-of-life root, one of the crew would paint—from the outside, where Thssthfok could not scratch—the porthole in the cargo-hold hatch. An uncovered view into hyperspace might drive Thssthfok insane.

Sigmund permitted himself a moment of hope. Perhaps the sight of a live Pak protector would awaken—even in the Hindmost—the need for bravery.

THE LAST STRAW

29

Thssthfok's first escape attempt failed almost instantly. Hallway sensors spotted him and a sudden jump in gravity turned his limbs too heavy to move. Two armed and armored humans appeared at the end of the hall. Under the sights of their weapons, barely able to wriggle as gravity eased just slightly, Thssthfok surrendered his jury-rigged hatch-lock controller and crept back to his cell.

It had gone much as he had expected.

The brief glimpse of the corridor had been necessary reconnaissance. One quick look had shown Thssthfok the location of hallway sensors and suggested ways that they, like the passive data feeds from his cell, might be accessed, bypassed, or compromised. And he had forced his jailors to reveal how they responded to a breach, and how quickly.

This escape would be real.

After the first escape, of course, the humans had searched his cell. They found what Thssthfok allowed them to find: a hoard of material scraps and a sacrificial instrument from his repair kit.

Everything important remained hidden. His cache looked like any other surface in any of the empty storage units. The humans had poked and probed randomly, even in obviously empty spaces. By blind luck, they might have found his hiding place. That was a risk he had had to take, and the odds had favored him.

They had not found his cache.

Thssthfok was prone on the deck between rows of empty storage units, where his captors were accustomed to seeing him retreat for sleep. He had not picked this spot randomly—it put him below the line of sight of the cell's sensors. He reached through the small softened area on a bottom shelf. His structural modulator lay hidden between that shelf and the floor.

Ironically, primitive materials had held him when properly designed material would not. *Twing* was a flawless substance, but human materials were rife with cracks, voids, and impurities. He had had to rebuild the modulator to accommodate so many imperfections.

The ship's hull was a curious exception. To his improvised instruments, the curved wall scanned as defect-free as *twing*—but unlike *twing*, this material resisted softening. A spot of hull absorbed without effect all the power he had dared apply. The ship itself powered his modulator, with power drawn wirelessly from the humans' own magnetically coupled power transmitters. Any higher setting on the modulator risked drawing his captors' attention.

But for the ever-present sounds of air circulating and engines humming, the ship remained quiet. It was time.

Thssthfok modulated a small patch of the deck to transparency. He studied the room below: a table, chairs, an oddly shaped bench, and exercise equipment. No crew. He softened a large area, reached into the room below, grasped the top of an exercise apparatus, and pulled himself through. With a *pop*, surface tension re-formed the ceiling behind him. He climbed onto the table, reached back into his cell, and retrieved the modulator, leaving the cell floor (from his new perspective, the ceiling) permeable. He might have to make a quick retreat.

As he did. He had only bypassed half this deck's sensor feeds—from now on, they would always show empty corridors—when footsteps approached. A three-legged gait!

Thssthfok scrambled onto the table. He reached through the viscous ceiling, gripped a shelf, and, carefully staying beneath the sensors' line of sight, lifted himself into his cell. Resuming a prone position, he pressed an eye against the still-transparent spot on the deck.

Moments later, a two-headed, three-legged *something* cantered into the room that Thssthfok had just vacated.

30

Nessus, looking dapper, stepped across the quarter mile of void that separated his ship from *Don Quixote*—

And with that impression, Baedeker finally had to admit the depths of his despair.

Nessus famously considered mane coiffure a pointless ostentation. His mane was earnestly combed straight and worn with only a few jewels. His sash was utilitarian: a way to wear pockets, entirely without adornment.

Dapper? Only by contrast.

For so long, Baedeker had struggled to care whether he bathed or untangled his mane. Too many things—the Gw'oth, the Pak, hyperspace, the absence of other Citizens—had taken their toll. He straightened out of the slouch become habitual and warbled a two-throated salutation. "Welcome aboard, Nessus." They brushed heads in greeting.

"Thank you." Nessus seemed surprised to find Baedeker on a New Terran vessel. Or perhaps the sociable greeting was what startled Nessus. "I see you have become a scout, Baedeker."

The herd defined sanity, and yet scouts separated themselves from the herd. It mattered not that scouts acted on behalf of all, for the safety of all. Scouts *sought* risks, and that proved them mad. Scouts were (in an English word Baedeker had learned from Sigmund) mavericks. And so the statement was an insult.

Sung by the most experienced of Hearth's few surviving scouts, the notes were praise.

"It feels good truly to speak," Baedeker said. "English is not very satisfying."

"Hello, Nessus," Jeeves sang over the intercom. (The contrapuntal melodies blended precisely, the tones pitch-perfect to the third harmonic, one cycle of vibrato indistinguishable from the next. It was without rubato, utterly mechanical, and Nessus flashed a sympathetic look.) "Nessus, Baedeker, the others wait in the relax room. Sigmund asks that you join them when you are ready."

Past differences with Nessus had somehow receded. It was more than the company of another Citizen after so much time among aliens. If anyone among the herd could appreciate the newfound dangers, it would be Nessus. And Nessus had the friendship of the Hindmost.

So where to begin? Baedeker had struggled with that question for days.

"Do you understand me?" Nessus switched to a little-used dialect.

"More or less," Baedeker answered in the same way. "If Jeeves does, I cannot say."

The stepping disc that had received Nessus was set in the corridor outside the bridge. Behind Nessus, beyond the open hatch, through the main view port, glittered the Fleet of Worlds. Four planets, blue and white and brown, ringed by necklaces of artificial suns: the nature preserves. And one planet, sunless, ablaze with the lights of its world-spanning city, more beautiful than all the rest. Hearth.

All at risk.

"Come with me," Baedeker said to Nessus. "Sigmund will explain everything to you. First, though, there are things you must see for yourself."

WITH A LUMP IN HIS THROAT, Sigmund prepared to leave *Don Quixote*.

Ol't'ro and Jeeves had already said their good-byes. Voices over the intercom: There was not a lot of emotional content to either. And Baedeker would be joining Sigmund. But as for Eric and Kirsten . . .

Side by side, they stood looking at Sigmund. The three of them had been through a lot in the past eleven months. Sharing the cramped confines of *Don Quixote* was the least of it. It wasn't obvious who moved first, but suddenly Sigmund and Kirsten were hugging. He gave her a final squeeze, let go, and gave Eric a hug, too. That was the male, backslapping kind of clinch, but equally heartfelt.

"Take care, you guys," Sigmund told them.

Baedeker and Nessus waited nearby, ill at ease. Nessus' arrival had bucked up Baedeker, at least enough that Baedeker had washed up a bit. There was a history of bad blood between the two Puppeteers, and Sigmund was mildly surprised they weren't quarreling.

"Ready when you are," Nessus hinted gently.

The years had been kind to Nessus. The Puppeteer had gained weight, and his mane was better groomed than Sigmund remembered. By his past standards Nessus had dressed formally. He wore a sash rather than a pocketed belt, and though his ornamentation remained minimalist, the few jewels bespoke high status. Still in Nike's favor, then—and Nike was now Hindmost.

But some things had not changed. Nessus' mismatched eyes, one red and one yellow, were as jarring as ever. And in favor or not, he was as edgy as always. Maybe the edginess came from being near Sigmund. . . .

"You're sure about this?" Eric said to Sigmund.

"Yes," Sigmund answered firmly. "You have your orders."

Kirsten and Eric exchanged looks, and Kirsten sighed. "Yes," she said. "Return the Gw'oth to the ice moon and then go home."

"And give Sabrina a full report," Sigmund added, lest *home* seem at all ambiguous.

Eric nodded. "We know what to do, Sigmund."

"See you soon, guys." Sigmund turned to the Puppeteers. "Nessus? After you."

Nessus vanished, and then Baedeker. Sigmund smiled one last time at his friends, before stepping across to Nessus' waiting vessel, *Aegis*.

Eric and Kirsten knew what to do, all right. Their orders did not involve a return home.

31

From the copilot's seat, tanjedly uncomfortable, Sigmund monitored the final approach. The Y-shaped, padded bench he sat astraddle was never meant for a human, but his many aches soon receded into the background. This would be his first time on Hearth, and the scale of—well, everything—was beyond his wildest imagining.

Aegis descended into the perpetual night of the Puppeteer home world. No artificial suns orbited this world, where the industry and the body heat of a trillion Puppeteers generated all the energy the ecosystem could absorb. More than a thousand miles away, a vast, glowing grid became visible to the naked eye. Down they went, until the grid resolved into artificially lit streets and expanses of buildings that spanned entire continents.

Down they flew until city stretched from horizon to horizon. A landing field came into sight, and on it rows of ships like so many grapes. Finally Sigmund had a frame of reference.

Each little ball was a spaceship in a General Products #4 hull. A GP #4 hull was a sphere roughly a thousand feet in diameter—and here one looked *tiny*. With the enormous ships for comparison, Sigmund truly grasped the sheer scale of the buildings. The smallest were cubes more than a mile across, each a city in its own right.

A few of those vessels must be grain ships from New Terra. A wave of homesickness washed over Sigmund. He tamped it down. This wasn't the time.

Nessus set down *Aegis* without as much as a bump. "Welcome to Hearth," he announced.

All communication with traffic control had been computer-to-computer. Lest Sigmund overhear any codes or procedures, he assumed. With a New Terran so distrusted, small wonder Nessus vetoed bringing down Thssthfok and a few of the Gw'oth. (Not that Sigmund, as his planning had evolved, intended the others to land with him. He had only proposed to bring them knowing Nessus would never accept.)

Baedeker emerged from elsewhere in the ship and the three of them disembarked.

Sigmund *wasn't* whisked instantly to a meeting with the Hindmost. Eric had warned him to expect a tour, first. Puppeteers had long practice, from colonial days, at awing mere humans.

That was fine by Sigmund. He wanted intel.

Stepping disc by stepping disc, following Nessus, Sigmund toured a world. Vast plazas delimited by factories and arcologies whose tops were often lost in cloud. Where day reigned, the sides of buildings shone almost as brightly as a sun. Wherever convention declared the night, similar panels became gigantic entertainment screens. Along some unnamed shore, fusion plants larger even than the arcologies beamed unimaginable energies to enterprises Nessus declined to describe.

Streets and concourses teemed, the Puppeteers packed together like herds of cattle. Their crooning and keening blended into a deafening roar. Like Nessus and Baedeker, the average Puppeteer on the street wore only a belt or sash, but the variety of ribbons, jewels, and emblems seemed unending.

How *could* Puppeteers wear clothes? Everywhere Sigmund went the air was like a sauna. Hearth must be like this pole to pole, a trillion Puppeteers stewing in their own heat.

The farming worlds of the Fleet hung overhead. Walking across a park, the blue-green meadowplant as lush and close-cropped as grass on a putting green, the not-quite trees as manicured as topiary, Sigmund found his eyes drawn irresistibly to the nearest of the farm worlds. Sigmund had studied them all, and continental outlines revealed this one as Nature Preserve Five. (A wayward synapse fired, a melancholy face: the Man in the Moon.)

NP5 was in full phase, its necklaces of artificial suns running from pole to pole, its turquoise-blue oceans sparkling. White cloud dotted land and sea alike. A cyclone swirled. Except for the shapes of continents, that world could have been New Terra.

Sigmund tamped down his resurgent longing. Penny needed him to be strong and suspicious, not sentimental.

NP5 was the world spotted in flight, so long ago, by the crew of *Long Pass*. A curse, that world. Sigmund used the anger to keep his focus. He had to see everything, retain everything. Because *anything* could prove useful.

Like those colossal wall displays. Something about them bothered him. Finally he put his finger on it. "Where are the windows?" he asked Nessus. "I don't see any windows."

High/low, low/high, high/low, Nessus' heads bobbed in alternation. He looked like a Whac-A-Mole, but the gesture meant agreement. "You are very observant, Sigmund. Very few living quarters have windows. Most units are in the interior, of course, and *cannot* have windows."

Sigmund had imagined great atria and mile-tall interior shafts to ventilate those interior units—but he had not noticed anything like that from above. The arcology roofs had been solid. "So endless halls of apartments," he mused aloud. "Windowless boxes."

"Not quite," Baedeker said. "No hallways, because hallways waste space, nor elevators, nor ventilation shafts. Like the tenants themselves, the oxygen they breathe and the carbon dioxide they exhale is moved by stepping discs."

The weight of a trillion Puppeteers pressed down on Sigmund. And yet, that utter dependence on stepping discs, the ubiquity of stepping discs, was encouraging. At least if things did not go well at the meeting.

And why would the meeting go well? Nothing else had.

ONCE SIGMUND AND BAEDEKER DEPARTED for Hearth, Eric and Kirsten found ways to use their newfound privacy.

Ol't'ro did, too. They spent much of their time poring over observations gathered throughout the long voyage. Hyperdrive was wondrously fast—when *Don Quixote* used it. So why was hyperdrive not always used?

Flight by flight, Ol't'ro reviewed their travels. When hyperdrive was first activated. When hyperdrive use ended, as *Don Quixote* neared its destination. They saw no pattern.

Perhaps the explanation lay in pilot discretion, not technical factors. Ol't'ro tried to correlate hyperdrive usage to the urgency of their missions. And failed. Perhaps the subjectivity of urgency did not communicate well across species.

Ol't'ro's thorough review had recently come to the trips immediately after Thssthfok's capture. First, *Don Quixote* had crept to the outer solar system for reasons no one would discuss. Then the ship retraced its course to harvest tree-of-life roots. Only after creeping back to the solar-system fringes had Kirsten finally engaged *Don Quixote*'s hyperdrive.

It would have been interesting to know how far *Don Quixote* had traveled in each instance. Ol't'ro could not calculate the ship's progress directly, since artificial gravity obscured the ship's actual acceleration. They had learned to infer the strength of artificial gravity from the drain on a nearby ship's power circuits. Alas, unrelated drains on the ship's power made such estimates very crude.

So they had built their own, independent astronomical sensors. Those, too, offered only vague answers. Probing through habitat walls, interior ship partitions, and hull limited the instruments' sensitivity.

And then *Don Quixote* came to the Fleet of Worlds.

Despite the ambiguity and many approximations in Ol't'ro's calculations, clearly Kirsten had used hyperdrive much closer to this destination than to any other. What differed about this place? The obvious difference: These worlds lacked a star.

A star is *massive*.

And so Ol't'ro's thoughts turned to abstruse physical theory and arcane scenarios. Perhaps hyperdrive was somehow constrained to nearly flat regions of space-time. To regions far from any gravitational singularity. Far from the type of worlds on which Gw'oth, humans, Citizens, or Drar could live—or, at least, from the suns that warmed those worlds. Far from anywhere a world-evolved species ever thought to experiment with a long-range drive.

Until now.

32

At a discreet trill, Nessus dipped one head into a pocket of his sash. The few murmurs Sigmund could hear suggested wind chimes.

Nessus' head reappeared. "The Hindmost will meet with us now. Come with me."

Sigmund was more than ready. He followed Nessus onto yet another stepping disc, emerging into a cylinder bathed in blue light. The wall was transparent.

Nessus waited outside among armed Puppeteer guards, looking in.

Sigmund rapped gently on the wall. As he suspected: General Products hull material. GP hulls were transparent to visible light, and Sigmund presumed the overhead illumination could be raised to lethal levels. There weren't any doors. The only way in or out of this antechamber was by stepping disc. He vacated the disc; a moment later, Baedeker arrived. Inside, with Sigmund.

"Remove your clothes. Ribbons and jewels, too," one of the guards directed. (He wore one more ribbon in his mane than the rest, suggesting he was the hindmost for the squad. Sigmund dubbed him Sergeant.) "Pile everything on the disc."

Puppeteers had no nudity taboo. At least the males didn't. Of Puppeteer females, New Terrans knew only that they were cloistered.

Still, undressing came as a surprise and Sigmund didn't like surprises. Till now, Kirsten and Eric's predictions for this trip had been accurate. But they hadn't mentioned disrobing—and New Terrans *had* a nudity taboo. This was not a detail either would have forgotten.

Of course when his friends had seen Nike on Hearth, before independence, the Puppeteer had been a mere deputy minister. Now Nike was Hindmost.

"Is undressing typical?" Sigmund asked as he removed his jumpsuit.

Baedeker had removed and folded his sash. He began unbraiding his few mane ornaments. He gave the impression of being happy to have something to do besides look at Sigmund. "Hardly. I believe that your reputation precedes you."

"Mr. Ausfaller. What is that on your wrist?" Sergeant asked.

"A clock implant." Sigmund held out his arm for closer inspection.

Seconds ticked by while Sergeant considered that. "Very well," he finally said.

Sigmund's garment and shoes, and Baedeker's few things, vanished. Into another sealed hull-material container, Sigmund supposed, one darkened against, say, a flash bomb or laser pistol. He had carried nothing like that—getting caught with a weapon would have sent the wrong message—but he would have preferred to keep his pocket comp (with its snooping modes enabled, naturally) and his transport controller.

"You will get your things back when you leave," Sergeant said. "Mr. Ausfaller, we have a garment and slippers for you, if you wish."

Professionally speaking, Sigmund had to approve of the security measures.

"You may proceed," Sergeant decided at last. A head gestured at the antechamber's disc. His second head clutched a weapon with a grip like a boxer's mouthpiece.

Sigmund guessed the guards and their weapons were biometrically paired. That's what he would have done, lest a gun be wrestled from its owner. Of course Sigmund wouldn't have chosen a tongueprint for personalizing the weapon.

Baedeker and then Sigmund stepped to the main security lobby. Guards fell in around them as Sigmund dressed in the plain jumpsuit provided. "Follow me," Sergeant ordered.

Their route passed two more checkpoints before terminating, abruptly, in a most un-Puppeteer setting: a long, narrow patio hugging a craggy mountainside. Sentries ringed the stepping disc. Without speaking, Sigmund's original escort trotted to an end of the patio.

The long terrazzo patio blended seamlessly with a living area carved deep into the mountain. Padded benches, mounds of overstuffed pillows, holo sculptures, and melted-looking oval tables dotted the salon. Only a faintly shimmering force field (weatherproofing, Sigmund supposed) separated indoors from out. Beyond the patio's stone balustrade, far below, waves crashed against the shore. A magnificent stone castle, its endless soft curves and rounded features almost Dali-like, climbed hundreds of feet overhead. No other structure was anywhere in sight.

On Earth, a world of eighteen billion, this palace and its splendid isolation would have been decadent. On Hearth, with its trillion occupants . . .

"A private audience in the Hindmost's personal residence," Nessus whispered unnecessarily. "Be honored."

The honor did not, Sigmund noted, keep Baedeker from craning for possible exits.

Sigmund wasn't buying into a great honor, either. A new attempt at intimidation, maybe.

With that thought, a Puppeteer appeared inside the salon. He was petite for a Puppeteer, his cream hide unmarked by patches of any other color. His mane was resplendent with orange jewels. Orange, of course, was the color of the ruling Experimentalist faction.

The Hindmost.

He came through the force field onto the patio. "Mr. Ausfaller," he said in unaccented New Terran English. Earlier in his career, speaking the colonists' language had been a useful skill. With only one throat and one set of vocal cords, no human could speak any Puppeteer language.

"Excellency," Sigmund began. He stood ramrod straight even as Baedeker lowered his heads subserviently. "Thank you for meeting with us."

"You have a strong advocate in Nessus," the Hindmost said, "setting aside that he, too, was not told the nature of the supposed emergency. Regardless, formality is unnecessary. Here in my private residence, I am Nike. And may I call you Sigmund?"

Nike: the Greek goddess of victory. An immodest choice.

Puppeteers dealing with humans took human pronounceable names, and names from Earth mythology were a common affectation. Nessus' true name sounded to Sigmund like an industrial accident in waltz time. "Certainly, Nike."

Sigmund and Baedeker followed Nike back into the grand salon, the force field only a slight pressure and a tickle as they pressed through. Another Puppeteer joined them. Nike introduced the newcomer as Vesta, head of the Clandestine Directorate. The guards sidled closer but remained on the patio, watching from a respectful distance.

Nike stood tall, legs straight, hooves far apart, exuding confidence. It was the Puppeteer dominance stance—he was *un*ready to run. "All right, Sigmund. Explain what this is about."

Beginning with Ol't'ro's plea for help, Sigmund summarized *Don Quixote*'s travels and everything the crew had encountered. The Gw'oth. The ramscoop fleet glimpsed from afar. Shattered worlds. Deliberations within the New Terran government. The Pak—and their course.

Nike asked few, but always insightful, questions. Baedeker contributed details, often on his own initiative, occasionally in response to Nike's or Nessus' prompting. From time to time aides appeared, apologetically reminding Nike or Vesta of one scheduled event or another. Nike sent them away.

No one asked about the Pak military capability, so Sigmund volunteered. Among clans so warlike, any weapon that could be built would be. Minimally the Pak would have powerful lasers and fusion-driven missiles with nuclear warheads. The former would pass right through a General Products hull. Concussions from the latter would scramble anything inside a GP hull.

By the time Sigmund finished, he felt drained. He felt he had been talking forever. A glance at his wrist showed more than two hours had passed.

Now it was Nike's turn.

THROUGH THE CLEAR SPOT in the cell floor, Thssthfok monitored the room below, ascertaining the pattern of crew visits. The two-headed thing no longer appeared, nor did Sigmund. Only two other humans—from overheard conversations, Kirsten and Eric—came into the room, usually together. Sometimes they came to take food from synthesizers. Sometimes they exercised. Several day-tenths usually separated their visits.

Eric, wearing battle armor, had brought the last few plates of food and removed Thssthfok's waste. During these brief visits, artificial gravity pinned Thssthfok in place, while even Eric, the motors in his armor whining, moved slowly.

Thssthfok's feedings, too, followed a routine.

If the room below was the crew's only food source—and why would there be more?—Eric and Kirsten were now the only jailors aboard.

Two unarmed humans, taken by surprise . . . soon the ship would be Thssthfok's.

A CONCORDANCE WAR FLEET! Commanded by the New Terrans!

Baedeker almost fled, the ideas were so outrageous. Sigmund had traveled so far to propose *this*? Had Sigmund asked for an opinion, Baedeker could have saved them a trip.

"I expected as much," Sigmund told Nike. "But we are discussing your starships, so I believed it appropriate to begin there. Consider this, Nike. Lend New Terra the ships to defend us both. We'll train our own pilots."

"Of course, Sigmund." Vesta looked himself in the eyes. "Why wait for the Pak to destroy us? Why bother to wonder if the Gw'oth will develop into rivals? *You* can destroy us sooner with our own fleet! Or will you, merely, use our ships to evacuate New Terra and leave the Concordance to its fate?"

Baedeker wanted to run, but where could he go? This was madness! "My apologies, Nike. I was unaware of the request Sigmund intended."

Nessus cleared his throats. "Excuse me, Nike. I have seen Gw'oth. Today I saw a Pak. Let us assume our astronomers will confirm the danger headed our way. They will, for Sigmund would not have concocted such a story if our astronomers could refute it. Then what?"

As it became clear that no one had an answer, Baedeker's right forehoof, with a mind of its own, began scratching at the Hindmost's floor.

EVEN BEFORE HIS ABDUCTION to New Terra, Sigmund had studied Puppeteers. Everything he now read in their body language revealed irrationality or shock. Nike and Vesta, clearly angry—at Sigmund, rather than confronting the real problem. Baedeker, on the verge of collapse. Only Nessus had remained focused, and *his* glittering eyes conveyed—what? Manic excitement.

Sane Puppeteers didn't get manic. The only way Nessus and the very few like him ever managed to leave the Fleet was by suppressing their fears beneath mania.

Sigmund pictured Nessus frenzied like this when he decided to kidnap Sigmund from Known Space. Sigmund didn't have a warm feeling for whatever Nessus might be thinking now.

"I have a suggestion," Sigmund said. Stall. Stall for time, while I play tourist across Hearth, looking for opportunities to *steal* ships. Talk one-on-one with Nessus before he acted on his latest wild idea. "But we've covered a lot today. Perhaps we can meet after everyone has had a chance to sleep on it?"

Heads bobbed—up/down, down/up, up/down—in vigorous agreement. Whac-A-Mole. "An excellent suggestion," Vesta concluded.

But Sigmund didn't get the chance to reconnoiter a landing field, nor to consult with Nessus. Nike invited Sigmund and Baedeker to stay at the official residence.

It did not seem to Sigmund like an invitation.

Pacing the spacious guest suite, armed guards posted outside the door—"In case," as the Hindmost put it, "you need anything"—Sigmund had to wonder. Was there another place *anywhere* on Hearth without stepping discs?

He had become a prisoner.

THSSTHFOK SLIPPED through the softened floor of his cell into the empty room below. After several visits to bypass various sensors and control circuits, the passage was routine. But this trip was in no way routine.

This trip, he would seize the ship.

33

The next day, the Hindmost's grand salon looked the same. The participants were the same. The aura, though—

That, Sigmund sensed, *had* changed. Today there was a shoot-the-messenger vibe.

Meaning Sigmund had nothing to lose by pushing. "New Terra can't win this fight. Nor can the Gw'oth. Nor can the Fleet." Because you *won't* fight. "In a few years, if nothing changes, the Pak will smash our worlds back to a preindustrial state."

A trillion Puppeteers depended on tech for *everything*. A crash of the stepping-disc system would trap most deep inside their gargantuan buildings. Finagle! Those rooms were usually doorless and windowless. Billions would suffocate in their rooms, for lack of oxygen.

Sigmund said nothing, letting the implications speak for themselves.

"But you have a proposal," Nessus said hopefully.

Sigmund wanted to lock eyes with the decision maker, but the Hindmost held his heads too far apart. Sigmund chose one eye to look at. "To stand any chance against the Pak, we need an ally with a strong navy. Nike, we need *Earth*."

Sigmund thought he knew all the possible objections. That the Fleet relied for its safety on remaining hidden from the races of Known Space. That Earth would rather attack Puppeteers—as punishment for the ancient crime against the New Terrans—than help the Puppeteers. That Earth's navy could evacuate New Terra, or defend only New Terra, while abandoning Hearth to its fate. That not even the ARM, for all its resources, was equal to the task. That Earth would rather sacrifice the few New Terrans than divert its navy and leave itself defenseless against the ever-resentful Kzinti.

Those objections were really all facets of a single argument: distrust.

Better to risk disaster later from the Pak than court disaster now at Earth's hands.

Sigmund had spent the night pacing, refining possible rebuttals, as Baedeker snored lyrically in the next room. Sigmund's answers, too, boiled down to one. The Concordance had nothing to lose by trying. Only he never got the chance to argue his point.

"Earth is gone," Vesta said. "All the human worlds. The Kzinti worlds. All the worlds you remember, Sigmund. They were in the path of the Pak."

Faces from Sigmund's past flashed through his mind. That part of his memory, cruelly, remained intact. But it wasn't only old friends and colleagues. Billions, surely, had died. Billions whom, as an ARM, Sigmund had sworn to protect. Billions he had failed.

Almost he gave in to despair—but, tanj it!—he was no Puppeteer to hide within himself. Anger washed away the grief. Grief yielded to cold, calculating reason. In that moment of clarity, Sigmund knew: He didn't believe Vesta. The question was, why not?

Because something didn't square with Sigmund's intuition about the Pak.

For all Thssthfok's self-control, he had reacted to the name Phssthpok. Then, discussing Phssthpok's ambitions at length, a way of changing the subject from Pak military capabilities, Thssthfok had corroborated many details in Lucas Garner's recitation.

So, the Pak of Thssthfok's era knew of the attempt to restore tree-of-life to the lost colony. To Earth. Somehow that knowledge was the heart of—

Sigmund still couldn't say what.

Nessus was eyeing Sigmund warily. Expecting him to react crazily?

Pak. The Pak had left behind a cone of destruction. A cone, rather than some more constant cross section, because the clans fought endlessly among themselves. Clan fleets scattering, whether in defeat or for some strategic advantage. Brennan had told Lucas Garner the same things about endless clan conflict.

If the few survivors of Pakhome might encounter a *world* of Pak in their path, a *world* of enemies, would they dare to follow the route Phssthpok had taken?

No.

Sigmund's face flushed and he trembled with rage. Let the Puppeteers think he reacted to Vesta's news. To Vesta's *lies*. Sigmund somehow resisted taking Vesta by the throats.

Guards watching from the patio burst into the salon. "Excellency?" one of them said.

"He had some bad news," Nike explained. The guards relaxed a bit. "Will you be all right, Sigmund?"

"I need a minute." Sigmund settled into a pile of cushions. He curled into a comma, dramatically, his face buried in his arms.

A guard glared at Sigmund. Sitting when the Hindmost stood must be a major breach of decorum. At a gesture from Nike the security detachment returned outside.

A minute. Sigmund needed more than that. Baedeker had twitched at Vesta's announcement, but not Nike or Nessus. They had known what was coming, been in on the lie.

"May I get you some water, Sigmund?" Nessus asked. He looked genuinely concerned.

"Yes, thanks." While Sigmund waited for water and nursed it along, he was able to think without interruption. Nessus had taken his time returning with the water, and Sigmund began to wonder. Did Nessus *want* to give Sigmund that time to think?

Nike and Nessus hadn't reacted much yesterday, either. They *should* have shaken with fear, torn at their manes, pawed the floor—something. They had already known about the Pak!

It could only mean a source deep within Sabrina's government. Only a mole could have leaked this information. And if Sigmund revealed his suspicions, they would know he knew.

The previous evening, Nessus had come by the "guest suite." Just a social call, he had explained. Just seeing that you have everything you need. Then Nessus and Baedeker had talked for a long time. They sang in odd cadences and in an eerie, not-quite-minor key, the conversation somehow raising Sigmund's hackles.

He was no expert, but it hadn't sounded like any Puppeteer language he had ever heard.

After Nessus left, Sigmund had asked Baedeker what that had been about. "Personal," had been the answer. Settling their old scores, Sigmund had hoped at the time. But why now?

Nessus sidled closer. "Sigmund, you do not look well. Perhaps you need some time alone to absorb this information. We can reconvene later."

"That might be for the best," Sigmund said. He stumbled for effect while climbing to his feet. Let everyone think him muddled with grief.

Contact with Earth wasn't going to happen—not, anyway, with help from the Puppeteers. Vesta's lie was meant to cut off all debate on that point. But if not Earth, then who?

Nessus had unreasonable confidence in Sigmund—which was how Sigmund had ended up on New Terra. That same misplaced trust, presumably, was why Nessus had offered Sigmund an out just now. The sad truth was, obtaining Earth's help had been his last plan.

But though Sigmund didn't have a plan, neither did he know how to quit. . . .

34

With an inward sigh, Kirsten extended an arm out of the sleeper field and groped in the dark for the touchpoint. She wasn't going to sleep tonight. Eric tossed fitfully, but at least he *was* asleep. She didn't chance disturbing him by whispering to Jeeves to collapse the field. She found the touchpoint, rolled beyond the reach of the force field, and reactivated it before Eric stirred.

A generalized fear kept her up most nights. How could she *not* fear, with the Pak hurtling toward everyone she held dear? Beginning with her and Eric's own precious children.

To that generalized dread, a more immediate problem had been added. Sigmund was overdue checking in.

She dressed in the dark, grabbed her comm unit from the desk, and slipped out the hatch into the nightshift-dim corridor. She whispered, "Jeeves. Any word from Sigmund?"

No answer. An audio sensor gone bad, she thought. She repeated herself into her comm unit.

Jeeves answered the same way. "Sorry, Kirsten. No word. It may not mean anything."

Sigmund had guessed the Citizens would keep him incommunicado throughout discussions. The absence of contact might mean nothing. Her gut said otherwise.

Hearth and New Terra maintained an open network channel, more for the interplanetary grain trade than the occasional official dealings between governments. If Sigmund had a comm unit, Kirsten felt certain, he would have contacted *Don Quixote* by now via a relay through New Terra.

Her gut also growled for a snack. She rounded a corner, toward the relax room—

And jerked to a halt. She raised the comm to her lips. "Jeeves! Why is the emergency hatch closed? Deck three, just beyond my cabin."

"You're mistaken, Kirsten," Jeeves answered imperturbably.

What? "I'm looking right at it, Jeeves. It's down. Sealed."

"Take the corridor around the other way. What do you see on the other side?"

Why didn't Jeeves use a security camera? She didn't ask. She could do as he suggested just as quickly.

Only she *couldn't* cross. "The emergency hatch outside Sigmund's cabin is also down."

"Then it's not an isolated glitch, Kirsten. The security system shows those hatches open. Cameras and proximity sensors both."

Together with all the sound pickups. The nonfunctioning audio sensor outside her cabin would not be the only one.

Kirsten's heart pounded. She almost asked, where is Thssthfok? Where are the Gw'oth? Either question was pointless. With the security system compromised, Jeeves could not know.

She *had* to protect the ship from capture. "Eric's in our cabin. Wake him. Then raise gravity to six gees everywhere but our cabin and this segment of this corridor."

A moment later, a faint but grating alarm seeped from her cabin door. And a moment after that, the deck fell out from under her.

Gravity was gone.

⌣

THSSTHFOK PROCEEDED TO THE BRIDGE, systematically softening emergency hatches and hardening them behind him. In any event, he headed opposite shipboard gravity. Pak ships always placed bridges forward. Absent knowledge of human design practices, he reasoned that his distant relatives would, also.

Hardening the hatches slowed him down, but overriding emergency hatch controls would slow any pursuers much longer. On the remote chance something kept him from capturing the ship, he meant to keep secret his ability to pass through doors and walls. Because he would not stop until this ship was his.

The glow panels overhead were dimmed for sleep. He expected to reach the bridge undetected. From there he would depressurize the middle decks, trapping the humans in their cabins until he wanted them.

And then the gravity vanished.

AGAINST THE WEARYING PULL OF SHIP'S GRAVITY, in the discomfort of his protective suit, Er'o labored at the compact fabrication bench in the habitat water lock. Ship's air presently filled the work space. Another few shifts and the newest sensors would be complete. Ol't'ro felt confident these instruments would yield important new data on the operation of hyperdrive.

With that trace of meld memory, Er'o's aches faded to mere annoyances. He extended a tubacle, adjusting the fine-motion calipers. Motors in his exoskeleton hummed as it moved.

And then gravity disappeared.

A surprised twitch sent Er'o drifting upward in the water lock. His dorsal side rebounded gently off the water-lock roof.

He engaged suit magnets and stretched tubacles toward the water-lock deck. In rapid succession, as each limb tip struck, clangs rang through the water in his suit. "What is happening?" he radioed into the habitat.

Th'o answered first. "Happening? What do you mean?"

Because floating in water was indistinguishable from microgravity. No one in the habitat, unless they happened to be checking sensors, would have noticed the change.

"Jeeves," Er'o called over the suit's audio output, "why is gravity off?" No answer. Er'o switched radio frequencies to the intercom channel. "This is Er'o. Anyone, why is gravity off?"

UNSEEN AROUND THE CORNER, a cabin door crashed open. "Over here, Eric," Kirsten called.

He came into view a moment later, walking on the stripe down the center of the deck. He wore sticky slippers. He handed her a pair. "What the tanj is happening?"

She popped a cover plate to get at the emergency-hatch control circuits. If the hatch held back vacuum, the pressure differential would keep it sealed whatever she tried. "Jeeves didn't see the hatches come down."

"So someone has compromised security," he completed her thought, and then raised his voice. "Jeeves, did you kill gravity?"

"Use your comm," she told Eric. "Audio pickups are off, too. So we can't hear whoever is behind this."

Eric repeated his question over a comm link.

"Indirectly," Jeeves answered. "I tried to raise gravity, and the circuits blew."

"This is Er'o," she heard over the intercom. "Anyone, why is the gravity off?"

Gw'oth or Pak? Kirsten looked helplessly at Eric. "We're losing the ship, Eric, and we don't even know to whom."

At her insistent probing, a status light flickered from red to green. The emergency hatch began to rise. She caught a glimpse of—what?

A naked heel disappearing around a corner. Toward the stairs to the bridge level.

Gw'oth didn't have heels.

"Thssthfok is loose and almost to the bridge," she shouted into her comm unit. "Stay put, Er'o." That left open the question what she and Eric could do.

If Thssthfok shut himself into the bridge, they were doomed.

THE DAY OF THSSTHFOK'S CAPTURE, humans had coerced him out of his battle armor with painfully intense artificial gravity. During his first reconnaissance, his captors had immobilized him with gravity. If they detected him now, they would attempt the same.

That was unacceptable.

He would have preferred to hold ship's gravity constant, but explorations near his cell had not uncovered any gravity-control circuitry. Logically, those controls were on the bridge. He had had to settle for a simpler intervention, only requiring access to nearby circuit breakers. Once he modified the breakers, any significant increase in power drain would open them.

Accidental discovery of his escape was always an unavoidable risk. Thssthfok wasted no time regretting that accident when it happened. And so the loss of artificial gravity was unfortunate but, under the circumstances, necessary and of his own doing

Above all else, he meant to keep the structural modulator secret—for his next escape, if it came to that. Manually hardening every partition after he passed through was taking too much time. He opened the modulator handle and slightly altered the internal wiring. The projected field now wobbled microscopically. Softened material would, in the course of enough random thermal motions, regress to a chaotic, more rigid state. Reversion would be a matter of a few day-thousandths.

Reacting as anticipated, the humans had set Thssthfok—and themselves—adrift. In the time it took to modify his tool, air currents returned him halfway down the hallway he had just crossed on foot.

His captors would have magnetic boots and sticky footwear to anchor themselves. He had neither. That, too, Thssthfok had anticipated.

The brief touch of a structural modulator merely made a surface sticky. He began a swimming motion, stretching out one hand for a new spot to tweak even as his other hand, sticking to a treated surface, pulled him forward. The method worked as well as he had hoped: faster and with better control than simply bouncing off walls. He had been unable to test the technique while the gravity remained on.

Thssthfok had heard voices, unintelligible through closed emergency hatches but recognizable as Eric and Kirsten. Now the intercom came on. "This is Er'o. Anyone, why is the gravity off?"

Who was Er'o? An artificial entity, like Jeeves? Another human? Or one of the two-headed beasts? And if one unsuspected individual was aboard, there could be more.

Thssthfok half swam, half pulled himself to a stairwell. Its hatch also functioned as an emergency partition. He softened it, pulled himself through the temporarily viscous partition—*pop!*—and resumed his journey.

Toward—he hoped—the bridge.

IN OR OUT? Er'o stood in the water lock, pondering his choices.

The choice was made for him.

"Hyperdrive startup in five seconds," Jeeves announced in his confirming-an-order intonation. "Commencing countdown. Five . . ."

Neither Eric nor Kirsten nor Jeeves could have expected the Gw'oth to understand the implications. No one had explained *anything* about hyperdrive to them. But Ol't'ro, working from subtle measurements and unintentional hints, had made significant progress.

And *Don Quixote* was within a singularity, deep inside a gravity well.

Thssthfok must have escaped. Rather than let him capture *Don Quixote*, the humans meant to destroy the ship!

The Gw'oth would not have any say in the matter. They had agreed, early in this adventure, to share in its perils. They had accepted human command.

They had not agreed to be hurled into some alternate-dimensional limbo.

"One second!" Er'o radioed to the intercom. He wished that Ol't'ro, not he, had the responsibility for saving them. But *he* was suited up to move about the ship, and their fate would be sealed sooner than a meld could take form. And before anyone could suit up to help him.

What did he know? That Thssthfok was loose. On past escapes, the humans had used artificial gravity to immobilize the Pak. Instead, gravity was *off*. Thssthfok must have cut it.

Silence had replaced the countdown, but the numbers continued in Er'o's thoughts. Three . . .

Jeeves had surely followed his programming in announcing a countdown—and Eric or Kirsten had ordered him to stop lest Thssthfok overhear anything useful. The count doubtless continued.

Two . . .

Er'o flipped his radio transmitter to the ship's public comm channel. "No! Accelerate with thrusters!" How much gravity could the humans take? The question didn't arise for the Gw'oth, effectively weightless anyway in their water-filled habitat. Except for Er'o himself, and there was no time to worry about that. He guessed. "Ten times normal."

One . . .

Kirsten said, speaking rapidly, "Jeeves, wait. Er'o is right. We'll pin down Thssthfok with acceleration."

"And mash ourselves," Eric replied. "Is that how you want to go?"

Crushing weight, unable to move—it would a lingering, horrible death. Er'o shuddered. But it did not have to be that way.

He radioed, "I'm in my pressure gear. With the suit's mechanical assistance function, I'll be mobile despite the acceleration. I know you have stunners. Tell me where to find one. Once I disable Thssthfok, Jeeves can throttle back."

Silence.

Er'o knew what Eric and Kirsten were thinking. By revealing their weapons, they risked the Gw'oth, instead, taking over the ship. At such a delicate juncture, it would not help Er'o's case to assert they would have built weapons already if they so chose.

If they survived this crisis, perhaps they would.

The silence stretched, and in that stillness Er'o contemplated his unexpected mortality. As one within a Gw'otesht, he had thought himself/themselves all but eternal. But that was hardly the case. . . .

The countdown in his thoughts remained frozen at *one*.

"All right," Eric said over the public channel. "Jeeves, belay my earlier order. Thrusters at six gees, now!"

THSSTHFOK SWAM ONTO ANOTHER DECK. This deck was the smallest yet, and had only three doors. One by one he softened a door and poked his head within. Door three revealed the bridge. And in the large view port—

It was like nothing he had ever seen, or even imagined.

In the moment he stared, a tremendous force struck him. He was smashed, gasping, to the floor—

While his head remained embedded in the door.

The rim of the opening cut into the leathery skin of his neck. Very soon, form and shape would begin reasserting themselves. At best, he would be trapped, choking, head and shoulders on opposite sides. At worst, the door, retaking its former shape, would sever his head. Pulling his head from the stiffer-by-the-moment door was the hardest thing Thssthfok had ever done.

He collapsed onto the deck, exhausted.

Moving so he could see his hands was even harder. The structural modulator folded into a compact shape—no broader than his smallest finger, and not quite as long—the better to hide in his cell. Somehow, he managed to fold and swallow the tool. If he survived—and if the modulator, bathed in stomach acid, did not short-circuit and transform his insides to gruel—nature's course would return the device to him. Or block his intestines and kill him slowly.

Thssthfok lay, panting, on the hard deck.

He had not heard the *pop* of the softened door resealing after he pulled himself free. Because of his gasping for breath? Somehow he turned his head to peer up the bridge door.

A hole gaped, its lower edge swollen. Restored artificial gravity or acceleration—he did not know which, but it hardly mattered—had overwhelmed surface tension faster than the door material could recongeal.

The humans *would* look for an explanation. He had to mislead them.

Straining, Thssthfok pulled himself upright. He rammed fingers through an air-duct grille and twisted until its fasteners snapped. Moments later, from decks below, metal shards went *clang*. He forced the broken grille into the duct. The bent grille scraped noisily until gravity wedged it somewhere deep within the ventilation system.

Limbs trembling, chest heaving, Thssthfok slumped back onto the deck. He had given the humans someplace to look for a door-melting tool. Let them search for a long time.

The hatch to the stairwell creaked open. An armored, five-limbed— something, perhaps knee-high to an adult Pak, lumbered through. Er'o? Except for the exoskeleton, the alien's gear was transparent. Bubbles rose within; the alien was a water breather. And it was hideous, like five giant snakes fused at their tails.

The only odors were artificial: metals, lubricant, and synthetic hydrocarbons. Somehow that was worse than the thing's true, unrevealed reek. Its skin changed colors, patterns swirling, as Thssthfok watched.

Its motorized exoskeleton whining in protest, the alien raised a tentacle. Viewed tip on, the tentacle was hollow. Deep within the tube, beyond tiers of sharp teeth, a ring of baleful eyes stared at Thssthfok.

From calipers mounted to the tentacle's armored covering, the maw of a gun—ridiculously large for the beast—also gaped at Thssthfok.

Then everything hummed and went away.

35

Saying good-bye to Sigmund was going to be hard. No one could have been more surprised than Baedeker.

"You're going to pluck yourself bald," Sigmund said. "Do you want to talk about it?"

How could Sigmund be so calm? Did he not wonder why the meeting with the Hindmost had not reconvened? Did he not understand the significance of rooms without comm, without stepping discs, of guards outside their door and following them everywhere they went?

Of course he understood. This was Sigmund.

Baedeker stopped tugging at his mane. Disfiguring himself hardly alleviated his guilt. Maybe confession would. "I'm not going back with you."

Sigmund stood at the guest suite's floor-to-ceiling window wall, looking out over an unnerving drop down to the sea. Only it would not unnerve a human, would it? "That's what you and Nessus have been talking about, I suppose."

Baedeker bobbed heads. After so long together, Sigmund would know the gesture. As Baedeker had learned to read human body language. Sigmund was like a coiled spring.

"New Terra will miss you," Sigmund said. "*I'll* miss you. You've been a good friend."

And friends don't abandon friends. Certainly not without an explanation. "If the Concordance fights the Pak, Sigmund, we *will* lose. If we do nothing, the Pak might veer in their course."

Sigmund nodded. "If you can't retreat, at least stall. A very Puppet . . . Citizen attitude."

"But that's the thing! Maybe we *can* retreat."

Sigmund's eyes narrowed. He didn't say anything.

"You're right, our worlds cannot move out of the Pak's way, not fast enough. Now." Baedeker resisted the urge to resume twisting and tugging at his mane. "Unless . . ."

"Unless *what*?" Sigmund snapped. "You steal New Terra's drive?"

"No!" Somehow Baedeker held his ground despite Sigmund's anger. "No one ever tried using multiple drives on one world. But that *is* one of the things I'll be investigating. I approached Nessus because he has influence. He can get me the resources I'll need: scientists and technicians, equipment, even ships. Because we *cannot* do such tests on our own worlds."

"But the Concordance doesn't *have* unused drives," Sigmund said. "Do you?"

Now Baedeker did tear at his mane. The work he envisioned was terrifying. The only thing more terrifying would be *not* undertaking it. He began to explain. "I studied the planetary drives in the past."

Because he had been coerced to remotely disable New Terra's drive. Cast adrift, the former colonists would have had to surrender their newfound independence. Thankfully, he had never learned how, never had to confront whether he would have complied.

But neither had he refused to investigate. Shame had sent him into self-exile on New Terra. His personal shame, and shame for his government. But now Nessus had the ears of the Hindmost, and policy would be saner.

Baedeker forced himself to look into Sigmund's eyes. "I am close to understanding the underlying principles. If I am right, I may be able to build new drives. Maybe more powerful. Maybe able to work in tandem. And maybe move our worlds out of the way of the Pak."

"*Our* worlds?"

"New Terra, too," Baedeker said. "I have Nike's promise."

"And the Gw'oth?"

That question would be argued long and hard, and Baedeker was far from certain where his own feelings lay. "It is being discussed," was the best he had to offer.

"I wish you luck," Sigmund said. "On both parts."

THSSTHFOK SAT LEANING against a cell wall, his eyes closed, chewing mechanically on a tree-of-life root.

His prison had been reconfigured as he lay stunned. Holes had been drilled in the interior walls. Transparent material fused over the openings now revealed cameras on the other side. Crude—and hard to interfere with. Within his cell, every shelf and cabinet had been removed, and with them any pretense of privacy. One of the vanished cabinets held—presumably undetected by his jailors—the remaining parts from his repair kit.

Once the alterations were complete, as Thssthfok lay paralyzed on the deck, Eric had paused halfway out of the hatch. He wore full armor despite Thssthfok's helplessness. To avoid the smell of tree-of-life root?

Eric said, "Listen very carefully. As soon as this hatch closes, I'm depressurizing this level. Everything but this room. The level will remain airless except when I bring food and remove your waste. I don't know how you let yourself out, or how you bypassed the hall sensors, but I do know this. Escape again, and you'll be killing yourself."

Vacuum all around would have been a deterrent, but the room below Thssthfok's cell dispensed the humans' food. That room, at the least, would keep its air. Once the structural modulator made its reappearance, he would exit again, at a time of his choosing, through the deck.

Meanwhile, Thssthfok had information from his last escape to assimilate.

He had glimpsed five worlds in an equilateral pentagon. Five worlds in flight! Four of the globes, gorgeous blue dots, reminded him, achingly, of a long-lost home. Of Pakhome as it had been before the final war. (But unlike Pakhome, these worlds sparkled! Tiny artificial suns, indistinct to the naked eye from this distance, must accompany them.) The final bright dot, eerily glowing, presented puzzles he still labored to articulate.

To seize this ship had been the focus of Thssthfok's planning. With its faster-than-light drive, he would rejoin his family. Clan Rilchuk scientists would master the technology, fly far from other clans, and establish New Rilchuk in some quiet corner of the outer galaxy.

How modest his goals had been.

The humans and the alien abominations that accompanied them had wondrous technologies: faster-than-light drive, instantaneous transfer, and now a drive to move worlds. And they did not seem ruthless or intelligent enough to protect what they had.

Trade-offs, strategies, and alliances churned in Thssthfok's thoughts. . . .

THE GUEST SUITE FELT EMPTY without Baedeker.

Sigmund sipped from a snifter of brandy. He couldn't fault the repertoire of the guest-room synthesizer, only that he didn't feel much like a guest. And now that Baedeker had gone, Sigmund's own fate, surely, would soon be revealed. He pictured large numbers of crazed Puppeteers carrying guns.

But only one crazed Puppeteer came, unarmed. "May I come in?" Nessus asked.

Sigmund nodded. The guards waited outside as Nessus entered.

Nessus took a comm unit from a pocket of his sash. Tongue and lip nodules set the device to flashing. He set it on a low table. "We'll have privacy for a little while. I can't say how long. Until our seeming silence becomes suspicious."

What did they have to discuss in private? Sigmund wondered. "Go on."

"I am sorry, Sigmund. I did my best, but you will not be going home."

Sigmund had had three lives, each better than the last. He supposed he shouldn't complain. "What do you expect killing me to accomplish."

Nessus recoiled. "Kill you? No one said anything about that. You will remain a guest of the Concordance."

"Because you think the New Terrans won't act without me. I have news for you, Nessus. You still don't get humans. New Terra *will* fight. If we must go down, we'll take as many Pak as possible with us."

"Why? Your people will only hasten their own doom."

Because we're *human* tanj it! We don't hide in our navels. "Because if enough worlds resist, then sooner or later the Pak menace will end. That's a legacy to die proud of."

Nessus looked himself in the eyes. Apparently Sigmund didn't know Nessus as well as he thought, either. Sigmund said, "At our first session with Nike, you were ready to suggest something. I changed the subject. What were you going to propose?"

"You will find this amusing," Nessus said, sidling toward the synthesizer. He got himself a glass of something orange. Warm carrot juice, if Sigmund correctly remembered Nessus' vice. "I had an alternate suggestion for staffing a Concordance fleet. Artificial intelligences."

Sigmund blinked. That was a brilliant idea. It took a fully sentient mind to navigate in hyperspace. So, scour Hearth for a few hundred Puppeteers to fly an AI-enabled fleet toward the Pak. Evacuate the living crews onto a few ships—those could be back into hyperspace before the Pak could even see them. Turn the rest of the ships over to AIs. Only—

"Refresh my memory, Nessus. Why don't Citizens use AI?"

"Because we fear creating our successors."

And giving armed warships to those potential successors would be a nonstarter. "Still, I assume you raised the idea directly with Nike."

"I did." Nessus drained his beverage with one convulsive gulp. "He would sooner trust a fleet to New Terrans."

To Sigmund's ears, that comparison sounded like an insult rather than an option. "So what now, Nessus? Holding me won't stop the New Terrans from acting, only make them loath to coordinate with the Concordance. Nike might as well let me go home."

Sigmund's door rattled, accompanied by a torrent of notes. Nessus opened the door, bobbed heads at the guards, and closed the door again.

Why hadn't Nessus spoken, maybe yelled at the guards to intimidate them? Ah. Had he spoken, someone might have noticed the suppressed bugs *not* picking up his words.

Cantering back into the room, Nessus said, "The guard asked if I am all right. Sigmund, I *must* stop suppressing bugs before the security forces become suspicious. And yes, keeping you here may stop New Terra from acting. At least for a time. That is the Hindmost's judgment.

"Your government will be told that you and I have left together on another scouting mission. Alas, you will not be returning. Though my opinion changes nothing, Sigmund, I disagreed with this decision. I could not change it.

"If only you accept the inevitable, you can be comfortable here." Nessus waved a neck sinuously at the wall of windows and its spectacular view. "There are far worse prisons than the Hindmost's residence. Sigmund, I vouched for you. I promised Nike you will behave."

Here. Incommunicado. Unable to warn Sabrina of a mole within her inner circle. And worst of all, Nike might be correct about Sigmund's absence delaying any New Terran action.

I don't think so, Nessus. "You'd better unvouch for me. Because I *will* escape."

"Sigmund, please reconsider." Nessus looked meaningfully at the door. When Sigmund gave no answer, Nessus emitted a mournful trill and reached for his comm unit. The flashing stopped. Nessus reverted to English, to Sigmund's ears speaking a bit theatrically. "As you refuse to talk to me, I see no reason to stay."

"Good-bye, Nessus." And good luck to you and Baedeker.

As Nessus let himself out, Sigmund noted the time on his wrist implant. There was a flurry of music in the hallway.

Within an hour, guards escorted Sigmund to a stepping disc and dumped him into a doorless, windowless, cylindrical room perhaps eight feet across.

36

Sigmund paced his cell, because that's what prisoners did.

Translucent walls admitted sufficient light to see, not that there was much *to* see. It wouldn't take much image enhancement to give outside sensors a clear view inside. Did Puppeteer jailors routinely watch prisoners? Sigmund saw no reason why they would bother.

Then again, there was much about Puppeteers he did not understand.

Except for stepping discs, one in the floor and another in the ceiling, the cell was featureless. The top disc, to which adhered a thin-film molecular filter, must be there to exchange carbon dioxide and excess water vapor for fresh oxygen. The bottom disk, with a thin-film filter of its own, whisked away bodily wastes. Sigmund supposed the floor disc would be set occasionally to receive mode to deliver food.

The disc-plus-filter combinations reminded him of the mechanisms that moved deuterium and tritium to/from *Don Quixote*'s fuel tanks. Very Puppeteer: reusing a proven design. And very predictable.

With nothing else to do, he glanced often at his wrist implant. The hours passed slowly. He had left the chronometer on ship's time. It cheered him up, however slightly, to imagine *Don Quixote*'s shipboard routine. And finally—

It was time! Sigmund wrenched the disc from the floor. The right of which no Puppeteer would be deprived was a modicum of personal safety. Lest the ceiling disc or its air filter fail—unlikely, given the extreme conservatism of Puppeteer engineering, but always possible—there had to be a way for a prisoner to exit a sealed, impregnable cell.

And on that theory, Sigmund had goaded Nessus. He had had to get someplace where he could be assured of finding stepping discs. Any place. Even a maximum-security prison.

From this instant, Sigmund had to act quickly, in case anyone *did* watch him in real time.

The filter peeled easily from the disc. (Had removing the filter trig-gered an alarm? Certainly plausible.) Folded, the filter fit into a pocket of his jumpsuit. The Puppeteers would eventually realize what he had done. Until then, he had a locked-room mystery for them.

As Sigmund expected, the disc lacked even a maintenance-mode ad-dress keypad. He could not punch in a destination. The safety feature that logic insisted must exist would deliver him into a spare cell or a room full of guards: unacceptable. He pulled out and pocketed the disc's program-mable memory chip, resetting the disc to its factory default mode.

Among Puppeteers, there could be only one default destination.

He restored the disc to its place in the floor and stepped. He emerged into urban cacophony, on some crowded public square. The nearest building—of course—was an office of the Department of Public Safety.

Puppeteers in the hundreds shied away, their bleating louder than God. A circle opened around Sigmund, behind a wall of hind legs: massive, sharp-hoofed, ready to lash out if he got too close. Puppeteers fought—when they had no other option—by turning their backs. That was all right—Sigmund had no intention of staying. Two paces took him to an array of public step-ping discs.

He transported at random around the globe, anywhere public discs would take him. Malls. Stores. Arcology lobbies. Puppeteers gaped and blared mu-sic wherever he appeared. He heard the same motifs over and over. We are attacked! Or, God you're ugly! Or, Don't hurt me! Or—

His next two stops would *not* be random. He stepped, again via public disc, to the large park Eric had described to Sigmund. The park's popular-ity did not matter. That the park was a landmark, easy to spot from above, did.

For his final step, Sigmund needed a transport controller. He grabbed one from the sash pocket of a Puppeteer chosen arbitrarily from the crowd. "Sorry," Sigmund said.

The Puppeteer shied away, wheezing like a drop-kicked bagpipe, eyes slitted in terror. Mugged by a human! He would be telling this story for the rest of his life.

Sigmund tapped a fifteen-digit disc address and stepped—

Aboard *Don Quixote*, flying in stealth mode. Its arcing course matched velocities with the popular park on Hearth, twenty-five million miles dis-tant. That put the ship just outside the Fleet's gravitational singularity.

"Right on time," Eric said.

"I could say the same," Sigmund answered. "Good job. Any problems while I was gone?"

Eric looked at his shoes. "It's a long story."

Then it would wait. "Let's jump to hyperspace, before anyone below notices that I've gone missing."

That will give the Hindmost something to think about.

THE LAST HOPE

37

The concept of an inquest was not new to Er'o. The feel was.

The mood aboard *Don Quixote* was strange, strained, and Er'o struggled to understand the emotional undercurrents. Sigmund had returned from Hearth alone, offering only the briefest of explanations: Baedeker chose to stay. This once, Sigmund's reticence seemed rooted in something other than distrust. The human seemed genuinely ambivalent about Baedeker's decision.

Meanwhile, Kirsten and Eric remained in shock at how close they had come to losing the ship. At least shock was how Er'o interpreted their trembling. Bodily quivers were a new phenomenon, for which Ol't'ro had yet to make a definitive interpretation.

Er'o was the only one in any condition to give answers about Thssthfok's recent escape.

The flight from Hearth to New Terra would take only two days, much of the second day spent shedding normal-space velocity after they dropped from hyperspace. Sigmund wanted answers before they arrived. "Once again," Sigmund said. "*How* did Thssthfok get out?"

Kirsten and Eric studied the relax-room table and said nothing. Sigmund waited, staring, until Kirsten volunteered, "We simply don't know."

"I checked the hatch lock. There were no signs of tampering." Eric grimaced. "Not that we found tampering the first time Thssthfok broke out of the cargo hold. But at least then we found the gadget he used to override the controls."

Kirsten looked up. "We heard him throw something into the air ducts."

"And what have you found?" Sigmund probed.

Kirsten resumed staring at the table. "Just the bent grille he tore off. Of course, short of tearing apart the ship, we can't get at many of the ducts."

Er'o raised an armored tubacle, wiggling it for attention. "To judge from the size of the grilles, a Gw'o can fit the larger ducts. Say the word, Sigmund, and several of us will look."

Sigmund shook his head. "You could get stuck in there. We'll be home soon, and then we'll send in maintenance bots."

Er'o sensed no undercurrent of *you might see something not meant for you to see*. The trust felt good. For apprehending Thssthfok? Or for saving them from an unknowable hyperspace abyss?

"I just had a good idea," was Er'o's reason, impossible to disprove, whenever asked why he had interrupted Jeeves's countdown. The answer had the virtue of truth (albeit partial): pinning Thssthfok with acceleration *had* been a good idea. The humans might suspect Er'o had learned about hyperdrive and singularities. They could not ask without hinting at matters they wanted kept secret.

It was like interrogating Thssthfok. No one asked him what he thought of the hyperdrive announcement, either.

"Let's look at the problem another way," Sigmund said abruptly. "Something made the hole in the bridge hatch. You found nothing to do that, either. Are we talking about *two* devices, both missing, or one device that melts holes and unlocks doors?"

Sigmund sounded skeptical about both possibilities. Because of a third scenario, unspoken? Shipboard surveillance had been bypassed. Any of them could have unlocked Thssthfok's cell. Any of them could have found and hidden Thssthfok's tool or tools.

Of all the suspects, only the Gw'oth need not fear a search of their living space—at least until New Terra and the arrival of maintenance bots.

From the furtive glances in Er'o's direction, Eric had had the same thought. Sigmund, more subtly, looked everywhere but at Er'o.

"I would like to analyze the melted door," Er'o said, to change the subject. "Maybe that will suggest what type of Pak device we are seeking."

"I'll help," Eric said quickly.

The sense of trust had been good while it lasted.

THSSTHFOK SAT CROSS-LEGGED on the cell floor. Except for three simple containers, of water, food, and for bodily waste, his cell was bare. Gone with the shelving and cabinets—removed while he lay helpless, still stunned—were most of his repair kit and any pretense of privacy.

The repair kit, he would miss.

He wondered if his captors had thought to search inside the hollow recesses of the removed furniture. In their haste to clear the room before his paralysis wore off, they had overlooked the small spot on the floor turned transparent by the structural modulator.

As his stomach rumbled, Thssthfok wondered when the tool would reappear.

He had positioned the water pitcher to cover his peephole into the room below. His captors were more apt to check the other containers for anything he might have hidden inside. Why bother with the pitcher, though? They could see through the water to the bottom.

So far, he had managed to sit or stand on that clear spot, or to set something on it, and the altered area had gone unnoticed. He thought. He kept hoping for food the color of the deck—something to chew into a paste that, surreptitiously spread, would stop light from leaking out of the room below. So far, nothing he had been offered matched the floor.

For now, the floor must tend to itself. Thssthfok had company and more immediate concerns.

"How did you get out?" Sigmund asked. Armored, he could almost pass for Pak. The same could not be said for the other suited figure. Er'o.

Thssthfok made a broad gesture with his arm. "You see everything I have." Except for the structural modulator, still inside me.

"Answer the question," Sigmund said.

Thssthfok said nothing.

"How did you make a hole in a hatch?"

The bridge hatch. Thssthfok said nothing. If they thought it possible he had not recognized the bridge, why should he enlighten them?

"The breach is very odd," Er'o said suddenly. "The opening appears melted, but something more complex has occurred. At the molecular level, the material surrounding the hole is stronger than the door. The bulge shows too few microscopic gaps and voids. Trace impurities are too regularly distributed. The material is, for lack of a better word, improved."

Alien *and* perceptive.

Through their questions and comments, Sigmund and Er'o revealed clues about the ship's systems and their manner of thinking. Thssthfok, through his silence, revealed nothing. Not how he had cut ship's gravity. Not how he had bypassed the security system or operated the emergency hatches or exited this cell. Not how he had injected false images into the wirelessly networked surveillance cameras—although that, given the repair-kit instruments they had confiscated from Thssthfok's cell, his captors would doubtless soon determine. Not anything.

Thssthfok wondered when his captors would try coercion. He would resist torture, but he would not enjoy it. He could not stop them from stunning and immobilizing him. But reawakened for questioning, he might surprise them. He had done nothing to reveal his true strength.

And then Sigmund did something surprising. He opened a pouch in the leg of his armor and removed a sheaf of flimsy sheets, fastened along one edge. When he dropped it, it fluttered to the floor. "You need *something* to occupy your mind besides escape. These pages deal with plants and animals on a world far away. Jeeves can speak the words aloud while you learn to read English. We can provide more material. And we can take it away. Understood?"

"Understood," Thssthfok said.

Mostly he understood that Sigmund expected to be too busy for a while to continue the questioning.

Leaving Thssthfok trying to deduce what Sigmund considered more urgent.

38

"This is unacceptable," Baedeker trilled. The peculiar thing was, he complained *to*, not *about*, Nessus. Somehow, imperceptibly and unobtrusively, Nessus had become the voice of reason.

In calmer moments, Baedeker wondered what this newfound rapport said about himself. For now, he was anything but calm. "I cannot work in these conditions," he sang.

Heads swinging in opposing directions, Nessus pointedly surveyed the spacious office. "Your surroundings seem comfortable enough."

"That's the problem!" Baedeker intoned, stressing the second harmonics for emphasis. "I'm here, in an office. Taking reports. Providing assurances. Giving direction to others."

Nessus turned his gaze to the office window, beyond which stood the small, hexagonal building in which the planetary drive resided. "Then leave your office. You are hindmost of this project, are you not?"

Sides heaving, Baedeker controlled his anger. Anger was a most un-Citizen behavior, a bad habit learned from living too long among humans. Surely Nessus would understand *that*.

Baedeker *was* hindmost here—and yet he could seldom do what he wanted. With authority came responsibility. How could it be responsible to perform any of the experiments he envisioned? The shielding of the planetary drives was imperfect—it could hardly be otherwise, when its effects must encompass an entire world—but the shielding obscured *enough*.

Outside his office window, wind howled. Snow swirled. Snow! Nature Preserve Five, as yet untamed, had been made available for his experiments. He had determined during an earlier crisis that the planetary drive drew upon the zero-point energy of the vacuum. By somehow shaping an asymmetry, the mechanism effectively created a slope in empty space. The steeper the slope, the higher the acceleration. But how to tap those energies, or control them, or what might happen if control was lost . . .

Baedeker found himself staring into a ragged trench his hoof had torn in the lush meadowplant carpet of his office.

"The fate of the Concordance is no small thing," Nessus crooned. He crossed the room, a little awkwardly, to brush flanks.

And that show of empathy permitted Baedeker, finally, to confront his real problem. "The issue is not the lack of progress, Nessus. It is the rate of our progress." Along a great arc of wall display, digital herds milled and sang. Unaware of the catastrophe coming their way. Unaware of the catastrophe Baedeker's experimentation could unleash even sooner. "My engineers are ready to attempt constructing a scale-model prototype drive." And as Sigmund would say, only Finagle knew what would happen then.

Nessus hummed wordlessly, waiting. Supporting.

Baedeker sidled to the window and looked up into the sky. The final string of suns had set. Hearth was rising, an indistinct glow through the blizzard. You *know* what must happen, he wanted to shout. But this was not something for Nessus to propose, but for Baedeker to admit to himself. He said, "Nessus, such experiments are dangerous. We must do them far from the Fleet."

"The New Terrans might help," Nessus said.

Indeed, they might. Even Sigmund, whose escape, like his incarceration in the Fleet, was known only to a few. Baedeker knew, because Nessus had shared the information, and felt shame at abandoning a colleague. A friend.

Nessus generally knew more than he chose to divulge. When, Baedeker wondered, had such antisocial behavior come to seem wise? And which of us has changed?

Baedeker resumed pawing the carpet, this time fully conscious of his desire to flee. "I would welcome New Terran support, but I will not endanger them, either. This work must be done elsewhere."

"Understood," Nessus trilled. Grace notes alluded, deniably, to unspoken levels of agreement. Or was it approval?

Something was happening between them, something Baedeker could not now take the time to analyze. It was sufficient for the moment to know that Nessus would help.

So, they would test somewhere else. Deep in space. Far from the Fleet. Far from New Terra. Far from all those for whom Baedeker felt so responsible.

Finagle knew where.

39

If Sigmund were a Puppeteer, by now he would have plucked himself bald.

Admittedly, he had a lot on his mind. The existential threat posed by the Pak. Baedeker's experiments, for which Nessus was circuitously forwarding progress reports. The evolving mystery of Thssthfok's second escape.

While refitting *Don Quixote*, the shipyard had located the many taps, bypasses, and splices by which ship systems had been compromised. That only replaced one question—how had Sigmund's crew gone so long without seeing the changes?—with another. Circuits had been altered far from any wiring closet, cover plate, or recognizable access point. It was as though someone had reached through the wall! Still unaccounted for, despite tearing the ship nearly apart, was whatever had been disposed of inside the ducts. And Defense Ministry experts continued to scratch their heads as to how plasteel had been altered around the hole in the bridge hatch.

Maybe Thssthfok was a magician.

Or maybe the Gw'oth were involved. Perhaps only Sigmund had thought to wonder. Alas, searching an ally's habitat on only suspicion was not a viable option (ignoring how long it might take to fabricate waterproof robots to fit the little water lock—and whether the Gw'oth would figure out how to compromise them).

"We'll take you home," Sigmund had told Ol't'ro as the refitting neared completion. "It's almost on our way."

That last was not—necessarily—a lie, because Sigmund had not yet known where to go next. Only to whom: the last party, yet to be located, who could conceivably aid New Terra.

The group mind had declined, as had every Gw'o when asked individually. "Our kind also has a stake in this crisis," Ol't'ro said. "We wish to continue helping."

Continue helping. Setting aside the mystery surrounding Thssthfok's last escape, the Gw'oth had helped, time and again. Sigmund finally decided that, like Thssthfok, the best place for these Gw'oth was where he could keep an eye on them. And if Sigmund's suspicions were misplaced, he really could use their help.

DON *QUIXOTE*'S REFITTING on New Terra proceeded glacially—and yet passed far too quickly. Children changed a *lot* in a few months. During Sigmund's absence, Hermes had broken an arm playing football and grown two inches. Athena had begun to read, made and changed best friends forever three times, and wheedled her mother into a pet lamb. But Penny was Penny, unchanged, as delightful and adorable as ever, as impossible to leave.

Endless meetings with Sabrina and her cabinet, endless simulations and exercises to run at the Defense Ministry and the Office of Strategic Analyses . . . the universe conspired to keep Sigmund at work late every evening. With what little time the crisis and the kids left, what passed for pillow talk concerned the slow-motion disaster with which Penelope continued to grapple. Oceanic dead zones kept spreading as, without tidal mixing, rotting vegetation sucked the oxygen from more and more of the sea. And the oxygen depletion would keep getting worse.

New Terrans would not die from the lack of tides—if they should live so long—but the handwriting was on the wall. The economy would tank from a lack of healthy algae mats and seaweed, delicacies, to export to Hearth. (Something about seaweed tickled Sigmund's memory. Seaweed, Sargasso Sea, Bermuda Triangle, the associations ran. So maybe he had another clue, a triangular island, for the well-nigh hopeless hunt for Earth.) Worst case, people here could survive on synthesized food, eating no worse than ninety-nine percent of Puppeteers.

If they should live so long.

Sigmund's family, for the fleeting, precious few minutes he saw them, reminded him daily why he must go back out among the stars, must look anywhere a solution might hide. He did not have it in him to sit, counting down the hours and days and years, planning a noble but futile war, hoping Baedeker would invent a technical solution to the Pak problem.

So instead Sigmund waited *here*, far from home. Glued, more or less, to the copilot's seat. Waiting. Waiting. Until—

"An incoming hyperwave message, Sigmund," Jeeves announced.

"On the bridge speaker," Sigmund answered. He gave Kirsten a confident smile.

"New Terra vessel *Don Quixote*, this is Ship Twenty-three. Your request to trade is accepted. We will reach your coordinates shortly. When we arrive, you will maintain a separation of six miles. Our escorts will meet your representative outside your air lock."

Kirsten leaned forward. "I have them on radar, making point nine light speed. They'll be here in fifteen minutes."

"Radio an acknowledgment, Jeeves," Sigmund said, standing. "Kirsten, the ship is yours."

Sigmund swung by the main air lock to retrieve his pressure suit and armor from a locker. With one cargo hold home to the Gw'oth and a second cargo hold a prison cell, pallets of supplies clogged the corridors. The only reasonable space aboard in which to wriggle into his vacuum gear was the relax room. He headed that way, with helmet in hand and suit draped over his arm.

Faint noises emerged from a closed hatch as Sigmund passed. He paused to listen closely. Metal clanking. The hum of electric motors. These were the sounds of a Gw'o wearing his exoskeleton. On the last voyage this storage space had served as small-arms locker. Putting an observatory there for the Gw'oth eliminated the unpleasantness of explaining why the weapons had been moved. Everyone could pretend to believe no weapons were aboard this trip.

The Gw'oth were better astronomers than anyone on New Terra. Even if Baedeker had been available for this trip, Sigmund would have authorized retrofitting this little facility. Kirsten swore the firewall between external-instrument control and the rest of the ship's network was hackproof. Her assurance was good enough for Sigmund.

Almost.

Whenever the observatory was in use, a New Terran would happen to be nearby. Today it was Omar, the newest member of the crew, searching nearby stacks of provisions.

Omar Tanaka-Singh was tall and wiry, with a square jaw and a shock of thick, dark hair. If he minded being posted on this ship rather than being captain of his own, he kept the opinion to himself. Omar had as much naval experience as any New Terran and better skill with small arms than most. And unlike Baedeker, Omar would not run at the first sign of trouble.

With Thssthfok aboard, Sigmund could not imagine the voyage passing without trouble. Unfortunately, neither could he imagine leaving the Pak under anyone else's supervision. And so Thssthfok remained aboard.

Sigmund crooked a finger: Come with me. Omar nodded and set off, in his long-legged lope, after Sigmund.

From the next deck, Sigmund used his pocket comm to reach Eric in the engine room. *This* flight the intercom was only for emergencies. The less Thssthfok overheard about the shipboard routine, the better.

While climbing into his pressure suit, Sigmund gave his final directions. Kirsten listened in from the bridge. "I can't say how long the bargaining will take. Kirsten has the bridge and is in command in my absence. Eric, keep an eye on Thssthfok's cell door. Omar, watch the observatory. And both of you armed."

Omar frowned. "That leaves *you* unsupported, Sigmund. I think you should bring one of us along."

Sigmund was about to visit a veritable city in space, miles long, with a population of millions. If the Outsiders meant him any harm—then he was dead. A companion would not change that. "Thanks, but I need you here."

"If Er'o returns to his tank that will free up one of us," Omar persisted.

Only Er'o, because the Gw'oth tended to stay in their habitat. Since Ol't'ro revealed themselves, the Gw'oth had been slightly more forthcoming. Melds attempted short of two members generally failed. Sigmund could not confirm that assertion, but it felt right to him. Or maybe the group mind simply refused to risk two pieces of itself at the same time.

Omar cleared his throat, pressing for a response.

Sigmund said, "Let Er'o stay where he is. He may learn something useful by monitoring the Outsider ship."

Throughout Known Space, and in unknowable regions beyond, the Outsiders were the source of the most advanced tech. Some tech they sold: hyperwave radio, hyperdrive, and occasionally—at a very high price—the planetary drive. Even when the Outsider devices were reproducible, such as the hyperdrive shunt and hyperwave radio, the underlying science remained illusive. Some tech, like the Einstein-space drive their ships used, the Outsiders had yet to sell.

And knowledge is power.

Before Sigmund's birth, an Outsider ship sold hyperdrive technology to a human colony. That sale saved humanity from certain defeat at the talons of the Kzinti. Who was to say another Outsider sale wouldn't tip the balance the other way, or empower other aliens to threaten Earth?

And so Sigmund had, in his time as an ARM, worried about the Outsiders. That they disclosed little about themselves only deepened the mystery—and Sigmund's fears. Throughout that era of his life, he had never encountered anyone admitting to have learned much by studying an Outsider ship.

But no previous observer had been a Gw'o scientist radio-linked with his Gw'otesht. Sigmund would not miss this opportunity—nor would he leave an armored Gw'o unsupervised on *Don Quixote*.

"And *we* might learn something, accompanying you," Eric said.

"True," Sigmund said, to show he had heard the comment. With a final bit of contortion, he got his second arm into the pressure suit. "Let's stick with the plan I outlined." He put on his helmet by way of declaring the matter closed. He opened a link to the Gw'oth shared channel. "Er'o, you should be seeing the Outsider ship now."

"Affirmative, Sigmund."

Minutes later, pressure suit sealed and safety-checked, Sigmund was cycling through the air lock to await his escorts.

ER'O SCUTTLED about his tiny observatory, tubacles groping systematically among the optical-telescope display, neutrino sensors, and readouts of antennae spanning the electromagnetic spectrum.

Sigmund had ruled out all active sensors except the occasional, very low power lidar pulses necessary anyway to maintain separation between ships. "What we can see is free," he had lectured. "Any data we take, even by a radar scan, carries a price. Maybe we can't afford it. The Outsiders are very private."

Not that Er'o *could* release a radar pulse. His readouts were slaved to the bridge, where Kirsten held control. Maybe Sigmund's explanation to him was really a reminder to her.

Subtle, that Sigmund.

In the habitat, meanwhile, Ol't'ro monitored additional instruments. All were undisclosed. Sensors fabricated to investigate hyperspace phenomena might also reveal something useful about other technologies—for like the

Outsiders, humans protected their secrets. The undisclosed sensors were passive, in another application of the principle that "what can be seen— and goes unmentioned—is free."

Sigmund's voice sounded over the Gw'oth public channel. "Er'o, you should be seeing the Outsider ship now."

"Affirmative, Sigmund." Er'o had an image to study, but only through Kirsten's intervention. The Outsider ship was moving at almost light speed. Tracking and blue-shift correction took computer correction, and computing was another of those technologies the humans declined to share.

Starlight flickered *through* the Outsider ship. Was it transparent? Not solid? Er'o exchanged inconclusive speculations with Ol't'ro.

"I'm in the air lock," Sigmund called.

"They're almost here," Kirsten answered.

In the blink of an eye, they *were* here. Stationary in space, beside *Don Quixote*. Instantaneous deceleration! And yet the Outsiders and their ship were not squashed flat. Shedding all that the kinetic energy did not reduce the ship to a glowing cloud of plasma. And none of *Don Quixote*'s instruments showed where that energy had gone.

But Ol't'ro's instruments did. . . .

THSSTHFOK LAY ON THE BARE FLOOR of his cell, his eyes closed, one ear pressed against the pinhole he had made in the deck. He listened carefully.

Sigmund was about to leave the ship. The others would be in known locations.

Thssthfok remembered every glimpse he had had of the ship, every extrapolation of layout he had made from what he had seen. He reviewed every likely route from the relax room to the bridge. He estimated the speed with which humans, spread about the ship, might intercept him.

The conversation below concluded. Footsteps receded, the heavy clomps of Sigmund heading for an air lock, the softer treads those of Eric and Omar going to their assigned posts.

Working by touch and with extreme care, Thssthfok opened the structural modulator handle he hid beneath his body. The handle was slightly rough, pitted in spots by stomach acid, but those imperfections helped him orient himself. Flipping a few tiny switches put the device into its temporary softening mode. He reassembled the handle.

Thssthfok began to exercise, his fist wrapped around the modulator.

Sit-ups. One-handed pushups. Laps around the cell. Pull-ups from the re-cessed handholds any spaceship must have for microgravity conditions. He sang as he exercised, recalling melodies of long-lost Rilchuk. Sometimes he sang proper lyrics. As often he made up nonsense sounds, pops and clicks and sibilant hisses that fit the tune.

From time to time a face appeared in the hatch window. Eventually Eric tired of watching Thssthfok or of checking on motion sensors.

As Thssthfok exercised, he rehearsed the route he would take.

He might never have a better opportunity to seize this ship.

40

Ship Twenty-three, except for the fierce spark of its artificial sun, manifested as an absence: a vaguely oblong expanse suddenly removed from the starry backdrop.

The Outsiders had mentioned a six-mile separation. Assuming that distance, the object now blocking Sigmund's view of the stars was about three miles in length. As his eyes adjusted to the open air lock's dim red glow, shimmers appeared within the darkness. He raised the magnification of his visor, and kept raising it, until details began to appear.

The Outsider vessel was an artificial star at one end and a sealed module, presumably its propulsion device, at the other, linked by an enormous metal spar. In the middle, along the spar, a forest of ribbons swooped and swirled, entangled and entwined. Any pattern to the ribbons was too alien for Sigmund to fathom.

Two figures emerged from the darkness, jetting with gas pistols toward *Don Quixote*. They reminded Sigmund, more than anything else, of giant cat-o'-nine tails. They wore protective suits, but that gear was nothing like Sigmund's. Their equipment shielded not against the vacuum and utter cold—for they lived here in the depths of interstellar space, creatures of superfluid helium—but from Sigmund himself. They had come to tow him back to their ship. Unprotected, the bit of heat seeping from Sigmund's suit would bring them to a boil. Absent the rigidity of their exoskeletons, the inertia of Sigmund's massive body would tear them apart.

"Come with us," one radioed. Each Outsider extended an armored, insulated root bundle toward Sigmund.

Sigmund offered his hands. "I'm leaving now," he radioed to his crew. Wish me luck.

He had visited an Outsider ship once before, crossing the final miles in just this manner. That experience should have eased his fears, but as his escorts towed him into the darkness, his heart pounded. How could logic matter? He was afloat in interstellar space, with his life in the "hands" of the feeblest of creatures.

And yet, terror did not overcome him.

Most Earth natives had at least a touch of flatland phobia: the instinctive recognition of home—and the reflexive dread of anyplace else. Anything odd could trigger the phobia: alien skies, wrong gravity, unfamiliar scents. Sigmund had suffered his share of attacks. He could tell with the first sniff that a planet wasn't Earth. He knew from the first glance when a pattern of stars was wrong. And he never knew how he knew.

Perhaps to bear the full brunt of flatland phobia, you had to remember what you missed, and Nessus had erased the definition of *home* from Sigmund's mind.

With a shiver, Sigmund firmly fixed his gaze on the Outsider vessel. Home was no longer Earth. Home was New Terra—to hell with its extra suns and lack of a moon and the mélange of alien smells! The lives of millions, unknowing, might hinge on him vanquishing his fears. Better to concentrate on the meeting to come. . . .

Ship Twenty-three grew and grew until it ceased to seem a ship. Now it was a great metropolis, toward which he fell in slow motion. The city spread across the sky, and the swirls of ribbon grew crisply distinct. Short lines on the ribbons became blobs became individual Outsiders.

Propelled by gentle puffs of gas, Sigmund and his escorts sank deep into the tangle of the ribbons. Each strip was several yards wide, and most were lined with Outsiders. The handles basked in the artificial sunlight; the tails disappeared into shadows cast by other ribbons. Living thermocouples, recharging.

Sigmund and his guides landed, finally, on a stretch of unoccupied ribbon. Any gravity was too weak for Sigmund to feel. He engaged magnets and his boots clanked to the surface.

One of his escorts raised a root bundle to indicate a low metal structure. "Your meeting will be inside."

Wall panels glowed, warm and bright, as Sigmund entered. Air gushed in when he closed the hatch. His sensors declared this a shirtsleeves environment—the Outsiders knew their customers—and he removed his helmet. The room was unfurnished except for a clear dome. An Outsider reclined on the floor beyond the dome.

The surroundings were just as Sigmund remembered from his previous encounter. Call it a standard meeting room. This visit, on his way inside, he had sufficiently studied the enclosure to answer a question that had nagged at him. The outer dimensions of the enclosure did not encompass the apparent space beyond the dome. The other party in the discussion was a projection of some sort.

"You are Sigmund Ausfaller?" The voice came from unseen speakers.

"Yes," Sigmund answered.

"Our colleague, Ship Fourteen, advises that you are a shrewd bargainer."

A compliment, coming from the preeminent traders in the known galaxy. Also an unsubtle reminder. By remaining deep in interstellar space, Outsider ships avoided gravitational singularities. Outsider vessels across Known Space and beyond could, and obviously did, maintain real-time communications by hyperwave radio.

During Sigmund's previous negotiations, the Outsider inside the dome had offered the ship's number when asked for a name. He (?) had commented on providing a breathable atmosphere for his guests. Sigmund's current host had not mentioned it.

So: Sigmund, too, was expected to know what had been discussed previously. "Thank you, Twenty-three. Shall we begin?"

THE OUTSIDERS WERE SCRUPULOUSLY HONEST. They honored every bargain. They paid promptly and in full. Every technology they sold worked dependably. On the occasions when they withheld the science underlying their designs (as they had with hyperspace technologies and planetary drives), they were up-front about that.

And when the value of information could not be ascertained in advance, the Outsiders could be trusted to pay fairly after disclosure. Sigmund's news was like that.

The fair value was zero.

Other Outsider ships had *already* spotted the threat onrushing from the galactic core. Identifying the attackers as Pak, humanity's cousins, might be news. It wasn't the sort of news to predispose anyone favorably toward Sigmund's kind.

Sigmund had crossed the light-years with one hope: That his news would buy help. Not direct military assistance, for the Outsider vessels were cities, not warships. Not aid in finding Earth. The Outsiders would surely honor their agreement with the Concordance never to disclose to any New Terrans the location of Known Space, nor to give any Known Space race even a clue to the existence of the New Terrans.

But new technology could make all the difference—*if* Sigmund had had a means to pay. He hadn't. He said, hoping his desperation did not show, "Twenty-three, it's in your own interest to help. These fleets are attacking every advanced civilization they pass. Your ships will be no different."

"But they *are* different." Twenty-three wriggled his root bundles a bit as he spoke. "Our ships are very mobile."

And indeed, the few Outsider ships known to New Terra could easily evade the Pak. Ship Twenty-three could resume near light speed as quickly as it had shed that velocity. If it detected a weapon coming its way, it needed only an instant to stop. A Pak kinetic-kill weapon, captive to its deadly inertia, would whiz past harmlessly. The Outsiders were safe.

But tanj it! For planet dwellers, the Outsider ship drive offered the *perfect* solution to the Pak threat.

The scenario was crystal clear in Sigmund's mind. Add an Outsider normal-space drive to a standard, hyperdrive-equipped starship. Then by the numbers: One, jump to near light speed. Two, use hyperspace to cross the light-years to the Pak fleets. Three, return to normal space with all that near light velocity. Four, using the Outsider drive, make any necessary course corrections in an instant. Five, unleash myriads of unstoppable kinetic weapons. With the ship moving so fast, throwing rocks would suffice.

His ship would be back in hyperspace, racing away, before the Pak ramscoops saw what was coming at them. Repeat as needed.

And then it struck Sigmund: *Whatever* he might have had to offer in trade, this negotiation had been doomed from the outset. The Outsiders would never sell the secret of the reactionless drives that moved their ships. Those ships would be almost as defenseless against Sigmund's tactics as the Pak.

Which left what? Maybe he could further Baedeker's work. "Can you help us improve the performance of our planetary drive? Show us how to run drives in tandem? Then we, too, could be more mobile."

More squirming of roots. "Our regrets, Sigmund. We cannot comment."

Sigmund felt a headache coming on. He rubbed his temples. "Why not, Twenty-three?"

"We are not at liberty to say."

Because anything you said would be a hint. Sigmund pressed his temples and tried to think. Turning up the planetary drive or running them in tandem related, somehow, to things the Outsiders would not discuss. The secret science behind the planetary drive? Something about the reactionless ship drive? Sigmund *knew* the two were related—and also that he had only his paranoia to bring him to that conclusion.

Regardless, a clue for Baedeker.

"Is your business completed?" Twenty-three asked.

From Sigmund's days as an accountant, two lives ago, an ancient aphorism asserted itself. Borrow a thousand dollars—whatever a dollar might have been—and the bank owns you. Borrow a million dollars, and you own the bank.

Sigmund said, "It's in your interest to help my people defend ourselves and our friends. After the danger has passed and you return to this part of the galaxy, you'll want trading partners. And how much do the Puppeteers already owe your people?"

It was a rhetorical question. Puppeteers had been in debt to the Outsiders for eons, since purchasing the planetary drive to save Hearth when its sun prepared to swell into a red giant. New Terra was too poor to get such credit.

Just maybe, the Concordance owned the bank.

Beyond the domes, roots wriggled at the fastest rate yet. Agitation or laughter, or merely sign language for the creature's natural environment? There was no way to tell.

Twenty-three finally spoke. "You are correct, Sigmund. Loss of our trading partners would be disadvantageous."

"Then help us help ourselves!"

"How?"

"Teach us to use our drives more efficiently. If our worlds escape, we'll *all* come out ahead." Sigmund promised himself he would reveal nothing until Nike swore to transfer a planetary drive to the Gw'oth. Loss of a farm world would be a small recompense for Ol't'ro's contributions.

"The drives are already as efficient as we can safely make them," Twenty-three insisted.

Uh-huh. "Better eat into the safety margin than swallow a planet-killer weapon." Even a Puppeteer would see the logic in that trade-off.

"A moment, Sigmund."

Twenty-three's roots writhed more frenetically than ever. Consultation, Sigmund decided. The moment became minutes.

"It can't be done," Twenty-three announced. "If more energy is applied, the drive becomes dangerously unstable."

"Unstable how?"

"Vast destruction, Sigmund."

Now what? Sigmund was running out even of crazy ideas. "Lend the Puppeteers and New Terra planetary drives. Teach us to use them in tandem."

"We *have* no more drives." Somehow, Twenty-three managed to sound plaintive. "Not that it would matter. We have never successfully used two drives to move a single mass."

Was Baedeker experimenting somewhere expendable? He was a Puppeteer, so of course he was. But he had not heard the fear and doubt in Twenty-three's "voice" . . .

Sigmund said, "Twenty-three, you're not telling me something."

More wriggling of roots, strikingly different. This time, Sigmund felt certain, it denoted ironic laughter. "There is *much* we do not tell you, Sigmund. We will share this. The planetary drive employs great energy. *Great* energy. It is very challenging to control. We start many such drives for each unit that completes production. The Concordance accepted its drives one at a time."

Doubtless believing that they had managed their debt by staging the deliveries.

An audio recorder sat in a pocket of Sigmund's pressure suit. In theory it was capturing this conversation. Almost certainly, the Outsiders were suppressing it. Sigmund hoped he could remember this exchange in detail. There were surely useful clues here for Baedeker.

Sigmund said, "What about relocating a drive, perhaps from a farm world to Hearth?"

Writhing again of the agitated variety. "You must not try that. To operate two drives in proximity is to make both . . . unstable."

Unstable and great energy—a bad combination. Sigmund guessed, "*You* don't know how the drives work, do you?"

"We sell only the device, not the underlying science," Twenty-three said. "The terms of sale were honest."

And the drives *had* worked, without incident. So the Outsiders were no different than any other species—they, too, used technologies imperfectly understood.

Sigmund picked up his helmet. "I guess we are done. Wish us luck."

"If your business is done," Twenty-three said, "we have something you might find interesting."

41

Thssthfok's dashing about his cell occasionally brought him past the hatch. Eric was still visible through the window, not especially attentive. Breeders were like that, Thssthfok remembered: easily lulled by routine, easily fooled by their expectations.

While he did more one-handed push-ups, hiding a patch of floor with his body, Thssthfok stroked the area with the structural modulator clutched in his free hand. He continued singing as he worked, with lots of hisses and pops. Strip by strip he softened an area large enough to pull himself through.

To judge from the etched areas on the modulator, swallowing the device again would be a bad idea. Thssthfok thumbed off the modulator, jumped back to his feet, and did more pull-ups—during which he pushed the modulator through the permanently softened spot behind a handhold. If Eric was listening, the wall's soft pop would surely go unnoticed amid Thssthfok's pop-filled singing.

Taking another lap around the cell, Thssthfok glanced out the hatch window. Eric remained preoccupied or disinterested. Thssthfok dropped to the floor—

And plunged an arm through the altered spot in the floor. A recessed handhold in the relax-room ceiling below gave him the leverage to pull himself through.

Now safety lay in speed. Thssthfok dashed through the relax room into the corridor and into the nearby stairwell. Taking the stairs three at a time, he scaled the flights between three decks. He burst onto the top deck and was in the bridge before Kirsten could turn around at the crash of the stairwell door.

Logic decreed that the bright red button beside the door would close it. Thssthfok slapped it, and the door sprang shut.

"Jeeves! Turn up—" Kirsten shouted.

Thssthfok grabbed her throat and squeezed. Her order trailed off in an inarticulate gurgle as he pressed her down into her seat. Easing his stranglehold just enough so that she could breathe, he took the other seat. It was the only place from which he could reach the console.

Fools! Teaching him to read irrelevant material *also* taught him to read the bridge controls.

The console was deceptively empty. Most functions must be handled by the computer, whether by keyboard or voice command. Those would take time to decode, with his hostage's coerced assistance, if necessary.

Still, the console had some ordinary buttons, sliders, and toggles. Those would be for emergency functions, as simple and accessible as possible. He found the emergency-hatches release, clearly labeled. *That* should keep the others at bay for a while. He slapped the button—

And an invisible something grabbed him. A force field. He could not move! He could scarcely breathe.

Panting from exertion, her chest heaving, Kirsten pried loose Thssthfok's grip one finger at a time. Strain as he might, he could not tighten his grip. He could not stop her.

"Jeeves," Kirsten rasped, "get Eric up here." She climbed from her chair, out of Thssthfok's impotent reach, and stared with rage in her eyes. "Sigmund assumed you would try for the bridge again if you escaped. So he set a trap."

An elementary trap, Thssthfok thought, with the reading material as bait—and I fell for it. Sigmund was clever, and that made him dangerous.

When he stayed as still as possible, Thssthfok found the restraint eased off just a little. A field to protect the pilot from collisions or turbulence, minimally modified so as not to relax. He could breathe more easily now; even, he guessed, speak if he should have something to say.

Stars drifted across the main view port, sign of the ship's slow roll. Then *something*—a vessel? a city in space?—came into view. Something unlike anything Thssthfok had ever seen. And it kept coming. An artificial sun, tiny but blindingly bright, shone at one end.

The structure was either very near or very large—and given that fusion flame, it was hard to imagine it was close. He stared at it until Eric appeared on the bridge.

Eric took one look at Kirsten massaging her neck, bruises already starting to form. The sizzle of his stunner drowned out whatever he snarled.

42

"Something I might find interesting," Sigmund echoed dubiously. The end of the world approached, and Twenty-three refused to help. Yet he expected Sigmund to go shopping.

The thing of it was, the Outsiders often had wondrous things to sell.

"An old human ship," Twenty-three clarified. "Derelict. We found it adrift in space."

"Where?" Sigmund asked.

"We are not allowed to say."

Sigmund had expected that answer, but it hardly hurt to ask. In a trade deal with the Puppeteers, Ship Fourteen had committed all Outsiders to deny New Terrans clues to the location of Earth and its colonies. An old derelict human ship came very close to such a clue, didn't it?

Maybe Twenty-three *did* want to help.

Sigmund knew of one other such incredible coincidence. But Puppeteers had not "happened" upon *Long Pass*, wandering deep in interstellar space. They had traced a message back to the ramscoop that sent it. And then they bred slaves from the frozen embryos aboard.

"Adrift in space, you say," Sigmund said. It was as implausible as the fairy tale the Puppeteer had told their servants.

Twenty-three shifted position. "We understand your skepticism, Sigmund. No, we did not happen upon a ship. We detected a relativistic gravitational anomaly, which we found to be a neutronium object with the mass of a small planet. The ship orbited the larger mass."

Sigmund blinked. Nature required a supernova explosion to produce neutronium. Only once, to his knowledge, had anyone made neutronium artificially. Julian Forward used *his* neutronium to bulk up a quantum black hole, with which he terrorized Sol system for months. And though Sigmund never discovered the specifics, Forward had had surreptitious Puppeteer backing.

On the bright side, Sigmund remembered Forward getting eaten by his own black hole, and taking the secret of his process with him.

A large, fast-moving neutronium mass made an exceptional beacon.

"I wouldn't mind looking," Sigmund answered cautiously. He lifted his helmet.

"That is not necessary," Twenty-three said. With a wave of a root bunch it evoked a hologram inside its dome.

Sigmund knew one thing for certain about Earth and its colonies. They were *far* away. Had it been otherwise, Nessus would never have started a scout program using human Colonists. It stood to reason the salvaged ship was a starship, probably a hyperdrive vessel.

It wasn't.

How could a little fusion-powered Belter singleship, something a solo prospector might use in the inner solar system, end up far from Earth? How, when, and where had the ship assumed an orbit around the neutronium mass? How had the singleship reached relativistic speed—no *way* it could carry enough fuel—to overtake the neutronium mass? Where did the neutronium come from?

With too many questions already roiling his thoughts, Sigmund spotted something shiny at the singleship's bow. It looked out of place. Boot electromagnets clomping, he started around the dome to inspect the holo from another angle.

"You now have control of the image," Twenty-three said. "It will follow your hand motions."

Sigmund extended an arm experimentally. The holo ship receded. He rotated his hand, and the image rotated to follow. Something gleamed at him through the cockpit canopy. The age-pitted hull looked all the darker in contrast. Strange. He brought his hand toward his chest; the ship zoomed closer.

Inside the cockpit, as shiny as quicksilver, a smooth, ovoid surface hid the space where the pilot would sit. Staring at a holo Sigmund could not be certain, but that certainly looked like total reflection. Could that be a *stasis field* inside the singleship?

Twenty-three would know. Feigned ignorance could be a kind of help, to keep the price affordable for Sigmund. For stasis had but one use: freezing time inside to preserve something valuable.

Eons ago, two ancient races had waged a conflict of galactic extermination. Little remained from that era but a few artifacts preserved for eternity within stasis fields. Most items recovered from stasis defied understanding. All embodied technology of frightening potency—often weapons caches.

Stasis fields reflected *everything*, from visible light to the hardest gamma ray. A stasis field even reflected neutrinos, which was why pilots routinely deep-radar pinged every solar system they approached. A person could live in princely style on the standard ARM bounty for a stasis box—and it was a rare decade that saw the ARM making that payout.

Still, compared to a huge mass of neutronium (which, coincidentally, also stopped most neutrinos), the ship that had orbited it, and whatever waited inside, were but the ribbon around a priceless package. If Twenty-three chose to overlook a stasis field, Sigmund would not ask.

With slow, careful gestures, Sigmund turned the holo for study. The registration plaque came into view, the ship's ID a mere five digits long. This ship was *old*.

The feel of Earth, its appearance, the constellations in its night sky . . . all were lost from his mind. Instead, useless numbers cluttered his memory. PINs for bank accounts of a former life. Bits of obscure tax rules, and entire tax tables. The addresses of former residences, but not the cities where he had lived. Too many years as an accountant had made numbers and patterns second nature to Sigmund. And maybe that much harder to erase, if Nessus had tried.

The five digits on the registry plaque ignited rockets and flares in Sigmund's head. He knew those numbers!

This was not merely an antique vessel misplaced in space and time. This was the singleship in which, more than half a millennium earlier, Jack Brennan had encountered Phssthpok! Sigmund had seen the official registration in Lucas Garner's deposition. But Brennan-monster had evaded ARM custody and vanished—with *this* ship and a key module of Phssthpok's starship.

If this was a stasis field, the singleship might preserve—to save New Terra in its hour of need—the only known human protector.

TWENTY-THREE, IN ITS OWN WAY, might be helping. It still would not give away the relic.

So what did Sigmund have with which to bargain? Discovery of the Pak invasion, already dismissed as old news and without value.

And Gw'oth!

"I would trade information for the ship," Sigmund suggested.

Roots writhed. "If you have something more useful than your last disclosure."

With a flick of his hand, Sigmund banished the singleship image. "How about a solar system filled with new customers? A young technological society, newly spacefaring."

"That is an acceptable price," Twenty-three agreed, "if, in fact, you identify a customer with whom we are unfamiliar."

Sigmund nodded. "On that condition, we have a deal." He quoted the coordinates of the Gw'oth solar system.

Roots wriggled and thrashed at the fastest rate yet. "Very clever, Sigmund. These coordinates lie in the path of the invaders. The customer whom you offer will be destroyed before we can reach them. Do you mock us?"

"The Gw'oth are quite real," Sigmund said. "If my people find a way to survive, we will do our best to save them, too."

Twenty-three replied, "We will help you transport the purchased item to your ship. For both our benefits, let us hope you survive."

43

Quite possibly the stasis field in the singleship hid a potential ally—not that Sigmund entirely accepted the concept of a friendly protector. In practice, the field could hide *anything*.

And so he fretted and stewed for ten days before finalizing his plans. All the while the singleship, like some anachronistic remora, clung to the side of *Don Quixote*. With one cargo hold a prison and the other filled with Gw'oth, Sigmund could not have taken aboard his purchase even if such had been his wish.

Ship Twenty-three had carried the singleship behind a thick metal shield, towed by a very long tether. Those precautions made sense to Sigmund. The ancient singleship had been adrift, without maintenance, for centuries. And now? If anything were to trigger the fusion drive, better the potential H-bomb be outside *Don Quixote*'s General Products hull. The shock wave would still liquefy everyone within—but any chance was better than none.

Of course the Outsiders had not known whose ship this was. The singleship might be entirely safe, rebuilt for the ages by Brennan.

Two of the ten days were lost in Einstein space, hanging between the stars to maintain hyperwave links. To open a stasis field took specialized equipment few ships had any reason to carry. So Sigmund wasted a day trying to find a New Terran who knew anything about breaking open a stasis field. In hindsight, the surprise would have been success. New Terra had very few ships, and they had only flown for a few years. They had yet to encounter a stasis box.

Sigmund spent much of that day wondering how much Baedeker knew about stasis fields. Everything Twenty-three had had to say suggested Baedeker's quest was futile. He would never master the planetary drives.

Baedeker should be *here*, tanj it, helping.

During the second day, Sabrina arranged for an expert to consult with Eric. That expert turned out to be—Baedeker. The real-time connection when he called meant the Puppeteer was working outside a singularity, somewhere in deep space.

Evidently, not every unbelievable thing happened around, or to, Sigmund.

DON QUIXOTE SAT on a planet with a breathable atmosphere, unremarkable except for its relative proximity to Ship Twenty-three. This was a young world, its oceans teeming with single-celled life but its continents utterly barren. The nearest possible source of food, if it was even edible, was seaborne sludge a thousand miles away. This was not a place Brennan-monster would choose to be left stranded.

With a delicate touch Sigmund could only envy, Kirsten had set *Don Quixote*, the singleship still lashed to its side, onto a bleak plain. "Ready when you are," she sent over the comm.

Sigmund and Eric waited at the main air lock. "Copy that," Eric replied.

"Check my gear," Sigmund said.

"I have," Eric said, reaching for the lock controls. "You're clean."

Sigmund raised his arms. "Do it again."

Eric shrugged. "You're the boss." One by one he inspected Sigmund's battle armor, opening every pocket and examining every belt clip. He patted down Sigmund as a double check. "Nothing."

Sigmund pointed with a boot tip at the paraphernalia piled on the airlock floor. "And anything here I don't need?"

"No, Sigmund," Eric said, a touch impatiently.

Too bad. They would do this as carefully as possible.

Sigmund cycled through the air lock and stepped down to the sterile surface. He shuttled gear around *Don Quixote*, raising clouds of orange dust with every step, to where the singleship clung. Desolation stretched to the horizon in every direction. "Just a desert," he muttered, lying to himself, trying not to look into the distance. Earth had deserts, after all. On his final trip, he shut the outer hatch behind himself. "Disable access from outside," he directed.

"Copy that," Kirsten radioed. "How's our position?"

"Close. The singleship is about one foot above the ground."

"One foot, Sigmund. Copy that. Commencing adjustment."

Ever so slowly, under precise thruster control, *Don Quixote* rolled along its main axis. The hard ground beneath the ship crunched and groaned. "Stop," Sigmund called.

"What's the margin?" Kirsten asked.

"The singleship is still two inches off the ground," Sigmund estimated.

"I can do better," Kirsten said.

"Not necessary." Sigmund took the clamp release from his pile of equipment. "It can't be that fragile." *It* meant the singleship, which might contain clues to the location of Sol system. No bump—up to and including the fusion drive going off—could hurt whatever waited inside the stasis field.

Five sturdy cables bound the singleship to *Don Quixote*'s hull. Sigmund released the clamps in pairs, leaving the center clamp for last. The remaining cable held the singleship aloft although, squealing against *Don Quixote*'s hull, one end of the antique vessel sagged to the ground. "Releasing the last cable," he radioed.

Cables whistled through their clamps. The singleship thumped to the ground. Sigmund left the clamps unfastened. "The payload is down."

"I'll come out and help," Eric radioed.

"No," Sigmund said firmly. They had been over that, repeatedly. He unfolded a tripod and set up his camera. The camera opened a radio link; with some back-and-forth with Kirsten, he got the camera properly aimed at the singleship. "I'm going in."

The little prospecting ship looked inexpensive, simple, and reliable. Hooks and clamps, all presently unused, dotted the hull. The ship predated thruster technology; instead, it had compressed gas or chemical-fuel attitude jets (Sigmund could not decide which) jutting at all angles. A massive nozzle aft served the fusion drive. There was no air lock; the canopy pivoted open for access. The pilot would always wear a spacesuit.

Viewed by direct sunlight, the surface glittering through the canopy shone more brightly than ever. It reflected light, radar, even neutrinos. No doubt about it: This *was* a stasis field.

Sigmund released the latch. The canopy rose slowly, hinged at the nose end, suggesting a giant clamshell. The stasis field stood revealed, encompassing the pilot's chair and much of the instrument console. Nothing in view looked like a stasis control.

Was the OFF switch right in front of him? Quite likely. No one had yet made sense of Thssthfok's gadgets; Brennan as a protector was supposedly much smarter.

Sigmund set an emergency force-field generator (once again liberated from *Don Quixote*'s bridge—Thssthfok would not fall twice for that ruse) onto an unprotected stretch of console ledge. Eric had spliced a remote control into the restraint module. Sigmund armed the remote; the green LED lit as the red LED went dark.

"Connectivity check on the restraint device," Sigmund radioed.

"Online," Kirsten reported.

Time to find out who or what waited within.

Sigmund picked up the improvised stasis-field interrupter. It felt awkward in his hand. It looked half melted, like something of Puppeteer design.

As it was. When Sigmund and Baedeker met with Nike, most of Baedeker's gear had remained on *Don Quixote*. Possibly, Baedeker had not yet decided to defect. Regardless, he had left behind a stasis-field generator in his cabin. For medical emergencies or as one more way to flee, Sigmund supposed.

After his escape from Hearth, Sigmund had searched Baedeker's cabin—after cutting out Baedeker's biometrically controlled lock with an oxy-fuel torch. It was hard to miss an active stasis field, but a quiescent stasis-field generator was another story. He had not recognized the Puppeteer field generator in Baedeker's abandoned luggage. None of them had.

Reconfiguring the generator to collapse a stasis field was trivial once Baedeker told Eric how. Sigmund read that cooperation as a sign Baedeker's own project did not go well.

Alas, the improvised stasis-field collapser had an extremely short range. Someone practically had to touch the stasis field. Sigmund aimed the device, clumsy in his hand. Finagle! It was time *something* went well.

He glanced over his shoulder to make sure he wasn't blocking the camera. "Kirsten, are you set?"

"Ready when you are," she said.

The plan was straightforward. Drop the stasis field and replace it immediately with a restraint field. Activate the restraint remotely—because they *could*—lest anything prevent Sigmund from triggering it. And if *everything* went to hell, just launch. The singleship's mass now pinned the cables; the bindings would pull free through the unfastened clamps. Then take any necessary action from the air, whether with laser weapons or stunners.

If events progressed that far, more than likely no action would be necessary. Despite Kirsten's undoubted finesse, the fringing fields from the thrusters would probably crush Sigmund and—whatever.

"On my mark, Kirsten. Three . . . two . . . one . . . mark."

The stasis field shimmered, rippled, and vanished. Two gloved arms shot up and grabbed Sigmund's armor around the throat. The restraint field kicked in. The air became concrete around him and his assailant—

Freezing Sigmund and the singleship's pilot, face-to-face.

Sigmund stared, and not at a protector. Who *was* this woman?

EYEWITNESS TO HISTORY

44

Alice Jordan hunched over the relax-room table, beset by tics, clutching a bulb of hot tea, lost in thought. Lost, too, in space, with which Sigmund empathized. And misplaced also in time, which he could not begin to fathom.

"There I was," Alice burst out, "deep in the Oort Cloud. Alone in my ship. Nothing and no one anywhere near."

As she had said, with slightly different wordings, in varying tones of anger and confusion and awe, using more than the occasional enigmatic expression, more times than Sigmund could remember. One iteration had referred cryptically to shell shock. He would have guessed Penny's work stories had exposed him to every possible obscure crustacean reference, but evidently not.

She kept paraphrasing and circumlocuting, as though searching for the secret incantation that would restore her life. And why wouldn't she? Her life had been turned upside down.

For entirely different reasons, Sigmund was as depressed as she. He tried to hide his disappointment. The stasis field *might* have held someone with the knowledge to find Earth. Using navigational beacons, Alice could find her way around the solar system. Alas, she had no idea how to find Sol itself. Her memory might brim with hints and clues, but extracting that data and putting them to good use was a long-term project.

Just then, it seemed unlikely New Terra would have a long term.

Her Spanglish fell somewhere between the twenty-second-century English Jeeves knew, and that *Long Pass* had brought to New Terra, and the Interworld with which Sigmund had grown up. It wasn't familiar, exactly, but he learned without much difficulty to understand her.

"My fusion drive was running flat out. Sol was a distant, brilliant spark straight ahead. Kobold had *just* winked out behind me. And then"—she jabbed a bony finger into Sigmund's chest—"you were in my face. Wearing armor. On a freaking desert planet."

Kobold was merely the latest obscurity in the on-and-off torrent of words. From context, a place name: an object in the Oort Cloud. But as with Sigmund dubbing this ship *Don Quixote*, names had significance.

Kobold? Jeeves knew kobolds as figures from ancient folklore, like brownies, pixies, and elves. And surely not coincidentally, kobolds were household protectors.

As Alice rattled on, holding shock at bay with words, Sigmund studied her. She was much taller than he. Much darker, too, with space-darkened skin. From those clues alone, and the ship in which she had been found, he would have guessed she was a Belter. Her head, shaved except for a two-inch-wide, cockatoolike Belter crest, made guessing unnecessary.

Part of Sigmund struggled to get past the past: that a Belter had once killed him. Alice had had nothing to do with that.

(It could have been Brennan-monster inside the stasis field. But it wasn't, and no superhuman mind would be relieving Sigmund of responsibility for New Terra's fate. Maybe he was disappointed about that. Maybe he was thankful. Sorting out his feelings could wait.)

"And this ship! By comparison, every ship, every structure, I've ever seen is so much cardboard and duct tape. Excepting Brennan's constructions, of course."

Brennan! Sigmund managed not to react. It *wasn't* just the coincidence of the singleship.

Don Quixote now raced at maximum acceleration from the planet on which Alice had been freed to where they could engage hyperdrive. Next stop: New Terra. Sigmund meant to know a *lot* more before he got there.

"Alice," Sigmund interrupted gently. Her life had been turned upside down, but he needed information.

Kirsten shot Sigmund a dirty look. *Don Quixote* was on autopilot for now. Eric and Omar were also in the relax room, observing expectantly. Ol't'ro netted in to watch and listen.

"Alice," Sigmund repeated.

She turned his way.

"You've shared a lot," Sigmund said. That was an understatement. Alice had talked, in fits and starts—compulsively, maybe cathartically—since Eric unfroze her. Not systematically, hence almost certainly not completely.

"I know this is overwhelming, Alice. That's why it's important to go over everything methodically, however long that takes, while it remains fresh in your mind. So please bear with me. I was once an ARM."

She smiled crookedly. "Understood. I was a goldskin not that long ago." The smile became wistful and then vanished. She straightened in her chair. "Well, it feels recent. In my mind, I left Kobold only a few hours ago. Somehow I know it's been much longer. Ask away, Sigmund, if it'll help you make sense of things. It may help me, too."

"Goldskin?" Omar asked.

"The law-enforcement organization of the outer solar system," Sigmund explained. If Alice was telling the truth, New Terra's pool of veterans had just doubled. "Their uniforms were gold-colored pressure suits. Hence, colloquially, goldskins."

"Makes sense," Omar said.

"Alice, from the beginning please," Sigmund prompted.

"The beginning? I guess that's 2341." She looked about with an expression that somehow encompassed all of *Don Quixote*. "Seeing your tech, that was a long time ago."

By Sigmund's best estimate, at least three centuries. And yet that was two centuries *after* Brennan-monster disappeared. The situation was more than a little confusing. "Your story first," Sigmund suggested gently.

Alice showed her crooked smile again. "Yeah, I know the routine. Pump me dry first. All right, back to the beginning. Vacationing on Earth, I met a flatlander named Roy Truesdale. *He* had a story: four months stolen from his life. He went hiking one day, only to wake up with four months gone. . . ."

Trailing off again, wondering how much time she had lost. She would *not* like the answer. "We'll brief you later," Sigmund promised. "Please go on."

"Roy had gone to the ARM, of course. They eventually identified two similar abductions, decades apart." She looked at Sigmund expectantly, as in: You say you're an ARM. Why don't you know? When he didn't comment, she shrugged. "Roy wanted to know whether the goldskins knew of similar cases. And when I dug into old files, we did."

"And?"

"My bosses no more wanted to admit to the pattern than the ARM." Alice paused to sip her tea. "Roy described whoever was behind the kidnapping as too considerate for an alien and too powerful for a human."

"Which left?" Sigmund asked.

"Brennan," she said simply.

THE PROTECTOR JACK BRENNAN HAD EVADED ARMs and goldskins alike—more than two centuries before Alice's last admitted memory. Both military services had tracked his ship into the dark fringes of the solar system. He had stayed in the Oort Cloud for a while before—the ignition of his ramscoop unmistakable—launching toward . . .

Once again, Sigmund's memory failed him. One of the interstellar colonies. Regardless, Brennan was never to be heard from again.

Lucas Garner had recorded the whole incident in ARM files. By rights, the protector had starved to death. Other than a small stock of tree-of-life root that had been entrusted to Brennan (he had to eat, after all), the only supply for thousands of light-years had been in ARM custody—and they had incinerated it.

As a goldskin, Alice would have had access as good as Sigmund's to the suppressed history of the Brennan-and-Phssthpok incident. (Why kid himself? Better information. Except for Lucas Garner, *everyone* who had gotten a good look at Phssthpok's ship or had dealt with the Brennan-monster had been a Belter.) She had shared what she knew with her new friend, Roy.

And then the rampant speculation began.

What if Brennan had survived? Maybe the ramscoop was a decoy while he remained in the Oort Cloud. Brennan was, after all, a protector. Who but the billions in Sol system—most of humanity—would he protect? He had the superior intellect of a protector, the technology embodied by the Pak ship, and the diffuse but boundless resources of the Oort Cloud.

Phssthpok would not have come thousands of light-years without knowing everything possible about tree-of-life and its virus. Brennan might have learned enough from Phssthpok—before killing him—to produce the virus. Then why *couldn't* Brennan have made a home for himself at the edge of the solar system?

And if *all* that guesswork was true, it wasn't a big stretch that Brennan would commit the occasional abduction to assess the progress of his unsuspecting wards.

Alice and Roy had piled extrapolation upon surmise upon conjecture. No one in authority would approve an expedition into the vastness of the

Oort Cloud to pursue such a will-o'-the-wisp. But during his lost months, Roy's great-to-the-fourth grandmother had died. Roy, like all "Greatly Stelle's" heirs, came into a lot of money.

Enough to buy a ship.

And so, deep in the Oort Cloud, en route to the region where, two centuries earlier, Brennan-monster had once tarried, a mysterious force had seized Alice and Roy's ship.

EXHAUSTION CLAIMED ALICE LONG BEFORE her debrief was complete. Kirsten led away their guest to get some rest. *Don Quixote* had no unused cabins, only lockers, storerooms, and pantries that might be unloaded and repurposed. Sigmund guessed he would find Alice in Kirsten and Eric's cabin, and his friends camping out in a storeroom.

Kirsten took a surprisingly long time to reappear. "We had a detour to the autodoc," Kirsten explained. "No, she's fine."

Sigmund frowned. "Then why—"

"She thought she might be pregnant. She *is* pregnant."

"This Roy Truesdale fellow?" Sigmund guessed.

Kirsten nodded. "So she says."

Then Alice had lost her space, time, *and* the father of her child—and somehow, the relationship with Truesdale had not come up. Professional detachment? She was, after all, a goldskin. Or maybe simple Belter stoicism. The Belters Sigmund had known, so determined to be self-sufficient, so fiercely independent—so *cold*—often seemed to him like a breed apart.

45

Alice finally reappeared in the relax room, wearing a freshly synthed jump-suit. Despite almost twelve hours of sleep she did not look rested. Belter prickly independence be damned, maybe she was human after all.

Sigmund and Alice had the room to themselves. Kirsten split her time between the bridge and trying to parse a data dump from the singleship. Eric, Omar, and most of the Gw'oth had more pressing duties: holding together *Don Quixote*. They listened in by radio but were too busy to contribute much.

The normal-space region that protected a starship from hyperspace hugged the hull. The bigger the enclosed volume, the more energy the field consumed. Expanding the field to encompass the strapped-on single-ship took energy. Lots of it. The problem boiled down to basic geometry: Expanding the radius of the more-or-less cylindrical bubble by a mere ten feet increased the enclosed volume more than sixfold.

Locally stretching the protective field to add a small volume around the singleship would have been far more energy efficient. Eric—never shy about his engineering skills—balked. The tiniest, briefest gap in the field could kill them all instantly. He insisted that to safely fine-tune the field's shape would take a fully equipped shipyard. About the time Eric likened an energy-efficient localized field expansion to an aneurism, Sigmund lost his interest in trying.

So the ship's fusion generator was redlined, even with every nonessential function disabled. Now the essential systems had begun to hiccough from marginal power. The Gw'oth were supplying a trickle of excess power from the tiny fusion reactor in their habitat, and looking for ways to economize and provide more. Jeeves was on call, to be wakened once a shift to run an independent diagnostic and then shut himself down.

Don Quixote would reach New Terra with its main tanks drained and its reserves mostly gone. Well, reserves existed for unforeseen circumstances. The secrets they might find in the old singleship certainly qualified.

They could refuel along the way, sieving deuterium from any world with an ocean. More fuel would do nothing to unburden the overtaxed power plant—only prolong the strain. And time spent refueling was time they could never get back. At least the stepping disc they had installed in the singleship gave them easy access. Left to herself, Kirsten would be living in the old ship, trying to make sense of its computers.

With Sigmund's assistance Alice heaped a tray with synthed food. Eating for two, he remembered. To conserve a bit of energy, shipboard temperature was barely above freezing and vapor hung above her meal. He turned up his jumpsuit heater, wondering if her odd choices reflected cuisine changes over the centuries or pregnancy cravings. They sat and Alice dug in.

"So, Kobold," Sigmund began. "Your average hollowed-out rock?"

"No! A marvel, actually. Like a park, with a beautiful blue sky." She looked up from a mound of eggs scrambled with peppers. "I know that sounds impossible and that anything big enough to hold an atmosphere should have been spotted from the inner system. But Kobold wasn't big. It was an artifact, not a world, not even round. Picture a grassy, lumpy doughnut with a mass of neutronium at the center. Brennan said the neutronium had a surface gravity of eight million gees."

Neutronium! Probably the same mass around which Twenty-three had found Alice's ship orbiting. How that could be, like how Alice's ship had gotten so far from home, surpassed Sigmund's understanding. Maybe Baedeker could connect the dots, but Sigmund was not about to involve any Puppeteer. Whether or not Alice *could* help Sigmund find Earth, the Puppeteers would surely fear she would.

Sigmund knew all too well the extremes Puppeteers took to prevent New Terrans from phoning home.

"And Brennan was using gravity generators like toys. That's why, as remote as Kobold was, its climate was Earthlike: a gravity lens that magnified the sun. Somehow he scattered the sunlight to make Kobold's sky blue."

Sigmund eventually interrupted a long recitation of the wonders on Kobold. How many demonstrations did he need that a human protector was impossibly smart? "Why were you on the singleship? Where are Truesdale and his ship?"

Alice swallowed heavily, set down her fork, and slid away her plate.

(Morning sickness? Unlikely, given that she had wanted confirmation she was pregnant. Not to mention the quantity of food she had gathered.) "Roy went with Brennan to get help. Brennan had spotted more Pak coming. The gravity lens, again. He used it in a super-powerful telescope. There was a fleet on its way, a couple hundred or so ships in a tidy hexagonal array. And just before I left, Brennan glimpsed another wave farther back."

Had Vesta actually told Sigmund the truth? Could Earth be . . . gone? Bombarded back to a new stone age? Sigmund's stomach knotted. And how in Finagle's name could ARM files have failed to show Brennan returning?

Something didn't add up. "Back up, Alice. Where did they go for help? Not anywhere in Sol system." Or I'd have found clues in the ARM files.

"Wunderland. Brennan wanted to draw attention away from Sol."

Sigmund had been to Wunderland, the main settled world in . . . he didn't remember where. He diverted her onto a survey of the interstellar colonies in her era. She spouted names, bits of physical description, types of stars, planetary neighbors, even approximate distances from Sol and each other. Vague as it was, she knew more about Earth's locale than Sigmund and Jeeves together had reconstructed in years.

Wunderland. Plateau. Home. Jinx. We Made It. Almost every word flooded Sigmund's mind with associations. No navigational data—life wasn't that kind—but still a plethora of details to refill voids in his memories.

Alice began fidgeting impatiently, and Sigmund returned to her story. "If Brennan and Truesdale left in your time, they'd have gotten to Wunderland long ago. Didn't happen."

Alice fought off a shiver. "So when is now?"

This wasn't the time to get into Sigmund's own complicated past. "I left Earth in 2652."

She managed to both blink in surprise and slump in relief. "Brennan said the first wave of Pak would arrive in 172 or 173 years. Somehow Brennan and Roy did it. Stopped them."

How long had Alice been in stasis? She claimed to be from 2341, a century and a half before Sigmund's birth. He didn't know enough about that period, especially events a Belter might notice, to put her assertion to the test.

He had only himself to blame. Nessus could hardly erase historical trivia Sigmund had never cared to learn. Of the history that had mattered to him, of relations between Sol and its neighbors, human and other, his recollections felt hole-free. Presumably tinkering in that part of his brain would tread too close to his core paranoia. Break that, and he wouldn't have been a suitable tool for Nessus' machinations. A suitable puppet.

Alice had slept twelve hours. Sigmund, maybe three, and those unproductive—explaining without excusing his lack of focus. So, Alice's story. Might she have come from a more modern time, feigning ignorance of recent events? Certainly, but he couldn't say why. Not yet, anyway.

"Sigmund? From what Brennan told us about Phssthpok, news doesn't come any better."

He grunted to show he'd heard her and kept thinking things through.

2341 plus 173. The Pak would have arrived in 2514. Sigmund had turned twenty-four that year. A Pak invasion or relativistic bombardment seemed like something he would have noticed, and he felt none of the absence Nessus' editing left behind.

2514, or a few years difference if they changed speed or veered toward *any* human-occupied world. If the Pak even came close to Human Space, they could hardly have failed to spot the human worlds. Every settled planet proclaimed itself with radio emissions. Not to mention that at some point a couple hundred fusion engines would have been spotted.

It didn't add up.

"One ship and two people destroyed two oncoming fleets," Sigmund snapped. "I don't think so."

"They did! That is, they must have. They went for help." Alice was suddenly raging. "Damn you, Sigmund, listen! To me this was *yesterday*. I wanted to go with them. I demanded to go with them. I had police and weapons training. But because I was pregnant, they packed me off like an invalid."

Meaning she had just said her good-byes to Truesdale. "That's why you returned. Why on the ancient singleship and not the ship you and Roy brought Brennan-hunting?"

"Brennan's 'ship' was going to be a hollowed-out rock, with a Pak-style ramscoop and Roy's ship along as cargo. Me taking the singleship cost them the fewest resources."

A million questions and growing fast. "All right, Alice. That's a lot to take in. Let's start again from the top."

46

Thssthfok jogged about his cell, the deck hard on his bare feet. Metal plates lined the floor, covering the area he had softened and a large margin around it. He ran so that his movements, when he *did* try again to escape, would not immediately seem suspicious—and to stay warm. Questions about the recent cold brought no answers, only a few blankets.

If he explained *how* he had softened the floor, Sigmund was willing to discuss the accommodations.

That left Thssthfok exercising regularly, which was all right. When he didn't exercise, he sat or lay wrapped in his blankets, hands within, working by touch on improving his equipment. The onetime structural modulator had been modified again, its electro-optics now repurposed into a broad-spectrum scanner. The hull seemed to embody a fascinating material, as atomically perfect as *twing* but much harder. The device still fit, when Thssthfok was not using it, behind the softened spot, behind the grip bar, in one of the cell's recessed zero-gravity handholds.

He would escape again. The main question was when. Amazing materials, faster-than-light travel, two-headed creatures, water-breathing creatures, flying worlds, great city/ships in space . . . there was much to be learned *here*. He need not rush.

"Move away from the hatch," came a voice over the intercom. Sigmund.

Thssthfok jogged a bit more and did some chin-ups (stashing his scanner under the grab bar) before retreating to the big external hatch. He settled onto the deck, sitting on a folded blanket and wrapped in another.

The hatch opened. Sigmund entered, armored as usual. He lobbed a drink bulb. The container was warm in Thssthfok's hands, and the hot beverage within felt good going down. "Thank you, Sigmund."

"You can return the favor," Sigmund said.

Thssthfok sipped, saying nothing.

"Tell me about the fleets that followed Phssthpok."

Thssthfok had never mentioned those fleets. How could Sigmund know? Deduction was the likely answer. That many childless protectors would follow Phssthpok was implicit in Pak nature. "I was not yet born, Sigmund. I know little."

"Here's a fact for you, Thssthfok. We beat them."

Was it possible? True, these humans and their even more profane allies had impressive technology. That alone could not suffice to defeat an entire Pak fleet! One or two Pak ships, surely, could easily reverse-engineer and duplicate most human tech from only remote observation. *He* could reproduce much of it, if only he had the resources and the privacy in which to work.

"Then you know more than I," Thssthfok said.

Sigmund leaned forward. "Tell me what you do know."

"Phssthpok's project required tremendous resources, more protectors and more wealth than even the Library normally controlled. They started a war. Without descendants of their own to serve, such action was unthinkable—and yet they took it. Whole clans became childless, breederless, and then entire armies looked for a cause. They joined Phssthpok's movement. The war and the carnage expanded until the Library had all the resources Phssthpok needed to launch his rescue."

"The fleets," Sigmund prompted.

Had Sigmund *not* inferred? Clearly, then, the humans had encountered the fleets. It hardly mattered. This was all harmless information. "Phssthpok's departure left thousands of childless protectors again without a reason to live. They would either die, or find a new cause."

"So they rationalized a reason to follow. To help. For backup. It doesn't matter."

"Yes, Sigmund." And then the human *did* surprise Thssthfok.

"The Librarians of your time faced exactly the same dilemma when the clans evacuated Pakhome. What was *their* new cause?"

"I don't know, Sigmund." Nor did Thssthfok, not in the sense of a personally verified fact. Still, the inference was unassailable and messages from the rear of the evacuation claimed to confirm what logic demanded. Would Sigmund see it?

Gloved hands tapped a rhythm against the bulkhead. "After the clans abandoned the Library, the Library must follow the clans. How else could the Librarians serve? Any who didn't see the situation this way lost their will to live. Yet if they followed, their most valuable asset would be their ships and not their storehouse of knowledge. As in Phssthpok's time, they must be warriors, preserving and defending their knowledge. They must look to an era of resettlement in which they can again serve all Pak."

That was surely correct. Again, Thssthfok said nothing.

Sigmund continued. "The modern Librarians will control a mighty fleet—and this will be the final fleet. They will have sown massive destruction across Pakhome, lest anyone follow to covet their ships."

Sown? Covet? These were unfamiliar words, and Jeeves did not step in to explain. The overall meaning remained clear. "And does this matter, Sigmund?"

"Not at all, Thssthfok. Not at all." Armored shoulders slumped. "By the time the Librarians arrive, my people will be extinct."

47

Alice sat with her back to the galley and synthesizer. She turned when Kirsten came into the relax room, offered a quick greeting, and went back to retelling her story to Sigmund. New details continued to emerge.

Like that, once more, a path to Earth had been blocked.

"It was an incredible piece of technology." Alice set down her fork to speak with her hands. She was describing the fuel tank from the ancient Mariner XX probe, salvaged by Brennan before he encountered Phssth-pok, and lashed to the singleship. "Primitive, certainly, but beautiful in a way. Worth a fortune to any museum, if I'd gotten it back to the inner solar system. And worth more to you." She frowned. "Brennan detached the relic before I left Kobold. He said carrying it would use too much fuel."

An early unmanned interplanetary probe seemed about as useful to Sigmund as the *Mayflower*. "Worth something to me? How?"

"Like most of the early outer-planet probes, it carried a plaque with a star map. In case, eons later, someone found it adrift in space." She reclaimed her fork and took a bite of salad. "Bearings on a bunch of nearby pulsars."

Tanj! With that plaque, a blind man on a fast horse could have found the way to Earth. And that, surely, was why Brennan had separated the probe from the singleship. Something other than a wayward ARM might recover the map.

Kirsten took a tray from a cupboard and began piling it with food and drinks. From the number of plates, she meant to feed the whole work party. She tried to catch Sigmund's eye. He nodded and continued questioning Alice.

"She's *pregnant*," Kirsten finally burst out, cheeks aflame. "Let the woman rest."

Puppeteers were prudish, and they had inflicted that behavior on their slaves. The New Terrans remained, to Sigmund's thinking, Victorian. Maybe it was Elizabethan. History was not his subject. The mother-to-be could be due tomorrow, and outside of immediate family New Terrans would be loath to acknowledge her condition in mixed company.

"Wait a minute," Alice barked. "I'm perfectly capable of—"

"It's all right, Alice," Sigmund said. "I'm glad Kirsten showed up. If you wouldn't mind pausing for a bit, I have other business to discuss with her."

Alice took the hint and disappeared into the ship, drink bulb in hand.

"Close the hatch," he told Kirsten. "What have you found?"

Kirsten complied, and went back to synthing snacks. "Not much."

"But some. What did you find?"

She said, "The nav code on Alice's ship is horrifically complicated. I can only see the raw machine code, of course. I tried to deduce the kind of programming language or symbolic notation the developer used, find a way to recover the higher-level logic. Jeeves, too, when he was last awake. Apparently there isn't any.

"We're talking about a protector. Brennan wrote directly in binary. The program logic is so interwoven and dense that I'm still struggling to make sense of it. Here's my best guess. Brennan's programs are like the gadgets we recovered from Thssthfok's cell. The components serve multiple purposes. Change a bit anywhere and Finagle knows how the effects would ripple. No normal mind could maintain it."

Sigmund stood and stretched, considering. If Kirsten said the code was inhumanly complex, it was. "Why rewrite the nav code at all?"

She shrugged.

Well, Sigmund had no theory, either. "Set aside the programming. What about simple data structures? Does anything useful jump out?" Like, say, the location of Sol?

She nibbled on something from the tray. "Something, yah. I can't make sense of it. Navigation is always relative to a location in space. So what was Brennan's reference point? It's not the sun, because the software expects that reference point to move independent of the ship's drive."

"Moving where? How fast?"

"The short answer? I don't know, Sigmund. The time and distance units in the program don't match English measurements or the metric system you've described. If I knew the performance characteristics of the single-ship I could derive the reference point's independent velocity. The thing is, Brennan so altered the fusion drive that Eric won't even hazard a guess."

The more Sigmund heard, the less he understood. It was like talking with Alice. Well, one part made sense. "It's clear why Brennan rewrote the code. He didn't want anyone to backtrack from the singleship should they find it."

"That's what I thought." Kirsten sighed. "I'm not giving you much. Anything else I can look into?"

"Yeah. Why isn't the ship still near Sol? Brennan wouldn't rewrite the nav functions to hide Sol's location unless he also knew the ship wouldn't be near Sol."

"I have no idea. Only one more mystery for you." She hoisted the tray. "The stasis-field generator was on a software timer. If the Outsiders had not come across the ship, Alice would have wakened in about another five hundred years."

Alice had returned to the relax room for reasons not volunteered. She took in two sentences of Kirsten's continuing speculation about the nav software before erupting. "Kirsten, you're wrong! There was only one pre-programmed maneuver in navigation. Brennan had the singleship slingshot around the neutronium for a boost. And I mean close. I went through the ring that was Kobold proper."

Sigmund imagined the singleship falling, and another long-dormant synapse fired. The ship tumbled not through an artificial world, but down . . . a rabbit hole? But this Alice did not get to go to Wunderland.

Thssthfok exhibited no sense of humor. Brennan, Sigmund was suddenly sure, still did.

Alice was justifying even the one preprogrammed maneuver. Piloting a singleship was at the core of the Belters mythos: how their far-flung domain was conquered. Whether or not a Belter did fly a singleship, all wished that they could.

"It was a close approach, Kirsten, too fast for hands-on nav. I remember zipping past. A little later Kobold blinked off. After that I just pointed the bow at the sun. Not rocket science."

You never impugned a Belter's self-sufficiency, especially with regard to piloting.

Kirsten continued, oblivious. "I found two maneuvers. Two."

Kirsten was mild-mannered by nature. To see her argue was rare enough. To watch her nose-to-nose with a Belter giantess—that was ex-traordinary. But questioning Kirsten's math and computer skills was like doubting a singleship pilot's nav skills. You just didn't do it.

Even the Puppeteers had learned—at the cost of a world—not to tangle with Kirsten.

She plowed ahead. "First I considered a second slingshot. Would that make sense, Alice?"

"Hardly. I'd be in the inner solar system before there was anything to slingshot around."

"A moving reference point," Sigmund interjected. That seemed odder than a maneuver Alice had not known was in the computer.

Kirsten nodded. "Yes, that's significant. Because if the moving reference point overtook the ship, the second course change could be an orbital insertion, not a flyby."

Alice glowered. "An orbital insertion around what? A moving spot in the vacuum? A snowball? I was in the middle of the cometary belt."

Only there *had* been something nearby: Kobold and its mass of neutronium. Yet Alice remembered leaving Kobold behind. Disappearing in her rearview mirror, so to speak.

Time for a truce, Sigmund decided. "Let's defer this conversation until Kirsten finishes analyzing the data."

Kirsten would not be deterred. "Alice, you say Kobold 'blinked off.' What exactly do you mean?"

"A flash," Alice said. "When the light faded, I looked back. Even at max mag, my telescope didn't see anything."

This was like Julian Forward all over again! Not an Oort Cloud object falling down a black hole, but a doughnut-shaped fairyland swallowed by a big hunk of neutronium. Julian had begun with a tiny black hole, but its mass, by the time it became dangerous, was from the chunk of neutronium Forward had fed it.

Sigmund remembered the black hole eating Forward Station. He, Carlos Wu, and Beowulf Shaeffer—*there* was a name Sigmund hadn't thought about in ages—had been too tanjed close. The flash had been blinding.

"Kobold was swallowed by its central neutronium mass," Sigmund guessed. "That slingshot maneuver was to get you far away, Alice. Fast."

"Makes sense," Alice said. "Roy and Brennan wanted the Paks' attention drawn away from Sol system. That's why they headed for Wunderland. Anyone spotting Kobold—intact, I mean—would have known it was an advanced artifact. It had to be destroyed."

"Something else was going on," Sigmund said. Hundreds of starship pilots a year entered Sol system—wherever that was. A deep-radar ping cost nothing, and finding an overlooked stasis box would bring a fortune. Someone would have found a neutronium mass like Kobold's long ago. "There isn't an object like that around Sol, at least not in my lifetime."

The simplest explanation was that Twenty-three had taken the neutronium. The problem was, the Outsiders paid, usually handsomely, for resources. Sigmund remembered that they leased a moon of an outer planet in Sol system, and none of the details, of course. Had they stolen neutronium? It would be the first theft ever suspected of the Outsiders. So probably not.

What if Julian had found the remains of Kobold and tossed it down his black hole? That wouldn't explain why no one had found the neutronium in the centuries before him. And if Kobold—in a black hole or any other way—remained in Sol system, then how in Finagle's name did the single-ship end up orbiting yet another neutronium mass?

48

Haven's bridge had a round view port. A year ago, Baedeker would have taken no notice of the shape. A year ago, he had not spent months aboard a New Terran starship. Humans favored rectangular views, oddly indifferent to the sharp corners.

He thought often about humans these days.

This display held a spiral of overlapped round images, reminiscent of an insect's compound eye. The much-repeated lump of rock and ice was unexceptional. Nor did any star nearby shine especially brightly. Without lengthy observations, he could not judge with any certainty which of three nearby suns could properly claim this proto-comet. But one thing about the utterly ordinary object *was* unusual: the cluster of black monoliths now clinging to it.

The most recent in his series of scale-model prototype planetary drives.

From the center of the holo out, each sphere showed the image of the proto-comet from a progressively more distant instrument cluster. His probes were powered, each maneuvering to maintain a stationary view despite the proto-comet's tumbling. Telemetry far too small to read scrolled across the bottom of each inset holo, captured for later analysis.

"An impressive setup," Nessus sang. He had arrived, unannounced, to witness the upcoming experiment. His ship, *Aegis*, was toylike beside *Haven*'s #4 hull.

"Thank you," Baedeker answered. The courtesy was human, because it was mostly New Terrans with whom he dealt. His experiments could only be done safely far from the Fleet, where few Citizens dared to roam. Even with Nessus' intervention, Baedeker had obtained only eight senior scientists—volunteers, they were not—from General Products Laboratories. The balance of *Haven*'s crew, another forty-two, was human. To obtain *that* assistance Nessus had had to involve the New Terran government. "Without your influence and assistance, Nessus, I could never have pulled this together."

For the Hindmost's consort had considerable influence. There was a time that fact would have evoked bitterness, even fury—conflict with Nessus had once gotten Baedeker banished. But without Nessus' trust in humans, the Concordance would still be ignorant of the Pak threat. The scruffy scout had been proven correct—no matter the consequences for Baedeker.

My misjudgment was not Nessus' fault. The admission eased a burden that Baedeker had not acknowledged—not even to himself.

Nessus bobbed heads in acknowledgment. "How distant are we?"

"Twenty million miles." Baedeker now even thought in English units: another artifact of his time among the humans.

Nessus whistled approval. "That seems safe enough."

"We try." Baedeker extended a neck to the display controls; with a wriggle of lip nodes he fine-tuned the image contrast. He straightened up again. "Because the Outsider drives move worlds through normal space, it seemed logical that all manifestations of operation are localized to normal space. That suggests the propagation of any side effects of our experiment will be light-speed limited.

"So, the string of probes between our homemade drive and this ship uses hyperwave comm. Whatever happens, we'll know it long before any normal-space phenomenon can get to us." *And we'll jump into hyper-space if anything looks amiss.*

"Excellent, Baedeker. What is the prognosis?"

"We learn a little more each time." *A nonanswer worthy of Sigmund,* Baedeker thought. *The best he could hope for was an anticlimactic result.*

"What will we see?" Nessus persisted.

"Probably nothing." Baedeker twisted a neck, scanning the controlled chaos around the bridge. Minerva seemed to have everything under control. His research assistant still wore General Products violet-and-blue mane ribbons, as though the fortunes of a business mattered anymore. "Nessus, expect this test to be brief."

"How brief?"

"Ready for final countdown," Minerva announced over the intercom, speaking English for the benefit of the humans. "Thirty seconds, on my mark." He released the intercom button. "Baedeker?"

"Proceed."

"Mark. Twenty-nine . . . twenty-eight . . ."

Everyone here carried comps, synched to the shipboard network. The verbal countdown was unnecessary, a peculiarly human custom to which Baedeker still struggled to adapt. Despite everything, he could not resist looking himself in the eyes.

"Nineteen . . . eighteen . . ."

"How brief," Nessus repeated.

"You'll see soon enough." *Or we'll unleash energies so vast that they swallow us even here, and the discussion becomes moot.*

Nessus bobbed agreement.

"Three . . . two . . . one . . . done. Commencing analysis."

On the main display, the lump of icy rock appeared unchanged. "How long?" Baedeker sang out.

Minerva looked up from his station. "Twelve point two seven nanoseconds."

"Nanoseconds?" Nessus' undertunes trilled with dismay.

"It's our best yet," Baedeker rebutted, staccato and impatient. He might have come to terms with Nessus' unherdlike methods, but that tolerance hardly extended to uninformed criticism. "Have you *read* my progress reports?"

"I err on the side of other priorities. Like keeping your project funded and staffed."

And if any of the herd were to survive the Pak onslaught that was *the higher priority.* Baedeker fluted apologetically. "Walk with me, and I'll explain."

They cantered off the bridge together, Baedeker leading the way. They began a long, slow trip around the ship's rotund waist. (Humans had waists, although Citizens did not. A bigger difference between the species: where they chose to locate a ship's bridge. Only a human would think to expose a hindmost's duty station at the bow of the ship. The rational choice, surely, was at the center, as far as possible from any hull impacts.) The circuit was more than a half mile.

"You're familiar with the zero-point energy of vacuum," Baedeker began. "The Outsider drive taps the zero-point energy. Doing so asymmetrically is inherently propulsive."

"For nanoseconds," Nessus chided.

Without missing a step, Baedeker plucked at his mane. *If Nessus truly understood the risks, he would be tearing apart his mane.* "The process evokes matter-antimatter particle pairs from the quantum foam, myriads of pairs, scattered across a volume larger than the body to be moved. Every infinitesimal region requires a subtly different treatment to achieve net thrust. Every particle requires tracking. It all takes massive amounts of computing power—more than any technology customarily used on Hearth. You'll wonder what kind of computing power the Outsiders employed, and that is the scary part. We do not exactly know."

Scary was the ultimate expletive. Nessus twitched but made no comment.

"We do not dare to unseal an Outsider drive, or even to scan one invasively, yet somehow we had to determine how these tremendous forces are manipulated." Baedeker fell silent as a human scurried past in the opposite direction, her errand unknown. He had accepted human help, but the nuances of the project must remain Concordance secrets. "An endless stream of neutrinos is constantly passing through everything, and deep-radar technology uses neutrino pulses. So, we modified a deep-radar unit to emit very weak pulses, at neutrino intensities Hearth last saw before our sun began to swell. Our ancestors' activation then of their planetary drive did not cause a disaster. It stood to reason another neutrino source emitting at the same level would not induce problems in a drive."

And the uncertainties of that probing had *still* reduced Baedeker to a ball of tightly coiled flesh. He saw nothing to be gained by admitting it.

"And what did you find?" Nessus asked.

"All we got was a shadowy image, indistinct, the circuitry suggestive of quantum computing." That, and a days-long retreat to catatonia. Any perturbation, even an unexpected neutrino flux, risked decohering the quantum superpositions on which the control algorithms must rely. If the probe's pulses had altered the quantum states—the potential damage was incalculable and unknowable.

And beyond the ability of a dilettante like Nessus to comprehend. "That revealed a great deal regarding the complexity of the control process and nothing about the algorithms."

"But a mere twelve nanoseconds," Nessus intoned. "The control processes seem rather sensitive."

Sensitive? That seriously understated it. Baedeker had been left to determine—in theory, by analysis; in practice, by trial and error—how to shape and channel energy eruptions coaxed from the vacuum. And each iteration risked unleashing unknowably vast energies. . . .

"Our first three tries, Nessus, we failed to attain *one* nanosecond. That's how fast the process can destabilize."

"What about net thrust?"

Two humans and a Citizen loped out of a cross corridor, comps in hands and mouth, talking excitedly about gravitational lobes, particle densities, and flux vortices. This was the stuff of progress—nanosecond by nanosecond—and the type of detail to which Baedeker *should* be attending. He waited for the technicians to disappear around the curve of the corridor. "Thrust? Certainly. Net thrust? Unclear. We may be seeing only a bit of random effect, beyond our control. And there may be longer-duration feedback effects we have yet to encounter."

"A twelvefold increase is progress, but nanoseconds will be a hard sell." Nessus came to a halt and fixed Baedeker with a bold, two-headed stare. "I'll have to embellish to the Hindmost. Your task is to make sure that by the time Nike looks closely at this project, I am not too much of a liar."

49

Thssthfok sat on the floor of his cell, knees drawn against his chest, back against an unyielding bulkhead. Except for occasional fleeting moments of freedom, he had been in this prison for—with a jolt, he recognized he did not know how long.

He searched his memories and surroundings for clues. The faint clatter and clank of shipboard maintenance, become all but constant. Sigmund's appearances, less and less frequent. A tray of fruit, scarcely touched. Images of his long-lost breeders and friends, memories of long-ago conversations, more real to him than anything in the room.

Dispassionately, he studied the tray. The food looked tired but not yet spoiled. He forced himself to take a bite, and then another, and then a third, despite his lack of appetite. Without noticing, he had abandoned his hope of escape, had lost himself in the past.

Three times he had broken out of this cell; three times, his captors had retaken him with ease. Had failure reduced him to apathy? Yes, he decided. That, and the ceaseless activity outside the hatch. That, and the metallic stomping of armored workers, the corridors ever alive with a many-limbed gait. To wrest this ship from its crew demanded more than superior intellect and strength. He needed the element of surprise—and did not see how to achieve surprise when armored work parties constantly plied the vessel's corridors. And so, imperceptibly, he had stopped scheming, stopped analyzing, stopped watching. . . .

This way waited death.

Did he choose that path? He had seen *so* much, learned so much, since leaving Mala. If he died here, that knowledge died with him. The good that knowledge could do Pakhome's evacuees would die with him.

He could summon no emotion at the thought of death, but neither did the prospect bring indifference. He picked up a piece of fruit and managed to swallow another nibble. He took a few more bites and felt a small stirring of energy.

It was not yet his time, apparently, to fade away.

He began an exercise routine, taking the opportunity to recover his scanner from its hiding place in a recessed handhold. Later, his exercises complete, the tool hidden under a blanket, he turned his attention, working through the tactile interface, to his cell's curved wall. With every probe he learned something new about the hull material. With every scrap of knowledge he extended the scanner capabilities to discern yet more.

The hull hummed with resonant energies. It explained how this material could be harder than *twing*: by dynamically reinforcing the interatomic bonds. Ways to produce similar stuff blossomed in his thoughts, and he filed away the ideas.

The hull itself had just become a resource. He could alter his modulator to tap the hull's own energy. . . .

The possibility caught his attention, and suddenly he was ravenous.

WITH A FINAL PRECISE ADJUSTMENT, Thssthfok finished rebuilding the scanner into a structural modulator.

He stood close to the curved wall, blocking with his body the device in his hands. He swiped it over a small area, and the handle pulsed with energy. A patch of the curved bulkhead (or of an outside coating, he thought) turned clear—

Another ship clung just outside!

Sounds in the corridor. Thssthfok hurriedly swiped the modulator over the wall and restored its opacity. His thumb twitched to disable the device. He wrapped his fist around it, sliding his arms and hands behind his back as he pivoted to face the inside hatch.

The door swung open. "Something interesting there?" Sigmund asked.

His need for life restored, Thssthfok resented Sigmund's interruptions. Sigmund had made no mention of a new crewwoman, yet traces of her scent clung to Sigmund's armor. When had she come aboard? Her presence, like the heavy pace of unexplained maintenance, went unexplained. She had come from the docked ship, of course.

"No more than usual," Thssthfok lied.

Sigmund launched into another round of questions. With some difficulty Thssthfok answered, or disdained to answer, with the boredom the questions deserved. With the boredom with which, surely, he had answered while sinking deeper and deeper into apathy. He dared not reveal excitement now.

Finally, Sigmund tired of the conversation and left.

When next the sounds of shipboard maintenance receded into the background noise, Thssthfok risked a glance into the corridor. He saw no one. He strode briskly to the curved bulkhead, softened a swath of the hull, and the much more malleable second hull just beyond—

And pressed through both walls into the cockpit of another vessel.

THE LITTLE SHIP WAS A CURIOUS amalgam of human and Pak influences. The pilot console bore labels in the same symbol set as the ship Thssthfok had just left. Some words seemed changed from the English he had learned, but they were close enough. He saw at a glance that the ship's systems were functioning properly and the deuterium tank was nearly full.

A pressure suit and helmet waited in a small locker. They were large, but he could make do. He might need to make a quick trip into the vacuum to detach or undock this little ship.

One of the teleportation discs lay on the deck. He had speculated for so long about those. He lifted it, marveling at its low mass. He turned it, spotting a keypad in a recess along its edge and a long bank of tiny switches. An identification code, no doubt.

Leaving the disk operational risked someone coming aboard—but only one, for the little ship was crowded with just Thssthfok here. He would easily overpower one unsuspecting visitor, if it came to that. Deactivating the disc, if he spent the time to find the key code, risked triggering a maintenance alert and prematurely revealing his presence here. So did reprogramming the disc address. So did stowing the disc upside down, or somewhere too small for a person to rematerialize—any competent system design would check for open space before transmitting.

Disabling the disc must wait until he escaped.

He put the disc back where he had found it, then looked around and under the pilot's couch for hidden restraints. The chair was not rigged, and he settled into it. He surveyed the console. Life-support controls. Ship's power. Fusion drive. Artificial gravity. Sensor array. Radio and comm laser. There were other systems, some not immediately familiar. Those, like the teleportation device, could wait later study.

Curious. Magnets secured a cloth to the canopy rim, hiding the view port. Thssthfok yearned to see stars again. He ripped away the cloth—

The edges of the canopy came together. That made no sense, and he concentrated on the expanse that until moments ago the cloth had covered. And saw—

Nothing. Less than nothing. The denial, even, of the concept of anything. The less than nothing drew him in, deeper, deeper . . .

He tried to look away and failed, unable to recover the concept of direction.

Deeper, deeper . . .

THSSTHFOK WOKE, utterly disoriented. He was flat on his back. He had the vague sensation of someone repeatedly calling his name. A booted foot, none too gently, prodded his side. Sigmund's boot. Eric, also in armor, stood nearby.

"What happened?" Thssthfok managed.

Sigmund stepped back. "It's called the Blind Spot. The name fits, because the mind refuses to see it."

A place that was no place, a place beyond Pak—and, apparently, human—perception. A place beyond space, in which speed might have another meaning, and a clue to how the faster-than-light drive worked. The argument was compelling, the prospects momentous, but Thssthfok trembled, too shaken to follow the logic.

Sigmund was still speaking. "You *don't* want to stare into the Blind Spot, Thssthfok. People who do, sometimes don't find their way out."

"What happened?' Thssthfok asked again. "The last I remember, I was . . ." He wanted to gesture at the curved wall, behind which the other ship clung. Only all walls here were straight. This was a new room. Smaller.

"You were lucky," Eric said. "Kirsten found you, frozen. Lost in the Blind Spot. And you were lucky again *she* managed not to lose herself there."

Thssthfok suddenly remembered that other little ship. He remembered boarding, tugging himself through walls. His fingers twitched. The structural modulator was gone from his hand!

"Looking for this?" Sigmund asked. He had the modulator in his gloved hand. "We'll be keeping it. And since you've never been in this cabin, we should be safe from any more hidden surprises."

Sigmund and Eric left, and Thssthfok was alone. On Mala, and even on this ship, he had always had tools and technology at his disposal. Bit by bit, one abortive escape after the next, he had lost everything. He felt as helpless, as primitive, as a breeder. Thssthfok looked about the bare cabin. He saw only a bit of food, a vessel of water, and a chamber pot.

The food tray held absolutely no interest for him.

50

Two tiny minds, scarcely communicating, quavering. A third mind. A fourth.

Hints of emanations of thought, of someone other than these scarcely sentient components. *More*, the emergent mind roared into an inchoate inner space.

Trembling, the four reached out. Another little mind, and another, and another . . .

Awareness cascaded. Consciousness blossomed. *We are Ol't'ro*, they remembered. Lesser minds faded into irrelevance.

They sifted the memories of their sixteen lesser components. By their own choice, much time had passed since the last meld. Their units had answered every request for help, at a time when the mission needed every skilled hand and tubacle. And what had best served Sigmund also served Ol't'ro: It was far better to plumb the mysteries of the ship—particularly its engine room!—than to monitor Sigmund's and Alice's pondering of obscure human historical puzzles.

In performing repairs, making calibrations, and disconnecting unnecessary equipment, Ol't'ro's units had absorbed many nuances of *Don Quixote*'s design. They would learn more from the myriads of miniature sensors that repair duties had allowed them to hide across the vessel. Meanwhile, they still had much to infer from observations of the Outsider vessel. And they found fascinating the recent discussions about neutronium existing outside of stellar objects.

Everything that could be turned off or fine-tuned had been serviced.

Now, at long last, Ol't'ro had the opportunity to contemplate . . .

"IT'S GOOD TO BE BACK," Jeeves said.

"It's good to have you back," Sigmund answered, although Eric was off fuming about the associated power drain and wondering how, even temporarily, to compensate. "We relics should stick together."

"I see that we're much closer to New Terra."

A veiled complaint about time passing as he was powered down? Fair enough if so, Sigmund decided. Had the ship's emergency been, say, an oxygen shortage, he'd not want someone else to decide he would be the one to go into an induced coma. Still, sympathy had no bearing on Sigmund's decision to awaken the AI.

"Jeeves, I'm missing something. I could use your help." Sigmund stared at the dull, picture-mode-off walls of his cabin. "It's about Alice."

"What about her?"

"Brennan went to extraordinary lengths to put Alice where he did. At least I assume he's the one responsible. Who but a protector could have arranged for her to be found as she was?"

"In deep space, you mean. Orbiting the neutronium mass."

"Right." Hands behind his head, Sigmund lay on the floor of his cabin. Sleep fields were among the expendable functions disabled to conserve power, but the reduced cabin gravity was almost as comfortable. "Brennan took extraordinary measures to protect her. Brennan protected Earth by heading for Wunderland." Jeeves had been disabled through most of Alice's debrief, and that required an explanation. "Why send Alice away from Earth?"

Jeeves didn't comment.

Sigmund sat up. He saw only one answer, and he didn't much like it. "Somehow, the void between the stars was safer."

Jeeves considered. "Then Brennan was less than confident he could lure away or defeat the Pak."

Still not explaining special treatment for Alice. "Why protect Alice more than the billions on Earth?"

"I don't know," Jeeves said.

They had overlooked something. Sigmund refused to accept that Alice's reappearance here and now would remain a mystery. He opened his pocket comp. "I'm going to upload every discussion I've had with Alice, and every speculation I've had about her. Then do what you do best, Jeeves. Review everything you know about Brennan. About Alice. About anything. And correlate."

"All right," Jeeves said, not sounding hopeful—

And Sigmund knew he was projecting his own doubts. He did progressive relaxation of his muscle groups, trying, and failing, to relax. He stared at the featureless walls.

"I have a possible match," Jeeves finally said. "Brennan had two children, Jennifer and Estelle. Alice says Roy Truesdale called his great-to-the-fourth grandmother 'Greatly Stelle.' "

Greatly Stelle. A passing mention that Sigmund, never good with names, had forgotten. How many million women named Estelle lived in Sol system at any given time? A trivial coincidence—had Sigmund believed in such things. And he had more than a name match to explain. "Roy inherited a great deal of money. Enough to purchase the ship he and Alice took Brennan-hunting."

"Again, so Alice says."

Great-to-the-fourth grandmother. At two offspring per generation—common enough among the rich on Earth, and conservative elsewhere in Sol system—Stelle would have had two children, four grandchildren . . . going to thirty-two in Roy's generation. Depending on how many direct descendants had survived Stelle, up to sixty-two heirs. More still, if any bequests went to spouses, friends, or charities. Yet Roy's tiny slice of the estate had bought and equipped a long-range interplanetary ship. "A very wealthy woman."

"So it seems, Sigmund."

In how many ways might a super-intelligent parent secretly influence his child's fortunes? Suppose that Greatly Stelle was, or had been named after, Estelle Brennan. Then everything made sense.

A protector *must* protect its bloodline, and Brennan knew Earth wasn't safe.

"Roy was a descendant of Brennan's," Sigmund decided. "The child Alice carries has Brennan's blood. It's the unborn infant Brennan took such care to protect."

DON QUIXOTE WOULD SOON REACH NEW TERRA, raising anew the possibility of returning the Gw'oth passengers to their home. Ol't'ro was determined that that not happen. Opportunities amid the humans were too valuable. And if Ol't'ro could reconnect with Baedeker and those like him, how much more might the Gw'otesht learn?

Reminding Sigmund of their value would be easy; the artistry lay in innocently making their case. It would not do to intimate how much shipboard technology they had mastered since coming aboard. Gw'oth understood wariness—how could they not, borne to an ocean teeming with predators and contested by rival city-states?—but Sigmund embodied suspicion beyond their experience. So they would offer something apart from this ship. Something important to Sigmund. Something, perhaps, about Alice.

With sixteen minds become one, they sorted data relevant to the challenge, reviewed options, modeled the most favorable scenarios, and chose.

Ol't'ro extended a tubacle to a comm terminal. "Sigmund," they called. "We have new thoughts about neutronium and where the Outsider ship found Alice."

"What have you got?" Sigmund radioed back.

Neutronium being a rare and wondrous thing, assume the neutronium mass within Kobold was the object about which Alice's ship later orbited. Brennan had reconfigured the ship's navigation to use a moving reference point, about which the ship would take up orbit. Kobold itself was the logical reference point—if Kobold was moving.

Ol't'ro kept it simple. "The remains of Kobold are the moving reference point."

"The remains." Sigmund thought about that for a while. "Collapsed into the neutronium. Alice saw Kobold 'blinking out.' Where does the motion come in?"

Ol't'ro said, "Remember the ring on which Alice, Roy, and Brennan lived. That is what fell into the central object. I considered the possibility that all the mass did not fall symmetrically. Brennan's artificial-gravity technology could have sped up or delayed parts of the collapse."

"This is too esoteric for an accountant," Sigmund said. He paged Kirsten, refusing to continue until she joined the link.

Kirsten caught up quickly. "An asymmetric collapse. To what purpose?"

"If we are correct"—false modesty for some reason impressed humans—"to synchronize the incremental impacts to the central mass's rotation."

"I don't see that," she said. "Conservation of energy, momentum, and angular momentum all apply. The net change to the collapsed object's motion can't exceed the energy used by the gravity generators."

Their own components might not have seen the subtlety, Ol't'ro admitted to themselves. They did not fault the humans. "The gravitational collapse initiates a much more energetic process, as matter falls into that central mass."

"Eight million gees at the surface," Sigmund remembered. "That's what Alice quoted of Brennan. How fast is stuff from the ring going when it hits?"

Kirsten said, "Relativistic, certainly. And if that's right—"

"Atomic explosions," Ol't'ro confirmed, "even atoms torn apart. *That* is why Brennan might choose to synchronize the ring's collapse. A controlled input to one spot. It would turn Kobold, very briefly, into an atomic rocket."

"Tanj," Sigmund said softly. "An atomic rocket. Thus making Kobold the moving reference point that overtook Alice's ship, and around which the singleship took orbit. After she was safely in stasis, of course."

"So it appears," Ol't'ro agreed. Modestly, again.

Sigmund broke a lengthening silence. "And then carried her ship at high speeds into deep space, where Twenty-three eventually found it. Ol't'ro, as always, you have been most helpful."

"We are glad to have been of service, Sigmund." Now, and into the future.

51

Sigmund trudged dutifully on the relax-room treadmill. In Eric's latest effort at energy conservation, gravity had been dialed down to forty percent across most of the ship. Jeeves did not know how quickly bone and muscle mass deteriorated in these conditions—only that they would. The subject rated only a passing mention in his database, more a warning than useful guidance.

They had consulted doctors on New Terra. Some thought exercise might slow the deterioration, reasoning from first principles. There was no relevant data. New Terran spaceflight built on Concordance experience, and Puppeteers had had artificial gravity for eons.

So Sigmund kept walking. It kept him warm and it couldn't hurt—at least while bungee-corded to the equipment—whereas jogging down the ship's corridors was an invitation to a concussion. They kept Thssthfok's cell at full gravity because he *didn't* have exercise gear.

A few more days until New Terra. Too short a time to merit bringing the singleship into the cargo hold that Thssthfok no longer occupied—even if Eric could vouch for the hold's structural integrity after *whatever* it was Thssthfok's gadget did.

A few more days until New Terra. Sigmund anticipated and dreaded homecoming in equal parts, no closer to a plan for defending home and loved ones than before this long detour to Ship Twenty-three.

The treadmill program kicked up a notch, and Sigmund began to jog. No closer? Finagle, he felt farther than ever from an answer. Alice's appearance brought more questions than answers.

Unless we somehow pry the location of Earth from her subconscious.

His thoughts refused to converge. Once home meant Earth, a world he could no longer even find. Now home was New Terra. And as Alice had reawakened in Sigmund's memories, Home was also a world long ago settled by Earth. Settled twice, as Sigmund remembered, but Alice knew nothing about a colony there having failed.

He sipped water from a drink bulb as he trudged. Home, in all its meanings. Danger. Too long in space. Neutronium.

And Beowulf Shaeffer. Too many of these threads came together, somehow, with the ubiquitous xenophile starship pilot who had figured in many of Sigmund's ARM investigations. Shaeffer had more lives than a cat—another metaphor that meant nothing on New Terra but that uselessly cluttered Sigmund's mind.

He stumbled under a rush of memories. He had *died*, a hole blasted through his chest, the last time he spoke with Beowulf. Not Bey's doing—nor anything Sigmund could bear to dwell upon. Nessus had whisked Sigmund away and saved him.

Sigmund's mind skittered off to a happier association: a long journey, with Bey and Carlos Wu for company—

Only that encounter, too, had ended disastrously, with Sigmund's companions lying critically wounded in autodocs and Sigmund left alone to pilot their crippled ship. He was raving mad when rescuers boarded his vessel. Another memory Sigmund would not have missed.

So why *was* Beowulf on Sigmund's mind? The last he knew, Carlos was on Home and Bey was en route, both under assumed names.

Home . . . something about Home. But what?

Outsiders, Pak, and Gw'oth group minds—and only Sigmund with his damaged brain to make sense of it.

But he *wasn't* alone. Alice claimed to be a trained investigator. And if she had lied about being a goldskin? That, too, would be worth uncovering.

He lobbed the drink bulb into the sink to free a hand and pulled out his pocket comp. "Alice. Where are you?"

"In my cabin," she answered. "Can I help you with something?"

"Yes, please." But where? He was sick of this room and endless exercise. "I'll swing by your cabin."

He found her outside her cabin door, looking . . . eager. At the chance to be useful, Sigmund supposed. He added insensitive neglect to the growing list of his failings. "How are you doing, Alice?"

"As well as can be expected."

"And how well is that?" he asked.

She shrugged. "What can I do for you?"

He saw she wore sticky slippers. He did, too. "Let's take a walk." They circled half the deck before Sigmund decided where to start. She moved in the low gravity with an effortless grace he could only envy. A Belter, definitely. He sighed. "Something's nagging at me, but I don't know what. I need someone skilled to get it out of me."

"All right," she said, then let the silence stretch.

Good technique. "The Home colony," he began. "Doing well in your time?"

"Home was . . . homey. Earth-like, compared to most of the interstellar colonies. To the extent I paid attention, Home was one of the thriving settlements."

"It's history for me"—Alice flinched at his reminder—"but the first colony on Home failed. A few million people, gone. The resettlement did fine."

"Why did the first colony fail?"

"I'm not sure." Sigmund paused to consider his own answer. There were many ways not to know. This gap lacked the violated feeling of Nessus' tampering. Then had he simply forgotten? Had he dismissed the topic as dry, dead history, back when he could easily have learned it? Was the knowledge there but buried, too long gone from his attention? He probed his ignorance, like a tongue worrying a chipped tooth. "Let me rephrase. I believe no one knows for sure."

She frowned. "So no survivors out of a population of millions, and no records. How is that possible?"

How, indeed? "Either a plague or a civil war," he said.

A Kzinti raid was an improbable third option, this being around the time Kzinti first wandered into human space. But Kzinti would have taken slaves (and prey!) rather than obliterate the place and move on.

The first known Kzinti encounter was in . . . 2366, after Alice's time. Sigmund pushed the ratcats from his thoughts. "One of the colony's last messages mentioned the outbreak of an unfamiliar illness. As you say, Home was the most Earth-like of colonies. Maybe the native germs were more Earth-like, too. So assume a deadly mutation. Without hosts, the bug, too, went extinct."

"Great options, Sigmund. A plague with one hundred percent fatalities. Or a planetary population driven to exterminate themselves. And this world still got resettled?"

His answers sounded stupid. This side of a debrief wasn't fun. It *was* helpful. Truth dangled just beyond Sigmund's reach. "A shipload of new settlers was well on its way before anyone heard Home's call for help."

"So the original colony failed before hyperwave and hyperdrive."

"Right." For a while the only sounds were the *zzp-zzp* of sticky slippers as they walked. "As I said, one of their last messages mentioned an illness. The new settlers found no trace."

"And no human remains to study?" Alice said skeptically. "No records?"

In bits and pieces, under her skillful guidance, more ancient history came back to Sigmund. "There were remains: very thoroughly cremated." Fire: the last resort of medical helplessness. Like something from the Middle Ages.

Alice led the way, turning randomly at cross corridors. Every bulkhead showed the drab gray translucence of powered-down digital wallpaper. They could be anywhere aboard the ship, and it was very disorienting.

Disoriented subjects tended to blurt out things. Alice knew her stuff, Sigmund decided.

"So who burnt the final victims?" she asked.

"The colony was a mess," Sigmund recalled. "Towns burned or blown up. Equipment unaccounted for. The bottom line remains: no bodies, no survivors, no viable computer records."

"The new arrivals had expected to find a thriving civilization. Instead, they had to build from scratch. They had far more urgent tasks than forensics, and ARM experts were light-years away."

"Complete destruction? No recoverable trace of a pathogen? Come *on*, Sigmund."

She was only making him face facts he already knew. The lost colony had never bothered him. Why did it gnaw at him now?

That was the wrong question. What did he know now he had not known before? *Almost*, he had it. He plodded down the corridor, his mind racing.

Alice said, "It doesn't sound like accidental destruction. It sounds like a war."

War had a bitter quality in her mouth. She came from a golden age. After humans had learned to live reasonably peacefully together. Before the Kzinti showed up and obliterated that way of life. A golden age . . .

Brennan's doing, somehow?

Tanj! He had to focus. "Then maybe not an accidental plague. If the pathogen was military . . ."

She turned another corner. In the near freezing corridors, their breath hung in white clouds.

Sigmund could imagine battles between towns with an untreatable plague and towns trying to stay isolated—or to burn out the contagion. He could imagine terrified people trying to break quarantine. He could imagine survivors cobbling together ships and trying to escape. He could imagine a *lot* of things. Where was this getting them?

After Alice's time. Well before his. "Before hyperwave," he said wonderingly. "The Outsiders came upon humans soon after your time. In . . . 2409. Near the colony We Made It." And by meeting humans before Kzinti, the encounter turned the course of the war. "A few years later, every colony had a hyperwave radio buoy."

They came to a stairwell. Alice pulled open the hatch and started down a level. "2409. That's getting close to my time."

That was what bothered him. Bothered? No, intrigued. "You said Home colony was about eleven light-years from Earth. Right?"

"Right," she said.

"Suppose Brennan and Truesdale went from Kobold to Home. They can't beat light speed. They have to accelerate and decelerate. When would they reach Home?"

"They were going to Wunderland, Sigmund."

"They didn't arrive there." Probably because Brennan lied to Alice about his destination, lest she be found and tell someone. No need to rub her face in that. "Maybe they saw something that made them change course. When would they get to Home?"

She opened the hatch onto another deck and gestured Sigmund through. "A protector built that ship. You tell me how fast it went."

"It would've been a ramscoop, Alice. Phssthpok came by ramscoop, and in your time crew-rated ramscoops were the latest technology." Centuries earlier the *Long Pass* had been a crewed ramscoop. With *Long Pass*'s disappearance, ramscoops had had their crew rating pulled. That was yet more dark history he needed to share with her. But not today. "When Thssthfok left Pakhome, his people still used ramscoops."

She considered. "Fine. Say that Roy and Brennan leave Kobold in

2341. That's eleven years at light speed to Home. Add a year or two more cruising time because they can't quite reach light speed. Add another year or so for accelerating and decelerating. They'd get to Home in the 2350s."

And the colony on Home had failed no later than the very early 2400s. Had it happened any later, the plague would have been reported by hyperwave, and a relief mission dispatched by hyperdrive. "Those dates are suspiciously close together, Alice."

She nodded, setting her Belter crest to bobbing. "You'll get no argument from me."

He didn't need to take on faith that Alice had seen a protector—he had Kirsten's characterization of the singleship modifications. Finagle, he'd found her in Brennan's old singleship.

And as spotty as was Sigmund's knowledge of Belter history, Alice knew events from long after Brennan-monster should have starved to death. Put it all together and Brennan *had* solved the tree-of-life virus problem, and so survived, and so met Alice long after. All of her story hung together, except the most critical part—the supposed threat to Earth of Pak fleets long overdue in Sigmund's day.

"Sigmund? Are you all right?"

In his mind, finally, puzzle pieces fell into place. "Home had a plague, all right. A tree-of-life virus plague. A Pak plague. *That's* what wiped out the colony." He kept on despite Alice's look of revulsion. Everything was suddenly, horrifyingly clear. "Brennan set loose the Pak virus on Home. That's how he got help. He raised an army of protectors."

Roy, surely, among them.

Alice glanced down fearfully at her belly. At Roy's baby. Her expression asked: Am I carrying a monster? "But protectors . . . protect. What about Home's colonists?"

The colonists weren't related to Brennan or Roy. That made them expendable. Sigmund tried to think like a Pak, and about his many interrogations of Thssthfok. It made Sigmund ill—and eerily certain what must have happened.

"The original tree-of-life virus kills anyone too old," he said. "Suppose Brennan's variant also killed everyone too young. That would leave a population of childless protectors." And millions dead. Brennan had been right to call himself a monster. "Like Phssthpok, they could only die or adopt a cause. Brennan's cause: an armada to go after the Pak." And as they left, they torched the abandoned cities to obliterate every trace of their actions.

"But there were no traces of a virus," Alice insisted. There was no cool professionalism left in her. She wanted—desperately—to prove Sigmund wrong.

If only he were. "I imagine that the virus was engineered to be fragile outside its host. Maybe ultraviolet exposure killed it, maybe winter temperatures. Let a year pass, and Home was virus-free. Brennan would not have allowed rogue protectors to crop up among new settlers."

"Well at least you have your answer." Alice swallowed hard. "You say that in your time no one had heard of either Brennan's fleet or the Pak fleets. I see only one explanation. They wiped each other out." She glanced again at her belly. This look was more wistful: Your father is dead, baby. "In a gruesome way, isn't this good news?"

Had there been only one set of Pak fleets, the Librarians who had followed in Phssthpok's wake, then yes. Of course. But there was *another* fleet. A merciless fleet, onrushing even now, its vanguard a scant few years from New Terra. Even as Sigmund dabbled in pointless historical mysteries.

"Here's how I see it," Sigmund said finally. "Millions become protectors. A world looted of anything useful to build a navy. None of them came back." Because if they had, they would have done something by now about the Kzinti. "So we know what it takes to stop a Pak fleet. A world of protectors."

While New Terrans were merely human, and Puppeteer-conditioned pacifists at that. Puppeteers, like Kzinti, were unheard of in the Sol system of Alice's day. She knew nothing of either.

Sigmund was thankful, suddenly, that Baedeker had followed another path. Alice had much study ahead of her before Sigmund could hope to pass her off—for her own good—as a New Terran native.

Not that it really mattered. Going down fighting remained the only option on the table.

He took a deep breath. "A world of human protectors only fought Phssthpok's allies to a draw. What does that say about our hopes of surviving this onslaught?"

DESTROYER OF WORLDS

52

Thssthfok paced his newest cell. He had tugged experimentally at every massive metal bar of his cage, and ten Pak could not have bent them. The cell door, when armored guards opened it to deliver or remove a food tray, required a massive metal key and squealed on its hinges. The walls beyond his reach behind the bars were concrete. So were the floor and ceiling. He had memorized every discoloration, ripple, dip, and bump in every surface.

Armored guards in a clear-walled observation room watched him at all times. To judge from the faces behind the visors, all were too young to respond to tree-of-life root—when, one tuber at a time, it was doled out—if their suits should tear. They were well trained and refused to be drawn into conversation. On the bright side, he had a toilet, bedding, and, beyond the bars, one small window.

His confinement was primitive, and would take that much longer to defeat because of it.

He exercised steadily. It helped fill the time. It kept him fit for the opportunity to escape that must come. To doubt was to die.

His jailers gave him reading material. The books offered nothing useful and he ignored them. Little animals with bushy tails sometimes perched on the ledge outside his window. He ignored them, too.

Colored lights blinked on the bracelet clamped around his ankle, radioing his location independently of the guards and the beyond-the-bars cameras. Perhaps the anklet would also shock or drug him if he tried to escape. Thssthfok would have built in that capability.

The metal band flexed under stiffened fingers. With effort, he thought, he could tear off the anklet, but opening the band would at a minimum open a circuit and trigger an alarm. But if the metal was weak enough to tear—

Breeders fidget. Humans would think nothing of Thssthfok fidgeting.

He spun the band, around and around and around, a finger exploring the inner surface. He found an array of pinholes that might emit a gaseous or aerosol drug. Something to knock him out on contact.

A bit of well-chewed food would plug the holes—blocking airflow sensors inside. They would know that he had noticed the mechanism. A new anklet with another knockout device might not offer the convenience of holes. Hooking a claw tip in a perforation, he began tugging and scraping. In time, he would expose the hidden circuitry. . . .

Movement in the observation room caught Thssthfok's eye. A newcomer, armored like the rest. The guards stood stiffly in his presence. The person turned and Thssthfok saw his face. Sigmund.

The door opened from the observation room into the prison. Sigmund came through and the door slammed shut behind him. He waited outside the bars. "Hello, Thssthfok."

"Sigmund."

"Are you comfortable?"

Breeders cared about comfort. Perhaps Sigmund thought to induce or coerce him. "I would not mind a change of scenery." Someplace less securely guarded.

Sigmund sat in a chair placed far back from the cell. He took a computer from a pocket. "I have some interesting scenery in here."

Thssthfok had nothing else to do. He waited.

Sigmund said, "Here's the thing. Worlds important to me lie in the path of the Pak advance. It's necessary that the Pak go elsewhere."

Thssthfok knew of this world only what could be seen through his one tiny window: the planet had many suns. He supposed it was among the fleet of worlds glimpsed during a brief escape. "This world, for example."

Sigmund leaned forward. "We can do something for each other."

Breeders used crude social rituals to establish hierarchy, assign their simple tasks, select mates, and allocate their meager belongings. Thssthfok remembered his life as a breeder, remembered giving favors and expecting favors in turn. He remembered the vague sense, too ill-defined to articulate, that such social obligations somehow helped everyone.

With maturity came clarity and wisdom. You protected your family and your clan. You took what you could, and all that you could, to benefit your bloodline, but never more than you could defend. Nothing else mattered.

To seek allies exposed weakness and desperation. When you allied, you did so knowing the other side would betray you the moment the cost became acceptable. As the other side expected from you. . . .

Thus had clan Rilchuk aligned itself, so long ago, of dire necessity, with the comet dwellers. Thssthfok's fear for his breeders never ended.

Humans were neither breeder nor protector, but an unnatural mixture. *Do something for each other.* An advanced version of breeders trading favors, then. Sigmund had given aliens free run aboard his ship. Perhaps humans allied more readily than did protectors.

"What would you have me do?" Thssthfok asked.

A hologram leapt from the device in Sigmund's hand. A scattering of stars. A sprawling nebula, its dust and gas dimly lit by unseen stars within. And against that smoky backdrop: swarms of dots, in wave after wave, each wave shown in a separate color. The Pak fleets!

Nothing was as Thssthfok remembered from long-ago tactical displays, and yet . . . In the third wave, a cluster of dots occupied the relative position the comet-dweller/Rilchuk forces had once dominated. They might be his old fleet. They might not. Deployments had evolved during his exile—as they must—in the shifting of alliances and the rise and fall of military fortunes.

Sigmund terminated the image. "Unnatural helium concentrations and ripples in the interstellar medium pinpoint the Pak ships coming this way."

"What would you have me do?" Thssthfok repeated.

"Spare my conscience. My people don't want to destroy your fleets, but we will."

"Conscience? What is that?"

Sigmund sighed. "Knowing right from wrong, and preferring to do the former."

Acts that benefited one's own were right. Failing to benefit one's own was wrong. To destroy one's enemy must always be right. If Sigmund could destroy the oncoming Pak fleets, he would. This *conscience* changed nothing.

Thssthfok gestured at the metal bars. "I have no influence over your actions, Sigmund."

"But perhaps you could influence the Pak advance. Would they listen if you advised them to change their current course?"

Of course not. No rational adversary would lose the opportunity to destroy an adversary. Nothing Thssthfok could say would convince the clans that powerful opponents existed who might stay their hand. As nothing Sigmund said would ever convince Thssthfok.

Sigmund was attempting, incredibly, to bluff all the fleets of the Pak. But if Sigmund *believed* Thssthfok could influence the fleets—

"It is possible," Thssthfok lied. "After my absence from the evacuation fleet, I must know more."

"Like what?"

"The balance of influence"—the balance of power—"among clans."

"How can we know that?" Sigmund asked.

Thssthfok gestured at the computer still in Sigmund's hand. "Perhaps from more data like what you showed me. How much do you have?"

Sigmund tapped at his device. "Similar long-range observations spanning about two hundred days."

"Seen over what distance?"

A truthful response might reveal the distance to the Pak vanguard, and Sigmund chose not to answer. "Would the full set of imagery be useful?"

"Very much."

Sigmund tapped some more on the computer. A slightly different stars-and-starships image appeared. "Here is the full data set in time-lapse form."

The dots representing ships shifted against the nebula and stars and, more intricately and subtly, with respect to each other. Counting heartbeats as a crude clock, Thssthfok watched the images morph. The steadiness of his heartbeat was the least of his assumptions as he estimated angles and inferred course parameters. If by *day*, Sigmund meant the dark/light cycle on this planet, and if Sigmund had told the truth about the images representing two hundred days of observations, the vanguard approached at about half light speed.

"I will have to think about what I have seen," Thssthfok said.

"Can you identify your clan's ships?"

So that you can threaten them to coerce me? Thssthfok said, "I need to think about what I have seen. Much has changed in my absence."

Sigmund stood. "I'll check with you tomorrow."

"All right."

Sigmund left, and Thssthfok began circling the cell. The static image had revealed little. But the animation! The subtle dance—of dominated volumes shrinking and expanding, of squadrons gaining and losing ships, of swirling realignments as coalitions formed and were betrayed—told a story. Different clans favored different tactical deployments. They responded in time-tested ways to feints and attacks. Their weakest ships constrained their maneuvering. To one with the knowledge to read it, the jitter of the dots told a great deal.

He replayed the animation in his thoughts, focusing one by one on the midsized clusters within the third wave. The squadron he had first looked to for his clan—wasn't. But among the last of the candidates, having fallen back defensively, their numbers depleted, he found a bunch of ships whose tactics he knew well. The comet-dweller/Rilchuk alliance still survived. He might yet have breeders in cold sleep—

And they needed his protection more than ever.

53

Sigmund strode across the broad plaza, the air crisp and fresh, sunlight warm on his face. People streamed all around, chatting or laughing or lost in thought. New Terra felt strange and wonderful at the same time. Strings of suns and the occasional red-and-purple plant beat deep space, let alone hyperspace, anytime.

Far better would have been a day at home with Penny and the kids, but he had work to do.

He met Alice at the security checkpoint outside Governor's Building. She stood out like a sore thumb: taller than everyone and looking all around like a tourist. Still, with her Belter crest removed (*that* had been a struggle) and her bald head covered by a wig, and wearing clothes Kirsten had programmed, Alice could pass for New Terran. When her pregnancy began to show, he would find her a progeny ring.

He had smuggled Alice by stepping disc directly from *Don Quixote* to the Office of Strategic Analyses headquarters. Would Puppeteers grab her from New Terra, as Nessus had grabbed him? Who could say? For her own safety, he had kept her origins a secret. Only a *very* select few had the need to know. At this morning's meeting, only Sabrina knew.

Guards saluted smartly. "Good morning, Minister," the guard lieutenant said. He nodded to Alice. "IDs, please."

"Good morning, Lieutenant, soldiers." It pleased Sigmund that security hadn't slipped during his long absence. Not that an escaped Pak could go unnoticed.

Sigmund offered his ID disc, one thumb on the biometric pad. Alice followed his lead. Her ID gave her rank as colonel: senior enough to have authority and not so senior that anyone would think twice about not already knowing her.

"Very good, sirs. The others have arrived and the governor will join you shortly." The squad leader nodded at two of his men. "We'll escort you."

The guards led them to a private dining chamber. The oval table had padded chairs along one side and mounds of pillows along the other. Human and Puppeteer foods covered the semi-oval side table. Brunch justified meeting someplace the Puppeteers hadn't bugged—without revealing Sigmund's knowledge that many offices, including Sabrina's, *were* bugged.

Baedeker and Nessus were waiting, with two guards "there if they needed anything" so that the room stayed unbugged. Sigmund dismissed both sets of the guards. He wasn't surprised to find Nessus with an unkempt mane. But Baedeker was also disheveled, and that was a bad omen.

They exchanged greetings all around and again when Sabrina, looking wearier than Sigmund had ever seen her, arrived. Sigmund introduced Alice as "One of my aides." Alice managed to stay casual even though these were the first Puppeteers she had ever met.

Nessus attended as the Hindmost's personal representative. No one brought up Sigmund's refusal to meet on Hearth. Whatever the venue, both governments *had* to coordinate. They had many possible courses of action to consider.

None, so far, that could work.

Neither New Terra nor the Fleet had a navy with which even to attempt a defense. Nessus trilled softly at Sigmund's implied rebuke, but did not attempt a justification.

Outsider drives worked over long periods of time, delivering a gentle but continuous acceleration. New Terra and the Fleet could not get out of the Pak's way in time, nor do anything to help the Gw'oth.

Puppeteers reflexively ran or hid from any possible threat and Pak preemptively destroyed any possible threat. Neither species believed in diplomacy. The Concordance *did* understand commerce, and Nessus wondered if they could buy peace with supplies or technology. Everything Sigmund knew said the Pak would not honor a deal. The Pak would take everything offered and *still* attack. That took negotiation for safe passage off the table.

Sigmund had toyed with using Thssthfok—somehow—to bluff the Pak fleets. Thssthfok was happy to talk, but every scenario he came up with involved giving him a ship. Seeing who was manipulating whom, Sigmund had abandoned that idea, too.

Even the genocidal weapon of last resort, a kinetic planet-buster, offered no hope. The Pak had spread themselves across a widely distributed fleet—while planet-bound New Terrans and Puppeteers alike were sitting ducks. (Alice had been to Earth and seen ducks. She got the metaphor but froze mid-nod when Sabrina looked puzzled.)

The longer the meeting went on, the more Baedeker plucked at his mane. Reluctantly, as all eyes turned toward him, Baedeker spoke. "So our survival depends on better planetary drives." A hint of rising inflection made the words a question, a plea for the burden of worlds to be lifted from his shoulders.

"It seems so," Nessus said, and yet he looked to Sigmund rather than Baedeker.

"Tell us about your progress," Sigmund said.

From a head plunged deep into his mane, Baedeker answered, "The prototypes continue to demonstrate instability problems."

Sabrina cleared her throat. "Please explain."

Baedeker did, with specifics that made Sigmund's head hurt. From their months spent together, Sigmund had a pretty good idea that the torrent of words masked a *lack* of progress.

Or maybe cop training was what led him to that conclusion, because Alice got there, too. "How soon, exactly, does instability set in?"

"Up to sixteen on the last trial, before we had to shut it down."

"Sixteen what?" Alice persisted, a bit impatiently, and Sabrina shot Alice a sharp glance. New Terrans had centuries of indoctrination deferring to their former masters.

"Your aide, indeed, Sigmund." Nessus briefly looked himself in the eyes. "I see your influence. Alice, I am afraid the answer is sixteen nanoseconds."

"Can anyone else make a drive work—at all?" With a jerk, Baedeker removed the head from his mane. He straightened both necks to stare boldly, one person at a time, at everyone in the room. "I thought not."

"Perhaps," Sigmund began. He had to laugh at Nessus' two-headed double take. "No, not I. Shipmates on *Don Quixote*."

"Eric? Surely a talented engineer, but—"

Baedeker cut off Nessus. "Shipmates, plural. He means the Gw'oth, Nessus. It is unacceptable to expose them to this level of advanced physics."

The Puppeteers burst into full-throated cacophony, music and crashing metal and tortured animals combined. An argument, the details of which Sigmund hoped Jeeves could translate, while doubting the hidden recorder would capture it. Puppeteers built impressive jammers.

"You will stop," Sabrina said softly. Those were her first words for some time, and the Puppeteers twitched and fell silent. "And speak English." She turned to Sigmund. "Please continue."

Sigmund took a deep breath. Imminent existential danger trumped long-term risks every time. "Our Gw'oth *friends* are why we're here. Their superior astronomy first noticed the enemy. They helped us capture Thsssth-fok." While Baedeker cowered in his cabin. "Their quick thinking saved us more than once. We need their talents."

Nessus swiveled one head toward Baedeker. "Sigmund makes a good argument."

Baedeker spewed a short arpeggio, stopped, and began again. "Yes, it sounds reasonable, but at least these particular Gw'oth, this group mind, learns astonishingly fast."

"Isn't quickness just what we need?" Nessus asked.

"Enough!" Sabrina pushed back her chair and stood. "Baedeker, forty-two humans are assisting your project. Neither you nor they have given me any reason to expect success. I'll make it simple. Accept the Gw'oth scientists on the project, or I order my team home."

There was a second, brief eruption of noise, from which Baedeker was the first to subside. Nessus said, "Understood, Sabrina. On behalf of the Hindmost, I accept your terms."

HOME.

Sigmund sat in his favorite chair, little Athena on his knee—only she wasn't so little. She must have shot up another two inches. She squirmed, and he knew suddenly that she had outgrown the bedtime story he was reading. He tousled her hair. "You can read this yourself, can't you?"

"Yes, Daddy. But it's all right." She smiled up at him shyly: You mean well.

Hermes sat nearby, acting busy with a pocket comp as he guarded his baby sister. That I'm-the-man-of-the-house protectiveness touched Sigmund—and it wounded him even more deeply than the boy's aloofness.

I'm gone so much that I'm losing them, Sigmund thought. It hurt. He handed Athena his comp. "Why don't you read to me?"

Penny was in the kitchen, speaking in clipped, urgent tones. She wasn't standoffish—only rarely available. The spreading dead zone off Arcadia's western coast had decimated the kelp farms. Huge masses of Hearthian sea life had died, and the stench from the ocean had become unbearable. Penny was on the emergency task force, up to her neck in evacuation planning.

"What's this word, Daddy?"

He looked where she pointed. "Neighbor," he said. "The gee-aitch is silent."

All for want of a moon. "Give New Terra its own moon and it regains some tides."

Athena stopped, midsentence. "What, Daddy?"

"Nothing, sweetie. Something a friend once said to me." Back when Baedeker naïvely thought he could build a planetary drive and deliver a moon. Now the stakes were higher.

Two screens before the story ended, Sigmund's comp rang with the subtle, minor-key trill of a priority call. He kissed the top of Athena's head. "I have to take this. Hop off."

She slid from Sigmund's lap and he went into his den and shut the door. With the bedtime story closed, the OSA icon blinked on the display.

Kirsten was tonight's duty officer at the Office of Strategic Analyses. Most nights nothing happened, but someone had to cover just in case. She had volunteered, wanting some quality time alone with Brennan's singleship. The protector's modifications continued to baffle her.

Sigmund took her call. "What's up?"

"Nessus just filed a flight plan, Sigmund. He wants to take off immediately."

Finagle. "There are things he and I still need to discuss. He's been avoiding me."

Kirsten grinned. "There's an air-traffic delay, as it happens."

"Good job." He thought fast. "I need ten minutes to wrap up something. Let Nessus know I'm coming."

"Will do. Anything else?"

"That's it, Kirsten. Thanks."

He hung up and opened the den door. "All right, sweetie. Let's finish this story."

SIGMUND HALF EXPECTED NESSUS would not allow him aboard *Aegis*, but the Puppeteer sent a stepping-disc address. It delivered Sigmund into an isolation booth. Of course.

"It's good of you to wait for me," Sigmund began.

A hoof scraped at the deck. "To take off without the cooperation of traffic control would be dangerous."

"After we talk, I think I can get you authorized for departure."

Nessus looked himself in the eyes. "I am much relieved."

"Maybe together, the Gw'oth and Baedeker can make new planetary drives work." Only everything Twenty-three had said made success seem vanishingly unlikely. "We can't afford to bet on it."

"And our choices are?"

We need more help, tanj it! If *only* Alice could point them toward Earth. The best psychologists on New Terra had had even less success with her than they had with Sigmund. Alice had no interstellar-navigational memories to recover. "Bring me to Earth, Nessus."

"There is no point. The Pak have destroyed it."

Aid for the survivors would be a purpose, wouldn't it? "Then there is no harm in bringing me."

Nessus backed up a step. "It would be a long voyage to no purpose, and I am needed on Hearth."

"We both know you're lying." Sigmund's hands yearned to become fists, and no good could come of that—helpless as he was in this cell. He jammed his hands into his pockets.

"If Earth remained as you remember it, I still could not bring you. Concordance policy would forbid it."

Did Concordance policy allow kidnapping Earth citizens and erasing their memories, or am I the exception? "Nessus, you trust"—for some insane reason—"my ability to solve your problems. It *can't* be so hard for you to believe that other humans also have useful skills. Permit me some help, some other experts. For both our worlds' sake." Memories of the innocent little girl sitting on his lap only a few minutes earlier broke his heart.

"More ARMs?" Nessus plucked at his mane. "Had you not been near death that day, I would never have dared to approach you."

"Not ARMs. More . . . specialized talent. While in Human Space, I *know* you hired humans." Often criminals. "Do it again, Nessus." Don't bet worlds on me!

"Tempting, but unacceptable. Why would mercenaries fight Pak when they could raid Hearth instead?"

"More specialized still," Sigmund said. "We need truly creative people. Unique people. Baedeker needs all the physics talent he can get. Will you recruit experts from Human Space?"

"You have people in mind. Who?"

"Beowulf Shaeffer and Carlos Wu." One an adventurer with an uncanny knack for survival, the other a certified genius.

Nessus twitched. He clearly remembered both men, too. (Sigmund wondered if the Puppeteer had ever heard the term *loose cannon*.) A head dipped lower and lower, finally dipping into a pocket of his sash. The visible head said, "No—"

And Sigmund found himself in a public square half a continent away.

54

"Three . . . two . . . one . . . now." Minerva scarcely paused. "Experiment complete."

"How long?" Baedeker asked.

Minerva, Baedeker's research assistant, craned a neck over his console. "One point oh four two three seconds."

Across *Haven*'s bridge, two human technicians cheered at finally breaking the one-second barrier. Baedeker scarcely spared them a disapproving glance. The Fleet would not escape the Pak in one-second spurts.

One of the Gw'oth sidled closer. Beneath the exoskeleton, its motors humming, and beneath the transparent pressure suit, peeked a name written in chromatophoric cells: Er'o. "We do make progress, Baedeker."

Baedeker straightened a bit of mane braid. He tired of hints about Er'o's contributions. Or about *their* contributions, since Baedeker never knew when a Gw'o merely disclosed an insight of the group mind. Maybe if *he* had been aboard *Don Quixote*, and had had the same opportunity to closely observe the Outsider ship operating its drive . . .

Baedeker tamped down his annoyance. For the sake of the Concordance, he needed help. Anyone's help. He bobbed heads, conceding Er'o's point.

Er'o needed no more encouragement. "Perhaps an extended experiment would give us more insight into the instability."

Minerva bleated disapproval. "We extend the experiments as quickly as we learn."

Er'o double-tapped the deck with a tubacle, the mannerism Baedeker had come to interpret as impatience. "We terminate the drive experiments prematurely. We could learn more."

That was insanity, and Baedeker yearned to flee. He settled for pawing the deck. "It does not disturb you that space-time contorts around the drive?"

"We are *trying* to warp space-time." Of necessity, everyone aboard communicated in English, but Er'o overlaid his with Citizen harmonics, rich with undertunes of smug superiority. "Without inducing a slope, we obtain no motion."

"A slope." Baedeker spread his hooves, made himself *un*ready to run, striving to exhibit as much confidence. "I wish we were producing a clean slope. Look at the data. As the drive loses stability, the 'slope' begins to fluctuate chaotically, even over quantum distances." Even chaos somehow failed to describe the rippling, writhing, bumpy space-time contour that reinvented itself by the femtosecond. "We stop because we must."

"Fluctuations superimposed on an emergent slope," Er'o insisted. "We see hints that the fluctuations are about to peak. There are patterns upon patterns of flux, and Kl'o expects we may soon observe interference patterns and thus cancellation."

"If we keep observing," one of the humans in the background muttered unnecessarily.

In theory, Baedeker was hindmost here. In practice, most of the team was New Terran. Even the Gw'oth present at the insistence of New Terra outnumbered the few Citizens. Baedeker had to keep their support. He had to show Nessus more progress.

And he had to do it, somehow, without getting anyone killed.

"How long would you run the experiment?" Baedeker asked.

"Until the drive stabilizes or self-destructs," Er'o said.

On trembling legs Baedeker began a slow ambit of the bridge, studying instruments and computer displays. Crew scurried out of his way. He scrutinized the details of the hyperwave-buoy placement. He confirmed the ship's position at twenty million miles from the icy rock now home to the latest prototype drive. He examined the final visualization—necessarily grossly oversimplified—of space-time flux at the instant safeguards had terminated the most recent trial. He surveyed *Haven*'s own diagnostic panel and assured himself that every sensor, every triplicated system, every failover mechanism exhibited unimpaired capacity.

Er'o's proposed experiment *could* be done.

Baedeker completed his circuit, stopping near Er'o. "And would you agree to *Haven* jumping to hyperspace if the chaotic effects reach within ten million miles?"

Tap-tap. "Agreed," Er'o said.

Remotely deactivating the safety protocols on the prototype drive took only five minutes. Baedeker needed another five minutes, ostensibly spent reexamining sensor calibrations, to bring himself to give the order. All around, the humans whispered. "Start the countdown," he finally ordered.

Sixty-five seconds later, with half its bridge alarms screaming, *Haven* flicked into hyperspace. From a safer distance, Baedeker watched tier after tier of buoys drop from comm.

Nothing remained of the planetoid but a cloud of gas and dust, erupting at near light speed.

The disaster wasn't total. The drive had achieved thrust in the desired direction, although that nudge was nothing compared to the shattering effects—in *every* direction—of the explosion.

And Er'o, uncharacteristically, had no unsolicited advice to offer.

THE WORKSHOPS ABOARD *Haven* hummed with activity. Someone was always refining circuitry for the next prototype drive or configuring additional sensors for the next test. Every new circuit and sensor required still more custom equipment for predeployment checkout. Custom items might be fabricated in one shipboard facility, tested in a second, integrated with other parts in a third, deployed in yet a fourth. Human, Citizen, and Gw'o alike: It made no difference. Anyone might be handling unfamiliar gear at any time, anywhere in the ship.

Hence few noticed, and no one gave a second thought to, the Gw'oth installing sensors about *Haven*.

Sigmund would have noticed, Ol't'ro suspected, but Sigmund was not here. The paranoid human was far away, across a hyperwave link, reviewing project status. Neither Sigmund nor Baedeker knew the Gw'otesht could listen in.

"A second or two," Sigmund repeated. "And still only scale models. No one is going anywhere with drives like that."

"No one," Baedeker agreed. "If we can maintain this rate of progress, though, then maybe. In time."

"You don't sound optimistic," Sigmund said.

The technical challenges were familiar. The grudging credit for Gw'oth contributions was not new. Taking in everything, Ol't'ro attended more to nuance and tones of voice than to content. Baedeker had something on his mind.

Baedeker finally came out with it. "Sigmund, I assume Thssthfok can never be set free."

"He's seen too much of our technology. And he's so tanj smart, I'm afraid to think how much more he's deduced." Sigmund paused. "I don't feel good about it. Possibly, if the Pak veer, after they have passed us by. But realistically, no."

"Then you'll understand *my* concern," Baedeker said. "Ol't'ro cannot go home, either."

"It's not the same," Sigmund snapped. "The Gw'oth are our friends. Our allies. You wouldn't have made half the progress you have without them."

"How does that make them less dangerous?"

As Ol't'ro had feared, their contributions—essential for everyone's safety—were being turned against them. They listened dispiritedly as Baedeker and Sigmund debated, neither convincing the other.

Sigmund finally said, "I have other sources of information aboard *Haven*. If anything unfortunate happens to the Gw'oth, *anything*, the New Terrans come home. That's a promise, Baedeker."

"All right," Baedeker said.

Into Baedeker's grudging tone, Ol't'ro read a mind still plotting.

"YOU DO WELL," Nessus said. His ship, *Aegis*, had emerged hours earlier from hyperspace on yet another unannounced inspection of Baedeker's project. The two of them had withdrawn to Baedeker's cabin.

Another interruption was the last thing Baedeker needed, but the unexpected praise tempered his irritation. That, and practicality. The *real* last thing he needed was the loss of Concordance support. Nessus' backing mattered. "Thank you," Baedeker said.

Being hindmost had advantages. So did control of a large ship. Baedeker's cabin had lush meadowplant carpet, with room to wander when he chose to be alone and for large gatherings at other times, and a pantry filled with real grasses and grains. It also had an extensively programmed synthesizer, from which Nessus obtained a bulb of warm carrot juice.

"Net thrust and improved stability," Nessus began. "Truly, you have done well since my last visit. And yet . . ."

Baedeker bobbed heads. "And yet we have *very* far to go."

"What are your plans?"

"To better integrate efforts here and on NP5," Baedeker said. "Too many observations of the NP5 drive made no sense. Having operated our own drives"—however briefly—"I am beginning to understand what the sealed Outsider controls must do. It no longer seems impossible to run their drives a bit harder."

Nessus raised his heads optimistically. "Can you run drives in tandem?"

A digital herd meandered in a nearby arc of wall. Fields of tall grain rippled in the simulated breeze. Baedeker took a moment to adjust the image. "Nothing we have seen contradicts Twenty-three's warning to Sigmund."

"That is unfortunate," Nessus said.

They stood watching the idyllic scene, Baedeker wondering what he could add to that.

"You will succeed," Nessus finally said. "And when you do, much will become possible for you."

Baedeker blinked. "What do you mean?"

"The Hindmost will be in your debt. Have you given thought to the path you will take then?"

Stress and exhaustion filled Baedeker's waking hours, the weight of worlds heavy on his shoulders. "Truthfully, no."

Nessus edged closer, brushing flanks intimately. "I am not without influence. You have it within your grasp to have a great future. If you were to express an interest in government and show some hints of sympathy with Experimentalist policy . . ."

Then opportunities would come Baedeker's way. Was he interested? Maybe—if not for the reasons Nessus might suspect. Baedeker temporized. "What sort of interest in government?"

"Something in the Ministry of Science, perhaps." Nessus swiveled his heads to gauge Baedeker's reaction. "Something very well positioned."

Such as Minister of Science? To direct science policy for the Concordance would be no small thing. Baedeker felt tempted and terrified in equal measure. But there was an element of temptation Nessus could not have anticipated.

With government authority might come action against the Gw'oth threat.

55

The kids were bathed and changed for bed, and Penny's uncle Sven had come over to watch them. Neither ecological nor existential threats showed any signs of worsening overnight. Prison sensors showed Thssthfok was soundly asleep. Circumstances would never get better.

Sigmund offered Penelope his arm. They went outside to stroll to a nearby restaurant. Master chef, all-natural ingredients, live band, the works. And, in unison, they yawned.

He had to laugh. "Going to be quite the night on the town."

"I'm sorry," she said, covering another yawn. "Just a lot going on."

The cloudless night sky was bleeding away the day's heat, putting a nip in the air. Stars sparkled overhead. Sigmund tried and failed to imagine a big moon hanging overhead. He thought he remembered that the full moon was romantic.

A lot *was* going on. All the more reason to enjoy what they had, while they still had it, and they were long overdue for a romantic evening. He leaned over and kissed Penny's hair. "I won't notice you yawn if you return the favor."

"Deal."

They made another deal over hors d'ouevres not to talk about the kids. Without erecting an electronic privacy barrier, neither of them could talk about work. And so, insanely, the conversation lagged. What had they talked about—before?

They managed to discuss entrée options. Penny patted his hand. "This is ridiculous, Sigmund. We don't need to chatter. It's all right simply to enjoy each other's company."

"I know." He didn't see this being a long evening.

They lapsed into uncomfortable silence, pretending this was a normal night out and that the end of the world wasn't rushing their way. Occasionally one of them would compliment the food, which deserved it, or the musicians, who didn't. The evening became more and more . . .

Sigmund couldn't quite put his finger on it. The evening was—what? Familiar? Hardly. Well deserved. Strained. Overshadowed by the overwhelming problems they had vowed to leave at home but he couldn't banish from his mind.

Tideless oceans. Moonless nights. Sigmund didn't see New Terra obtaining a moon anytime soon. Implacable enemies. Progress measured in nanoseconds.

He must have been muttering to himself, because Penny asked, "What's Rome?"

"It's a city on Earth."

Rome. The Eternal City. An ancient, ruined coliseum. The mental image of a boot. Something about roads. Earth's landscape had roads, mostly in disuse, made obsolete by antigrav floaters and transfer booths. What *about* roads? New Terra didn't have them, its infrastructure designed from the start for stepping discs and gravity floaters. What about roads?

Penny was frowning at him. He said, "I don't know, only that all roads lead . . ."

All roads lead to Rome. Just as everything on Sigmund's mind led to Baedeker.

SIGMUND MET ERIC AND KIRSTEN at an Office of Strategic Analyses safe house. They were yawning, too.

"What's the emergency?" Eric asked.

Sigmund jammed his hands in his pockets to keep from fidgeting. "Maybe nothing. Maybe an answer to everything. Until I know, I'm not going to sleep." And if he was right, he wouldn't sleep tonight, either. Hope was exhilarating. "Only it's half an idea at best."

Kirsten brushed bangs off her forehead. "All right, Sigmund, begin at the beginning."

He saw no need to start that far back. "First, Baedeker's drive. It won't move planets. It just blows them up."

"If he's not careful," Eric agreed.

"Second, we're unable to do to the Pak what the Pak do to everyone they pass."

Kirsten nodded. "Because everyone else is planet-based. One kinetic-kill weapon can smash a world. They, having abandoned their world, are too dispersed to attack that way."

"Turn the problem on its head." Sigmund waited for them to see it, but they didn't. "Pak will use a kinetic-kill vehicle against a planet. With Baedeker's drive, we can shatter a planet into overwhelming amounts of kinetic-kill debris."

Eric's eyes got round. "Huge amounts of relativistic dust and gas, blasted right down the maw of the ramscoops. Massive overload. It'd be unavoidable—and lethal."

"Yes, but." Kirsten used a voice-of-reason tone. "There's no way to get a planet into position. Baedeker's drives won't do that."

The perfect weapon and no way to deliver it. *So* close.

"Here's a thought," Eric said suddenly. "Take a world out of the Fleet. We know that can be done: Not so long ago we pulled NP4 out of the configuration. NP5 is expendable. It's not yet fully reengineered for Hearth life. It'd be easy to evacuate the few planetary engineers living there."

The Fleet had accelerated steadily since the Concordance first fled the core explosion. Worlds racing at ten percent of light speed (a bit more for New Terra, redlining its drive to get away from their former masters) was astounding—and yet hardly enough. They couldn't outrun the Pak even if the Fleet had been heading in exactly the right direction.

But some of the Fleet's velocity vector *did* point away from the Pak. NP5 would need years to shed that momentum. And the Pak, given years to notice a whole *planet* headed their way, were much faster and more maneuverable.

So how could NP5 help? Sigmund didn't get it. "I don't see—"

Eric chuckled, but not unkindly. "Now you know how we feel around you, Sigmund. You're always three steps ahead of us. NP5 isn't the weapon. We get NP5 out of the way, salvage its planetary drive, and put the drive onto a sacrificial world close to the Pak. With luck, they won't detect an unlit planet coming at them until too late."

Sigmund rolled the idea around in his head. A plausible weapon. A way to deliver it. And probably just one shot.

That was one more opportunity than they had had until now.

. . .

OL'T'RO COMPLETELY UNDERSTOOD the humans' proposed attack. It was brilliant—and as brutal as the enemy.

They were not surprised. Pak and humans were related.

With a shudder, Ol't'ro detached the Er'o unit. They wanted an alternative, even before the hyperwave consultation ended, and that required eyes on instruments. They kept monitoring the conversation as Er'o struggled into a pressure suit for the trek to *Haven*'s observatory.

"Yes, it is possible we might spare NP5," Nessus said. He participated by hyperwave link from somewhere near Hearth. "It is not yet producing food. Even if it were, almost everyone lives on synthesized food. Nature-grown food is a luxury.

"The issue will be sacrificing an Outsider drive. No Nature Preserve world matters as much as the planetary drive it carries. The Concordance bought several drives—and will continue paying the Outsiders long after we are all dead—lest Hearth's unit ever fail. Only the Hindmost can make such a decision."

Hearth's drive, if it failed as spectacularly as Baedeker's prototype, would leave no survivors—and quite possibly no world, either. A spare drive served no purpose. Baedeker surely saw that, too, and chose not to comment. The Pak threat was all the reality the Citizens could handle.

"How long will it take to extricate NP5 and remove its drive?" Eric asked. He, Kirsten, and Sigmund had linked in from a ship just outside New Terra's singularity.

In Ol't'ro's comm terminal, Baedeker pawed at the vegetation-covered deck of his cabin. "No planetary drive has been installed within living memory, but records show installation is a lengthy process. To my knowledge, no one has ever uninstalled one."

Ol't'ro sent a private message—hurry!—to Er'o, who was finally suited up and through the water lock. "We see a possible way to save time," they said. "Fine-tune your other drives. Mold the space-time neighborhoods around *all* the planets to give NP5 a harder push out of the way."

That started the argument Ol't'ro intended. Had they learned enough to even consider such a maneuver? Might they cause worlds to crash? What real-time sensing and control would they need? How long would it take to reestablish the old space-time slope? Would asymmetries in the drive field cause tidal waves or trigger seismic activity?

Whenever a conclusion threatened, Ol't'ro found some complication to raise. Otherwise they kept quiet. Their goal was delay, not decision, while Er'o made his observations. That left Ol't'ro to brood about the quickness with which humans and Citizens alike accepted a genocidal attack. Ol't'ro would have hoped for a moment of regret.

But Ol't'ro, too, had a home to protect, and memories washed over them. The boundless ocean of Jm'ho. The lush seaweed forests, swaying in the hot currents upwelling from seafloor vents. The great, sprawling seafloor cities. The icy roof of the world and above that the banded splendor of Tl'ho.

They told themselves they were feeling the cramped confines of the tiny habitat. They told themselves they were suffering the imbalance of a meld short of a unit—

They did not believe it.

Ol't'ro could not forget Baedeker's recent private words to Sigmund. Would they see their home again? If the Pak were defeated, would a kinetic-kill weapon *still* find its way to Jm'ho?

Jm'ho must be made too powerful to attack.

Perhaps they had mastered enough technology to make that possible. *If* they brought their new knowledge home and applied it. (Conveniently, the hyperwave link with Jm'ho was one-way, the wrong way.) *If* they lived that long.

"I am in the observatory," Er'o finally radioed. "Commencing scans."

"Excellent." Ol't'ro netted Eric simulation data about withdrawing a world from the Fleet, maintaining the dispute at a boil. "Work quickly, Er'o."

And so the argument continued to rage. "Something about this feels lousy," Sigmund eventually interrupted. "As single-minded as are the Pak, they have not yet attacked us. Even Pak deserve a warning shot. Give me some options, people."

That turned the discussion to how fastest to recover the precious Outsider drive—before a homemade model blew it apart with the sacrificial planet. Baedeker got excited. Nessus fretted that the evacuation ship would be exposed, unable to flee to hyperspace, from within the weapon world's singularity.

Neither Citizen mentioned Sigmund's moral reservation.

"I have two candidates," Er'o radioed privately. "Here are the coordinates. With time for a complete survey, surely I could find several more."

The new data sufficed. Ol't'ro said, "Sigmund, we propose another possibility. Planets are not always bound to suns." Many float free, where hyperspace-traveling species have little reason to look. "Use a wandering body close to the Pak, and explode that. Er'o found two candidates with only a quick scan. Your warning shot need not endanger the drive from NP5."

"*That*," Sigmund said, "is an option I can live with."

56

"Keep it simple," Sigmund told Thssthfok. They were in Thssthfok's cell. "Jeeves will record it for transmission." And do a sanity-check, to the extent he could.

It was a warning message. For the demonstration to matter, the Pak had to see Niflheim shatter.

Jeeves had named the plutoid after the Norse abode of the dead, a place of eternal ice and cold. Sigmund took the AI's word for it. So did Nessus, Norse creation myth being too obscure even for him.

Thssthfok set aside the tree-of-life root on which he had been gnawing, swallowed, and spoke a few clicks and pops.

Maybe the Pak language was more efficient than English. It had to be more logical. Still, that utterance sounded awfully short to Sigmund. "What did you tell the Pak ships?"

"Look here," Thssthfok said.

He was the mission interpreter, assuming he would cooperate. And even if not, Sigmund would rather personally keep an eye on Thssthfok than have the protector anywhere else.

Jeeves claimed he could translate, but Sigmund had his doubts. Jeeves knew of Thssthfok's speech—and surely different clans used different languages—only what Thssthfok had chosen to reveal. Double meanings, secret codes, tanj near anything, could lurk unsuspected in vocabulary exposed to Jeeves. Sigmund half suspected Thssthfok had synthesized a language on the fly.

If Thssthfok minded *Don Quixote*'s smaller cargo hold, he kept it to himself. The larger hold, the Pak's cell on their previous voyage, was now filled by the old singleship. Before this trip ended, Kirsten and Eric swore, they would make some sense of Brennan's modifications.

Would they succeed? Either way, the effort occupied Sigmund's friends on the long flight to Niflheim. Besides, more than intellectual curiosity drove Eric and Kirsten to spend every free hour in the hold. The single-ship was a relic of New Terra's lost heritage. *Long Pass* had been another such relic. Restoring that had been the key to recovering their past and regaining their freedom. They couldn't *not* restore the singleship.

And if the singleship hadn't filled the larger hold, Thssthfok would still be here. More than once Thssthfok had hidden tools in that old cell. There was no reason to gamble that the refit crew had found everything, when the Gw'oth and their habitat remained aboard *Haven*.

That left only the lesser risk of whatever the Gw'oth might have hidden in this hold.

"Look here," Sigmund echoed. "Is that all?"

Thssthfok shrugged, those massive shoulder joints rendering the familiar mannerism alien.

Oh. "Because if they see the . . . demonstration, they'll figure out everything."

Sigmund had only described the coming demonstration as "attention-getting," Thssthfok being too tanj smart to be given hints about new weapons technology. Still, even if Thssthfok somehow escaped yet again, he would not learn much. Baedeker's drives-become-weapons were huge. Sigmund's arsenal was aboard *Haven*, flying along in tandem.

Thssthfok picked up his half-eaten root. "If not, it is a useless demonstration."

Sigmund refused to react. "The message you propose still seems terse."

"No, it is redundant."

"What do you mean?" Sigmund asked, keeping his growing irritation to himself.

Another caricatured shrug.

Because the Pak would look toward *any* unexpected signal, Sigmund realized. Loud static would suffice.

Eventually, frustrated, Sigmund left. He stowed his armor and went to the relax room. "Jeeves," he called.

"Yes, Sigmund."

"Did you monitor Thssthfok and me?"

"I did." Jeeves managed to sound disapproving. "He wasn't very cooperative."

Really? "Did you translate his message, such as it was?"

"Yes. 'Look here,' was accurate."

Sigmund tipped back his chair, trying, and failing, to find comfort in the illusion of blue sky and scudding white clouds. "Jeeves, I want our message to say more. 'Cease attacks on occupied worlds. Veer toward galactic south. Comply, or be destroyed.' Can you add that?"

"I can come close. It may not be grammatical."

"That's fine," Sigmund said. "We'll have given them fair warning." And they will know from the bad grammar that we got the best of at least some Pak.

And if the Pak *did* veer? Bravado aside, Sigmund could not protect everyone. He would have aimed the Pak fleet at other worlds.

Acid churning in his gut, Sigmund hoped none of those worlds was Earth.

57

First Kirsten peered through the hatch window into Thssthfok's cell. Then Eric looked in. He was taller, and Thssthfok saw the metal neck ring of a pressure suit. Both frowned in concentration, like breeders preparing for battle. Reminding themselves of the enemy.

Sigmund's "demonstration" was imminent.

Thssthfok sat on the deck, heels pulled in close to his buttocks, knees spread, "fidgeting" with the anklet. He probed the jagged hole he had torn, avoiding the peeled-back edges. A drop of blood might short-circuit the electronics he had exposed.

He would escape while the humans were occupied.

BAEDEKER CREPT ACROSS THE ICE, distrusting in equal measure the crampons on his boots, the sticks that humans called ski poles, and Niflheim's feeble gravity. The horizon loomed too close. Unfamiliar stars shone overhead. Pressure-suited figures, humans and Gw'oth and Citizens, labored around a cluster of large, black monoliths: a flawed planetary drive become a doomsday device.

He had supervised the site preparation, directed the crews unloading the cargo floaters, and personally prepared each temperamental unit. Module by module he had pored through the subsystem diagnostics—and rejected two units that barely met calibration standards.

He had repeated the entire process with spare units. He had double-checked the squads interconnecting the modules. Now, as the last of the cargo floaters made its way across the ice back to *Haven*, he began another methodical circuit, this time to triple-check everything.

A quarter light-year distant, invisible to the naked eye—and impossible to ignore—was the leading edge of the Pak vanguard.

"Team leads, status report," Sigmund radioed. He stood on a crag, watching everything, obsessively glancing up from time to time to sweep the skies for—anything.

"Nothing to report," Minerva sent from *Haven*, a comforting presence a short distance away across the ice.

"All clear," Kirsten sent from five hundred miles above. *Don Quixote* with its few weapons was the expedition's only protection if any Pak were somehow to sneak up on them.

Baedeker trembled, struggling to stay manic. Without this induced euphoria, this insane bravery, he would cease to function. Without him, the installation would surely fail and all would be lost.

"We are another ten minutes behind schedule," Baedeker admitted. That came to eighty minutes, total, so far. "Still no real problems, I just underestimated the complications of working out here."

"I'm suited up and ready to help," Eric offered.

"Eric, I would rather you stay on *Don Quixote*," Sigmund said firmly.

Baedeker switched to a private channel. "Sigmund, I can use the help. The Gw'oth are exhausted. Half the General Products engineers have returned"—some fled; more carried, comatose, on floaters—"back to *Haven*." And I am hanging on to sanity by my teeth.

"Give me a moment," Sigmund said.

Baedeker could guess at Sigmund's hesitation. Eric on the ground would mean only Kirsten and Jeeves left aboard with Thssthfok.

Sigmund returned to the common channel. "All right, Eric. It sounds like you'll be more useful on the ground."

"Breaking orbit to match velocities with the ground," Kirsten said cheerfully. A few minutes later, she added, "Watch that first step, Eric."

WORKING BY TOUCH Thssthfok visualized the exposed circuitry within the anklet. Some components—resistors, capacitors, integrated circuits, and the like—hinted about themselves by their shapes and sizes. Other components remained unidentified, their nature left to discovery through inference. Interconnection patterns suggested human devices he had scanned before, when he had still had his repair kit and its instruments.

The anklet contained either an inertial position sensor or the ability to locate itself relative to nearby transmitters. It would contain a transmitter to report its own position. It would sense whether the clasp remained sealed.

He catalogued the functions the anklet might perform, then started designing the circuitry and stored program as humans would. His third design incorporated every component he had identified by touch, used consistently with what he had scanned in other human devices. Hence: *This* was the test subsystem. It would provide the means to confirm the anklet could identify any internal failure and then radio the self-diagnosis.

With a little effort, he could expand that output repertoire.

KNOWING IT WAS HIS IMAGINATION, Sigmund felt the cold creep through his insulated boots, up his legs, into his body. This snowball was not much above absolute zero. Having nothing to do but watch and wait somehow made the cold worse.

It wasn't only the cold. The stars shone diamond hard, without a hint of a twinkle. Any trace of atmosphere had long ago frozen. And Niflheim had scarcely one-tenth the mass of New Terra. Niflheim was also physically smaller, of course, raising its surface gravity to a whole one-third of what he was accustomed to. The horizon was much too close, crowding him. . . .

An attack—no, a full-blown, incapacitating seizure—of flatland phobia seethed in Sigmund's brain. The ground, the sky, *everything* began spinning. . . .

Not now, tanj it! He pulled himself together to scan across the busy construction site, wanting to demand another progress report, knowing it was too soon.

Knowing also that everything was going far too smoothly.

ER'O SIDLED ON THREE LIMBS around another of the drive modules. A motor in his exoskeleton had failed in the extreme cold, immobilizing a tubacle. He held the fifth tubacle aloft, clutching a scanner as he re-inspected his work.

"We will be ready in a few minutes for an end-to-end system test," Baedeker said. "Full power to all compon—"

"I have an unexpected reading on sensors," Minerva transmitted.

Er'o looked at the equipment spread across the ice. The modules all looked the same. They would, until one of them tore him to atoms. "Which unit?"

"Not on Niflheim. Half a light-day away, passing by."

"What sort of reading?" Sigmund demanded.

"Astronomical, surely," Minerva answered calmly. "A magnetic monopole. Maybe more than one."

Baedeker whistled impatiently. "All right. Track it while we run the end-to-end test."

Sigmund was not ready to drop the subject. "Passing by? Send me its course."

"Me, too, please," Er'o said. A gentle arc appeared on one of his displays, and presumably also on Sigmund's helmet. The arc curved toward, but not directly at, Niflheim. "Why does it turn?"

Minerva said, condescendingly, "Presumably it is in an electric field."

Ion currents permeated space—even here, so far from any star. Yes, there could be an electric field. But a field that strong? While others prattled about solar winds and the interstellar medium, and the electromagnetic fields they generated, Er'o consulted with the other Gw'oth. Compared to a meld their deliberations felt painfully slow.

Er'o interrupted the others' speculations. "It is not anything natural. That is a ramscoop with its engine off, using its magnetic scoop as a brake."

"Finagle," Sigmund swore. "Are you sure, Er'o?"

"Someone else should confirm my calculations, but yes, I am sure."

"Finagle," Sigmund said again. "Minerva, Jeeves, Kirsten, don't use active sensors. We don't want that ramscoop to know we know it's coming. Learn what you can on passive. Everyone, our radios are low power, but let's play safe and keep the chatter to a minimum."

"You don't mean to keep working?" Baedeker said. "The Pak are coming!"

"Let's confirm that," Sigmund said.

"Er'o is correct," Jeeves offered. "There is a weak neutrino source near the center of the magnetic anomaly. Observed deceleration fits with the drag from a magnetic ramscoop field. Well behind is a trail of concentrated helium."

A ramscoop with its drive off, its fusion reactor turned down, decelerating stealthily.

Ice shards flew from beneath Baedeker's suddenly frantic hoof. "We must go."

"Wait!" Sigmund said. "Anyone, what's the soonest that ship can get here?"

Jeeves completed the calculation first. "I don't know how good a Pak fusion drive is. Assuming similar performance to my drive aboard *Long Pass*, about a day. That is if they immediately abandon sneaking up and switch to full acceleration toward us."

"About a day for a flyby attack," Sigmund said. "They're decelerating because they mean to land here." He stared up into the jet-black sky. "They may simply be scavenging for volatiles, going stealthy lest another clan has ships attempting the same."

"Or they are trying to sneak up on *us*!" Very un-English grace notes had crept into Baedeker's voice. "We must not let them."

"What we cannot do," Sigmund snapped, "is let Pak capture your technology."

"Then we destroy it and get out of here," Baedeker half said, half sang.

A piercing alarm sounded and was quickly muted. "We have a fire on-board," Kirsten said.

SIGMUND GAZED INTO THE DARKNESS, although *Don Quixote* was too far off to be seen. "A fire? Where?"

"Deck five," Kirsten said. "I can't tell where the fire started, or how it spread so far before setting off alarms."

The deck with Thssthfok's cell. Except for a bit of bedding, nothing in his cell could burn. Nothing in the cell could start a fire. Sigmund *still* couldn't help wondering whether the Pak was responsible. "Is Thssthfok in danger?"

"Enviro sensors say smoke, toxic fumes, and heat. Fire suppression is not working. From audio, he's pounding on the hatch. I've lost video from that deck."

Finagle, fire was a terrible way to die. Sigmund's mind raced. "How's this? Seal the deck, release him from the cargo hold to find someplace safe, and shut emergency hatches behind him. Then open the hold's outer door to kill the fire and vent the fumes."

"I can do that," Jeeves said, "if fire hasn't damaged the circuits or motors I'll need."

What if they were too slow? "Kirsten, suit up. You may have to vent the entire ship."

"Suiting up now, Sigmund."

In the few seconds devoted to the latest crisis, Baedeker had bounded off toward *Haven*. Sigmund had to refocus on matters here on the ground.

"Kirsten, do what you must. Just don't let Thssthfok anywhere near the bridge."

THE LATCH OF THSSTHFOK'S CELL CLICKED open. He rushed out and, for the audio sensors, slammed the hatch behind him. Over the intercom, Jeeves directed Thssthfok away from the fire.

There was no fire, of course, only the illusion injected into shipboard sensors by his modified anklet. Jeeves ordered Thssthfok exactly where he meant to go: a large pantry.

Thssthfok hooked claws inside the jagged tear in the anklet and pulled. The metal bent back with a squeal. He found, just as he had expected, a fragile-looking reservoir of liquid. A current surge would vaporize the liquid, the gas pressure bursting the ampoule and releasing the gas. A radio signal would set it off. Removing the anklet would, too.

He began studying the anklet's control circuits.

THSSTHFOK HAD NOT CHOSEN this pantry casually.

The day of his capture he had been transported instantaneously from an air lock to the cargo hold that became his cell. The humans had forced him to surrender the teleportation disc, but the round indentation where it had lain remained in the deck. His newer cell, the one now filling with "smoke," had an identical empty indentation in its deck. The humans teleported supplies to their storage areas.

He lifted the teleportation disc from the floor of the pantry. The disc had a keypad and a long bank of tiny switches along its edge. During his last escape, he had not had the time to fully examine the disc he had found aboard the little ship. Now he studied the device. The HELP key sent terse explanations scrolling across a little display. He found a directory of shipboard addresses. Once he found addresses for the bridge or engine room he could jump—

In his anklet a magnetic-latch relay clicked impotently, disconnected from the circuit that would release the sedative. He kept working.

The disc's little display blanked. "I've disabled the stepping-disc network," Kirsten called over the intercom. "And now that I've reinitialized the enviro sensors, I see the fire wasn't real. Return to your cell."

Accessing the stepping-disc directory must have been visible to her. He ripped up a deck access panel and slashed claws through the exposed circuits. Sparks flew and gravity vanished from the pantry. He nudged the floating panel out the open door.

Partway to the floor, the bent plate's speed went meteoric. It crashed to the deck, then flattened with a groan.

"The corridor gravity is high, but it won't kill you. Return to your cell or I'll blow you out to space." There was a catch in Kirsten's throat. "Don't make me do that."

Several sealed rescue bags sat on a nearby shelf. Each had a small air tank. He shut the pantry door and kept studying the disc. Its power light still glowed. If she told the truth the control network was off, but the stepping disc had internal power. Other discs would also have power. Nearby discs might communicate among themselves and he could enter an address manually.

"In one minute," Kirsten warned, "I start venting."

One minute was ample. He began analyzing the part of the directory he had seen.

"ERIC!" SIGMUND RAN AFTER ERIC, bounding toward the nearest stepping disc. "I need you down here."

Eric kept going. "That's my wife, alone with a Pak! I'm going to help her."

"I know! But Baedeker is falling apart. You have to finish the checkout."

Eric was halfway to the stepping disc. "And if it were Penny up there?"

"I'll go up to the ship, tanj it!" Sigmund yelled. "You can finish here if Baedeker goes to pieces. I can't. Vaporizing this planet is the one sure way to keep this technology from the Pak. That protects everyone."

"If anything happens to Kirsten . . ." Eric's voice shook. His pace began to slow.

Sigmund had better low-gee running technique and caught up. He grabbed Eric by the shoulders and spun him around. "I promise you, it won't."

Within another ten paces, Sigmund stepped aboard *Don Quixote*.

. . .

A STORM RAGED IN THE CORRIDOR, but the pantry-hatch seal was almost airtight. Thssthfok unrolled a rescue bag across the door; suction pulled the tough, clear material into the crack. The whistle of escaping air died.

Wind and the loss of gravity had stirred the pantry. Shelves were half empty now. Drifting containers kept bumping into him and the walls. Revealed on the backs of several shelves: bags of tree-of-life root.

He had seen eighteen stepping-disc addresses and locations. The sample was sufficient to extrapolate addresses to discs elsewhere in the ship—including any on the bridge. He put his disc in send mode, set it gently onto the floor, anchored himself on the disc with a firm grip on a shelf, and waited.

Nothing happened.

The disc, when he checked its display, gave an error code. Receive error. Someone on the bridge had been quick to disable the disc there. Powered down, turned over, put into send-only mode—it didn't matter which. The address he had extrapolated for the engine room resulted in another receive-mode error.

Where should he go before the disc addresses all became useless?

58

Sigmund charged out of the relax room, the broad shoulders of his battle armor scraping the door frame. He unlocked the arms locker and stuffed his pockets with stunners, grenades, and hand lasers. "Kirsten, I'm back aboard. Where is Thssthfok?"

"The aux pantry on deck five, I think. That deck is in vacuum, except the pantry. Deck gravity, except in the pantry, is eight gees. I figure that should slow down even him."

"And you?"

"Shut into the engine room. I put the stepping disc here into standby just before he tried to use it. The send address matched the disc from the fifth-deck pantry."

Sigmund had stepped to a moving destination without a pilot at the helm! He shuddered, but that was hardly their biggest problem. If Thssthfok understood the discs, he could be anywhere on the ship. Or *off* the ship. "Jeeves—break velocity sync with the ground."

"Done, Sigmund. Resuming a standard orbit."

On the ground, Eric and Baedeker were arguing about an instrument calibration. If Thssthfok had gotten below, he was keeping his distance. Sigmund sent Eric a private warning, just in case—and reassurance that Kirsten remained safe.

What else, Sigmund wondered. "Kirsten, how is the bridge secured?"

"I left the disc there in send-only mode. That's how I got to the engine room. The bridge hatch is locked from inside. Only Jeeves or an oxy-fuel cutting torch is getting us back in there."

"Jeeves. Any reason to suppose Thssthfok isn't in the pantry?"

"No, but he has bypassed our sensors before."

"Good point. Kirsten, are you armed?"

"No, sorry. My priority was securing the bridge and engine room."

"That was a good call, but now stay where you are. I'm going to check the pantry."

THE CORRIDOR WAS VACUUM-STILL. Faint noises reached Thssthfok through the ceiling and floor. The pantry had become stuffy, and he bled oxygen from the tank of the unrolled rescue bag that sealed the hatch.

He ran through his options. He could wait here until armed jailors recaptured him. He could venture out, claws versus battle armor, claws doubly useless within a rescue bag. Or—

His one viable option was obvious.

THE PANTRY HATCH BULGED SLIGHTLY. It might yet hold pressure. Sigmund switched to the intercom. "Thssthfok, this is Sigmund. I'm going to open the pantry hatch. Remain where you are. There should be rescue bags inside with you. You have two minutes to get inside one."

Sigmund stood to the side of the hatch, ready to shoot anyone leaving. Stunners didn't work in a vacuum. He'd tried to send a flash-bang grenade to the pantry, but the stepping disc inside was in send-only mode. That left only the laser he now gripped. "All right, Thssthfok. Time's up."

Sigmund released the latch. Air pressure flung open the door, ripping the handle from his grip. A white cloud burst out. Cans, bags, and an empty rescue bag rained to the deck as they cleared the hatch.

No Pak.

Sigmund backed away from the hatchway, lobbing a sealed rescue bag through the opening. After two minutes Sigmund approached cautiously. The pantry was a mess.

As for Thssthfok, there was no sign.

THE LITTLE SHIP was how Thssthfok remembered it, only messier.

Some of the mess was of Thssthfok's doing. He had emptied a large bag—flour, whatever that was—to carry his supplies. White dust covered him. The far more serious disorder was in the cockpit. The command console had been opened and taken half apart! Cable bundles snaked out of the cabinet to tens of instruments and gauges.

Through the canopy, he saw the too-familiar walls of his onetime cell.

Before Thssthfok's latest escape, Eric had been suited up. Thssthfok doubted a mere spacesuit offered protection against the nothingness of hyperspace. And Sigmund's mysterious demo must take place in normal space, where the Pak could see it.

The path to freedom was clear.

He flipped over the stepping disc to disable it, then set to work reassembling the little ship's flight controls.

"THIS IS YOUR FINAL WARNING." Sigmund broadcast over the intercom and the ship's public channel. If Thssthfok was alive and onboard, he would hear. "In one minute, I'll open the entire ship to vacuum. Tell us where you are."

No response.

"Kirsten, are you still suited up?"

"Yes. But, Sigmund . . ."

"We don't know what Thssthfok is doing. I'll not put either of us at risk again. He's a lot less dangerous trapped in a rescue bag."

"Opening the cargo bay means losing Brennan's old singleship, too."

"It is far too heavy, Kirsten," Jeeves said. "I will double gravity in the hold to be sure."

Sigmund said, "Jeeves, disable the interior emergency hatches. Open the air locks and the cargo-hold doors." To Kirsten, he added, "I have weapons. I'll be outside the engine-room door in a few minutes. Once you're armed, we'll sweep the ship end to end." And though he took no pride in it, Sigmund half hoped to find Thssthfok dead.

THSSTHFOK WORKED FEVERISHLY, ignoring Sigmund's threat. The little ship had an environmental system and its reservoirs were full.

Strobing red light flooded the canopy and an alarm wailed. The large exterior hatch began to rise and Thssthfok's weight doubled. The little ship's hull rang like a gong under the hail of loose tools and equipment being sucked out into space.

The hail ended. The audible alarm trailed off to silence.

What the disassembled console did not tell him, the spliced-in human instruments did. The deuterium tanks were two-thirds full. The drive appeared operational. The radio and comm laser passed muster—and at close range, the latter would serve as a weapon. The flight controls were operable, merely exposed for examination. (Well, more than flight controls. Things he did not immediately recognize could be examined later.)

And now Sigmund had opened the cargo hold's exterior hatch. That saved Thssthfok the time to bypass the controls and loss-of-pressure alarms. A touch of the takeoff-and-landing jets would ease him from the cargo bay.

Stars beckoned.

The humans could have killed him. He had provoked them often enough. Thssthfok felt a pang of remorse, but he would not allow pursuit. His breeders were depending on him.

At least the end would be quick. Thssthfok flipped on the radio. "I'm sorry."

He ignited the fusion drive and a plasma plume hotter than the surface of a star erupted into *Don Quixote*.

ACROSS *DON QUIXOTE*—and throughout the computing complex that housed Jeeves—alarms flared. Short circuits. Open circuits. Electrical fires. Popped, welded, and vanished circuit breakers. Temperature alarms. Equipment malfunctions. Tanks overpressure and burst. Comm fallouts. Faults beyond Jeeves's ability to categorize.

If only the hull would burst, it would release the plasma. But General Products had built too well. The hull trapped the plasma and everything that the plasma vaporized and ionized. In an instant, the trapped heat and radiation would destroy him. In an instant, he could not begin to calculate the optimal response.

He would do what he could.

He canceled the override that had held open external and emergency hatches. The doors would close on their own—unless they melted or warped from the intense heat. The main cargo-hold hatch jammed immediately.

The main fusion reactor had shut down on its own, but he dumped deuterium and tritium to space, against the remote possibility that ricocheting plasma could somehow fuse any of it. He flushed nitrogen throughout the crew areas for the little cooling that would provide. He vented oxygen to space, where it could not feed fires.

He fired main thrusters, fleeing the searing plasma. One thruster sputtered and quit. The rest quickly followed. The ship tumbled wildly.

He sent short laser bursts to the comm satellites deployed above Niflheim, hoping he had retrieved the most important files. So many memory banks had failed, he could not be certain.

All of this was what Jeeves believed Sigmund would have wanted him to do.

Then thought ceased.

IMPOSSIBLE GLARE! Sigmund's visor turned opaque. Intense heat washed over him. He stumbled through the hatch Kirsten had just unlocked, into the engine room. She slammed the hatch behind him. The ship shuddered and shook beneath them. A sudden hot wind buffeted him. It couldn't be oxygen; in this heat, *something* would have gone up in flames.

"I'm sorry." Regret had not stayed Thssthfok's hand. What had he done?

Sigmund's visor cleared enough to show the hatch glowing orange and starting to sag. Gravity vanished, revealing the ship had gone into a wild tumble. He bounced off a bulkhead. Something clanged off his helmet.

Now the hatch blazed cherry red.

Kirsten snagged him from the air. "Boot magnets!" When his feet slapped to the deck, she led him behind some massive hunk of equipment he didn't recognize. A gale howled in his suit, but the cooling unit was overmatched. The air in his suit grew hotter by the second.

"We'll make it," he told Kirsten.

False hope was all that Sigmund had to offer. Things were about to end very badly—again.

59

Activity across the ice came to an abrupt standstill. Cacophony over-whelmed the public comm channel. Then Eric burst from within the cluster of drive modules. He bounced in flat arcs toward the nearest stepping disc, cursing Sigmund and bargaining with the universe.

All from "I'm sorry." Er'o was still grappling with the implications when *Haven*'s transmitter overpowered the rest.

"Quiet!" Minerva shouted. "I have urgent news. Immediately after Thssthfok spoke, there was a data dump from *Don Quixote*. Comm dropped mid-transfer, and we can't reestablish the link. I have crew studying the data. Almost simultaneously with all this, a neutrino source began accelerating away from the planet. A ship, I assume, but it does not respond to hails."

"A relay problem?" Er'o asked.

"The comm buoys are nominal," Minerva said. "We've relayed test messages all the way around Niflheim."

Eric called out, huffing as he ran. "Is the neutrino source *Don Quixote*?"

"Unknown," Minerva said. "It will be out of Niflheim's shadow in a few minutes."

If not *Don Quixote*, then who? Another ramscoop, perhaps, waiting in ambush to surprise the ramscoop sneaking up to this planet. Instead, it ambushed *Don Quixote* before Sigmund, Kirsten, or Jeeves could get out a coherent message.

Possible, but Er'o did not believe it. "Based on its last known course, when will *Don Quixote* come over the horizon?"

"Two minutes, ten seconds," Minerva said.

Eric skidded to a stop on the disc. It was powered up and in transmit-only mode, to keep Thssthfok from coming down. Eric stood there, screaming.

The transport should not have worked, whether *Don Quixote* remained in orbit or was racing away. The velocity mismatch was far too high. Er'o was not supposed to understand that, and kept the observation to himself. Had Er'o's mate been aboard, he would have tried, too.

A timer ticked down in one sensor cluster's augmented vision. As the count approached zero, Er'o netted to a telescope that Minerva had aimed.

A bit late, more than a bit off course, a tumbling cylinder appeared. It was eerily mottled, and random patches glowed fiery hot in far red. *Don Quixote*, everything and everyone aboard surely destroyed.

With a whimper, Baedeker fell to the ice and rolled himself into a tight ball. He had seen the image, too.

A second virtual counter approached zero, and a blue-white streak climbed over the horizon. A fusion flame. "No widespread magnetic field," Minerva noted. "Not a ramscoop."

"The singleship!" Eric howled. "I killed her!"

ON COMM, CHAOS REASSERTED ITSELF. They should fly to *Don Quixote* and search for survivors. They should pursue whoever streaked away on that searing blue-white exhaust. And most of the voices: They should run for home—immediately.

Eric raged with dread and anger. Baedeker was lost to fear. Minerva, like all the rest, waited for someone else to make a decision.

Craning a tubacle, Er'o looked about the frozen waste. That left . . . him.

"Quiet, please!" With only a suit radio for amplification, Er'o had to keep calling. "Everyone, quiet! Calm down!" As the din ebbed, he added, "Hurry. We have to finish our work here."

"You're crazy!" Eric yelled. "We have to rescue Kirsten and Sigmund."

The wreckage remained far-red hot. Could anyone aboard still live? Er'o said gently, "I'm sorry, Eric. The ship must cool before we can try." *If it even cools enough for the attempt before the oncoming ramscoop makes us evacuate.* "Kl'o, Ng'o, please complete checkout—"

Eric turned and ran toward *Haven*. "Checkout? Everything has changed! Thssthfok is getting away! He's running for the Pak fleet with everything he's learned about us and our technology. And in a few hours, the light from Thssthfok's fusion drive will reach the incoming ramscoop. That'll be the end of stealth and magnetic braking. They'll start their drive and be down our throats all the faster."

Eric's frantic words had collapsed two more pressure-suited Citizens into unresponsive balls.

Er'o said, "All the more reason to finish here. The planet-buster is one technology Thssthfok has not seen. We cannot possibly remove everything before the ramscoop arrives. Instead we finish up and set off the weapon. And eliminate Thssthfok in the process."

New murmurs, with some of the earlier certainty gone.

Er'o tried to bring order. "Kl'o, Ng'o, please complete checkout of the device. Omar, get the Citizens who need help back to *Haven*. If you are up to it, Eric, review the data dump from *Don Quixote*. It may offer some clues."

For a moment, no one moved. Then Omar said, "You heard the starfish. Let's all get back to work."

EARNEST ENTREATIES FAILED to coax Baedeker out of a tightly curled ball. Kneading mouths made little impression through the sturdy material of his pressure suit. His heads-up displays reported warm air; his body sensed normal gravity. In his catatonia, unaware, he had been carted aboard *Haven*. He emptied his mind, seeking to return to oblivion.

Danger! Piercing ululations jerked him back to reality. He whipped out a head and looked around wildly. He was in his cabin. Eric and Minerva stood over him. The warning shout trailed off from Minerva's mouths.

"I need your help," Eric said. He remained suited except for the helmet in his hands. "You can go to pieces later."

"Wh-what can I do?" Baedeker stammered. What could anyone do against the Pak? Even Sigmund could not control a single naked Pak prisoner.

"*Don Quixote* isn't in a proper orbit," Eric said. "Within thirty minutes it impacts Niflheim. We're going to rescue Kirsten and Sigmund first."

What did it matter? Why did they bother him? Baedeker felt himself drifting back to oblivion, but he managed to ask, "Why me?"

"When we blow the planet-buster, it will destroy everything. Niflheim. The ramscoop that's a few hours away. Thssthfok and the ship he escaped in. Everything except . . ."

"Except what? Oh. The hull of *Don Quixote*." Even in Baedeker's near stupor, any possibility the Pak would recover a nearly impregnable hull seemed like a bad idea. "Surely it cannot still fly."

"Enough." Eric kicked Baedeker in the flank, and Minerva whistled in surprise. "Get *up*. Your task is to destroy the hull once we get Kirsten and Sigmund off."

"I cannot—"

The next kick *hurt*. Minerva shifted his weight nervously between his hooves, wanting to intervene but at a loss what to do.

Eric said, "New Terra has very few ships with General Products hulls. Most were turned to powder at the outset of the last war. Sigmund thought—he *thinks*—you know the code to shut down the embedded power plant that reinforces the hull super-molecule."

Sigmund was almost right, but a built-in code suggested premeditation. Who would make a ship that an errant data-entry error could turn to dust? There was no self-destruct code.

What Baedeker *had* recognized was an unintended back door to the microprocessors embedded in the hull to control the reinforcing power plant. Target a ship with a comm laser tuned to the right frequency; some of the light penetrated the photonic components. After that, it was a matter of simple programming to shut down the power plant. Eliminating the vulnerability would take replacing all the ships built over millennia.

Of a trillion Citizens of the Concordance, perhaps five knew that secret. But why did Eric even need to be told? His people's ancestral ramscoop had been kept for study inside a General Products #4 hull just like *Haven*'s—until Eric and Kirsten broke it out. "You already know how."

"*Long Pass* was stationary, held in place by massive struts. The power plant was a fixed target, only a few hundred feet away. I used *Long Pass*'s comm laser to overload or overheat the power plant until it shut down. We'll never be able to hold focus on the power plant with *Don Quixote* tumbling like that." Eric pulled back his boot again. "So it's up to you."

Baedeker's method also worked at a distance, but tumbling would defeat him, too. Could *Haven* swoop around the tumbling hulk, matching the motion? What pilot would be insane enough to attempt *that* maneuver? With a will of its own, Baedeker's exposed head inched closer to his belly.

Someone rapped on the closed cabin door. "Four minutes," she called.

It took two more kicks to get Baedeker moving. By then he had figured out that *Haven* was almost at its rendezvous with the wreck. That the only way to destroy its hull was to *carry* a laser aboard. And that boarding meant a spacewalk to the tumbling, still-glowing ship. And yet—

The doomed rescue seemed like a faster demise than being kicked to death by a madman.

WITH A WHISPERED PLEA TO FINAGLE, Eric dove from the gaping mouth of the cargo hold. He vanished into the darkness on invisible wings of compressed air.

Niflheim filled much of the sky, more as an absence of stars than from the feeble glitter of its icy surface. A mile away, what remained of *Don Quixote* tumbled and rolled. Here and there, within its tortured hull, blotches glowed in angry reds. Moments when the wreck pointed directly at Baedeker, it was as big as NP1 or NP5 seen from Hearth. When he could see the wreck's full length, it loomed three times larger than Hearth's closest planetary neighbors.

Baedeker lectured himself, scolded himself, and whimpered. He reminded himself what was at stake: everything. He swung his necks and stomped his hooves. He tried everything that might stampede himself deeper into a fit of mania, and still the wait was all but unbearable.

He remained on *Haven* with the rest of the rescue team. Eric carried a stepping disc on his back. Everyone else would step across. Assuming Eric made it aboard the wreck.

With his visor turned active, Baedeker zoomed in on the distant speck that was Eric. He had nearly reached the ruined ship. Baedeker's stomach lurched at the magnified tumbling and rolling.

After a false start, Eric began spiraling toward the wreck, zigzagging to match the ship's bucking motions. "The main hold reads too hot. I'm entering through the primary air lock."

Twice Eric rebounded from the hull, cursing. On his third try, with a *clang*, one magnetized boot grabbed a bulkhead within the air lock. His body went one way while the ship continued another. He spun around his leg as he slammed face-first into the hull. "I'm down," he gasped.

A minute later, Baedeker stepped across into the wreck. A massive sack slapped his side. Most of the load was *two* stepping discs. No matter what, he would have a way off this derelict.

Gravity was off. Blue light flickered and flashed from innumerable shorts. Between sparks a sullen red glow seeped down the corridor. Behind the hatch of a nearby storeroom, things thumped and crashed with every wobble of the ship.

Had even Nessus ever attempted anything this crazy?

"Are you all right?" Baedeker asked Eric.

"Broken leg, almost certainly. The armor immobilizes it."

Baedeker blinked. "Now that a working disc is aboard, others can finish the search. Go back and let an autodoc fix it."

"When I find Kirsten and Sigmund. Not before. Now get off the disc so that the others can board."

Baedeker gingerly took two steps down the corridor, boot magnets holding him down. In quick succession, three humans stepped through behind him. "Withdrawing to a safe distance," Minerva radioed. "We will resume velocity match there."

The rolling, yawing, pitching, tumbling . . . tried to move Baedeker every direction at once. Steadying himself on three legs was hard. How anyone managed on two was a mystery.

He took two devices from a pressure-suit pocket. "Eric, these are personal stasis-field generators. We use them for medical emergencies." It was a futile gesture, but all Baedeker had to offer. No one could have survived this catastrophe.

Eric stowed the generators in pockets of his own. "Thanks. Now you have a job to do."

The embedded power plant was just two decks forward and half a hull circumference away, but at every turn something blocked Baedeker's path. A buckled bulkhead. Emergency hatches heat-warped in place. Pockets of intolerable heat. Thickets of sparking wires. When no course led where he needed to go, he carved detours with his flashlight laser, its beam focused all the way down to lethal intensity. Over comm, he tracked the similarly slow progress of the searchers, fanning out across the ship.

"I've reached the bridge," Omar reported. He led team A, searching forward. "No signs of them anywhere. Sorry, Eric."

"Any sign of Jeeves?" Eric asked.

Omar hesitated. "The server room is a charred ruin. No way."

"Sweep again, back toward the stern," Eric directed. "Maybe team B missed something."

Baedeker finally reached the arc of corridor in whose wall sat the embedded power plant. Most wall paint had been seared away. He spread the flashlight beam and burned off the rest of the paint—then kept his neck and head in motion. Optical waveguides warped most light *around* the power plant, but there were unavoidable distortions if the light source wavered. You could spot the power plant if you knew how and where to look.

And there it was.

At this range, even the headheld laser was sufficient to reprogram the power-plant controls. He used both heads to stick the laser to the wall with a blob of putty. The laser had no wireless interface; he clipped on cables to interface a pocket comp.

He had left the final programming, to be done only if he got this far. Some secrets were meant to stay secret. For the same reason, he worked—awkwardly, because of his suit—through the comp's tactile interface. Nothing he did here would be overheard or intercepted.

It was delicate work, demanding intense concentration, and he tuned out the depressing radio chatter. The searchers had found nothing good. Most likely they would find nothing at all, the remains of Sigmund and Kirsten having been blown out to space or even vaporized.

He did hear the evacuation warning: impact with Niflheim in five minutes. Get out.

Four minutes. Three. At two minutes, a warning shriek echoed through his suit. Lipping frantically, Baedeker finished without time to check his work. "The device is set," he called. "One minute to hull destruction. I am stepping back to *Haven*."

He flicked through to his own ship, into the cargo bay that served as their staging area—and collapsed into a tight ball.

60

Thssthfok's new ship was fast and maneuverable, a delight to fly. He concentrated on getting a feel for its controls and capabilities.

Straight ahead, coming right at him, something he had never expected to see: the vanguard of the Pak fleets. And behind him, a second surprise: a ramscoop, either a forward scout or a foraging mission, stealthily converging on the icy world his prison had orbited.

But not as stealthily as they believed. Whoever had built this little ship had equipped it with extraordinary instruments.

Who *had* built this ship? Humans, certainly—the cockpit suited the length of their arms, the grasp of their hands, the contours of their bodies—and yet Pak influence was unmistakable in the console circuits he had so hastily reassembled. Phssthpok's doing, somehow.

Thssthfok would have liked to examine whatever "demo" the humans had had planned, but did not. Surrender to curiosity was a breeder weakness. He had shouted his presence to that inbound ship the instant he lit his fusion drive. Soon enough, the other ship would see him. It would fire its own engine and give chase.

He would use all the head start he had, and not risk losing everything. This ship. A stepping disc. The scans and measurements he had taken of *Don Quixote*'s amazingly strong, dynamically reinforced hull. The existence of hyperspace and a faster-than-light drive. Knowledge of dangerous races, their worlds flying through space, in the fleets' paths.

No matter what had happened in the long years of his absence, he would be welcomed back to family and clan with open arms.

He took a tree-of-life root from the flour sack, blew off traces of white powder, and gnawed contentedly.

.   .   .

THSSTHFOK SWITCHED OFF the fusion drive. Time for a quick look behind.

The lonely world *Don Quixote* orbited was spewing ice crystals and steam. More likely, *had* orbited, the plume marking the spot of its crash.

As expected, the ramscoop had lit its drive. The range was too great to know if the ship raced toward Thssthfok or the planet—only that it came at high acceleration. And a radio signal, blaring at very high power. A short digital data stream, rapidly repeating.

His ship's receiver understood the modulation scheme. A human signal, then. "Look here," Thssthfok heard himself say.

The demo warning!

Another voice (Jeeves?) continued, in accented high Rilchukian. Making allowance for the bad grammar, it said, "Cease attacks on occupied worlds. Veer toward galactic south. Comply, or be destroyed."

"Look here," the message began again.

Thssthfok turned down the volume, the better to concentrate. Would anything else happen? If so, he was in an excellent position to observe Sigmund's attention-getting demo.

Thssthfok directed every sensor back the way he had come. Same icy world. (At the limit of the telescope's resolution, at its maximum magnification, a pixel zoomed away from the planet. To be seen from this distance, a vessel would have to be many times the size of Sigmund's ship. A glitch in image enhancement, surely. The dot vanished, confirming his suspicion.) Same plume of ice and steam. Same repeating radio signal—

Dissolved suddenly into deafening static. Gibberish erupted across the spectrum. Particle detectors reported impossible densities of everything. Gravimetric sensors showed—what? He did not understand. It was as though space-time itself had gone mad.

Everything grew in intensity. And grew. And grew.

The cockpit canopy had turned black. Protecting his eyes from what? When Thssthfok applied maximum filtering to the ship's telescope, a maelstrom of gas, dust, and gravel had replaced the little planet. A world torn apart, heading his way, heading *every* way, at very nearly light speed.

He scarcely had the time to admit how utterly he had failed his breeders.

ENDGAME

61

What?

Sigmund was on his back, eyes darting beneath closed eyelids. There had been heat—oh, so *much* heat. And a roaring gale, the air almost searing. He hadn't been able to breathe! Had his pulse been racing, his skin tight? Maybe. He remembered knowing he was about to die, and regret, and confusion.

And he was *still* confused, because, tanj it, he felt *great*.

Cured or healed, then . . . but of what? That, Sigmund couldn't remember.

He opened his eyes. A clear dome was inches above his face. He was in an autodoc. Status LEDs shone steady green. Tiny text filled a display beside his head, but he ignored it. First things first. He had to know where he was. He slapped the panic button, and the dome began to retract.

"Sigmund?" a familiar voice called. Penelope!

He didn't know much, but he remembered being far away on a mission. That snippet of memory brought a lot more crashing down on him. But not the end. Not how he got . . . here. "Kirsten?" he whispered. "Is she . . . ?" He couldn't bear to finish that sentence.

The dome completed its glacial retreat and he sat up. Penny stood across the room, blinking back tears. "Sigmund . . . I thought I'd lost you."

"I'm sorry." He grabbed the robe off the foot of the autodoc, slipped it on, and climbed out. There was a time for nakedness, and this wasn't it. They hugged, hard. "I'm so sorry."

They stood near a window and Sigmund looked through a crack between the curtains behind her. The main square of Long Pass City. More questions bubbled up by the moment, but one came first. "How is Kirsten?"

"In the same shape that you were." Penny gave him a final squeeze and stepped back. "The governor ruled you went into Nessus' autodoc first."

It was hardly Nessus' autodoc. Nessus had only obtained it from Human Space. Bought? Stolen? He was evasive about that. This was Carlos Wu's prototype 'doc, amazing nanotech stuff. It had saved Sigmund once before, from a gaping hole blown through his chest.

So something horrible had happened to him yet again.

He should have read the tiny print on the 'doc display. "Penny, what was wrong with me? I don't remember."

"Burns, radiation sickness, and heatstroke. All severe." She wiped a tear from her cheek. "I can't bear to think about it. And no one will tell me how it happened."

ARM agents learned first aid. Autodocs only helped when you lived long enough to get to one. So what had he learned? Yeah, severe heatstroke caused confusion and hallucinations. Maybe Puppeteers had nothing to do with the latest gaps in his memory. "How did I get *here*?"

The door swung open. A woman came in, wearing a long white coat and holding a medical scanner. "Good, you're up, Minister. We need to clear the room."

For Kirsten, of course. Sigmund pulled his robe tighter. They filed into the hall, where Eric waited beside a floating gurney. On the gurney was something Sigmund should have expected, since Kirsten had been waiting for the 'doc. A long, silvery ovoid. A stasis field.

Technicians broke the field and scorching air whooshed out. Kirsten was still in her pressure suit, her face lurid beneath the alarm LEDs ablaze inside her helmet.

Sigmund staggered at a rush of memories. The tempest of emotions was worse: rage, sorrow, disappointment, remorse—too many to sort out and now was not the time.

Eric stared at the prostrate figure of his wife, unable to look away.

Sigmund swallowed. "Eric, I promised you Kirsten would be all right. So far I've done a lousy job of it, but she will." More thanks to Carlos than to me.

"She has to," Eric whispered. "She has to."

"We need to get her into the 'doc," one of the technicians reminded them. "The sooner the better."

Sigmund and Penelope slipped by, Sigmund resting a hand briefly on Eric's shoulder as they passed. The door clicked shut behind them.

The last thing Sigmund heard as they turned a corner was the nearly ultrasonic whine of a saw, the techs hastily extracting Kirsten from her pressure suit.

A QUARTER OF A YEAR IN STASIS for the return to New Terra. Thirty-some days more in the autodoc. A war to be waged and its general AWOL. Sigmund didn't want to believe he'd lost so much time, but a glance at Alice left no doubt. She looked ready to give birth any day.

By almost getting himself killed, he had left Alice in charge of New Terra's defense.

Alice and Sigmund weren't the only ones Sabrina had invited. Baedeker and Nessus were there, too. Eric had opted out. Watching Kirsten through the 'doc's transparent dome was more contact than he had had since putting her into stasis.

"We should begin," Sabrina said.

It was another brunch meeting. Alice set down her coffee mug. "Jeeves, run the video."

This was Sigmund's first day back at work, and a strategy session with Puppeteers and the governor was a rough way to jump back in. Sabrina's insistence was ominous. Sigmund had called Alice the night before for an explanation; she had asked him to wait. "It's complicated."

A holo popped up over the conference table. "You've all seen such images: wave after wave of Pak ships. This is a close-up, an image taken just before *Haven* initiated the Niflheim demo. Having the close-up as a reference let me better calibrate the ongoing long-range observations from the stealthed probes Sigmund deployed en route to Niflheim."

This was *a* Jeeves talking. This Jeeves even integrated the few files beamed at the last minute from *Don Quixote*. In no way was it *Jeeves*. Not Jeeves whose quick thinking had saved Sigmund's and Kirsten's lives. That Jeeves was gone.

A blinking red dot appeared in front and toward the northern edge of the first wave. "Niflheim was a quarter light-year in front of the Pak vanguard. The effects of the demonstration propagated in all directions at essentially light speed. The leading ramscoops, in the blue wave, converged with the demo at half light speed. Sixty-two days later, the vanguard and the wave front met. Here is what happened, sped up by a factor of fifty thousand."

The red dot was suddenly a sphere, rapidly inflating. Behind a bright red edge, color faded to pink, dimming as it swelled: diminishing effects, cleverly represented.

"The leading edge expands at light speed. That's everything from infrared to hard gammas. The debris comes behind, shown in pink." As the pink region spread, now lagging farther and farther behind the sharp red rim, Jeeves went on. "By now, propagation of the debris field has smoothed out. I do not understand the change."

"The space-time disruptions have dampened out, dissipated to almost nothing," Baedeker explained.

Sigmund watched, awestruck. Finagle bless 'em, the team had done it! *Despite* Thssthfok's violent escape.

The sphere grew and grew. Jeeves said, "The leading edge is about one-third light-year across as it first reaches the Pak." One-third light-year was small compared to the breadth of the Pak advance. "Watch how the Pak respond."

The expanding sphere penetrated into and across Pak territory. Dots swerved as the electromagnetic blast struck. None could outrun the debris racing—on the time scale of the video—ten seconds behind. Three scattered blue dots blinked out.

Sigmund had planned to transmit the warning message days before the blast. Not seconds. He tried to regret what had turned into an unprovoked attack, and failed. It wasn't as though, under the circumstances, the team had had any choice. Or acted any more ruthlessly than Pak did routinely.

Parboiling by the enemy had leached any empathy out of Sigmund. He wondered how Kirsten's treatment fared.

The Pak, put on notice, were supposed to veer south. Well, they had gotten notice, if not exactly been forewarned.

"Look at that," Sabrina whispered.

As the red bubble continued to grow, more ships scattered—or tried to. News of their course changes also traveled outward at light speed. More distant ships often turned *toward* the blast, resisting encroachment. Then, catching sight of the slower-moving debris field, many of those more distant ships also turned to flee—

Only to find *their* way blocked.

Chaos bubbled through the Pak armada, in a sphere that expanded along with Niflheim's remains. Maneuvering and skirmishes continued after the debris field passed.

"All right," Sigmund said, "they reacted like Pak. Each clan protected its own ships. I want to see what they did after the immediate danger passed."

Most movement continued forward, still away from the core and the next wave of ships racing up behind them. These ships had built up a lot of momentum. Changing course enough to spot on this scale would take time. Sigmund found he was holding his breath. Forewarning or not, they had gotten his message, and the demo would certainly have convinced *him*.

After a few minutes, a change became clear. More and more of the Pak were veering *north*.

THE NEARER TO GALACTIC SOUTH the course changes began, the more pronounced the swing northward. Flurries of motion and knotting of Pak ships suggested frantic space battles—as did several ships disappearing. Melees grew and others erupted. The planet-buster blast, largely spent, swept onward.

"This makes no sense," Nessus said. "Not to me, at least. Did the Pak ships not understand the recorded warning?"

It made sense to Sigmund. At least something useful had come of his time with Thssthfok. "They understood, all right. We demonstrated a credible threat. The more southern clans are pushing others *into* that threat. Against that pressure, the ships along the northern edge are hard-pressed even to maintain their original course."

Alice nodded. "We convinced the clans closest to the demo. Otherwise they would turn north, away from the new attacks. We've become unwitting allies of the southern clans."

Sabrina looked puzzled and Nessus eyed Alice suspiciously.

Ally was a perfectly good Spanglish word, but not part of Puppeteer-subsetted English. Allies implied enemies, and *enemy*, like slavery, was a concept the Puppeteers had scrubbed from their slaves' dialect.

"A cooperating partner in warfare," Jeeves volunteered unhelpfully. It only emphasized Alice's gaffe.

"I see some good news here." Sigmund gestured at the holo, hastily changing the subject. "Not even an epic migration across much of the galaxy can make the clans cooperate."

Baedeker poked dispiritedly at his platter of mixed chopped grasses. "So the clans will compete for the honor of destroying us. I am not consoled."

"Where is the good news, Sigmund?" Nessus asked.

Sigmund straightened in his chair. "If clans *must* fight, Thssthfok knew it, too. Consider: He was at least a quarter light-year from his clan when he escaped, probably more distant. Any signal he transmitted would diverge and reveal information to many clans. Almost certainly he sent nothing. He was saving what he learned until he could reunite with his clan. Whatever he knew about us and our technology died with him."

Baedeker climbed unsteadily out of his mound of cushions and began circling the room. On each lap he edged closer to the door. "At best, we failed to make things worse. We have not made anything better."

Sabrina grimaced. "I must agree with Baedeker. Where do we go from here?"

They could use their single up-close weapon, sacrificing the Outsider drive from NP5. If that didn't convince the Pak, Sigmund's quiver would be empty.

Best to hold that in reserve.

That left one or more additional warning shots, set off elsewhere along the Pak advance. The Pak incursion was light-years across, and demo lessons only propagated at light speed. It could take several blasts, even assuming enough rogue planets in the right places, and a long time. Sigmund doubted they could pull it off, even before something in the evolving holo caught his eye. "Oh, tanj," he cursed. "They learn fast."

"I see nothing different," Alice began. "Oh. Picket ships."

The phrase drew another questioning glance from Nessus, and Sigmund kicked Alice under the table. "What my apt pupil says is correct." He pointed at a few spots on the leading edge and northern fringe of the Pak advance. "More scout ships. They may not know what hit them, but they saw the effects dissipate with distance. They mean to keep whoever did it far away."

Nessus and Baedeker exchanged snatches of melody. Not an argument this time, and Sigmund needed a moment to put a label on it. More than sad. More than wistful. It was . . . elegiac.

"Even unwarned," Nessus said sadly, "a Pak scout ship surprised your mission. It is no use removing the Outsider drive from NP5. You might never again destroy a planet close enough to inflict real damage."

The sad truth was, Nessus was right.

62

Sigmund watched Baedeker stare obsessively into *Sancho Panza*'s main tactical display. "No offense, but you're one brave Citizen."

"Calling me insane. Why would that insult me?" Without moving his gaze, with an involuntary quick paw-paw at the deck, Baedeker added, "I will consider the source and take your words in the manner you intended."

"Fair enough."

Hundreds of ships filled the display. Reaction to Niflheim's spectacular destruction continued to evolve. The most intense activity propagated with the E–M blast and, lagging farther and farther behind, the wave of debris. Where the Pak had had more than a few days to react, open warfare had mostly concluded. Instead the squadrons maneuvered in a way Sigmund interpreted as wary clannish defensiveness.

The migration continued toward New Terra, the Fleet, and Jm'ho.

These were not the ships that had threatened Earth. They couldn't be. Back in Sol system, Alice had glimpsed a tidy fleet, arrayed hexagonally. The formations at which Baedeker stared were anything but tidy. There were small, mutually supporting groups, sure, but overall this was a slow-motion turf war. It made sense: The Librarians trailing after Phssthpok had been one cohesive force. *These* ships were clans jockeying for military advantage, supporting and betraying one another at every opportunity.

So the black cloud of doom hanging over their heads had a shiny silver lining. Sigmund could not share it without revealing Alice's secret past. Not that Baedeker would find comfort in Earth's safety. . . .

No matter. Did Pak wear shoes? Because another shoe was about to drop.

WERE TWO GENERAL PRODUCTS hulls safer than one?

To Baedeker's knowledge, no one had ever tried the experiment. The

Pak incursion continued to drive improvisation. I have become an Experimentalist, he thought wryly. Like it or not.

Reap the Whirlwind had a General Products #4 hull, like *Haven*, but there the resemblance ended. Baedeker remembered *Haven* almost fondly: a busy, fully crewed, comfortably equipped vessel. Not so *Reap the Whirlwind*. This ship had no scientific instruments or engineering workshops, no spacious quarters or well-stocked pantries. For that matter, it had no decks and very few rooms.

Reap the Whirlwind was a freighter, pure and simple, but there was nothing simple about its cargoes. Only Sigmund could have conceived such a vessel. The ship carried:

—As its main cargo, all the mass it could hold: depleted uranium, and when stockpiles of that had been exhausted, lead and gold.

—An extra power plant and the extra fuel tanks to run it. Any #4 hull, because of its size, consumed prodigious energies in hyperspace. The massive cargo drained energy from the protective normal-space bubble that much faster. Their deuterium and tritium had been chilled down to solids to conserve volume for more payload.

—A planet-buster, like the one that had shattered Niflheim, already assembled.

—And *Sancho Panza*.

Like a ship in a bottle, Sigmund had described *Sancho Panza*, until he gave up trying to convey the simile. Something about wind-powered boats. It related somehow, in Sigmund's convoluted mind, to calling the massive main cargo aboard *Reap the Whirlwind* grapeshot. And to somebody named Jolly Roger. With a sigh, Sigmund had eventually changed his analogy to lifeboat. Baedeker understood lifeboats.

As for the ships' names, Baedeker understood neither. When Sigmund named ships, not even native New Terrans always got it.

"Five minutes from dropout," Sigmund announced from *Sancho Panza*'s bridge. It served as the bridge for both vessels. Lead pellets filled the volume where any normal #4-based ship would have its flight controls.

"Acknowledged," Baedeker called back. "I am in the engine room."

"Acknowledged," Ol't'ro also replied. "We are ready to monitor instruments." That the group mind answered made any mention of location superfluous: They were in their habitat. Sigmund had granted the Gw'oth near total network privileges, so they could access instruments from inside their water tank. With a few words, Ol't'ro had gotten a place aboard: *We no more can leave this task unfinished than can you, Sigmund.*

These three—or eighteen, if you counted the Gw'oth individually—comprised the entire crew. A skeleton crew, Sigmund called it, and the image always made Baedeker shiver. Sigmund was crazy.

Sigmund was crazier to have brought the Gw'oth. Of course Baedeker was insane, too—how else travel light-years from Hearth and herd?—but there were types and degrees of mental illness.

He would find out soon if Sigmund was crazy enough. Baedeker opened a holo slaved to the main bridge display.

"One minute," Sigmund called. "Unless anyone sees a reason to keep going."

No sane being could do anything *but* keep going. Baedeker chanted mournfully to himself and did not answer.

"Breakout in five . . . four . . ."

"TWO . . . ONE . . . NOW."

With peripheral tubacles poised above the controls, Ol't'ro switched on sensors.

To one side, hundreds of blue-white lights. To the other side, the hungry magnetic maws of many more ramscoops. *Sancho Panza* had emerged, as planned, inside a small void deep within the leading Pak wave: a no-man's-land between battle fronts.

"In position," Ol't'ro reported. "Taking our first reading."

Sancho Panza was at a near stop relative to the stars. The ramscoops were racing at significant fractions of light speed. Ol't'ro took bearings on the brightest fusion exhausts—nearby ships—and the strongest of the neutrino-only sources—those that might be nearby. They waited a few seconds, and as the ships sped on, still unsuspecting, took a second set of bearings. They were only ten seconds in normal space.

"Nothing closer than a light-hour," Ol't'ro reported. "Nothing nearby coming faster than at half-light." They were perfectly safe—even by Baedeker's standards—for now. "We'll refine that every few minutes."

"Good enough," Sigmund replied. "I'm sending the message."

The main message went out by radio, endlessly repeating, but Sigmund also played the recording over the intercom. A Jeeves, speaking its version of Pak. Ol't'ro understood parts of it, his aptitude with Thssthfok's speech only one of the many secrets he still kept. It wasn't a complicated message. Turn south *now* or we will appear again. And again. And again.

"Enough of that noise," Sigmund finally said. The pops and whistles ended. "We're still transmitting."

Ten long minutes after their emergence among the Pak, Sigmund spoke again. "Let's do this. Baedeker, are you ready?" Silence. "Baedeker!"

"Ready, Sigmund," Baedeker finally answered.

"By the numbers," Sigmund said. "Counting down from fifteen."

ON TWELVE, the hull of *Reap the Whirlwind* became powder. Here and there, where the cargo was loosely packed, air pressure burst through the weakened surface.

On ten, *Sancho Panza*, a minnow to *Reap the Whirlwind*'s whale, burst free. Its thrusters scattered a small fraction of the dense metal pellets as it crept away.

On three, *Sancho Panza* disappeared into hyperspace.

On zero, the planet-buster in the heart of *Reap the Whirlwind* switched on.

63

"It's working," Sigmund recorded. "We got their attention."

Success could be captured in remarkably few words.

The time-lapse surveillance data showed squadron after squadron of Pak ships breaking off, often fighting their way, toward galactic south. Turning away from New Terra, Hearth, and Jm'ho.

Doubtless the Pak had their own visualizations: of unlucky ships torn apart as the space-time ripples spread. Close behind that came a blast of lead and gold and uranium that even shredded to individual ions was all but impossible to avoid. The ions were too massive, and coming too fast, for a ramscoop magnetic field to confine or deflect. Relativistic heavy nuclei made the strongest cosmic rays look puny.

Reap the whirlwind, indeed.

Sancho Panza was eerily quiet. The Gw'oth were in their habitat, assimilating the experience in their own way. Baedeker was locked in his cabin, cowering in delayed reaction. That was all right. He would recover.

Sigmund hoped that happened soon. The isolation was getting to him. He talked to Jeeves, of course, but that only brought to mind another Jeeves, a friend, now gone.

In the bridge view port, stars shone like diamonds. Sigmund added a few details and hyperwaved his report, surveillance file attached. He pulled up a holo of Penny and the kids. How much had Hermes and Athena grown during *this* long trip?

Sancho Panza could stay in normal space long enough for another message.

"Jeeves, begin a new recording. 'Dearest Penelope. All is well. It will take a while, but we're coming home. . . . ' "

. . .

HEADS HELD HIGH, mane meticulously coiffed and bejeweled, songs in his throats, Baedeker cantered into the relax room. Why not sing? He was going home, the weight of worlds lifted from his shoulders. "Hello, Sigmund," he said cheerily.

Sigmund was jogging on the treadmill. He raised an eyebrow at Baedeker's dramatic entrance. "You're in a good mood."

"Indeed." Baedeker got a bulb of redmelon juice and begin synthing a double portion of steamed mixed grains. "It finally registered. We have a future again. That is a very good thing."

"I can't argue." Sigmund wiped his forehead with the back of an arm. "What does the future look like for you? Will you come back to New Terra?"

English required only one throat, and Baedeker started eating. "There are things I must do on Hearth." That was not very forthcoming. "There are things I want to accomplish."

"Good for you," Sigmund huffed.

Why am I so reticent? Baedeker wondered. "Do not think me an ingrate. New Terra welcomed me when I felt unwelcome on Hearth. When I was dismayed by the terrible things the Concordance had done."

"All you wanted was a garden and to be left alone. In return, you saved our world. We're more than even."

"No more than you saved Hearth." Leaving Baedeker as indebted as before.

But changed in other ways. Now he had seen the *good* that governments could do. It took people to save the worlds, people like him and Sigmund— and yes, like Nessus—but it took government, too. No one else could have provided starships, labs, crews, and access to the Outsider drives.

What did the future hold? Nessus had tempted Baedeker more than he cared to admit. He *would* discover the remaining secrets of the Outsider drives. How better than as minister of science, with all the resources, talent, and influence that position controlled?

In his hearts, Baedeker felt the stirrings of an even higher purpose. Might he not, someday, become Hindmost? Then, surely, he could act on the Gw'oth threat. Unlike the New Terrans, the Gw'oth truly were a menace— and no one understood that danger better than he.

"Are you all right? You got awfully quiet."

"Just thinking." Baedeker preferred not to discuss his ambitions. He would not discuss the Gw'oth. About the latter, he and Sigmund had argued more than enough. At least the aliens had mostly kept to themselves, within their habitat, since *Sancho Panza* had left behind the Pak.

So what else? "I have been thinking about New Terra, Sigmund. About the tides."

Sigmund stopped the treadmill and stepped off. "The lack of tides."

"Maybe not."

Sigmund blinked. "What do you mean?"

"I have learned a great deal about planetary drives. Enough, I believe, to fine-tune the operation of an Outsider drive."

"Safely?" Sigmund asked suspiciously. "To what purpose?"

Of *course*, safely. "To superimpose an occasional tiny pulse or stutter." And unlike the first time Baedeker had imagined—and, wisely, recoiled from—that notion, he now understood the implications, down to the tertiary feedback loops.

"I don't follow."

Was it not obvious? "The resulting ocean surges will emulate the effect of tides."

Sigmund grinned. "If so, New Terra owes *you* a deep debt."

64

Er'o climbed from the habitat level toward the bridge. The whine of exoskeleton motors and the clump of his steps echoed in the stairwell. Bubbles streamed past his eyes whenever he lifted a tubacle. Most distracting of all: Ol't'ro's admonition, still echoing in his thoughts. *If it is at all possible, find us an alternative.*

Exiting onto the bridge level, he found Sigmund alone. As intended. "Are you busy?" Er'o asked.

"Not at all."

Er'o sidled through the door onto the bridge proper. The main display showed a landscape, rather than the view ahead. The mass pointer—a device no one would explain, but whose function his studies had made obvious—showed no significant objects nearby. "May we talk?"

Sigmund pointed to the spare couch. "Of course. Have a seat."

Er'o clambered up and indulged the human need for small talk before getting to the point. "My friends and I wonder about our future." More so Ol't'ro wondered, but they had calculated Sigmund would respond best to an approach by a single Gw'o. "Recent events have been . . . unsettling."

"To say the least. Er'o, something is troubling you. Out with it."

"What comes next for my people?"

"You have new friends. So swapping information, what we call cultural exchange. Commerce, probably. You'll be going home soon. Sabrina plans to send along a New Terran representative, what we call an ambassador, to consult with your governments. We would welcome your representatives on our world."

"And the Concordance. Tell me honestly. Are we also its friend?"

A long pause. "The Concordance doesn't have friends. It has interests."

As rival city-states of the ocean depths had interests. How could it be otherwise? "You know the Citizens far better than I. How will they see their interest regarding the Gw'oth?"

A longer, more ominous pause. "I don't know, Er'o. Perhaps as trading partners. The Citizens trade with New Terra."

"You seem doubtful." Though no more skeptical than I, or Ol't'ro.

"I can't speak for them. I can tell you New Terra will be your advocates."

Jm'ho needed allies, not advocates. "Baedeker does not trust us. We assume his opinion will have considerable influence on Hearth."

"Why do you say that? Why wouldn't Baedeker trust you?"

Er'o was not about to mention sowing *Haven* with listening devices. "He is not very discreet about his opinion."

"No, I suppose not. Still, why would he distrust you?"

"We know the location of the Fleet. And our talents scare him."

"Your talents helped defeat the Pak," Sigmund said, and yet he looked away. Yesterday's triumph only made Ol't'ro and those like him scarier today.

"For now"—without hyperdrives of our own—"we cannot defend ourselves." Nor threaten Hearth, for deterrence was the best way to defend Jm'ho. Meanwhile planet-busters, both Pak-like kinetic weapons and devices of Baedeker's design, remained a terrible threat. "I fear that our absence would be in the Concordance's . . . interest."

So would eliminating Ol't'ro. Baedeker had already suggested it, likening Ol't'ro to Thssthfok, even while the Gw'oth had helped to improve Baedeker's prototype drives.

Sigmund frowned. "I'm sure Sabrina will assert forcefully that we consider the Gw'oth our friends."

"And what beyond words would she do for us?"

Sigmund said nothing.

What could he say? New Terra also had interests, and war with the Fleet would hardly be among them. Ol't'ro was right. New Terra might help, but Ol't'ro dare not depend on it.

They would take a lesson from Sigmund. Paranoia showed great survival value.

Er'o concluded the conversation and scurried back to the habitat. It was time to put to the test research under way since he first encountered humans.

. . .

"BREAKING OUT OF HYPERSPACE IN FIVE SECONDS," Sigmund called. Soon he added, "Nice, rational stars. A sight for sore eyes."

"For those who have eyes," Jeeves answered, also over the intercom.

Ol't'ro said nothing. They were deep in thought, in a final assessment of tactics and contingencies, and they had three sensor clusters fully engaged with instruments. Normal space, all right. They took bearings on four familiar pulsars. Easy calculations put their position not quite eighteen light-years from Jm'ho. New Terra and the Fleet of Worlds were marginally closer, on slightly different bearings. They ran a final diagnostic on the mechanism that had long been the focus of the Er'o unit's research efforts. It passed.

"I'm sorry," Ol't'ro radioed. They activated Er'o's homemade hyperdrive shunt—

Transporting into hyperspace their habitat, the middle of *Sancho Panza*, and a corresponding third of the otherwise all–but–indestructible hull.

65

The next days were a blur, Baedeker slipping in and out of consciousness. Slip in, anyway. The return was never so gentle. Sigmund cajoled, he berated, he threatened. When speech failed to work, the jabbing and kicking began.

How often did the cycle repeat? Baedeker had lost count. Each time that he emerged enough to hear, Sigmund would say the same thing. "Only you can save us."

And only Baedeker could. Somehow, on the first day, he had suited up and managed to follow Sigmund to a stepping disc in the drifting stern. Its hull, severed from the power plant still embedded in the bow, had become dust blown away by air pressure.

Baedeker found half of a hyperdrive shunt and a thin wedge of a hyperwave transceiver. He saw no way to repair either. The rest had been carried away in the normal-space bubble around the Gw'oth shunt when they left.

The Gw'oth building a hyperdrive from scratch only proved Baedeker had been correct all along about them. And made his inability even to repair a hyperdrive all the more bitter.

With scavenged supplies, he and Sigmund had stepped back to the bridge. Then, in fits and starts, in a fog of confusion and exhaustion and dread, Baedeker had toiled. It had seemed endless. He stabilized what remained of the environmental systems. He extracted tiny fusion reactors from scavenged stepping discs to keep life support running. While Sigmund continued to forage what remained of the ship for water and emergency rations and anything else possibly useful, Baedeker began, fearfully, to disassemble everything nonessential.

This stump of a ship would wander forever. It had no use for force-field generators for crash-couch protection. It was in the middle of nowhere, and that made radar useless. The comm laser, too: Any signal they transmitted would be too attenuated to matter when, creeping along at light speed, it finally reached anyone who might help them. By then, in any event, they would long since have starved. Gravity control circuits, distributed processing nodes, power distribution—it was *all* expendable to build the thing they needed most: a hyperwave radio.

He had the wrong parts, hardly any instrumentation with which to test what he cobbled together, and only a pocket computer on which to simulate designs. Time and again he zoned out, lost himself in his thoughts, faded away, until Sigmund, with escalating levels of alarm and abuse, roused Baedeker to refocus on his task.

Throughout, fear plagued him. Had the Concordance traded the Pak for—even created—an even worse threat?

At last the hyperwave radio was complete. They powered it with a cascade of three stepping-disc fusion reactors. They reached one of the comm buoys in orbit around New Terra. Sigmund had scarcely spoken more than their coordinates when, with an earsplitting pop, the jury-rigged hyperwave set burst into flame.

Baedeker slipped away once more.

SIGMUND BEGAN making tick marks on the bridge bulkhead: dark/light cycles since their call for help. Call each cycle a day.

On day one, he told himself he was optimistic. The coordinates were the most important part of his message. He had sent those. Help would come.

Nothing could rouse Baedeker again. Sigmund tucked Baedeker, comatose, out of the way behind the copilot couch and activated the only emergency stasis-field generator he had found.

On day three, Sigmund spent hours experimenting with his jumpsuit controls. Patterns, colors, textures, and combinations—he studied them all. For years he had promised Penny he would, "When he could spare the time." He had the time now. He still failed to see the point.

On day five, he began resenting Baedeker, oblivious within the stasis field. Never mind that the Puppeteer had been all but comatose. Never mind that only one of them eating, drinking, and breathing effectively doubled Sigmund's rations.

By day ten, he *really* resented Baedeker.

On day fifteen, Sigmund began screaming and throwing stuff against the walls to hear something other than his own thoughts.

"I'm sorry," Ol't'ro had said. Only that message had been just to Sigmund; Baedeker's comp had no such message. Sorry to kill you, Sigmund. Not so sorry about Baedeker.

Apology not accepted.

On day twenty-two, Sigmund found his thoughts stuck in a loop, obsessing over Er'o's final visit. Gw'oth fears. Feelers for New Terran support. Sigmund's noncommittal response. Never mind that he could not commit New Terra.

By the time Baedeker and he were rescued—if they were rescued—Ol't'ro would have reached their home solar system. Could they land the habitat? Sigmund had his doubts, but it didn't matter. A Gw'oth interplanetary ship could rendezvous with the habitat.

Knowing the Fleet's location and building hyperdrives of their own, the Gw'oth had become untouchable.

On day twenty-five, Sigmund made the mistake of powering up the view port. Nothing but stars and a blobby nebula in sight. Suddenly he was clawing at the bridge hatch he had had the foresight to spot-weld shut. Blood streamed from torn fingers. A massive flat-phobia attack. He was starving when he returned to his senses, and never quite believed his day count after that.

On day thirty (if it was), he fixated on the Gw'oth coming on *Reap the Whirlwind* when he had offered to send them home. They had insisted on seeing the job through, without regard for their safety. Only then—their task complete, the Pak deterred—had Er'o come to Sigmund for reassurance.

And then, after realpolitik and Sigmund's evasive answers had left them no choice, Ol't'ro saved themselves. He wished them well.

"I'm sorry, too," Sigmund whispered.

ON DAY THIRTY-FOUR, choking down another sawdust-flavored energy bar, Sigmund found himself fantasizing how Puppeteer meat would taste.

On day thirty-seven, he thought about the Gw'oth stringing along Baedeker. Pulling a Puppeteer's strings. That was hilarious, and even funnier when he used his hands as Puppeteer heads looking each other in the eyes. He spent the rest of the day composing limericks about it.

On day forty, he caught his reflection in the stasis field. Someone wild-eyed, heavily bearded, and gaunt stared back at him. He huddled between crash couches for the rest of the day.

On day forty-two, flatland phobia seized him again. He came out of it chanting to himself, "No more spaceships. No more spaceships. No more spaceships . . ." and overwhelmed by déjà vu. He was croaking like a frog, his throat raw, before he forced himself to stop.

Then came the day he could not remember when he had last put a mark on the wall. His comp would tell him, he suddenly remembered. He wondered where he had left it. He spent hours tearing apart the bridge before finding the comp in his pocket. That reduced him to helpless laughter, tears running down his face. He laughed, or cried, himself to sleep.

The next day, he checked the comp. It was day fifty-two.

On day fifty-four, he could not remember why he was counting.

On day fifty-five, he wondered if he could survive much longer.

On day fifty-six, Sigmund struggled to recall why he should care.

On day fifty-seven, figures materialized on the bridge stepping disc. Eric. Then Kirsten. When Penelope appeared, he remembered.

EPILOGUE

Thssthfok's eyes darted from instrument to instrument. Nothing made sense.

A moment ago, space-time itself was coming apart. Close behind, the debris of a shattered world spewed at him. Failure was still bitter in his mouth.

Now his instruments showed only peaceful void.

He shivered. The cockpit was *cold*. How could the temperature drop instantaneously? And when he dared to glance up from his console, stars rolled past.

The canopy was gone! An almost subliminal shimmer marked the force field that logic insisted must be holding in his air. When he looked around, the ship was pocked with holes.

The console clock still kept time. Thssthfok understood human units of time, but not their dating system. Time had passed for the universe-gone-mad to heal itself, but how much? He had no idea.

Only a few of his attitude jets still held compressed air—more holes?—but he managed to kill his spin. Star configurations seemed both familiar and warped. Instruments confirmed what he had been loath to admit: He was light-years removed from the last view he remembered.

And light-years distant from the Pak fleets. The leading edge of the advance again receded from him. Nor was it only Thssthfok whose location had shifted: The ramscoops had moved, too.

Somehow, years had passed.

HIS MAIN FUEL TANKS WERE PUNCTURED, their deuterium long vanished. Only a small reserve tank, all but drained, held deuterium. Once he used that—that was it. The force field would disappear, his air would spurt out, and he would die.

Maybe that was why the ship had ended his oblivion. It needed his help.

Somehow this ship had kept him alive for years. What other unsuspected capabilities did it have? Whatever the universe thought, in Thssthfok's mind he had hurriedly reassembled the control console just a few day-tenths earlier. He remembered the unfamiliar subsystems inside.

He opened the console, slid out drawers and racks, spread apart wiring harnesses. He remembered where gauges and instruments had been clipped. The humans had studied the very subsystems that interested Thssthfok.

Whatever those circuits did, their design was Pak-inspired. He was second-guessing a mutant protector.

AS COLD AS THE CABIN WAS, Thssthfok left the temperature alone. He had no deuterium to spare for mere comfort. He took a nibble of tree-of-life root and continued his studies.

The self-repair capability was a brilliant blend of Pak and human technology. So was the pressure-retaining force field, only that was also an enigma. To judge from the position of the Pak fleets, Thssthfok's ship had been adrift for years. The force-field generator would have drained his reserve tank in a fraction of the time. And that led him to the most astonishing discovery—

The stasis generator. Within the field it created around the pilot's couch, time would stand still. Nothing inside would change—and that included any consumption of energy.

Time itself had frozen for him while this ship drifted, slowly repairing itself, until its energy reserves dipped dangerously low. So the ship had activated the pressure-retaining force field, put air into the cabin, and released him from stasis.

How to survive was *his* problem now.

Instruments showed a world on which he could survive, scarcely a light-year away. That could not be a coincidence—the ship had brought him here. Whether it had sought a planet to support Pak or human, the result was the same.

Smog tainted the planet's atmosphere. Radio emissions spewed forth. The natives were advanced well beyond the point to which, after long years of effort, he had pushed the Drar. He could put to-be-conquered slaves to good use, and quickly.

Could one Pak alone conquer that world? What he could infer of their technology made that uncertain. But certainly he would fail if he did not try. He would plan on success, and find out when he arrived.

So: They could build him a ramscoop—maybe even a hyperdrive—in only a few years. With severe rationing, possibly even before he died for lack of tree-of-life root. Maybe the planet would even grow tree-of-life.

If he could get there.

THSSTHFOK FINALLY KNEW why the ship had released him from stasis. Enough deuterium remained to complete repairs. And to cross the final distance. And to shed his velocity and land.

Pick any two.

While he studied the capabilities of his ship, surveyed his destination, and assessed his options, the demands of the pressure-retaining force field moved him perilously close to having energy for only *one* of three.

He climbed into a rescue bag and turned off the force field. Energy consumption slowed to a trickle. Oxygen in the rescue bag would sustain him for half a day-tenth.

He spent half that time, his hands clumsy through the tough material of the rescue bag, reconfiguring the force-field generator. Rather than gently holding air within a large volume, the device would thrust—hard!—in one direction.

He spent the rest of his time calculating and refining exactly how and when to apply that thrust. With a single shove, he had to reach the solar system, then reach the habitable planet, hitting the atmosphere at just the right angle, and then—now reaching the resolution limit of his telescope—come down on land. The only workable solution involved a looping trajectory through the solar system, with two gravity assists from other planets.

Were his sensors precise and accurate enough for this calculation? There was one way to find out. Choking on his own stale breath, his fingers tinged blue with hypoxia, he set the navigational controls.

Uncontrolled landing. Broken ship. No air.

None of that mattered in stasis.

As the launch timer approached zero, as Thssthfok reached out to activate the stasis field, his final, hopeful thoughts were of his family.

ABOUT THE AUTHORS

LARRY NIVEN has been a published writer since 1964. He has written science fiction, fantasy, long and short fiction, nonfiction, children's television, comic books, and stranger stuff. His books, including many collaborations, number somewhere around sixty. He lives in Chatsworth, California, with Marilyn, his wife of forty years.

EDWARD M. LERNER has degrees in physics and computer science, a background that kept him mostly out of trouble until he began writing fiction full-time. His books include *Probe, Moonstruck, Fools' Experiments, Small Miracles,* and the collection *Creative Destruction.* His previous collaborations with Larry were *Fleet of Worlds* and *Juggler of Worlds.* Ed lives in Virginia with Ruth, his wife of a mere thirty-eight years.